Praise for TRENT JAMIESON

"*Roil* is a compulsive, action-packed adventure, set in a dark fascinating world, rich in menace and challenges."

Rowena Cory Daniells

"The first novel in Trent Jamieson's "Death Works" series is a brilliant opening to what promises to be an enthralling series. The narrative runs at a good pace, interspersed with the kind of humour that has made Jamieson's award-winning short stories must-reads."

Bookseller & Publisher

"Jamieson writes a fast-paced story studded with action-movie beats."

Financial Times

"Trent Jamieson is well known in speculative fiction circles as a significant talent, writing beautifully crafted tales that often have a baroque sensibility and resonate on an emotional level."

Terra Incognita

"*Death Most Definite* is a darkly absorbing debut novel, compelling from beginning to end. Jamieson is a skilled writer who has earned his stripes in the short story craft and enters the novel scene with a bang – I see a big future ahead!"

Australian Speculative Fiction in Review

"I predict that Trent Jamieson will deservedly be Australia's next big genre expert."

Chuck McKenzie

ALSO BY TRENT JAMIESON

Death Most Definite
Managing Death
Reserved for Travelling Shows (collection)

TRENT JAMIESON

ROIL

THE NIGHTBOUND LAND
BOOK I

ANGRY
ROBOT

ANGRY ROBOT

A member of the Osprey Group
Midland House, West Way
Botley, Oxford
OX2 0PH
UK

www.angryrobotbooks.com
Into this world we're thrown

An Angry Robot paperback original 2011
1

A catalogue record for this book is available from the British Library.

ISBN: 978-0-85766-183-8
EBook ISBN: 978-0-85766-185-2

Set in Meridien by THL Design.

Printed in the UK by CPI Mackays, Chatham, ME5 8TD.

For Mum and Dad

PART ONE
DISSOLUTION

When you talk of great victories, remember, too, the defeats. I was there when McMahon fell. I was there for that Grand Defeat. And let me tell you, there was nothing grand about it.

Raven Skye

CHAPTER 1

Since the founding of the first city, with a few obvious exceptions (see Connor McMahon, also Julian Hardacre), two political parties have ever battled for dominance: the Engineers and the Confluents. The Confluents were always regarded as too emotive, too populist in their endeavours, the Engineers too focused on civic structures and their construction whatever the cost to their workers and their people (see The Levees Built on Blood, Milde & Whyte, *page 125). A gross simplification, perhaps, but all such political narratives are (if they are to survive) and both parties played upon this perception in each of the twelve metropolises.*

Throughout the centuries, Confluent and Engineer would have torn each other apart, and on several occasions almost did (see The Right Bank Insurgency *page 878), but always the Vergers stood between them, the knife-bearers keeping a brutal peace.*

That ended with the Dissolution.

Considering the Roil's rapid expansion, and the stinging memory of the Grand Defeat (and the flood of refugees it brought with it) a decade prior, it was surprising it didn't happen much sooner.

Dissolution: The Bloody Avenues of Bloody Mayors,
Deighton & Bogert

THE CITY OF MIRRLEES-ON-WEEP
300 MILES NORTH OF THE ROIL EDGE

Midnight, and Council Vergers reduced the front door to splinters. They dragged David Milde's father onto the street. Kicked his legs out from under him. And, their long knives gleaming in the streetlight, slashed his throat.

David watched it all from his bedroom window with a cold impassivity fed by Carnival.

He slapped his face, once, twice. Hardly felt it. He'd taken the drug, as he often did, after his father had accused him of taking the drug. The argument had been loud and wild, and of utterly no consequence now.

They'd be coming for him next. David hesitated as his father bled to death down below, the rain washed the blood away: it never stopped raining in Mirrlees, blood was always being washed away.

Run.

Run.

Run.

David's hands shook as he gripped the windowsill.

He blinked a heavy Carnival-induced blink. The world lumbered into a brutal sort of focus.

Bundles of Halloween orbs, strung down the street just the night before, coloured everything in reds and greens. Windows from here to the next suburb banged shut. Lights switched off.

David's father lifted himself almost to his feet, his head loose on his neck; barely on his neck at all. Oh, what kind of strength the man possessed! But it meant nothing now. The Vergers kicked him back to the ground, where he lay and did not rise again, and David knew his father was dead.

Footsteps and the hard voices of men not needing nor desiring to hide their approach echoed up the stairs. David considered crawling under the bed. But they would find him and drag him kicking and screaming out into the rain, and they would slash his throat, and he would lie there with his father.

The thought held some temptation.

He wasn't stupid. The Vergers would keep hunting him, and the realisation filled him with a great and awful weariness.

He didn't know where to run. He knew that if they had come for his father, they'd have come for everyone else. There'd be no one he could turn to. Not James Ling or Medicine Paul or the Cathcart Sisters. Any survivors would be running for their own lives.

All these considerations in under a second and, while he thought them, he opened his window and slid out, with just the clothes on his back, clinging to the slimy windowsill with his fingertips – the Carnival-calm in tatters – and knowing it might end here with just one slip.

It nearly did.

David lost his grip and dropped into the dead tree beneath his window, its rotten limbs snap-crash-snapped under his weight. He landed in a heap on the soft mud beneath and clambered to his feet – no bones broken as far as he could tell. He leapt a stone wall, almost tripping, and sprinted onto the road.

Someone shouted from his window. Whistles blew.

David did not look back, because if he did he would stop, and stopping would end him.

Such are politics in Mirrlees.

• • • •

MIRRLEES – DOWNING BRIDGE

David wiped the vomit from his lips for the third time in under an hour.

He knew what was coming, just as much as he knew he couldn't stop it, which was almost as terrifying as the Vergers that hunted him.

The Carnival's claws tightened. How could something get so bad, even as it left your body? It was just another awfulness to add to his collection, only this one would grow, and quickly.

He tried to occupy his mind with other thoughts, possible options of escape, the long term, anything but the drug and his body's rising hunger for it.

The north was his best choice now.

If he could make it to the city of Hardacre he would find refuge. He had an aunt who lived there, and she would take him in; they had always been close.

But the road to Hardacre was impossibly perilous; the Margin and Cuttlefolk, half wild and with long and bitter memories of war, lay between here and there. And the one bridge that crossed into those lands, on the edge of the Northmir, was heavily guarded. He may as well be striking out to the moon. But then again, he had proven himself more adept at survival than he had first thought.

All night he had been running, hiding, keeping to the shadows, moving only when the Vergers in their whistling packs had passed.

It had been surprisingly easy, perhaps because escape was all he could allow his mind to focus on. As he had run he had found himself instinctively heading to the one place he might hide. Once or twice he had scored Carnival there, though only when most desperate.

Usually, he'd not needed to look far to find people willing to supply him. After all, he was the great Confluent Leader, Warwick Milde's son. And if his father's currency had decreased in the last few months, well, he had never expected it to go so low.

Downing Bridge loomed out of the murk. David was familiar with it, had often come this way as a boy with his father. The master engineer would point out its various structural peculiarities, its size being the least of them, for Mirrlees was a city of excess; its levee banks blocking out the sun, channelling away the rain. Once the River Weep had been just a trickle between the embankments, a trickle two hundred yards across. Now it had climbed their walls to a height of nearly fifty feet and was rising every day.

The *Dolorous Grey* rattled overhead; David could just make out its plumes of smoke. That's what he really needed, to be on the train, steaming away from Mirrlees. Even though its destination couldn't be considered safe it was better than what faced him here, and he could lose himself in the colour of the Festival of Float.

But the train was beyond his reach now. All he had was the sanctuary of the bridge. Or, more correctly, what lay beneath it: Mirkton, the undercity.

Water streamed from the iron lips of the bridge. Through the falling water he could see a few dim lights, around which darkness lurked like a hungry dog.

He only hoped it was a darkness deep enough to swallow him.

THE CITY OF MIRRLEES – RUELE TOWER
302 MILES NORTH OF OBSIDIAN CURTAIN

"So the son escaped?" Stade's tone made it more of an accusation than a question.

Mr Tope nodded. Dry blood caked his grey suit; he picked at it with dark, cracked nails, and Stade wanted to slap those hands away even though they had just given him uncontested government.

"It's a minor setback." Tope's voice suggested he wasn't used to setbacks (minor or not); there was a kind of wonder in it, and dismay. "We'll find him: he is an addict, his options are limited, and only decrease with every hour he runs. He cannot go to ground, because without Carnival in his veins the ground will swallow him and spit out his bones. We have staked out his usual suppliers. We have eyes on all his friends and family allies, and there aren't too many of them now."

"If you can get to him, then *they* might as well. I don't like loose ends."

Tope's lips pursed. "We've few loose ends left, and the boy is the least of them. Both John Cadell and Medicine Paul have evaded us." Again that wondering tone.

Stade's gaze dropped to the withered fingers floating in the jar on his desk, the brass Orbis on one of them thick with verdigris. Medicine had acquired a new ring, of course, but Stade would always possess the first. He should have never been so lenient those decades past. Perhaps none of this would have happened if he had cut off Medicine Paul's head instead of his fingers. "You are right, and those are loose ends enough. The Confluents are broken, all credit to you and your Long Knives; fine and bloody work, indeed, but you have not removed the threat in its entirety."

"We will find him."

"Good. We have limited resources and not much time. Milde's death was unfortunate, but he let the Old Man out. Such open dissent could not be without penalty, and not just the death of his brother. The Engine… what he had proposed... actions with consequences far too dangerous. We could not let it continue, knowing what we know."

Tope's eyes were inscrutable. He never gave much away, and he certainly didn't now. "Knowing what we know, yes."

Stade sighed. "I should have killed him sooner. The day he defied me. The day he crossed the floor. I should have cut his throat, then the Old Man would not have been set free and none of this would be necessary. But I was a gentler soul in those days. And we had been friends. Ah, Tope; it's always the ones I don't kill that I regret. Blood and murder, how else do you reach the top of the Tower?"

He turned to the window, glared down at Mirrlees as though it might reveal his enemies if he scowled hard enough. Ruele, the Tower of Engineers extended into the sky, almost as high as the low layer of cloud from which rain fell and fell and fell.

Stade's offices had an unmatched view of the city, from the outer orbit of radio arrays, round which Aerokin circled – their flagellum twitching in ceaseless hungry jactitation from their underbellies, water tumbling from their flesh until they breached the cloud bank – to the vast bulk of Downing Bridge and the levees, nearly five hundred yards high, yet barely containing the River Weep. The *Dolorous Grey* crossed the bridge, bellowing smoke, the train making its way south to Chapman and the edge of the Roil.

Rain wormed along the office windows. Wind whistled through a crack in the lower edge of the window frame, bringing with it the smoky, rotten odours of the city and dribbles of water that pooled upon and stained the carpet. Stade grimaced at the mess. Such was the pace of work required with other endeavours he had no one to spare for even the simplest maintenance.

"Not long for this city," Stade said. "The bastard had to die. Now tie up those loose ends, Mr Tope. We're running out of time."

CHAPTER 2

That the city of Tate could have survived its absorption by the Roil was unthinkable. That Shale lost its brightest minds in the Penns was an absolute tragedy.

The Penns, though, had never been popular leaders outside their city, seen in the north by Confluents as too much in their sympathies like Engineers, and by the Engineers as far too much like Confluents. It could be argued that little effort was expended by the three Allied Metropolises of the North to aid their southern cousin, and that all parties were complicit in it.

The Roil baffles radio signals but, without a doubt, more energy could have been applied in trying to contact the city.

However, it must never be forgotten that those first years of the Roil's rebirth were madness, its creatures (outside popular fictions and fairytales) unfamiliar and terrifying.

Night's Engines, DEIGHTON

THE CITY OF TATE
600 MILES SOUTH OF MIRRLEES: WITHIN THE ROIL

Margaret's parents were late. She sat in the basement of the family home beneath the Four Cannon, seeking distraction in weapons prep and failing. It was a mindless sort of work (charging vascular systems, checking regulators, resetting clips) that set your thoughts wandering, and all her thoughts wandered in one direction.

Two days ago a bullet-shaped balloon drone flew over the Jut and the wall, passed beneath the Four Cannon of Willowhen Peak and the vast and twisting buttresses of the Steaming Vents, and landed on the forecourt of Tate's Breach Hold Chambers, meeting place of the Council.

Within the balloon's storage nacelle, along with various letters to Ministers and Engineers alike, had been a short note to Margaret written in her mother's crabbed hand:

Tests successful. The I-Bombs drove back the Roil and we saw the sun. Hah! Knew you'd be jealous, my child. This will be an end to it all. Combined with my iron wings we can destroy the Roil. A new age is begun!

A few things to conclude, then we'll begin the journey home. Your father sends his love. Back tomorrow, no later than six.

Both anxious to see you

A

Margaret read the note again, it was particularly jubilant for her mother, beginning of a new age or not.

Margaret had finished her sentry duty for the day – a twelve hour shift, dull, nothing to mark the time but the occasional opportunity to launch a cannonade at Quarg Hounds, or a dusty-winged Endym, or practice her marksmanship on Hideous Garment Flutes – though so many of them filled the skies it was harder to miss than strike one.

She hadn't even spied a Walker: those driven to despair who clambered down the spiked and ice-slicked Outer Wall of the Jut and walked into the dark, never to be seen again. Of course, such despair was unjustified now.

Margaret had barely slept the night before, and her superior officer, Sara, had ordered her off the Jut, promising to alert her as soon as her parents arrived with three rings of the intercom bells.

Margaret had agreed wearily, but her head was buzzing and soon there'd be no need for such vigilance. The I-Bombs had been successful. The Roil could be forced back. She would see the sky, the real sky, and its sun and moons and stars.

Her parents had achieved what many had considered impossible. No less than a means of destroying the Roil that did not involve the near mythical Engine of the North – the ancient saviour and scour of the world.

But it hadn't happened yet. She cleaned her guns, swapped the old fuel cells for new, and set to charging the drained ones.

She checked her watch. Her father had given her that on her seventeenth birthday. All it did was remind her of him. Why were they late?

Nearly six. As her watch reached the hour, the Four Cannon fired, launching endothermic shells out into the darkness of the Roil, driving its substance away from the Outer Wall – though it would quickly return. The Four Cannon – designed by her parents, like every other endothermic defence in Tate – were the city's heartbeat. Without that regular cannonade Tate would have long ago succumbed to the Roil.

Conventional weapons did little harm to the creatures of the Roil, other than encouraging them to fury. However, Roilings could not survive in temperatures below three degrees Celsius, and Roil spores themselves were killed by temperatures below freezing. All the city's weapons took advantage of this, creating a zone of cold around Tate that kept the Roil out.

Margaret stretched her arms, appreciating the quiet. As much as she looked forward to seeing her parents again, she knew that once they drove through the gates it would be non-stop, starting with her flight down the wireway to see them.

The bells rang three times.

Margaret sprinted up to the Wire Room and responded with three rings of her own. From here she could ride the wires down the slope of Willowhen Peak to the Outer Wall itself. She took a moment to admire the view before all the noise and fury of her parents' return.

Tate was about to change: the I-Bombs had been a success. She glanced from the Outer Wall and the Jut, and the beginning of the white thread of Mechanism Highway leading north, then back over the Wall Secundus to the ice sheathed inner walls and the Steaming Vents.

These monstrous chimneys rose high above the Four Cannon, their buttresses lit with low voltage electric lights and crammed with all manner of endothermic weaponry. Keeping the city cold generated heat and not all of it could be recovered and distributed back into the city's engines. The waste heat released by the Vents was a constant draw to Roil spores and other more horrible entities. An endless battle raged around them. A unit of men and women called Sweepers garbed in cold-suits and more weaponry than any Sentinel, clambered over vent and chimney or rode the thermals on sharp-winged gliders into the spore cloud.

A knot of them slid down, and the next shift rose up. Their mocking whistles echoed over Tate as they passed one another; tallies added up, kills expressed in swift signals; the sign language of the Sweepers.

Men and women died above the city in the dry and ceaseless heat, but there were always more to take their place, drawn by the glamour and the terror of it. Margaret herself had hinted at such a career path; her parents promptly made her swear she would do no such thing, as if her parents did not risk their lives every day.

She grabbed her harness, just as another bell began to toll. And another. She stopped and tilted her head towards the city beyond the Wire Room, and the cacophony that was building there.

The ringing rippled over Willowhen Peak, taken up in watchtower after watchtower. In every house, in every quarter of the city, lights came on and doors swung open. Searchlights broke up the city airspace into grids of brilliance, revealing the nets and the dense darkness rising beyond.

A gun-prickled dirigible rushed east. Something flashed, from beyond the walls. The dirigible fell, a long exclamation mark of fire. And the bells kept tolling.

The city was under attack.

Tate's heartbeat raced. The Four Cannon loaded and fired, their huge engines turning, trying to cover as much ground as possible. Their grinding movements vibrated through the earth and into her feet.

Bells tolled. Smaller ice cannon fired all along the outer walls. What the hell was happening? An explosion shook the house, but not from above – this vibration had come from below. Another series of bells started ringing. Margaret, raised on the language of the bells, knew at once what it meant.

The Roil had breached the Jut, the gatehouse of Tate's outer wall. Even from here she could see it burning.

Another explosion and the Jut was gone, nothing remained of the gatehouse but a shower of blazing stone falling into the city.

The Four Cannon picked up pace. Margaret stumbled back inside. She strapped two belts of pistols to her waist and grabbed an ice rifle. She reached for her harness again, but stopped before her fingers closed upon the leather.

The wire thrummed as though the line were in use. She sighted along the wire, east. Her breath caught in her throat.

A Quarg Hound slid towards her, hooked claws gripping the wire perfectly. The beast's black eyes widened as it saw her, then narrowed. It opened its mouth. A black tongue flicked out over tiers of jagged teeth, and lashed at the air.

Margaret lifted the rifle to her shoulder, took aim and fired. The endothermic bullet hit the creature squarely; the hound spasmed and dropped.

If the wires were compromised her father's armoured carriage the *Melody Amiss* was the only way she would be able to get down to the wall. The wire thrummed again, startling her. Another dark shape raced over the city. She reached for an axe to break the line then thought better of it. The creature was a minute or so away, at least, and breaking the high tension wire was as much a danger to her as it. Margaret left the axe where it was, bolted the door to the wireway behind her, grabbed her weapons, rime blades and guns, and ran through to the Carriage Room.

The ceiling was high. Her footfalls echoed loudly, melding with the distant clamour of bells. She pulled on a cold suit: time-consuming but necessary. The black, rubberised substance clung to her and it chilled her to the marrow, but the suit would protect her from the Roil. Over the suit she shrugged on her long coat, its pockets already filled with ammunition and spare fuel cells. She'd been taught from childhood to dress as though the sky might fall in at any minute and decide to eat her. She considered the *Melody Amiss,* inside which she'd be something of an indigestible meal.

The *Melody* was a brutally elegant carriage of streamlined steel and brass, an electrical-fuel hybrid her father had kitted out with more than the usual ice weaponry. Coolant fans streaked its tail. Her father regarded it as a barely tested prototype, but Margaret's faith in it, and his designs, was far stronger. The cockpit could fit two at a stretch, but it was cramped, and the air within bitter with coolants.

She jabbed at the starter buttons, the engine hummed beneath her. She engaged the automatic doors to the driving room. A Quarg Hound raced on stiff limbs through the opening. It leapt at the *Melody Amiss*. All Margaret saw was teeth and scrabbling claw. She released a burst of cold air and the hound shrieked and slipped away and under the carriage's wheels.

The *Melody Amiss* lurched out the doorway and on to the street.

A body fell from the sky, striking the road with a wet thud – a Sweeper, the glider they had been riding torn to shreds. Its fall dragged her gaze up, to the tops of the Steaming Vents, the air around them was black with Hideous Garment Flutes and other Roilings. Gliders were being attacked from all angles. Sweepers fell here and there, broken, no grace in their descent, just a plummet.

There was nothing she could do here. But she could get to the front. She could help in the battle, and she could find out what had happened to her parents.

Even now, there was no panic. People gathered at the evacuation points. Lifts were already taking groups down to the caverns beneath the city; Margaret didn't even consider heading for their safety.

She drove as quickly as she dared. Wan-faced Sentinels let her through the first gate with a quick wave.

In the next zone, endothermic weaponry was being passed out to cold-suited Sentinels, and men and women in daywear or dressing gowns or Halloween costumes. It was an incongruous army that marched towards the walls – almost as varied as the creatures of the Roil itself. Every one of them moved with absolute economy, eyes lit with fear and a terrible determination.

Pride blazed within her. These people did not cower before the immensity surging over the gates; they stood their ground and fought.

At the second gate, a guard stopped her. She recognised him at once, a friend of the family and an old teacher at the rifle range. She released the door of the *Melody*.

"Howard, the Jut… I have to get through. Please let me through."

"I can't, Margaret, the Jut isn't there anymore. You know better than most that we have evacuation protocols to follow. The gates stay shut until we get everyone we can to the caverns below."

Behind him, Sentinels, straining against harnesses, dragged cannon to the edge of the Wall Secundus, then winched them up. The weaponry already on the wall thundered ice into the attackers.

"I know about the protocols. But I have to get through."

"You will do no such thing," he said, folding his arms. "Of all the people that I would expect trouble from… Margaret, this is not the time. We need you up on the ramparts."

Margaret's gaze turned frantically to the gate. "My parents are out there."

"So is the Roil."

"Has it reached the Secundus?"

Howard shook his head. "Its agents are close, though, and getting closer. I relayed Sara's message. I *know* your parents were at the Jut. I need you here. I'll send someone out for you, when we can spare them, once this is contained."

Another explosion shook the earth, ice crashed from the Secundus and fiery steel shards hurtled overhead, searing the air, striking the wall and exploding again. White-hot metal showered the Sentinels, igniting their cold suits so fast it was as though they had instantly become flame. All along the wall people shouted and screamed, pointing back at the way Margaret had come.

"One of the Cannon!" Howard rushed towards a burning Sentinel, Margaret followed, though she daren't get too close. Howard beat the flames away with his hands, then signalled to a stretcher crew.

"One of the Four has blown." He said to her as the Sentinel was taken away. "Get back, Margaret. You're a Penn, we need you safe."

"I can't, the Cannon sit above my home. And as to needing me, it's my parents you need, and you know it."

Howard said nothing. Margaret watched his eyes take in the blazing Cannon, the burning walls.

Fires everywhere. Ash darkened the sky until it was almost indistinguishable from the Roil.

Margaret knew the Penn home was gone. Where the cannon and the house had been was a wild ribbon of flame. The other three Cannon picked up speed, endothermic shells arcing out beyond the walls.

More ice smashed into the ground nearby. Gutters choked and water gurgled.

Her boots were soaked, as were the tips of her coat. The ice sheathes were failing and all that water freed was filling the streets.

In the middle of a firestorm the city began to drown.

CHAPTER 3

The Bridge was lost long ago, or won. Mirkton, after all, allowed such freedoms within the dark that no other suburb provided.

If Mirrlees was the beacon of the North, then Mirkton was its shadow. Life was cheap there, but still it was life.

Until the spiders came.

The Shadow City: An Economic History, MOLCK

THE CITY OF MIRRLEES – DOWNING BRIDGE

He'd been a fool to come here.

Mirkton crowded the gloom beneath the bridge. Its rough shanties were stacked precariously on and over each other, bound up in Aerokin-ropes, supported by rude poles, the shells of old carriages, whatever was solid and might bear weight. They sat in heaps that made them look more like midden piles than houses. Gas lanterns and stolen electrics gleamed in the dark. David was surprised by just how many people lived in this small city beneath the bridge. And every eye seemed focused on him. He realised that he stood out here perhaps more than anywhere, and in Mirkton he had more than Vergers to fear.

The place stank of the river and rot, and too many people pressed too close together, a raw smell that lingered and stung the back of the throat. The dark sang with the noises of the enclosing Downing Bridge: groaning metal; the dim thunder of the run-off from the rain; the chatter of Mirkton's markets, of deals being made. People lived their lives down here, and to a large extent had dragged the world that they had sought to escape from with them. David could see that there was commerce of a sort; he just didn't understand how it worked.

He found himself a quiet safe place, down a stinking, rubbish-strewn alley where he could gather his thoughts. But every thought brought him closer to utter paralysis. There was nowhere he could go, no plan or direction that could provide him with more than a few hours' life. Maybe he would have been better off just letting the Vergers take him. There'd be no worrying now.

Carnival's pangs struck him again, a body-wide shaking that dropped him to his knees. He vomited loudly. Sobbed when he was done, a frail sound, the sort of weakness you didn't want to project here.

He stopped almost at once, covering his mouth with his hands. But someone had heard him.

Heavy footfalls drew near, kicking their way through debris.

Quiet, safe place no longer, if it had ever been.

"You," someone shouted in the dark. "I've need of your clean skin. I've a hungry piece of meat for you."

A man, a good foot taller than David, two feet broader, at least, shuffled closer, his cock in his hand. "See how hungry it is."

David backed away. Not far, rough, sweating bricks pushed against his spine. Dead end, kind of appropriate, he thought.

David clenched his hands into fists. "Come no closer," he yelled.

"Oh, I'll be coming closer, fancy boy." The man grinned. "See it?" the man said. "Now feel it."

David kicked at his groin, and the man caught his foot, throwing David off balance. David landed on his back, and choked as more vomit crowded his throat. "Now, let's see what we can do with you, eh."

He bent down, slapping David's hands away. "Let me se–" The man's eyes rolled up in his head. He groaned and fell, crushing David in a hot and stinking embrace.

The body lifted, an inch or two, and David stared into lifeless eyes. "Ah, he's a heavy bastard," someone muttered. The body dropped. "You know, the least you could do is help me get him off you."

David pushed. The body rolled away, a knife in its back. A Verger's knife. David looked into a boy's face far younger than his own, but harder, even though he was smiling. "Ain't no Verger, by the way. May tell you how I came by that knife one day, if you make it." He reached out a hand and David grabbed it, scrambling to his feet. "You're not going to last long down here, without help."

"I'm not going to last long anywhere," David said.

The boy crouched down and extracted the knife from the dead man's spine. "Well, you've got a chance now, the name's Lassiter."

"David."

"Well, David, you can come with me. I've a bolthole, away from all this noise. You're welcome to share it."

"And why would you do that?"

"Because two's better than one here. Someone to watch your back. You wander through Mirkton alone and unknowing and … You want to be someone's meat puppet, David?"

David shook his head.

"Then step to it. I've no desire for death tonight." He kicked the corpse. "One kill's enough, don't you think?"

Lassiter led him away from the dim bulk of Mirkton and into the darker regions, where shanties lay broken and empty, and their boots crunched on glass, and kicked up a dust made of bone and death and desertion. Lassiter flashed a grin. "Here we're alone, some parts of Mirkton even the scum avoid."

Soon the paths they took were criss-crossed in gossamer threads.

David brushed past a web, and something stung his arm. He cursed, shaking out his hand to free it of the web, and was stung again. David slapped his palm down over the bite; whatever had bitten him smeared beneath his fingers.

"Spider," Lassiter said. "Keep away from the webs. There's a lot of them down here. Closer you get to the levee, and under the main part of the bridge. Mirkton was much bigger a couple of years back, but the spiders drove them out of the deeper parts. Some say that's the Council's doing. I don't know about that, but it's interesting that when the Vergers stopped patrolling this place the spiders started to swell in numbers. There's still refuge to be found in a few of the spider territories if you know what you're doing." Lassiter puffed up his chest. "And I know what I'm doing."

Another spider bit him. David snarled and squashed it definitively with his thumb. "Are you sure this place is safe?"

Lassiter laughed. "Nowhere's safe down here, but it's safer than most."

They passed down long-abandoned streets lined with dipping, treacherous-looking houses, their walls mould-black or furred with web, and finally reached Lassiter's bolthole. There was some light here: a small electric lantern, the power taken, Lassiter told him, directly from the levee itself.

There were also a couple of paper-thin mattresses, and a few books stacked neatly in a corner, mostly pulp adventures: *The Night Council, The Ragged Poet*. David picked one up, a *Night Council* title. On the cover, Travis the Grave was fighting an Endym, its wing blades bloody. David stared at the lurid cover like it was a picture of home.

"Got to get your mind off all this crap sometimes," Lassiter said.

"This was a good one," David said.

"Yeah, that Travis the Grave is crazy. No-one takes on an Endym that way," Lassiter said, as though he had considered the tactical elements of a one-on-one fight with an Endym and worked out the best way. David almost thought to mock him, then realised that he had done the same thing many a time as a boy, not too long ago, before the Carnival gripped him. It saddened him in an unfamiliar way to think of that boy – where was he now?

Dead as his father, and his mother.

"You hungry?" Lassiter asked and hurled David a bruised apple before he could reply. Lassiter grinned a proud and clever grin, as though this feat matched any conquest over an Endym. Perhaps it did. "Nicked 'em a week ago, valuable as gold, what with all this rain."

David was starving. He wolfed the soft and floury fruit down. Lassiter tossed him another. David ate it more slowly. When he was done, while hardly full, he found himself wearier than he could have believed possible.

"Oh, and you might want this." Lassiter slid a small package into his hand.

David almost wept.

"It isn't much, but it'll see you through the night."

David didn't ask how he knew, he just slipped the three dark pills into his mouth and dry-swallowed them.

He yawned. Too early for the drug to take effect, but knowing that it would was enough to calm him. True calm would follow.

"You're tired." Lassiter said. "We're safe enough here, won't let nothing hurt you. You rest up, and we'll talk properly when you wake. World's changed for you, David. You've a lot of work to be done, if you're going to live."

David wondered just how Lassiter could know all this about him. Some of it was obvious, he guessed. After all, here he was in the darkest of the dark of Mirkton. Few came here because they wanted to.

He had questions to ask, yes. But not now. He'd run too far that night, and he was bone weary.

Answers for the morning.

And if Lassiter slit his throat in his sleep, well, at least he would be sleeping.

He knew there were worse ways to go.

The *Dolorous Grey's* shrill whistle echoed down the streets. The sound tightened the muscles in John Cadell's neck. He should have been anywhere but here, standing in the dimly lit vestibule of what was somewhat contentiously considered a safe house.

Surely, the last twenty-four hours had put paid to the concept. No place was safe for members of the Confluent Party, or their allies. Ha, there wasn't a Confluent Party any more, just a list of corpses. And he was responsible. They'd died protecting him. That thought was enough to set the earth spinning. He yearned just a little for his old cage.

"All of them are dead?" Cadell was almost certain they were being watched. Well, let them come. Right then he would have happily broken a few Verger skulls and indulged his less than savoury hungers.

Medicine Paul nodded. His hands shook. Those hands a perpetual reminder of what Stade was capable of. After all, Stade had ordered the severing of his index fingers ten years ago and ruined Paul's career. He'd been a fine surgeon. Ultimately such punishment had merely strengthened Paul's resolve. Stade had gotten that one wrong.

A burst of wind rattled the windows to the rear of the house. Medicine jumped. "All of them, *except* David."

"Milde's son? Where is he?"

"Beneath the bridge. I've a man with him."

Cadell snorted. "Lassiter is hardly a man, he's younger than David, scarcely a tuft of hair on his chin. What is he, the last of your agents? The Council has its Vergers and we have boys and old men."

"We've got you," Medicine said.

"And you'll jeopardise all of it for his son?"

"Warwick's boy."

"Hasn't he suffered enough? He's an addict for all that he's barely a man. We've no use for him."

Medicine's eyes were cold. "You know enough of addictions, one would think, to feel some sympathy."

Cadell nodded. Yes he did, though his were cruel and far bleaker than anything the boy was acquainted with. "You mock me and my purpose with this request, and you do nothing but ill to the boy. The son hates me, and with good reason. What happened with his uncle..."

"Cadell, everyone is dead. And it is precisely what happened with Sean... you could make amends."

"Make amends! Make amends? This is no mere slight to be fixed with a kind word." Cadell folded his arms. "I could refuse. Where I am going is dangerous. I'm dangerous."

"You could take him to Uhlton."

"My plans would have to go seriously awry before I ever did that. They hate me there."

Medicine laughed, a little hysterically to Cadell's mind. "You do have a way of making enemies."

Cadell didn't laugh with him. "I've already organised the Aerokin, the Mothers of the Air have agreed to my request, a miracle in itself. I could refuse what you ask of me. "

"But you won't. You will pick him up from Lassiter and you will take him safely to Hardacre. You owe him and his family as much."

Cadell had nothing to say to that, his hard eyes just stared at Medicine, and Cadell was surprised that Medicine held that awful gaze. "But you won't refuse," Medicine said.

And Cadell knew he was right.

CHAPTER 4

A city twice lost, and more than double the tragedy. Here, what should have been a bulwark of civilization, a clarion-call to the Roil's defeat, became nothing more than a sad footnote.

What might have been becomes instead the thunderous ruination of a world. It is the historian's duty to avoid hyperbole, but it is hard not to use such language in this case.

Dark was the loss of Tate, but darker days were to follow for all.

Engine of Madness, MINGLEE

THE CITY OF TATE

Something dropped heavily to the ground behind them. Margaret was ready with her rifle, but she did not fire.

The Quarg Hound squatted on its four legs, its head high as her waist. It splashed furiously in the water, then with a whine, rolled over dead.

The streets were still too cold, but not for much longer. The firestorm intensified, leaping from roof to roof, devouring houses and coolant in a terrifying quiet flame. Nothing crackled, everything hissed thin as a dying man's last breath.

Another Quarg Hound fell, landing on a Sentinel. Saved by his armour, the man stumbled and swung to face the beast. It was already dead, slain with a single shot from Margaret's rifle.

Howard blinked. "You've been practising." He raised his gun and fired behind her. Another Quarg Hound died. "Good with the blade, but never so good with the gun."

A wave of heat rushed over them, coming from the centre of the city. The ground rippled, Margaret fell.

Howard reached down to help her up, his mouth moved and she read his lips as much as heard him. "You all right?" Debris crashed all around; fiery shards of metal punctured houses and set tarred roofs burning. A nearby coolant tank caught alight. She could smell flesh burning, people dying.

But Margaret hardly noticed. Willowhen blazed, fires swirling around the ruin of two of the four Cannon. Tate's heartbeat had grown wild and empty. She imagined the men and women up there, working frantically, desperately, because without the Cannon the city was lost. Screams echoed down to her, and laughter, human, but wrong, as though the Roil had warped it.

There wasn't much time left. But for those distant cries, everything had grown silent. All around the crowded street people paused and stared at each other, weapons in hand. Margaret could feel their fear, and see it in their eyes. But then they got to work, they clambered onto the Wall Secundus and brought rime blade and gun to bear on Quarg Hound or Endym.

Perhaps it was her presence, what she represented, but Howard's reaction was different.

"Another one, they've taken out another one." Howard's voice cracked. "This is no time for argument. Go back now or you–"

The third cannon exploded, its muzzle collapsing onto the streets of the inner city, buffeting them with stinging heat. Margaret's ears rang. Ash fell everywhere, squalls of darkness, buffeted by heat and cold. The remaining cannon launched its icy shells futilely into the beast-crowded sky. Far above, black shapes jeered and cackled.

Howard seemed smaller, his shoulders slumped and his hands shook. His fear, if that was what it was, passed almost at once. They'd been at this battle all their lives. His face shone with the light of some new kind of resolve… or madness.

"Tate is lost. Betrayed, there can be no other reason for its swift fall." His words came hard and fast, he grabbed her hands. "In those early years no one believed we stood a chance, but then your mother fell pregnant and we knew hope remained. Please remember that. You were, and have always been, a symbol of hope to us."

And there it was, that which hurt her the most. The thing she was supposed to be.

Howard led her to the *Melody Amiss* and signalled that the gates be opened.

Sentinels stepped into the breach and fired their rifles. Howard's words came fast; he did not look at her. "Drive through, quickly now, I have to shut the gate behind you."

"Come with me." She reached for him.

Howard shook his head, changing his hold on the rifle and pulling back, almost as though her touch was all it would take. "No, my family is here. Go, find yours."

Margaret clambered back into the *Melody Amiss*, its engine idling, and drove through the gateway into chaos and flame.

The inner city blazed behind her, throwing the road ahead into sharp relief. Most of Tate's coolants had finished their shift of allegiance from ice to fire. What that fiery treachery revealed was a flowing, flickering image of madness. Throughout the city, ice cracked and melted, lit red and orange as though already given over to the flame. Quarg Hounds and other Roilings cavorted in streets that streamed with foaming bloody water, cold enough that they had to jump from claw to claw or prey to prey, hacking, slashing, feeding. And she had never seen such wild joy grip them, nor seen before the dark cunning in their brute faces.

Here, more terror bloomed than any lone ice cannon or armoured carriage could ever hope to halt. Twenty years it had taken them, but at last the siege was over and the Roil triumphant.

The Roil had always been a mighty fist wrapped around the city, biding its time. The fist was closing now, without pause, and she, just as horribly resolute, drove towards the Jut.

Where were her parents?

Just moments before the attack began, the bell had rung with news of their arrival. Perhaps the last thing Sara had done. Margaret tried to separate the bare facts from the deaths and found she couldn't. Her thoughts were muddied by them. There was too much to consider and far too much to do. Surely, her parents had tried to enter the city, perhaps begun mobilising the defence. Yet she had seen no sign of such mobilisation, nor had any word reached her, as it most surely would.

Her thoughts returned to that first distant explosion, of the Jut disappearing in fire and black smoke. It had happened in an instant. She doubted anyone near it could have survived. A bleak chill overtook her and she forced it down. Down. Far deeper than her waking mind could follow.

Margaret needed the facts.

Until then, everything was speculation and possibility, and leanest possibility at that.

To find out required her driving on, through every cruel nightmare that had ever haunted her, racing towards what may be her worst fear of all.

The cockpit's thick glass and metal shielded her from all but the loudest, shrillest screams, but it was a guilt-tainted mercy. She should be out there. She should be helping, but the city was lost, and her parents were before her. When she reached the outer gate, she found it a blasted ruin. The bridge beyond smouldered but remained intact.

She paused, not sure what to do. Margaret had expected to find her parents at the gatehouse, dead or alive, but there was nothing – just stony, smoking ruins. Few Roilings had gathered there: the gate's defences had been engaged. Jets of cold slush shot over the bridge, the run-off flowing back down and around the gatehouse.

Sick to the stomach, she drove the carriage slowly towards the ruin.

A sentry lay dead directly in front of her, and she could not make herself drive over the body. Arming all her guns, she leapt out of the *Melody Amiss* and dashed to the corpse.

It was Sara.

As Margaret approached, Sara sat up. Blood darkened her uniform, and the cold suit beneath. She lifted her rifle and aimed it at Margaret's head.

CHAPTER 5

Cadell, where he fits in the Grand Narratives of Time grows ever more tenuous. Surely he is mere apocrypha, as likely a creature as Travis the Grave or Ray Normal.

Everywhere Cadell is mentioned there is chaos, blood and despair. Excise him from history and the fable of the past is pulled away. Excise him from history and hear the wind howl through the holes that are left.

That is the problem of Cadell. He makes no sense, but without him, nothing does.

Myths, Meanings & Memories – Letters to a Historian,
GUY NURRISH

THE CITY OF MIRRLEES

David woke in the bolthole under the bridge, as the spiders ran across his face, trailing silk. He couldn't see the creatures, but he could feel them in the dark. He batted them away with a hand already sticky with web. It could have been a dream, it had that light touch, and his dreams that night had been vivid and frequent.

"Go away," he mumbled.

The spiders started to bite.

David hissed, awake all at once, and scrambled from the bolthole into the lesser dark, slapping his skin, scraping the web from the back of his hands.

The spider bites stopped, though the stinging did not.

Where was Lassiter?

David peered into the dark. "Lassiter?" He could just make out the boy's legs, further in the bolthole. "Lassiter!"

Lassiter's foot twitched.

David reached out and grabbed at a shoe. It was coated in silk and spiders, each the size of his little fingernail; they started nipping again. But David clung on. He pulled Lassiter free. He scraped the web from the boy, ignoring the bites of the spiders. Then he remembered the electric lantern. He switched it on, and wished he hadn't

There wasn't much left of Lassiter's face. The spiders had already devoured his eyes. David opened Lassiter's mouth to check his breathing, as his father had taught him, and found it filled with the creatures. They poured out over Lassiter's lips.

Lassiter had saved his life. They'd fed on him first.

David backed away from the corpse. But not before he saw the photograph. He remembered that one, his mother had paid for it to be taken. He picked it up. Who had Lassiter been working for? And where were they now?

He turned and ran.

Straight into the Old Man. "And where are you going, lad?"

"You!" David swung a fist, and the man caught it, gripped it in a hand that was shockingly cold. David's knuckles stung, he wrenched his hand free, but had a sense that he had only been able to because Cadell had let him.

"Good, there's some fight in you yet," Cadell said. He pulled the photo from David's fingers and peered at it.

"How else could Lassiter find you?" he said.

"Lassiter's dead."

"I know that." The old man's voice cracked. "That's another one to the tally. Mr Milde, you're coming with me. Long as I've some conscience left I'm keeping you safe."

"There's nothing safe about you," David said.

"No, there's nothing safe. But everything is relative, and I would suggest you swap certainty of death at spider bite or Verger's knife for the uncertainty of me. I am dangerous, yes, but even more so to those that hunt you. Surely it is the obvious choice."

"The obvious ones are hardest," David said.

"Ah, as obstinate as your father."

"It did him little good."

"Exactly, but it might serve you better. Put that will into your flight with me, and you may yet live out the day, and those that follow."

"And where will you take me?"

"Away from here, for one." Cadell peered into the bolthole. "Hurry, we can discuss the future at length where there are no spiders listening or dead boys to drive another nail of guilt into my heart."

David didn't say anything, just stepped a little further from Lassiter's tomb. He felt another pang of addiction, bent over and was sick. Not much to bring up, but it came painfully nonetheless.

He wiped his mouth. Cadell stared at him. It was too dark, even with the lantern, to know what he was thinking.

"Come on, Mr Milde," Cadell said, and his voice was gentle, no hint of the danger of which he had just spoke. "We've such little time left to us. Oh, and I've your drug… your Carnival."

Cadell turned and walked from the bolthole, not looking back, and David followed him, away from the electric lantern and Lassiter's corpse, and into the dark.

"I don't trust you," David said.

They had been walking some time, Cadell leading them on a path beneath Downing Bridge that kept well away from Mirkton, their only company being drops of rain and the occasional scratch and scurry of rats. Once a shape the size of a very large dog came lumbering out of the gloom at them, and the old man snatched a blade from the handle of his umbrella, but whatever it was wasn't interested in them; it passed by, quickly lost again to the dark. Twice they came upon the corpses of rats smothered in spiders, bringing back to David the image of Lassiter. David had been but minutes away from the same fate. Where he was headed now he had no idea, just the looming bulk of Cadell before him. He realised that the old man was laughing.

"I wouldn't trust anyone right now. Lack of trust is an extremely useful survival mechanism. But I am all you have," he said. "I am sorry that your life has taken this turn, Mr Milde. I really am, but there is nothing for it, but to keep walking."

Soon enough that walking led them to the eastern edge of the bridge, it was wet and murky beyond, a typical sort of day. A fog had lifted from the levee and settled on the streets.

"I brought you an umbrella." He pushed it into David's hands and David took it, wondering if it contained a sword as well.

"It doesn't," Cadell said. "See, I don't trust you either."

The sky was dark, with rain, and the deeper darkness of Aerokin and the Cuttlefolk's messengers, swift racing smudges through the air. Looking back, he could see the pale lights of

Mirkton. Stale air from beneath the bridge washed over them. "Where are we going?" David opened the umbrella.

"My room," Cadell said. "Then we're going to catch a train."

"North or south?" David asked.

"South."

David still wasn't sure he'd heard him properly. There was only one train that went that way: The *Dolorous Grey*. The Roil was down south. Nothing safe was down south.

"Yes, south," Cadell said. "We have to get you out of here. I will get you to Hardacre, I promise. But the direct route north is too obvious, and too dangerous. There's the drowned suburbs, the Margin, Cuttlemen, and not the refined folk we have in the city, but the ones for whom the war is still fresh and bitter." Cadell said. "We're travelling to Chapman. We're going to the end of the world."

There was a slight sucking sound as the machine disconnected itself from Stade's skull. Stade hated that noise, the wet extraction of filaments from his brain.

Stade blinked. He tasted blood in his mouth; he reached for the glass of water by the chair. Tope stood in one corner of the room and Stade glared at him. He didn't like the Verger seeing him in such a vulnerable state. Stade spat the bloody water into a bowl.

He was almost glad that the spiders had never extended their territory beyond Downing Bridge – something to do with the great quantity of iron in the structure he'd been told. Whatever it was, it meant he didn't need to use them very often.

He shivered. All that information, all those eyes. His skin crawled every time he entered that space, his teeth ground away at the inside of his cheeks. Old tech, it never really translated to these new situations. He'd caught flashes of other images, other spaces beyond the interface between him and the arachnids: a pyramid of skulls, a spherical particle accelerator, and his mother's face.

"David got away. The spiders are hard to control, always have been, too many of them, too many thoughts; they settled on the other one."

"Who has him then?"

"Cadell."

Tope frowned. "Well, *that* is something of a challenge." Stade spat out another mouthful of water, clearer this time. "Yes, chances are Cadell will kill him before we ever find them."

"I'll find them, and I'll kill them both."

"You've Cuttle in your blood, Tope. But he's an Old Man."

"I'll find them and I'll kill them both." Tope left the room, shutting the door behind him.

Stade laughed, and he dug through the pockets of his coat for a cigar. "The thing is you really think you can, and you might just be right."

CHAPTER 6

Death, when it comes, is always unexpected. But a reawakening to something else, another shifting mental space, how peculiar that must be. When the churches speak of this, surely they do not mean the deathlessness of the Roil.

The Death cults, the Birthers and the Renewal, their resurrection could not be thus.

This was madness and hunger and dreams.

Histories, DEIGHTON

THE CITY OF TATE

"Stay where you are," Sara said.

"It's me." Margaret raised her hands above her head. "It's me."

"How can I be sure?"

"It's me. What are you talking about?" She searched her friend's face. Sara spat a little blood onto the ground. Her brow creased with some sort of decision and she lowered her gun. "Doesn't matter now," she said. "Dead bodies, coming back to life, I've seen them. You don't want to stay here. You strike the heads from their shoulders. I die and you do that for me. Promise me now or I'll shoot you where you stand."

"I promise," Margaret said.

"There's moths everywhere," Sara's eyes grew unfocussed, she clutched at her gun. "Even in their carriage."

"You saw them," Margaret demanded. "My parents..."

Sara shook her head. "Something happened. Whatever was driving your parents' carriage wasn't human." She lowered her voice. "They're dead, and if not, perhaps it's better to consider them that way."

"I have to find them."

"I don't think that would be a good idea. I don't think you would like what you found. Margaret, believe me, what came through the Jut was no more your parents than the Quarg Hounds they guided to the wireway." Sara rolled her head, towards the blazing heart of Tate. "But you can't go back. There's no way you can go back, there's only death in the city for you now, for all of us."

"Get out of here, north, along Mechanism Highway. That's an order. You might have a chance."

They let what they both knew was a lie stand there between them. Margaret shuddered, took great gulping breaths. Calm down, she thought. Slow your breathing down. She was her parents' child. She was a Penn, and born of the city of Tate. Her breathing slowed, her mind stopped its flailing, she even managed a grin. "Well, you're coming with me." Finally, she had the comfort of her resolve.

Sara stared up at her, silent. Dead.

Margaret dragged the body to the side of the road, the trail of blood she left behind revealing the extent of Sara's injuries. She brushed Sara's face with her fingertips. The heat was already going from her flesh.

She gripped her rime blade in her hands and cut her

friend's head from her shoulders. She had promised, she owed Sara that much at least.

Margaret sprinted to the *Melody Amiss*, struck by a horrible epiphany. The first glimpses of an answer to what was going on, how the Jut had been obliterated just seconds after the alarm bells started ringing and why the Four Cannon had fallen so quickly. The Roil was affecting people, transforming them as it had transformed the land beyond the Outer Wall.

What had happened to her parents? She could not bear to think of them as changed.

Margaret guided the *Melody Amiss* through the broken gateway. As she drove onto the bridge, she took it all in, not daring to get out; there was no one left standing, just human wreckage amongst the bare stone. More death than she had ever seen, sightless eyes and still, bloodless limbs. But that was not the worst of it.

As the *Melody Amiss* passed them, they rose. Sentinels, faces wreathed with moths, their movements stuttery at first, as though their muscles were new to them. Soon they quickened, their shambling turned to sprinting as they shook free the cowl of their deaths. They rushed the carriage, their fingers reaching. Eyes not empty but alien and terrifying, black as the moths that crawled and tumbled from their wounds and their lips. But they were not as swift as the *Melody Amiss*; she left them behind as she had left everything else.

A hundred yards from the gate, rubble was all that remained of the Jut. Roilings massed there, some humanoid, others sluglings or crab-octopuses, and around them in their thousands, barking and baying, circled packs of Quarg Hounds. Into the monstrous clamour dived Endyms: huge eyes shining in the fire, their leathery wings showering the ground with dusty Roil spores as they scooped up creatures and dropped them over

Tate's walls. Above it all, the city's nets blazed and fell in great fiery clumps. A few battle drones remained, raining endothermic weaponry upon the enemy, but they were not enough. Even as she watched, Endyms dashed them from the sky, the burning remnants tumbling to the city, setting even more buildings alight.

Margaret neared the end of the bridge. The whole structure shook and the valves that had before ejected icy slush now churned with a liquid fire.

The moat beyond was still thick with ice, but it would soon grow warm as blood. Bodies floated on the surface, drifting backwards and forwards as more water rushed in. Margaret wondered how many of her people the Roil had infected.

Not now. Do not think of it now.

She was running out of time. The banks of the moat would not contain the rising water for much longer. She could already see dark cracks spreading across its outer edges; water seeped from them as blood from a wound.

A crab-like Roiling, legs spiked and furious, almost as big as the *Melody,* scurried in front of her. Its fore-claws slashed out and its mouthparts flexed.

Margaret slowed almost to a halt, gave her front cannon a full charge and fired, tearing the Roiling apart.

Fingers tapped against the *Melody's* side window: a little girl struggled frantically with the handle. Margaret popped the door open.

"Get in! Quick!" A blast of cold air shot out into the night. The little girl screamed as the air crashed against her face. Her head folded back, unveiling grasshopper-like mandibles. Luminous eyes stared from the pit of the girl's skull. The creature hissed at her then bound away on prickly legs that had been hidden by the little girl part of its body.

Margaret slammed the door shut.

CHAPTER 7

Carnival. The sweetest dreams for the darkest times. No common opiate, it was wilder, crueller in its denial. It had appeared upon the streets of Mirrlees, in its dens and its parlours, only a decade before the end, and grown ever popular.

In those last days its use was commonplace, both lowlife and highborn drawn to its comforts. It did not discriminate. Only the most paranoid would suggest it was addiction as assault.

Drugs & Damages, DOYLE

THE CITY OF MIRRLEES

Cadell shook him awake, the Old Man's touch cold enough that David could feel it through the sheets. He shivered.

Cadell pulled his hand away; there was something almost contrite about the movement.

"You were talking in your sleep." Cadell's breath stank of liquor, David blinked in the burning wash of it. "Bad dreams?"

"Yes," David said. "Bad dreams." Churning, horrible dreams that he'd fallen into every time he closed his eyes: knives and blood and Downing Bridge itself, drowning bridge in truth, with its dribbling levee-bed, its profusion of spiders and their hungers.

Cadell chuckled. "Curse of these times. The city's rotting as the Weep swells, no one has pleasant dreams. Of course the lack of Carnival in your veins wouldn't help."

He nodded to the table; David's skin prickled, a small syringe of the disposable type lay there. Not more than a few feet away.

"I've powders for the journey ahead, better for travelling, less chance of breakage. But today you've need of the purer stuff," Cadell said. "Much as I might wish it otherwise, we've no time for you to break free of the Carnival. It's a maintenance dose, but a quality one."

David's mouth was dry. It was all he could do to stop himself from leaping out of the bed and driving that syringe straight into the fattest vein he could find. He already had three in mind. He'd shove it into an eyeball, if it meant he could have it now.

"I understand such hungers," Cadell said, drawing David's attention back from the syringe, though his voice sounded distant.

David's tongue stuck to the roof of his mouth, but he worked it loose. "You were a user?" he said thickly.

Cadell shook his head. "No, but there are other addictions, believe me, and some much more harmful than sticking a needle in your arm or your foot. When you're done, there are clothes in the bag by the dresser; they should fit."

Cadell left the room then, and David did the one thing that he'd desired since he'd fled his father's house into the dark and the rain. These were no sere old pills. This was the good stuff.

When he was done, and the Syringe disposed of, he slumped in the chair, breathing deeply, a stupid smile broad across his face. Cadell hadn't been lying about the Carnival's purity. The tension left his limbs and the deep grief that had threatened to overwhelm him evaporated. It was almost as if none of it mattered, and it didn't really. Not one little bit.

But he'd kick along with Cadell, of course he would. He didn't want to die – unless it was right now. *That* he *could* handle

David finally dragged himself from the chair and picked his way through the bag of clothes. Cadell was a man of impeccable sartorial taste, and a good judge of size at that. David cleaned himself up, dried himself down, and dressed.

He winked at his reflection in the dresser mirror. He could almost imagine he was young, free and single again, and not a fugitive on the run from knives.

"If you're done…" Cadell said, startling him.

Everything had increased in clarity. Cadell's bloodshot eyes gleamed. David blinked.

"You look better now," Cadell said. "Much more the man about town than the fugitive fleeing through it."

"Clothes and Carnival maketh the man," David said, feeling stupid as soon as the words left his mouth.

Cadell sat down. "We've a while yet, and time to talk. Ask what you will."

David nodded. "What do you know about the Roil? Your name always came up when father spoke of it."

"More than I ought. More than what's good for a man. And so will you, before this is done." He reached over to the table, picked up his hat, ran his hands along its brim, turning the hat around and around, perhaps to keep his fingers busy and his eyes focused on something other than David. "But that's the way of this decaying world, and I owe your father this much at least."

This much? Was David, this much? "What do you owe my father?"

"Plenty," Cadell said. "Just believe me, when I say this doesn't even begin to square the debt, perhaps it even adds to it."

To David this wasn't much of an answer. "What would square the debt then?"

"I hope you never have to find out." Cadell stood up, dropped his hat on the bed and walked to a cabinet near the mirror. He splashed something in a glass, swallowed it down in a gulp. Grimaced. "I should have warned him, more than I did. More forcefully, should have kept a closer eye on your house."

"He knew this was coming?" A dark bitterness rose in him and raged. Why hadn't he fled? Why had his father risked both their lives?

Cadell nodded his head. "He knew that as soon as he crossed the floor of Parliament, soon as he joined the Confluents, something was coming. He just didn't expect it to be this. Thought they were all working towards the same thing. Stade proved him wrong. Oh, lad, there are secrets that layer Mirrlees and Shale, sediments of madness and lies more damning than you could believe. Missteps, and murders, from the First Ships down." Cadell lifted his empty hands in the air. "There's blood on these, as much as Stade, more." Cadell stopped. "I'm sorry, David."

"People die, Mr Cadell," David said, and his voice was colder than even the Carnival could account for. "People die."

And that was all he allowed himself.

Cadell took his time in responding. "But you're not dead."

David didn't argue the point, but he knew Cadell was wrong. Something inside him was dead. Not too long ago, a few years, no more, he'd been maybe fourteen or fifteen, he had woken in the middle of the night, and realised that he was going to die, that the night was smothering him. He'd started screaming then.

His parents had rushed into the room. His mother had held him, and he had told her, that he didn't want to die, that he didn't want any of them to die. She'd kissed his brow, and assured him that he had a very long time indeed before he needed to worry about such things.

Well, it had turned out that they hadn't had that long at all. The next day the rain fell, and it really hadn't stopped. His mother was dead six months later, his father increasingly obsessive and cold. Was it any wonder he had succumbed to addiction by his seventeenth year?

"Stuffy in here," Cadell muttered and opened a window. The rain had picked up a notch; it cooled the air but a fraction.

Better than nothing, David thought.

"I'm sorry, lad. Not least of all that I'm all you've got. You're right there; people die, and most of your father's allies died with him last night. The Engineers have played their dissolution and rule Parliament now. And the Vergers have taken sides. These are desperate times, and Stade really thinks he's doing the right thing. But he isn't."

David was thirsty. He found a glass and filled it with water from a jug. A revolver sat on a bench nearby. He stared at it a long time, then considered the broad back of Cadell. Carnival made all things possible, steadied the shakiest hand, if he moved quick he could avenge at least one death in his family.

"Well, *are* you going to shoot me, Mr Milde?"

David shook his head. Something about Cadell changed then, and even though David could only see his back, he knew he was grinning. "Do you even know what I am, David. Did your father ever tell you that particular secret?"

"My father never told me anything. All we did was fight."

"I guess that was all he knew at the end. How to fight. He told you I killed your uncle, but he never explained the circumstances. Oh, where to begin?" Cadell turned from the window, the rainy city behind him, dark and streaming, and him sharing some of that darkness.

Perhaps David should have used the revolver.

Cadell walked over to the table and flipped open the revolver's drum, no bullets. "Never leave a loaded gun where an enemy might use it. Of course, we aren't enemies. Have you ever heard talk of the Engine of World?"

What? David thought. Fairy tales?

"It's a myth," David said. "Tearwin Meet, Land Crash, the Battering of Gillam Hall, those I can believe in. But the Engine… an impossibility."

"It's not an impossibility. I was there. I helped build it."

It was then David knew without a hint of doubt that Cadell was mad.

CHAPTER 8

If one event can be counted as the beginning of the final days, then, arguably, one need look no further than the fall of Tate. The true fall, the one revealed to us so unexpectedly.

Some equilibrium was upset, what had been expected to take decades, a slow and steady transition into the dark, became instead a sprint. The Roil, ever vast and ponderous, transformed, grew predatory, and found an urgent hunger to match its size.

Histories, DEIGHTON

THE CITY OF TATE

The fourth cannon fired a few more times before succumbing to gravity and sabotage like its siblings. Its last two blasts came perilously close to the *Melody Amiss*, clearing the path before her in great bursts of ice, but also striking the ground so hard that the carriage bounced, Margaret rattling around inside it as she struggled to gain control, the wheel jerking in her grip.

The falling cannon struck tanks of coolant on the eastern quadrant. A storm of flame lifted the carriage up and slammed it into the ridge.

Margaret blacked out and, for a moment, she was home with her parents in their library.

Here, alone in the Penn household, clutter ruled, books, notes, schematics in their most incubate form (iron ships of the air, scurrying many limbed metal transports, a hand-held device for the calculation of arithmetic), even political cartoons. On the wall was suspended the terrestrial Orrery, a map traversed by a metal band that depicted the Roil's progress across Shale. The band had long ago crossed McMahon in the North and now was on the verge of sliding over Chapman. Many times Margaret had run her fingers over the Orrery, imagining lands and metropolises beyond the Roil. Places that had a blue sky not black, that saw the Sun, the Moon and the stars.

A huge wooden table, surrounded by plump leather-bound chairs, dominated the centre of the library, a grand old man deliciously besieged by books.

Margaret slumped into a chair, glancing over the books and papers stacked up high before her. On the armrests were her father's plans for a system of pneumatic railways, and an old copy of the *Shadow Council*. The lurid cover showed Travis the Grave racing over a burning rooftop, sabre in his mechanical hand, proving that even her father still liked to relax a little – though he had annotated it with stern pronouncements on the scientific and engineering flaws within the text.

Her mother had been reading Deighton's treatise on the *Engine of the World*, and receiving much mockery as a consequence.

"It's just legend and the whimsy of mechanics who should know better," Marcus Penn muttered. "Deighton, little more than folklore dressed up as history and science. Mechanical Winter is just a way of explaining the Ice Age. Engine of the World! Why do you insist on stretching credulity so?"

Arabella Penn arched an eyebrow, her lips curling into something too scathing to be a smile. "Then how was the Roil stopped? How do you explain the fact that this world is colder than it ought to be, even with the Roil?"

"Hmm."

Her father raised one hand vaguely, jabbing at the air. "For the latter, our astronomical mathematics are wrong, much as it chagrins me to admit. And, for the first, obviously it is a natural process. Perhaps a kind of tide. The Ice Age came, the tide turned."

"Ha! I can't imagine this tide turning. As for natural, I'm not quite sure the Roil is natural. If it is, it is nature gone wrong."

"Bah, nature goes wrong all the time. One could say it is the very nature of nature to go wrong. What is wrong anyway? Just because it doesn't agree with us doesn't mean it's wrong. But then again it's not humanity's nature to agree with nature, otherwise we'd all be living in trees, which wouldn't be all that bad I suppose as I'm rather fond of trees myself. Natural or not there are no engines." Her father cleared his throat. "Margaret, my dear, could you see to that damnable ringing."

Ringing!

She snapped awake with a gasp and touched her stinging forehead. Her fingers came back wet with her blood. The cut was deep, but she barely felt it. She could hardly feel anything.

The firestorm had turned the carriage around so that she faced Tate. A howl cracked her lips.

Sheets of fire consumed the city, from the foot to the crown of Willowhen Peak, even the stony, spiked walls burned with a coolant-fed blue flame – a terrible ghost light. The Four Cannon were stumps of iron glowing with a white heat. The Steaming Vents, too, had mostly fallen, caved in on themselves or blown apart. In the blazing sky, the battle was nearly done. An Endym tore a Sweeper's glider from the air. Another glider plummeted, weighed down by Hideous Garment Flutes.

There was a furtive movement in the corner of her vision.

Grey moths, more winged smoke than insect, fluttered against the cockpit window closest to her head. There were at least a dozen of them, similar to the wisps that had tumbled from the lips of the dead sentries. They appeared too frail for flight; each brush of their wings against the glass diminished them. And yet they remained. They battered at the window a few more times then burst away and flew towards the city, joining a half-mile wide plume of their brethren, almost indistinguishable from the smoke boiling over the walls.

Margaret had had her first kiss on those walls, and in all that awfulness the memory rushed back to her.

An older boy, Dale, who'd gone on to become a full time Sentinel, had kissed her hard then turned to gaze out into the Roil, hiding his embarrassment or his excitement, Margaret didn't know which, the blood pounding in her own head scarcely letting her breathe let alone consider anything else.

"Do you ever think we'll see the sun?" he'd asked her.

Of all the questions she'd expected, if she'd even expected any, that wasn't one of them.

"Some days, yes. Other days, I think those that don't climb down the wall and walk will be overcome, and the Roil will grind out every light, and us with it."

Dale's eyes had widened and Margaret felt a thrill rush through her, almost as potent as that first kiss. A Penn could never admit doubt and yet she had.

"Kiss me again," she had whispered. "If we're doomed what does it matter? Just kiss me."

But Dale was already walking away; he'd avoided her ever since.

She wondered where he was now, then let the thought slide away from her. There could be no good answer to that question.

Margaret checked the *Melody's* instruments. The carriage was designed to withstand extreme conditions, but it had its limits. She studied the array of valves and meters, and exhaled slowly. Everything was as it should be, or near enough: no spikes in temperature or noticeable leaks. The *Melody Amiss'* fuel remained contained. Of course, if the fuel tanks had ruptured, there would not have been enough of Margaret left to know it. Margaret eased the carriage forward; nothing crunched or groaned or detonated. The city burned behind her, and an icy shaft of guilt drove through her heart.

How was she any better than a Walker?

She shook her head, whatever had so easily destroyed the Four Cannon and the Steaming Vents would tear apart the seals to the caverns beneath with ease. Tate was gone. Doomed, perhaps, to rise again as the bodies of the Sentinels had risen.

And she didn't leave in despair, but rage.

All she had was the North. And the slim chance she could escape, and wreak some sort of vengeance upon this dark.

The Engine. She would find the Engine, and she would turn it to her will.

She turned the carriage that way, onto the three hundred mile straight of road, and fled her city, its fires lighting the way for miles ahead, driving the shadow of the *Melody* before her.

Not far along Mechanism Highway she found one of the I-Bomb expedition's carriages, crushed flat. She scanned around for survivors but failed to see a single body, nor what might have destroyed it.

She did not stop, nor try to think who might have been in the vehicle. Her parents were gone, the city taken and all she had left was the distant promise of the north, and that, for now, was all she could cling to. She dare not think of anything else, or she would stall and stop and never make it beyond the Roil.

When she passed the wreckage, she did not look back. She didn't need to. Every time she closed her eyes she could see it all.

CHAPTER 9

Cadell. Cadell. Everything returns to Cadell. Were he to walk into this room I would shoot him dead without hesitation.

Of course, he would kill me `ere I reached my gun. Or draw out my death, in the manner of a Verger. Yes, he might just at that.

Cadell is the monster. The black heart beating at the core of our grim history.

A Whinger's History, Molck

THE CITY OF MIRRLEES

"You like to read, boy?" Cadell asked, pulling something from his bag.

"Yes," David said. "I like to read. And would you stop calling me boy."

"If you wish, though this is a world of infants to me. Children scrambling about in their own shit and fear. You've felt life's whiplash enough to be called a man, I guess. But if I call you boy again, I don't want you thinking it's through any rudeness. I've the memory of a sieve these days, a weight of years poking holes in the fabric of my mind," Cadell said. "Here."

He held a Shadow Council novel. On the cover, Travis the Grave fought some sort of beast, maybe a Quarg Hound, though it was the size of a bear, beautifully, wildly ridiculous. And yet Cadell, the man before him was no less fanciful than Travis, but here he stood, quietly handing over a book. "For the train ride."

"Thank you," David said.

Cadell was already at his bag, packing the last of his things – hopefully he wasn't lying about there being Carnival in there, too. "Don't be so quick to thank me."

"Sorry, I–"

Cadell grunted. "Don't be so quick to apologise either. This isn't a Sunday trip. We're going into danger, but, if we're lucky, safety after that; safer than here for you, anyway. When we reach safety, if we reach it, then you can thank me, and Medicine Paul."

"He's alive?"

"Was the last time I saw him. He sent me to get you."

David was disappointed that Medicine hadn't come to get him himself.

"He thought it safer that you come with me. Yes, that is how grim things are." Cadell shut his bag. "How old are you, lad?"

"Sev– Eighteen," David said.

"Do you not know your age? There's no shame in that, I'm a bit fuzzy when it comes to my own."

"I know how old I am," David said. "It was my eighteenth birthday last week."

A whole range of emotions passed across Cadell's face. David thought he saw pity there, and it made him angry.

"Happy birthday then." Cadell said, and closed his bag.

David realised that he barely knew the man, other than that he had killed his uncle Sean. Which, until these last twelve hours, was all David had ever thought he needed to know.

"How did you meet my father?"

"Your father was a very wise man. He's the reason I'm free. Well ... maybe not wise, but clever. Knew a lot about the Roil. "

"Taught me a lot, too. Well, before we started fighting," David said, *except when it came to you*. In the weeks after his mother's death, his father had been most attentive and that attention had expressed itself in lessons concerning the Roil. In David's mind he'd just exchanged one horror for another.

"I don't doubt it," Cadell picked up the bag. "But your father didn't know as much as me. Nobody does, and as sincerely as I wish it were otherwise, that's no idle boast."

Cadell was obviously mad. The Engine of the World, if it had even existed was at least two thousand years old. He'd said as much to Cadell and he'd corrected him. "It's four, four thousand and eleven years and three months old."

No one lives that long. Vertigo welled in him at the thought of all that time, and a dim anger. This man had lived that long, but David's parents were dead. He stopped himself, how easy it was to fall into belief. Cadell was not four thousand years old, maybe seventy, and a well-preserved seventy at that. He'd seen young men less spry.

Cadell seemed to read his thoughts. "A lot of it hasn't been living, not in the sense you'd recognise it. I'm one of the Old Men. You know, the Punished? Those that were cursed and locked beneath the Ruele Tower for their wisdom and their folly. The Engine's my business, lad, and you'll believe me by the end, or you won't." Cadell laughed.

"What's your curse?" David asked.

"Hunger and sanity. You don't know what that's like all those ages, and to crave and crave and not even have madness to slide into." Cadell's voice fell away to a whisper. At last, he cleared his throat. "Now, we've got a train to catch."

He slung the bag over his shoulder, as though it were nothing. David had tried, and found himself barely able to lift it off the ground. Strength of a madman, nothing more, he thought.

They walked out of the building and into the rain. David turned right, towards the crowded Shop Lanes. "Where are you headed, lad?"

"Central station."

"Too obvious. We're going to the bridge."

"The train doesn't stop there." David regarded him quizzically, his opinion of Cadell's sanity only confirmed.

Cadell opened his umbrella. "And it isn't going to tonight, but that's where we'll board. Easy."

It wasn't.

CHAPTER 10

The railway had ever been the transport of the middle and lower classes: flight is not cheap.

When the rail declined the world shrank for many. So, too, did the threat of the Roil. That which is beyond the horizon may as well be another world.

The Dialogue of the Tracks, Edwards & Leer

SOUTHERN TERMINUS SOUTH OF CHAPMAN
ROIL EDGE

The stationmaster of the Southern Terminus despised the seven days of Halloween, the heat and the faux haunts, but he dreaded the nights, and night was coming, from the east and from the south. Night and the Roil were coming.

He stood upon the edge of the southernmost platform and stared south, through brass binoculars greasy with his fingerprints. He lifted his gaze past weed-drowned marshalling yards, crammed with carriages given over to dry rot and rust, focussing on the obsidian curtain, the point where the Roil rose into the sickly, luminous sky.

It flexed and bulged, ripples of concavity and convexity played ceaselessly along its face. The damn thing was hypnotic. But then, how could the end of the world be anything but hypnotic?

He fished in his pockets for the most recent letter from his wife, and when his hard fingers closed about the soft paper, he found some comfort. He did not read the letter. He had memorised every word. He yearned for her touch. But doubted he would ever know it again, nor hear his children's laughter. Each letter had become a whispering domestic hope and a terrible rising fear.

Things had been different when he started this commission, no Southern Terminus then. Multiple lines had branched from here and, almost on the quarter hour, the tracks sang to a train's approach. The *Dolorous Grey*, the *Eastern Line Galvin*, the *Consolation City Four* or the Southern and Western Suburb's *Clattering Eights*.

Now they serviced the *Dolorous Grey* alone. By the time the eight wheeler reached the Southern Terminus all the passengers had disembarked and there were only empty carriages to clean and the dim hope of mail and the even dimmer hope of orders to return north.

The line extended south but ended in darkness and no train had come from there in years.

No train from the south, but over the last year, as the Roil closed the distance between itself and the station, other stranger, crueller rolling stock had followed the tracks. They did not come when the winds blew cold from the Ekalb Mountains in the north, but when the winds were hot and from the south, and those days were ever on the increase, they washed in; drear and dangerous driftwood carried on some bleak tide.

"Hot night," came a voice from behind him.

Startled, the stationmaster jumped, his heart pounded and rattled in the cage of his ribs. But he did not turn around, just refocused the eyepieces of his binoculars. There was Chill in the office. He'd never thought to keep some with him.

"Where have you been, Jeremy?" he asked, his voice cracking. "We believed you dead."

"I've been away. Hunting. Or so I thought. It's the merest slip twixt cup and lip til the hunter becomes the hunted."

Thc stationmaster jerked around, raising the binoculars before him like a shield. "What are you talking about?"

Jeremy grinned, a wide and terrible grin. An actor's grin, or a mask, for surely it was not his own. "Heat is the issue here, the draw and the reasoning; furnace heat, blood heat. The Roil told me, in its loud old voice. Can't you hear it?" His smile grew and grew and it came spilling from his mouth, dark and frangible, a softly hissing shadow; moth-like they fluttered. So many of them, the man must be filled with them "Witmoths," Jeremy whispered. "Thought and madness and command."

The stationmaster stepped back. Too late of course, but it had always been too late. You can only watch the end of the world for so long before you get caught up in it. He took another step backwards.

"Don't worry," Jeremy said. "It hurts but briefly."

The Witmoths struck at his eyes and ears and mouth, and where they touched burned with a pure and terrible agony. His head filled with noise, louder than the thick, stupid racing of his heart. He tried to scream. The moths poured through the useless split of his lips, crammed it with fire. He bit down on his tongue, blood rushed into his mouth and the moths found another portal to his brain.

The binoculars dropped from his fingers, and he dropped to his knees after them, scrambling towards the brass tubes.

But no salvation lay there, only mindless grasping amidst the cloud of stinging moths that followed. His wife's letter fell free and the stationmaster swatted it across the platform. He raised his head and howled. Or tried to.

No sound came, just darkness, from his mouth and eyes.

Cognisance fled, drowned out by a voice: dim, distant, and old.

Get to your feet. It's still too cold here.

He rose unsteadily. The binoculars lay on the platform, one lens cracked, a dent marring the left barrel. He kicked it over the edge.

"You're right," the stationmaster said, bending to pick up the letter, and slipping it into his pocket. "Hardly... hardly hurts at all. Now, let's get out of this cold."

The clock had just struck two when the *Dolorous Grey* arrived at the Southern Terminus. Despite the late hour, it was still sweltering hot as the driver and his crew disembarked. The moons Tacitus and Argent were both low on the horizon, and the stars were dimmer than the driver remembered them.

He shook his head. No matter, they would drink their tea and eat their biscuits, stoke up the engines, clean the carriages and head north again, and the sooner the better. The Southern Terminus was one rest stop that his staff were happy to see truncated. He did not blame them.

He hated being this close to the Roil.

Deserted suburbs surrounded the station. Once these areas had been bustling and crowded and had names like Willingvale and Worryon. Now they were a ghost city, serviced only because the Council demanded appearances be kept up.

Like most people of Northern Shale, the driver preferred to give the Roil as little thought as possible. It was all too much. Of course, it was easier to avoid such dark thoughts in his offices in Mirrlees. However, this far south it was impossible.

The Roil permeated everything and with every trip its presence increased, darkening not just the sky but people's souls as well. Down and up down and up. He'd gone this way enough times to feel it there, that awful horror which would rise and build with him with every mile. For north or south, he was always coming here, always returning.

He prayed he was not around when the Roil crossed that last mile. The Grand Defeat was still a fresh memory for him; he had lost his father there and an older brother. Damned if he was going to let the Roil take him as well.

The stationmaster, dressed in his greatcoat, as though it was the middle of winter, came out of his office, whistling cheerfully. Odd, the fellow was at the best of times a grim duck.

"Ted, why is the furnace blasting?" The driver asked, wiping sweat from his brow and pointing at the fuming chimneys.

The stationmaster smiled a wide tenebrous smile and showed him.

CHAPTER 11

Lithdale Expedition Missing

Lithdale's eighteen-man expedition into the Roiling Darkness has not returned. More alarming is the spread of the darkness itself. While authorities assure this paper that there is no real danger from the newly sprung equatorial phenomenon, they have requested caution.

Rumours continue of things, as one local has put it, "Not right", coming from the darkness.

So far all reports are unsubstantiated.

Lithdale of Lithdale Triumphant Industries, and of no little standing in Confluent circles was described as a man of alarming virtue. He will be…

McMahon Times JB1287

MECHANISM HIGHWAY WITHIN THE ROIL

The *Melody Amiss* rolled past column after column of creatures – Quarg Hounds for the most part though there were other beasts there too, some humanoid – padding towards Tate. Few used the road and, though she came from the city, such was the intense focus of these Roilings that she went ignored.

Tate blazed, its call far stronger than the draw of her tiny carriage.

Every mile she drove was a mile away from her home, and every mile was another to add to her betrayal of it. For she had fled while the others remained.

Not long after the city had passed beyond the horizon, with only a smudge of flame discernible, there was a silent blinding brightness behind her that lasted a heartbeat, and the earth shook as though one of the Vastkind had stirred then fallen again into sleep.

Outside, dust-darkened flakes of snow drifted down and shrouded everything in white.

Behind her, the Roil had thinned though not enough to reveal the stars, she was too far from the epicentre.

In Tate, she knew, the sky would be clear for the first time in decades. But there would be no one to see it, just the shattered and frozen remains of the city for moon and starlight to pick over and wonder what had been? What might have happened here?

Margaret knew.

Someone had managed to ignite an I-Bomb, perhaps several of them.

Tate was dead, its suffering complete. The ice would melt, and the night would roll back in over lifeless, broken stone. Even as she drove, the snow faded like the faintest of dreams and the Roil closed over her again.

Mechanism Highway had emptied of Roilbeasts and grown crowded with ghosts.

Margaret could not escape the memory of her city aflame. She had time to think, and her thoughts plunged her lower than she had ever been. And always there were questions. Where were her parents? Who had set off the I-Bomb?

She slipped between rage and fear, cold clinical plans and theories and deep, deep sadness.

Most worrying of all was the question of the Roil's new-sprung awareness. Its beasts had howled and battered against Tate's walls and moats, not through any desire for conquest but because it occupied space in the Roil. Such dull-witted assaults had been relatively easy to resist. This though, this new cunning could not be stopped.

If it had gained a kind of mind, then it was a creature that covered half the world with a colossal consciousness.

While she knew she could not even begin to understand its motivations, or the depth of its intelligence, growth must be one of them, growth as swift as possible. Humans were a threat to it. Out there somewhere to the north lay the Engine of the World. Did it know of this? She hoped not, but there was no way she could be certain.

A dim flickering in her mirrors focused her attention. At first, she thought it nothing more than her imagination for it was so faint, so questionable in its existence, and the miles behind her were pure darkness. However, she embraced the diversion and found her attention drawn to the soft uncertain light, until she had to force herself to focus on the road.

Over the next few hours the light increased in intensity and, finally, she recognised it for what it was – a drone. It had been set to follow the straight line of the highway. However, it had slipped a little off course. An hour or two further north and she would never have seen it.

She slowed the *Melody*. Not daring to stop nor turn back. Not daring to hope it might be from her parents. The drone caught up at last and threatened to pass over her.

Margaret shot the drone down.

It hit the ground in a spray of dust and metal.

Margaret charged up her cold suit, fumbling over its controls, her hands at once numb and feverish. She left the engine idling and scrambled out of her carriage, pistols at ready. Such was her haste that she almost tripped over her feet getting to the shattered drone.

Her footsteps scarred the ground, the Roil spores that coated it, sliding away from the touch of her boots, and growing pale as bone.

She kicked at the half crushed message pod's door until it swung open. Smoke moths rushed out at her. Margaret stumbled backwards, batting at the air. The chill of her cold suit did its work and the moths fell away. Margaret stared into the pod.

A book lay within, well-thumbed, curling up at the edges. Her father's notebook! She snatched it out and flipped to the back.

Be careful, and swift. They'll be coming for you. She'll be wanting you. Run and keep running.

Trust no one. There is no one left to trust.

Who wanted her, and why? Margaret desperately desired to read it now, glean whatever she could from its pages. But that note filled her with fear.

She could not stay here. It was too exposed. A Quarg Hound yowled in the distance and far above some great winged beast churned through the Roil. She sensed things drawing in, closing around her.

She had no time to dig into the wreckage. She snatched up the notebook and ran back to the *Melody Amiss*. The engine clicked into gear smoothly and Margaret drove away, picking up as much speed as she dared.

She'll be wanting you. Trust no one. There is no one left to trust.

She had hoped for answers and found only more questions.

CHAPTER 12

To blame Cadell for what happened on the Dolorous Grey *is to blame a wind for blowing, a storm for raging. Cadell is Cadell, disaster comes easily with him.*

He is the hungry man, the whisperer in shadow that comes just before the flutes descend. You see him, you run.

Cadell: A Picture Book, JAQI

THE CITY OF MIRRLEES

A little down George Street a horse had fallen at harness, stone dead before the carriage, tipping the whole thing forward. The driver roared, then moaned. He jumped from his seat and beat at the beast's scrawny rain-soaked hide with the handle of his whip.

The sight struck pity into David's heart. He turned away.

"Horses are dying," Cadell said. "Every day feed grows scarcer, what remains is often bad, rotten before it leaves the fields. And the best of that's already earmarked for the Council. Not long for this city, lad."

A long low whistle echoed down the street.

Cadell didn't need to point – there was a curfew, post Dissolution, the streets were empty. David saw the Vergers at once.

Cadell spat on the ground.

"We are going to have to run," he said, pulling his bag close around his shoulder. The muscles in his forearm's flexing.

And we were so close to the bridge, he thought. "Do you think they know where we are headed?"

Cadell flashed his teeth. "I hope not."

Perhaps the Vergers didn't to start off with, but there wasn't enough time for them to try and lose their pursuit. The *Dolorous Grey* would be crossing the bridge and soon. As they reached the nearest abutment of the Downing Bridge, and began to climb its superstructure, Vergers were coming from all directions. David followed Cadell, throwing himself up ladders, fingers burning as they gripped the rusty rungs. David could hear both the train in the distance and the Verger just behind them, his feet clanging loudly on the metal.

Cadell jabbed a finger below, and grunted. "That one's Tope. High up as they go, he's been after me a while now."

David recognised him as the one who had slashed his father's throat. A cold anger filled him, and a fear. Both spurred him on, as they made their way higher up the bridge.

They reached the top of the Downing and a small walkway that ran over the tracks.

David glanced down, a truly vertiginous experience, not because the bridge was so high, but because the water was so close, dark, angry, and on the verge of swallowing the city whole. The city had turned every contrivance, every levee bank and pump to taming the untameable. The river roared and engines bellowed ceaselessly, wounded by their industry; like the rain, they did not stop, whatever the hour.

Above it all, the *Dolorous Grey's* whistles blew shrill as some blood-hungry Roil beast.

"Nowhere to run," Tope said, from behind them, which was exactly what David had been thinking. If they missed the train they were done for. He could see its lights in the distance, crashing nearer. One man Cadell could probably handle, but other Vergers were converging on the spot.

Cadell laughed. "Is that what you think I've been doing, chimera?"

Tope hurled his knife. David didn't even see the throw; just the blade in the Verger's hand, and its absence, like a masterful piece of sleight of hand. Cadell was faster. Somehow he snatched it out of the air, and the knife buried itself to the hilt in Tope's arm. The Verger snarled, wrenched the knife free, then stopped still; blood shot from the wound.

"Major artery there," Cadell said. "I wouldn't do much if I were you. Wouldn't want to bleed out."

The knife clattered on the walkway. The Verger clutched his arm to staunch the flow of blood, and slowly sat down.

The *Dolorous Grey* whistled beneath them, smoke washed over them.

"Time to go, David." Cadell's eyes burned with such fierce and rapacious delight that David wondered just who he was travelling with.

"No time for doubts." Cadell nodded to the train racing beneath them.

"No time," David repeated.

But there would be time later. His blood raced, he wasn't scared of the leap, not now. He realized Tope was watching him, the Verger's eyes shining in the bridge light. Not so much fun when you're the one doing the bleeding, is it? I hope you die.

They leapt from the bridge, and onto the *Dolorous Grey*.

All David could hear and smell was the train, it enveloped him in choking smoke and clattering heat. His heart pounded in his chest. He could just see the silhouette of Tope, shrinking rapidly with distance, one arm thrown out to bear his weight.

David wondered how anyone could remain conscious after losing that much blood. Other Vergers closed on the scene. A knife thunked onto the roof before his boots, then clattered away.

Cadell yanked David down. An iron beam crashed overhead.

"Watch it, lad. Or you'll dash your brains out." He jerked his head to the left. "This way."

They reached the edge of the carriage, where a ladder dipped over the rear, and clambered down it and through a door.

"Won't they throw us off the train?"

"No stopping this train until Chapman. Old tech, not even radios. Stade has been investing the city's considerable sums in the Project, and the Project alone." Cadell laughed, he patted his top pocket, and put his ear against the nearest cabin door. "I've got our tickets. I don't think it matters how we board. As long as we present these." He nodded his head. "Now, this cabin sounds empty. In we go."

Stade stood before the broken door.

Halloween, what better time to be surrounded by these dead and whispering things, he thought. Well, not so dead. The Old Men were simply that... old. Very, very old. And hungry.

Stade examined the door, as he had from time to time over the past two years. It was cracked through the middle, the locks shattered.

He regarded the door next to it; its bolt was intact, the eight seals unbroken, the same for the other six doors but that first one. He put his hand against the heavy wood. It was cold. He put his ear against it and heard the endless muttering. Stay down here long enough and you heard it everywhere. After a while you could hear it throughout the tower. Though it was only here he had a chance of gleaning words from the noise. The Old Men never slept in their cages, or if they slept it was a restless chattering sleep.

He'd had one of the doors opened once, the key that opened the lock was said to be protection enough from the room's denizen. Though he'd held a revolver too. He'd seen the withered thing within the room, its eyes boiling with rage, lips moving, muttering. "Shut the door." It spat. "Shut the door, or I'll suck out your bones." And Stade had, forgetting the protection of the gun and holding the key in his hands. He was swift, but not swift enough, for he had seen it. A little humility had infected him then, but not much.

Stade ran a hand down the broken door. The metal was cold, even now, even after these past two years.

The Mildes and Paul had done this. Two years ago, after they had freed the Old Man, Stade knew Dissolution was the only adequate response. And while he should have enjoyed it, even he quailed at such bloodshed. These were good capable men. Debate he could handle, but this had amounted to an utter betrayal of the Project. Warwick had sacrificed his own brother to this.

The problem had been to deal with the Confluents without admitting to the general public that the Old Men existed. Stade would have acted faster, but Warwick's caution had stayed his hand, there'd been no mad dash into the north, and the fact that Cadell had proven something less than an asset to the Confluents.

Cadell had not destroyed the Roil, he had not reactivated the Engine, and Stade knew why: the same reason that the

Project had to succeed. The Engine was a weapon of last resort, a weapon that the Old Men feared. After all, it had caged them here as punishment for daring to use it.

"Cadell," he said. "How did they get you out? What madness drove them to give you freedom?"

The other question he did not ask. How Stade's men had not managed to catch him. Stade had lost more Vergers to that task than any other; their cracked and cleaned bones more often than not left stacked outside his offices, sometimes with little effigies of Stade resting upon the heap and, one time, a single red rose.

The broken door, of course, did not answer.

CHAPTER 13

Who knows what darkness lurks in the heart of the Roil? Who knows what sleeps within its cities, and dreams?

Travis knows.

Travis the Grave – series introduction, AF Scott

MECHANISM HIGHWAY WITHIN THE ROIL

The bleak landscape extended for hundreds of miles in every direction and every mile was crowded with such inimical life. This had been farmland for centuries, whole hundred mile long tracts of it, feeding the voracious hunger of the Twelve Metropolises. But those days, while but a couple of decades gone, had been wiped almost completely from the land. The Roil alone fed here, a single shadow ecology where no crops or livestock could survive.

Margaret passed the occasional ruin of a farmhouse or the shattered wreckage of a village. Round these remnants of civilisation Roil beasts tended to gather, as though commemorating past conquests.

Endyms perched on silos and the fragmentary eruptions of

barns, their huge eyes staring down. Packs of Quarg Hounds, that most ubiquitous of Roil predator, circled beneath.

All watched her passing with some interest. Though none followed or harried her. It was the intensity of their gaze that she found disturbing. Quarg Hounds, which she had always considered as little more than target practice, gazed at her with dark and too intelligent eyes. These were not the creatures she had slain from the ramparts of the Jut, here they were curious and cautious. It was almost as if the lands surrounding Tate had been seeded with lesser beasts, cannon fodder, smart enough to pose a threat but not enough to reveal the true quickening of the Roil.

The hours passed slowly as the Roil flexed and rolled its livid bulk about her. It was hard now not think of the land and the air as one. A beast as cruel as it was opaque, and every ounce of that cruelty and hatred, for all that it held back, seemed directed at her.

She thought of Tate, and what she had lost in a single night. Sadness and anger competed within her, becoming finally something cold and hard in her mind. Her emotions fell away, or hardened and grew as sharp as a knife blade and a terrible purpose filled her. She would destroy the Roil. No matter the cost, she would see this darkness broken and should nothing else remain, so be it.

The city of McMahon did not come upon her all at once, but piece by piece. Deserted farms became villages, villages became towns and finally the city, well the corpse of one, swelled up around her. Though she had studied maps of this place since childhood, McMahon was at once an alien and all too familiar environment. Where Tate had been built upon a hill, McMahon sprawled and stretched in a scale that amazed her. Broken towers thrust out of the scarred ground, fire-gutted houses rose up like rotten teeth.

At the edge of the city proper, where buildings thickened and reached high into the dark, sat McMahon's Tower. It had been destroyed, but still a good third of it remained, jutting into the sky. And what was left was higher than the Willowhen, the Four Cannon and the vents.

When whole it would have been an incredible sight. Still it stole her breath. Around its peak circled Endyms tiny in the distance.

While not the capital of Shale (for Shale had never been a unified continent, regardless of the Council of Engineers. The Lands of the Council of Engineers would have been better called Lands of the *Councils* of Engineers. Each city had almost been a state unto itself) it had the bearing of a capital.

In all the books of geography Margaret had read and the travel pamphlets written before the Roil had so much as stained the ground, McMahon was referred to as the Jewel of Shale.

Ice cannon far mightier than Tate's were piled around the tower, broken and discarded as though they were little more than toys. They would have been awe-inspiring, launching their frozen munitions into the dark. But they had failed, vast and ponderous weapons swallowed by, and rotting in, the Roil.

Something dark curled about the top of the tower and, as Margaret passed beneath it, that darkness stirred and the building shook.

For two decades it had crouched in mourning upon the ruin that it had wreaked. Motionless. Eyes fixed upon the city, pores gaining sustenance from the Roil itself. A quiet rage swelled within its breast as it saw the small carriage pass beneath it.

So this was what the mothish smoke hunted?

How could this cause so much consternation through the dialogues of the Roil? It was so tiny.

The human within was wrapped in metal and ice – venomous, loathsome cold. Ah, but it had seen such ridiculous devices before and dealt with them. Just as it had destroyed those ice launchers, eating their human guards one by one.

The still air found sudden life around the creature as it rose up, spreading open dark wings the size of steam engines. Endyms nesting in the ridges of its spine flew for their lives, dust and stone tumbled from its broad back. Its muscles clenched and bunched for flight. All but ready to leap into the sky, it paused and swung its heads south.

Something else was coming, and fast.

After ten years, so much was going on all at once. Its many eyes narrowed.

It paused and waited, like some monstrous tide on the verge of turning.

CHAPTER 14

Steam is already a tired medium. We have the air, and now New Fuels. Their integration into the transport system is assured. New Fuels are safer, more reliable, and their engines less likely to explode.

Engine of the World, MOLCK

THE DOLOROUS GREY, THE SOUTHERN LINE
280 MILES FROM THE ROIL EDGE

"Now, lad, the thing is we don't want to look like fugitives. So relax, appear as though you are enjoying yourself. Here, read this, if the book I've given you isn't to your taste." Cadell passed him a pamphlet advertising Chapman's upcoming Festival of Float. David put the pamphlet down, and folded his arms. "Suit yourself then."

The rain streamed across the window and Mirrlees-on-Weep streamed with it. The city's lights nothing more than glittery tears tracking down the glass. David had not cried. He let the city do it for him. It cried too much. He wondered when he might return. Not for a long, long time, if ever. Which suited him fine. He didn't want to go back. He let out a long breath and let himself believe that he was out of the city, that things might just be getting better.

He started to whistle a tune that his mother used to sing to him.

"Whistling, I can't stand it. Stop that now," Cadell said, with a vehemence that surprised David.

"All right," David said. "Sorry."

"I'm sorry too. Just that tune brings back bad memories." Cadell frowned and mumbled under his breath. "Hot in here. The air's stale and I don't like the way it smells."

David held off suggesting that that smell was probably them, after their flight in the storm; the Vergers trailing them, down street and along creaking bridge. He considered opening the window, but thought better of it, preferring to leave the rain outside for a while. So he ignored Cadell and watched his home – the city that he had lived in all his life – slip behind him, becoming a single wavering brightness that, in turn, faded to nothing.

Cadell, despite his misgivings, fell asleep almost at once. David envied him bitterly; he had no such luck. He shut his eyes and that dark space only served up memories he did not want, his father or an eyeless Lassiter, spiders bubbling from his lips. He thought of his Aunt Veronica in Hardacre, she ran a school there. He wondered if she would even recognize him. They'd never been close. She hadn't even been able to make it down for his mother's funeral. But then again the cities of Hardacre and Mirrlees were hardly on good terms. She was family, a good woman, and he knew he could start his life again up there. Of course he had to actually reach Hardacre first.

He kept his eyes open and gazed at Cadell. In sleep he became, somehow, older, frailer – though not nearly as old as he claimed. Cadell moaned, rolling away from the window; drool pooled onto the engineer's shoulder.

David peered a little closer. A single tear, gleaming in the cabin light, followed the line of Cadell's left cheek.

David looked away, embarrassed. He didn't understand his own grief, it shamed him. Someone else's tears were worse.

Outside, buildings rushed by in the murk – fragments of metropolises and structures that pre-dated Mirrlees-on-Weep and the Council. Most of them had been deserted centuries ago but not all. Lights burned fitfully from narrow windows, figures moved from shadow to shadow.

Old men, smoking pipes, stood framed in ancient doorways and raised their hands at the passing of the *Dolorous Grey*. In greeting or as a ward against evil, David could not be sure.

David wondered what their lives were like, here, away from the city. How they could survive? These train-swift fragments were not enough to give him any answer. He knew you could survive pretty much anywhere: the two obvious exceptions being within the Roil and in the far north. And here he was on a train racing to Chapman and the edge of the Roil.

He gave up on sleep, Cadell was right; it was stifling in here. He wondered where Cadell had hidden the Carnival, perhaps he could just... Cadell snorted in his sleep, and shook his head.

David opened the window a touch, scowling when it did nothing but let in damp hot air.

He picked up the pamphlet.

The illustration printed on it was masterful in its detail, crowded with Aerokin, balloons and even a kite or two above the famous Field of Flight.

HEED THE CALL

There has never been a better year to attend Chapman's aerostatic event. The release of ten thousand BALLOONS, to represent the

fallen. The sky a fury of fliers, a fantasy of flotation, the Roil an imposing and majestic backdrop. Security and delight are assured.
At prices undeniably reasonable and reasonably undeniable.
FLY ONE, FLY ALL! HEED CHAPMAN'S CALL!
The Mothers of the Sky have approved this event, a portion of the proceeds of which will go to the maintenance of Drift.

The whistle blew ahead. Once, and then again, a shrill and mournful sound.

Heat and sadness.

There was so much noise: the clatter of metal wheels running on metal tracks, thc shrillness of whistles and the animal growls of steam.

So much noise, and yet so little.

That thought gave him pause.

Where was everybody?

Surely people should be walking up and down the train. Children exploring, folk gossiping, or even someone snoring. But he had not heard a thing.

Too quiet.

Too hot and too quiet.

The door handle rattled as the train jolted round a bend, as though someone was trying it, turning it, soft and slow, so as to be barely perceptible. A Verger, perhaps.

It rattled again. Violently.

David jumped, wished he had a gun, or a little more carnival.

He shook his head. Just a few rough spots on the track, that was all. He was being paranoid.

He took a deep breath and stood up. Then crept towards the door and flung it open. The hall was empty; lights flickered along its length. He poked his head through the doorway; nothing grabbed him.

David carefully observed the aisle from the rear carriage door to the front.

No one.

No movement.

He waited a few breaths, then stepped into the hallway closing the door behind him, after checking that Cadell was asleep – and he was, dead to the world, another tear tracking down his face. David considered waking him and decided against it. He'd be gone a minute or two, no more.

He walked to the cabin next to his and put his ear against the door. Silence. He opened the door slowly. The cabin was vacant.

And the next. And the next after that.

He turned to stare back at his cabin. Just one more door, then he could give up and go back. He swung it open. A porter sat within, dressed in his uniform, looking down at his hands. He blinked, turned towards David, and smiled.

"I can't remember why I'm here," the porter said. "It's a little cool, don't you think?"

David was about to say that it was anything but cool, then thought the better of it. The porter shivered; looking at him was enough to make David feel cold.

"Have I seen your ticket?" The porter asked.

"Yes," David said, and hoped that the lie sounded believable.

The porter's eyes narrowed. "I think I'd better see it again."

"It's here somewhere," David patted his pockets, then remembered Cadell had them. "Um, it's back with my–"

The porter slapped his hand down on the seat. "It is of utmost importance that the passenger keep his ticket with him at all times," he said, his voice rising alarmingly in pitch. He frowned. For a second, David caught a glimpse of some sort of shadow leaking from his lips, and then it was gone. The porter raised a hand to his face. Tapped his head. "There's all sorts of buzzing going on in here." He made an odd snorting sound that David took some time recognising as laughter. "It's all right, come in here, with me. Just having a joke."

"I think I better get my ticket." And wake up Cadell. David didn't like what was happening at all.

"I said it's all right. Sit with me."

"I better get my ticket, after all there are rules." He wished his paranoia had extended to waking the old man up.

David took a step back.

The porter bounced to his feet and strode towards him.

"I said it's all right." Something slipped from between his teeth. It fluttered moth-like, then dropped, the porter tried to snatch it out of the air and missed. "Odd, but it is too cold." His voice was a whisper. The porter was out the door, blocking David's path back to Cadell.

Another moth tumbled, dead, to the floor where it sprayed a little dust. The porter bent down, picked it up, and put it back in his mouth. "Much too cold. Now, come here, there's things I can do. Things I can put in you. Just come to me, eh."

David did nothing of the sort. He turned on his heel and ran fast as he could, towards the dinning car.

Whatever had gotten into the porter, he did not want in him.

The rain poured down, hot fat droplets driven north by wind and Roil. The engine of the *Dolorous Grey* raged and roared, blasting heat and noise against the driver's face. His lips peeled back in a rictus of pure joy. The train had never been pushed so hard or fast. He felt connected, utterly connected with Roil and engine, furnace and fire and speed.

And it was glorious.

"On with you, lads!" he roared at his men feeding the

steamer. "On with us all, to the heat and the dark and the cities what dream."

Heat. They had to keep their bodies hot. Here, they were in a fortunate situation, but those behind, in the carriages. So new to this, and having to deal with the comparative cold, he pitied them a little, poor, new-sprung things.

If worst came to worst, body heat was enough, but the hotter the better, and the closer one came to the Roil, the easier it was to think clearly. The easier it was to hear the Roil's voice.

One day all this would be theirs. In his mind, he could see the land as it had been and would again, swallowed and warmed by the Roil, its glorious croon echoing, echoing in his skull. But, for now, they could only visit, briefly and madly, this chillier Roilless place.

It was just too far away from the Roil itself. The dreaming city's commands were too fractured, nonsensical.

From the cabin behind came a growl, then something else snarled in reply.

"Settle," the driver whispered. "You will get your run, in the dark and in the heat."

The snarling stopped, though it took its time about it.

The driver stared into the rain. The Roil, two hundred miles south, roared in his blood, a violent glorious siren song.

Faster, he had to drive the engine faster.

DOLOROUS GREY
170 MILES NORTH OF THE ROIL EDGE

Was the train running faster? It took a corner and jolted, David stumbled through the door to the dining room hall, ready to shout out a warning.

He stopped, mouth agape.

Maybe this had not been such a bright idea after all.

It was the poetry that disturbed him, and the music, utterly unlike anything he had ever heard. No, *everything* about this room disturbed him. It was off in the way the world was off after a day or two straight without Carnival. Two fiddlers played loudly, and in an odd tempo, coming to abrupt halts and sudden bursts of quiet and crescendo.

Fiddlesticks, toothpicks, drown 'em in sweet
Shadows are singing. Shadows are singing
Buried in me from my nose to my feet
'orrible 'orrible cascading shoes
'orrible 'orrible singing with youse.
Moths in the cradle. Served with a ladle.
Shadows are singing. Butterfly's eaten
eaten my brain.

The smoky dining room was, like the rest of the train, far too hot and almost airless. Bodies pressed together here, too close; almost the entire population of the train had to be in this long room. There was something almost insectile about them, as though he had just opened the top of an ants' nest.

Popular place, David thought. Odd as it was, he should be safe in here. There were plenty of witnesses.

He took a couple of steps into the room. The music ground to a halt, every eye in the dining carriage trained on him: as though he just might be dinner.

"My eyes, but he isn't one of us," someone chortled.

"Soon will be." The crowd took up the call. "Soon will be." Men, women and children their lips edged with darkness, crowed. "Soon will be." And around them all, in spiralling streams, the moths moved, from eye to eye and mouth to mouth. Then they lifted into the air and dipped, crashing towards him.

Tiny wings made a soft soughing noise like the first breath of wind. One brushed him, burning his skin. David stumbled back to the door.

The porter stood there. Moths slid from his lips, bearding his chin with fluttering darkness. His eyes were more focused now, sharp and cruel.

"Not so fast," the Porter said, and walked towards him. "Much warmer here."

Another moth touched David's arm. He yelped, brushed it away.

"That's it, give 'em room to fly into that mouth of yours. Let 'em kiss your blood."

David clamped his mouth shut.

"Don't matter they'll find a way in."

The dining car door slammed open, and with it a whip crack of cold. The whole room chilled.

Moths tumbled around David, a rain of ash-veined shadow, blasted back. People, who were no longer people at all but something else – something monstrous that David did not understand – shrieked.

"Well hurry up, lad." Cadell was bent over, his face curiously pale and dark as snow. Cadell's arms were raised; blood streamed from his nose. From where the Old Man stood, frigid air howled as though he were a portal to another frozen realm. The glass in the windows nearest him had cracked; so swift had been the change from heat to cold.

"Hurry." Cadell breathed

David bolted towards him.

Someone grabbed at him, their boiling fingers curled to claws that caught his arm and held on. The Porter. It tightened its grip around his arm.

"No. You're staying here," he said. "With us. You'll like it."

David lashed out with an elbow and the porter groaned and fell.

The room warmed. David's heart pounded in his ears, and his only thought was, out.

Out.

Out.

Out.

He reached the door and was through. Cadell slammed it shut behind them and pressed his hand against the panelling; ice sheathed the door at once.

"What was that?" David demanded.

Cadell waved the question away, his fingertips blistered, blood oozing from one dark nail. "No time now. Just run."

The door behind them jumped in its frame, and David jumped with it.

"Hurry."

The ice cracked. The door creaked. They sprinted down the aisle.

"They'll all be back in there, or in the engine room where it's hot," Cadell said. "Those bound by Witmoths do not like the cold. And thank goodness for that, this far from the Roil, and this newly sprung, they're confused."

"Witmoths?" David asked, looking back at where they had come. There was another loud crack, and the doors panelling fell away. But they were in the next carriage, and Cadell was locking the door and sheathing it in ice as well.

"Witmoths, moth smoke, it goes by many names. But it's what happens when the Roil gets inside you," he said as he worked on the door. "Haven't seen its like in a long time, and then it was the desperate gambit of a desperate enemy. It's as though I've stepped into a corridor of ghosts."

They crashed down the carriage, the door behind them already taking hits. Boots slapped on the roof above, people cackled and screamed.

They worked their way back through the carriages until

they reached their own. Cadell grabbed his bag, gesturing that David leave his where it was, and then they continued on.

"Where are we going?" David demanded, his heart pounding in his ears. "Where will we be safe on this train?"

Cadell stopped at the last exit, leading outside, and paused, panting. "Nowhere," he said, his hands working the bolt on the door. He tugged at it and the metal creaked then cracked. Behind them a window smashed, people howled and laughed.

Cadell flung the door open with an ease, despite his breathlessness, that David would not have credited but a few hours before.

The rain-smeared world rushed by, lightning flashed in the murky distance and thunder followed. David didn't like the look of that darkness, of all that space, but it pulled at him. Or was it the nightmare things coming after them, the cloying heat driving him out?

"On the count of three," Cadell said.

"One."

Back down the aisle, they rushed towards them, a knot of angry cackling flesh, moths running from their chins like blood.

"Two."

Moths and smoke boiling and billowing before the crowd. Cadell raised his spare hand and the air cooled again, the moths and the smoke scattered, and tumbled, and all along the aisle men and women screamed, but this time they did not stop their pursuit. A hand reached down over the exit, Cadell touched it, and it jerked back, a scream coming from above.

"This is madness," David exclaimed.

"Indeed, it is," Cadell said, quietly. He hurled the bag through the opening, then grabbed David's arm, fingers digging painfully into the muscle as though to illustrate the truth of it and, with that confounding and illogical strength, he hurled him out the door.

"Three."

CHAPTER 15

The Mothers of the Sky. These progenitors of Aerokin were politically moderate, and utterly unfathomable. Their impact upon history negligible.

The Scales of History, Michael Pompis

THE AEROKIN *ROSLYN DAWN*
THE OPEN SKY

"You will do this. He is to be treated as one of us, unless or until we tell you otherwise."

"No," Kara Jade had said. "This is madness, absolute folly, and besides there are plenty enough Aerokin in Chapman. I will not risk the *Dawn*."

Of course, she hadn't actually. If you wanted to fly, if you wanted to serve your Aerokin, then you did what the Mothers told you, even if it meant danger, even if it meant doing things that you would rather not, like coming down out of the air, like having to deal with people. All she wanted was the air and her *Roslyn Dawn*. There were plenty of Aerokin in Chapman too, for the Festival, but none of them were like hers.

Kara Jade did not like flying this close to the Roil. The *Roslyn Dawn* liked it even less. It hadn't stopped complaining in its slow deep tongue since they'd left Drift.

Mirrlees-on-Weep dominated her mirrors. The river metropolis was not as wondrous as the pilot's city of Drift, but impressive in its way, with its monstrous bridges and its crooked towering skyline. Though now it languished beneath masses of dark storm cloud like a beaten dog. What did her sister call it? That's right, the Sump. Just one big drain with a city circling around it.

Kara half wished that Raven was with her. Of course she would have been bloody intolerable. Old pilots always were, and Raven was more a mother to her than a sister.

The river Weep had swollen. Suburbs north and west of the central boroughs, right up to the old forest known as the Margin, were stained with it. Cranes, another mighty and genuflecting forest, worked ceaselessly along the levees, extending them, repairing damage, thickening the levees bases, but it was ultimately a pointless industry, for the rain fell not just around the city, but further west, in the catchments. And there seemed no end in sight to its fall.

Mirrlees she could deal with, corrupt government or not, there was money to be made there. But the Mothers of the Sky had directed her south, and on this ridiculous and dangerous mission, and there would be a man, on board, an Old Man no less, and that was enough to make her sick.

Away from one darkness and too soon into another.

A hundred and fifty mile wide ribbon of dry air stretched between Mirrlees and Chapmen, broken on the Chapman end by Roil.

From up here it was easy to see everything, and that was why she preferred the north. The weather had been crazy that way for some years, but there was no darkness rising, no obsidian curtain, you could almost believe it wasn't happening. Here though there was no doubt.

If the Mothers hadn't commanded her, there was no way she would have flown this way. But they had.

"We wait a week," she said to the *Roslyn Dawn*. "Until the beginning of the Festival, no more, and if he hasn't come, we go."

The *Roslyn Dawn* accepted that, but barely – she was as stubborn as her pilot.

CHAPTER 16

Let us speak of the Grand Defeat. Let us speak of lightning and a city's fall. Let us speak of refugees driven north, and the city of Mirrlees-on-Weep whose citizens greeted them with less than welcoming arms. Do not be so harsh to judge.

Who could face what they represented? A world's ending. A prophecy apocalyptic. Hardacre was more accommodating. Though many didn't survive the journey through the Margin and the Cuttlelands, enough did to swell that Metropolis' population to almost double its size.

To say it had ramifications for Hardacre and Mirrlees' relationship is an understatement. Their alliance was in name only. McMahon's defeat a poisonous wound that could not be healed.

Grand Defeats & Great Deceptions, DEIGHTON

THE RUIN OF MCMAHON
WITHIN THE ROIL

Margaret consulted her maps, more through a nervous need to keep her mind occupied than to check where she was going. She had pored over these since her earliest memory, imagining lands where the sun still shone, where the light did not just radiate from lamps and lanterns and huge glowing machinery but from the heavens.

Beyond McMahon the land plunged away into Magritte Gorge, a canyon extending from the Sea of Cage to the deep interior of Shale. That canyon was why the city had been built here. McMahon was designed to impress, to mark the earth with its glory. Only six bridges spanned the mile-wide gorge and four of those, complex structures of wire and rods, were in the city proper, the other two were many hundreds of miles west. If she wanted to cross the gorge, without risking running out of fuel, she would have to drive through the city.

Margaret had known that, of course, but now she was here there was something frightening about these empty streets.

Unlike Tate, McMahon followed an asymmetric pattern, little more than a sprawl of suburbs and outlying townships. McMahon was too big to have ever been walled and too young to have ever needed them. By McMahon's time, the Council had stopped its aggressive expansion and the war with the remaining Cuttlefolk had moved to the north and south.

In a period of relative peace, McMahon had grown rapidly.

There was evidence of the city's swift collapse everywhere – cannon piled high like a child's blocks, their muzzles so pale that Margaret doubted they had fired at all, and buildings torn down and strewn all over the road.

Worst of all were the burnt remains of the residents in market squares and other public meeting places, rough pyramids of skulls long ago picked clean of flesh.

Though there was no human meat to consume here, Quarg Hounds crammed the streets, scattering like cockroaches before the beams of her carriage. Nothing had come this way in a long time and the noise unsettled them.

However, as in every other part of the Roil through which she had travelled, their fear quickly gave way to curiosity, and they followed her passing with huge indolent eyes, jaws yawning wide then wider, revealing teeth-crowded mouths.

As tempted as she was to let fire with all her endothermic weaponry, Margaret held back.

She was starting to run low on everything. She could see a time when her ammunition ran out, when all she had left was, if she were lucky, her rime blade and a bullet for herself.

The *Melody*'s passage through McMahon couldn't come fast enough, every second within the city a callous weight. Many of the bone-towers had collapsed, covering the roads to such a height that Margaret often had to double back and find a different route. Hours passed before she drove beneath the Tower of Engineers with its raw edges of stone reaching up into the sky: a vast architectural howl that never stopped. Her skin prickled at the sight of it, and she was glad to have it at her back. But it remained another memory of ruin and despair that she had fled.

The ground shook, and bones tumbled from a nearby pile.

"What on Old Earth is that?" Her voice startled her. Her throat was dry, her head ached, and the words had come out shrill and barely recognisable as her own.

Perhaps she had imagined it; it wouldn't have been the first time on this journey. She checked her instruments; the *Melody* was running a little hot, but not enough to explain the vibrations. The carriages were sensitive to such things, quite often such sly beats were the only warning of Sappers or other digging Roilings lying in wait beneath the road.

Moths tapped gently against the glass.

Her lips twisted with hatred. She released a blast of cold air through the side vents of the *Melody* and the moths were gone.

The vibrations increased in intensity. Margaret pulled into a narrow side street, stopped the carriage and extinguishing the lights. In the darkness she waited and she did not have to wait too long.

Something glowed, an indistinct light that quickly became stronger. Twin beams of light, and then more, illumining the entire road. A whole convoy of vehicles was coming.

Hope swelled within her, dying when the first carriage became visible through the murk.

The cockpit cabin had been blown open or torn apart; only tattered fragments of metal remained. Sara hunched over the wheel, her head bound with a smoky halo of moths. A Quarg Hound crouched beside her – much larger than the creatures she had seen throughout the city. Another and another carriage rounded the corner, all with cabins cracked, moth-smothered drivers and Quarg Hound companions.

By the time the first carriage passed the side street in which she had hidden, nine cars in total had turned the corner.

Nine cars, all of them heading for the Perl Bridge.

She could think of only one reason they would be travelling that way.

They were hunting her.

She waited until all of the cars had passed, then she pulled out her maps. If they were going to the Perl Bridge to the west she would take Pascal's Bridge in the east. Margaret just hoped the bridge remained. Quickly, she worked out the fastest route, then started on her way.

CHAPTER 17

Quarg Hund, Quarg Hund Burning Bright
In the Suburbs of the Night

The Hund, RALLY

THE WILDERNESS BETWEEN MIRRLEES AND CHAPMAN

David yowled and crashed into the dark, hitting the soft wet ground and rolling.

The *Dolorous Grey* roared by. All he could hear were the carriages, its wheels but yards away. All he could feel was its rolling, boiling breath.

He hit something and stopped so abruptly that his teeth slammed together, biting the inside of his cheek and filling his mouth with blood.

He lay there a moment, trying not to choke or throw up. The muscles in his legs shook as he pushed himself to his feet. He knew that much, you always got up. He fell on his arse again.

Cadell came into view, bag over one shoulder. "You right, lad?"

"Think so," David said.

"We better get moving. They won't let us go that easily."

True enough, a little down the line, the *Dolorous Grey* shrieked and rumbled and came to a furious halt.

"I suggest we run," Cadell said. He motioned over at the *Dolorous Grey*. Smoke billowed from the train, wreathing the air in clouds veined with fluttering darkness.

David blinked. His head rang with all the discordance of a half dozen broken bells. He knew he should get up and start running, but his body resisted the babble of his thoughts. He wondered if he would have taken it all so calmly if he'd not a little Carnival remaining in his veins.

And that thought had its own terrors. A little Carnival! A little wasn't enough, not nearly enough. He could be here crooning at the moons and the rain, instead he had the spiders of his addiction crawling in his veins.

Cadell was saying something. David blinked at him. "Up now. Up."

"What?"

Cadell grunted, bent down and gripped David by the shoulder, dragging him from the edge of the railroad and onto his feet. "Anything hurting? Can you walk?"

David nodded. He felt his body finally listening to what he required of it.

He had more aches than he could catalogue but, at the same time, fear dulled them, a short-lived remedy no doubt, but one for which he was oddly grateful.

Cadell made a noise in his throat. "Then we'd best get out of here."

Sounds echoed from the *Dolorous Grey* through the dark and the pounding rain, doors slamming open, boots crunching hard on gravel and the stuttering, shrill laughter of the Roilings. From the engine room, something howled.

David shuddered, he had heard an imitation of that sound

on one of the radio serials he used to listen to as a child. "Is that what I think it is?"

Cadell nodded; his face wreathed in shadows that failed miserably to hide his dismay. "Quarg Hound, and a big one. I haven't heard that cry in over two thousand years." There was another howl and another and another. "Three of them, time to run, Da–"

David was already sprinting into the darkness, away from the train. He turned, Cadell stood by the tracks staring at him.

"Well, hurry up then," David said.

Behind them the *Dolorous Grey* returned to rumbling life, and its whistles shrieked until the Quarg Hounds shrieked back. David was not sure which was the more terrible, but he had no doubt what those hounds would do if they caught him.

So he ran, and ran hard, his breath coming fast and hot in the driving rain. The train behind him – wheels slipping loudly, whistle shrieking – continued on its journey south, down to Chapman.

David could not see how he and Cadell were ever going to make it to the city. The *Dolorous Grey* raced there, the Roil was down there, and all of it was intent on stopping them.

The land quickly became overgrown. Lantana and a dense and prickly scrub known as Meagre's Knife closed in around them, but it did not stop the rain. The sodden ground sucked at his boots with every step. Twice they stumbled into overgrown streams, Meagre's Knife tearing at their faces and hands, blood-warm water thigh high, the stones beneath treacherous. David was soon shivery and exhausted.

However, there was no stopping for them, the Quarg Hounds were always close behind, their guttural ravenous howling drawing nearer by the minute.

Cadell closed with him, glancing left and right.

"That's funny," he said, his voice thin and hopeful. He lifted a hand and David couldn't shake the feeling that he smelt the air with it. "I remember this place. Vaguely and distantly. Bah, David when you get to my age things blur and each turn of the road or rise of the hill becomes familiar."

David looked at him askance, opened his mouth to speak, and a Quarg Hound crashed into his back.

David grunted, the wind knocked out of him, he fell forward, arms flailing about.

Then he tumbled, through the tangle of lantana, the scrub giving way, cracking and scratching. David tried to hold on, but couldn't. All he could think of was that Quarg Hound coming down behind him. David pitched headfirst into a much broader, much deeper stream.

The water rushed up and it was cold, then he was through, his head clipping a rock. He gasped with the cold and the pain, and sucked water into his nose and mouth.

As though on springs, he jumped to his feet, retching, head swinging this way and that. *This isn't good.*

He raised one hand as though to point, or perhaps to ward something off. He couldn't remember, so he lowered it again, turning in a shaky circle as he tried to clear his head. What was he doing here?

The cold stream tugged at his knees, slowly pulling him down; knees, thighs, groin and belly.

The Quarg Hound that had tumbled down after David yelped and pushed away from him towards the edge of the stream, convulsing so savagely David could hear its back cracking. David watched it die, the Hound's shuddering limbs folding up, and it sank into the water, dragged down and away by the current. He knew he should be afraid, but he just couldn't manage it.

"David!" Cadell shouted from above.

David's vision narrowed to splotches of light and dark and pain. He tried to focus on Cadell's voice but couldn't, his head pounded as though a hundred hammers were trying to beat their way out. The pain dimmed, and he wasn't sure if that was a good thing.

He blinked.

"I'm here," David yelled. Or tried to because no sound escaped the torpid cage of his lips.

His voice failed him, followed by his legs. David fell forward, a numb and silent weight; his head slipped under the water and cold darkness found him.

Lassiter was laughing, and David's parents were egging him on.

"David! David, wake up." Someone shook him. "You must wake up."

"I–" David said, coughing up more water. He stopped at last, wiping his mouth with the back of his arm and whispering, "Are they gone?"

Above the stream, from behind the thick shield of lantana, came two rough growls. Cadell jerked his head in the direction of the sound. A Quarg Hound tumbled out of the dark, shrieking as it struck the water. Cadell walked over to it, gripped its shuddering head and snapped its neck. He let the beast drop back into the water, swung around towards David, and winced. "It's all right." Obviously, it wasn't or the old man wouldn't be saying it. "Now, you must try and stand."

David struggled to his feet and stumbled, falling forward, the cold had seeped into his muscles turning them stiff and sore and clumsy. His nose ran. His knees were raw. And his head, what had happened to his head? "I seem to be having difficulty."

Cadell nodded, pulling David up again and letting him lean on his shoulder, one arm reaching around David's back and gripping his right arm so tightly that it hurt, numbed only a little by the chill radiating from Cadell's fingertips.

"I'm just so tired." David tried to pull away, but he couldn't manage it.

Cadell nodded. "Of course you are, so we'll just keep going. This water is colder than it ought to be. What say we follow it to its source? I suspect what we find there might help us." A shadow of a grin passed across his face. "I thought this place was familiar."

Even with Cadell's aid, each step was a challenge. When he closed his eyes, the whole world would spin and tumble in too many directions, and yet, several times he found himself almost falling asleep. This was worse, because Lasslter waited behind his eyelids, or his father, both mocking corpses, already beginning to rot – things rotted fast in the rain and the heat. David batted at spiders, the memory of their webs.

Everything had become so fractured and dreamlike that he took some comfort in the increasingly believable hypothesis that he *was* in fact asleep, his head lolling against the window of the train or better yet, in bed; his parents still alive.

"Don't do that!" Cadell shouted, shaking him hard. "You must stay awake."

"Absolutely," David said, vomiting explosively into the river. "Nothing easier. Where did you say we're going?"

Cadell patted his back gently, though his grip on David's arm did not loosen.

"Too hard to explain while you're so addled, but we've not far to go, then you can rest, I promise."

Cadell's not far to go turned out to be quite the opposite. They walked for nearly two hours, harried by the remaining duet of Quarg Hounds. Cadell chattered constantly, apologising, demanding, cajoling, and drawing every single step out of him one at a time.

Did they walk the length of Shale or had time been arrested somehow, beyond the trudge of weary feet, the howl of hounds and the continuous stream of talk that tumbled from Cadell's lips?

But the scrub came at last to an end, opening onto a flat clearing a mile in diameter at least. A small hill marked the centre of the clearing. The source of the stream was a tiny spring at the foot of the hill, the water gleamed, a single silvery eye.

Cadell grinned. "A Lode of the Engine. Lode B1914 in fact," he said almost smugly. "Ah, yes. It's all turned out rather well, considering."

Before David could ask him what he meant by that and how anything that had happened to them that evening could be construed as going even remotely well, the Quarg Hounds howled again, paws slamming into the water.

"David, you're going to step out of the water now. The stream is broadening and deepening. There is no way we can continue to walk in it. Once we reach the shore, you are going to have to run. I know how difficult that is, but you must. Run as hard and as fast as you can towards that hill. The Quarg Hounds will be running too."

David glanced from hill to hounds to Cadell. "What about you?"

Cadell shook his head. "I must stay in the water. If I could I would have you stay here with me, but it would be... dangerous."

The Quarg Hounds were already sprinting towards the edge of the stream. "But–"

"David, don't ask questions; questions are for later – now run."

David shuddered, his cold lips clung to his teeth, all he could taste was blood and snot, and all he wanted to do was curl up and die.

"Run!"

He dragged himself to the edge of the stream, clambered over its grassy bank, and ran on legs ready to collapse beneath him. Ran, towards the hill.

Ran towards the Quarg Hounds.

CHAPTER 18

Two enemies united, by a common, greater foe. Such alliances are fragile. The Vergers had been formed to ensure such alliances remained whole. Of course, it was open to corruption.

What isn't?

Vergers: Knives & Knaves, DEIGHTON

THE CITY OF MIRRLEES

The *Dolorous Grey* made its smoking, juddering progress out of the station, picking up speed on the slippery tracks as it clattered past the final gates of the platform. The driver released the horn and, all over Mirrlees, people paused and listened to that mournful sound. Medicine, in his hiding place in the shadows by Central Station, was one of them.

He crouched in a nest of iron beams and watched as smoke and the storm devoured the train.

"Good luck, David," he whispered, and rubbed with aching fingers at the tension turned to knots in his neck. "You're going to need it. At least the Council won't have you now. Your father would be pleased with that if not the company that you keep."

Desperate times demand desperate measures.

He slid from his hiding place onto the street, gripping his umbrella in both hands. The damn thing was heavier than his usual, a sabre hidden in this one's wooden neck. When he moved too fast he could feel the blade rattling.

Medicine hurried down Argent Lane reflecting that while you could not see that bright moon in Mirrlees' sky, the downpour did little to obscure this street's luminous stretch. Red lights glowed in every window, and the whistles of painted ladies, from doorway, corner and alley, pierced the crashing rain with their lascivious promises. Some of them calling out to him by name.

He was tempted, very tempted. Just to get out of the rain, he told himself, but his funds were dangerously low – most of his money had gone into Cadell's wallet. Medicine still had his supporters, people he could call on, though every day that number decreased. And those remaining were, perhaps, suspect. Just who had they made deals with? A few more weeks and Medicine knew he would have to flee the city; but there remained things to be done. At least David and Cadell were gone.

He considered Cadell, and the two years it had taken before he was ready. So much had gone wrong, starting with Sean's death. After which Warwick had discovered a mad recklessness within him, as first he lost his brother, his wife and then, finally, let his son float away from him into addiction. Medicine regarded this recklessness, as much as Cadell's release, as the cause behind Stade's Dissolution.

Their allies in Chapman, Lord Mayor Matthew Buchan and his advisor Whig, had been banished from that city and the Confluent party effectively broken there. Cadell had lingered in Mirrlees, drifting from safe house to safe house, indulging his hungers with any Verger that sought him out. The man had been afraid, an odd prospect, considering how terrifying Cadell could be in person, and that fear had kept him confined in the city. And, every day, the Roil moved north.

Medicine's face flapped on a nearby lamppost (WANTED. DANGEROUS. DEAD or ALIVE), a terrible photograph. Medicine tore it down and hurled it onto the streaming street. If only everything could be that easy.

At the end of Argent Lane, after he'd ripped up another wanted poster, he realised he was being followed.

The painted ladies had stopped their whistling, and all along the lane, red lights died.

Not now.

He knew of only one thing that would silence the Ladies of Argent Street. Not coppers, nor thugs, nor gangs from the Northmir.

A Verger.

Medicine gripped his umbrella even more tightly, loosening the sabre it contained with a flick of his wrist.

He peered behind him: just rain and fog. The Verger filled the silence, perhaps in honour of Argent Lane, with his own whistling. Medicine felt the blood drain from his face, his lips thinned to a single nervous and angry line. The Verger whistled an old Confluence tune, a call to arms.

Bastard. Fucking Bastard. How dare he? Do not take up the challenge. Just keep walking. Bastard. Fucking Bastard.

Once round the corner, he ran, heading for a safe house on Wisden Street: a place that he had held in reserve for years. Most safe houses had burned in the last few days, greasy smoke rising into the rain. This one remained, empty, but its windows were broken. Blood stained the living room floor.

Footsteps echoed from outside. His nerve broke, and he ducked through a bolthole hidden in the living room that led, via a narrow stone tunnel, to a street two blocks behind. All the way, he walked with his sabre unsheathed and held shakily before him.

No one was waiting in the back street, but he did not hang around. Soon enough, the Verger was whistling again.

One place remained and he made his way there, all pace, through slivers of broken suburbs, wading along half-drowned streets, clambering over walls and under bridges.

Little traffic came this way. Those roads that weren't covered in water were potholed, devourers of cart and horse. Empty side streets coiled and wound away from the city and the river. The city here had clenched around itself like a wounded beast. Medicine's wet boots slapped down Cove Street and over the Cove Bridge. If luck were with him, he might lose his pursuer in the northern district, then come back via the Shine Bridge and into the rear of the Ruele Tower. The Verger's tune followed him all the way.

At the Shine Bridge, Medicine stopped and peered down into the white water of the Weep. A steamer, one of the sail-steam hybrids, was making its slow progress against the river. A snarl of logs struck the boat. In a puff of flame it was gone, leaving a brief pall of dirty smoke to be snatched away by the wind.

The water seethed and what could only be bodies, dim desolate shuddering shadows, passed beneath the bridge.

Portentous and terrible, he thought, somewhat hysterically, and continued on his way over the Shine. When the Verger was done with his games, Medicine was certain he would find a turbulent rest in the belly of the Weep. He was not Cadell, he could not fight these men with their Cuttlefolk blood, nor could he bribe away the edge of their knives.

Once across, he glanced back along the Shine and started. A single figure slouched there at the end of the bridge, he blinked and the figure was gone.

Medicine sprinted down the next few streets alone, and there were no whistling or solitary figures to disturb his thoughts. He cast glances behind him every time he reached a street lamp, most of them bearing his portrait. Nothing.

In the absence of obvious pursuit, Medicine sprinted first down one lane then another, through back streets as narrow as doss house corridors. The city reeked, stonewalls covered in a patina of fungus. Dead things floated, bloated and stinking, in the shallows of gutters. This was Mirrlees now. Death's rotting signature scrawled everywhere.

When he made the secret entrance to the Ruele Tower, he threw furtive desperate glances over his shoulder and found some small relief in the empty lane and the silence – if pounding heart and pouring rain could be called silence.

He tapped the wall in five places, and in the right order, and the wall slid back and opened a crack wide enough to admit a grown man. He frowned at the darkness beyond, unsheathed his sword, and slipped through the gap, letting the secret door shut behind him.

Inside, he dropped to a crouch and reached for the torch hidden to the left of the door. Nothing. His fingers brushed the floor. Something ran over his ruined knuckles. He flicked it away.

Where's the damn torch?

The Verger's knife pushed into his neck not hard or deep enough to draw blood. Medicine breathed deep the stale air. This last air, obviously, once the Verger was done with him.

"What do you want?"

"Mr Paul," the Verger said. "Let me introduce you to an old friend of mine."

The Verger's old friend hammered into the back of Medicine's head and he fell into the merciful dark.

CHAPTER 19

The lodes were wretched, their master cruel. Locked here. Locked here. Locked here.

Old Man D3

LODE B1914

The Lode stung him with its rising awareness, its memory of his blood and his guilt.

The water conducted the Lode's power and as Cadell walked further up the stream it focussed on him. The water grew dense around his limbs, began to defy its natural tidal inclinations. Shapes took form within its depths. Lights winked into being. And all around it was an odd and breathless sort of shock. *You are here. Why are YOU here?*

Cadell reacted to the Lode's shock, its recognition, with a sort of shock and recognition of his own.

Strange, the things you forget, he thought. The power and the agony.

Old code words, old data flickered to life in his memory, dim at first, they increased in intensity, beacons of energy to which he was drawn.

But he also sensed a hesitancy, a distant doubt. Was it his own?

Ah, but he always had doubts. Always. They rang in his bones and rattled, ancient as fear, in his skull. The Engine merely magnified them, as did its cruel punishments.

The Quarg Hounds howled, no doubt about their hungers.

He glanced over at David then back to the Hounds. They were at the hill, racing towards the pale bare rock of its summit. Fierce as they were and deadly, this weather was still too cool for them – the run and the rain had taken their toll. The beasts whined between each howl; dark blood streamed from their jaws. They were weakened, but what strength remained was more than enough to rend David limb from limb.

Cadell clenched his teeth. He could not put it off any longer, already his stomach was cramping, his ears ringing in anticipation. He took one final breath and raised his hands.

This was going to hurt.

"Now," he cried. "NOW!"

And his bones turned to ash. Pain hammered into his skull.

"Now."

The Quarg Hounds had reached the summit. On that final "Now" they stopped, as though yielding to his command.

But it was not the Roilbeasts that Cadell's words commanded. The Quarg Hounds' bloody snouts rose up quizzically.

One of them opened its mouth, then shut it, swiftly, cocking its head, as though it were listening to something distant but racing nearer.

Silence. The air cooled, something hardened within it, became crystalline and deadly.

Ice enclosed Cadell's skin, burnt and bit deep. His body shook with energies and their absence, because that was the wounding truth of it.

His power was an absence, a vacuum, and a slowing, and all that lived quailed from it.

Insects fell, dead and frozen, out of the air, an entomological hail.

At the top of the hill, the Quarg Hounds yawled, thrashing and screaming, as all that cold struck them. David had fallen forward, on to his hands and knees, in a field of frost-coated grass, his face a mask of winded agony.

The Quarg Hounds howled again, a beaten horrible sound that dropped at last to a whine. They crumpled in on themselves, all their menace, all their strength gone and only their blackened skeletons and brittle skin remaining. And that was somehow more horrible than claws and howls and hunger, perhaps stillness always is.

The ice around Cadell's legs turned to slush, and his blood started stinging, singing and stinging, as it forced its way back into constricted veins. The stream began to flow again almost as it had done before. The icy skin on the stream cracked and drifted away.

The Lode continued to burble inside his head, its ache rising to freeze much more than it already had, to wake its siblings and blanket the land for hundreds of miles around with cold. But only the Engine was capable of unlocking all that ice, of slowing the shuttling atoms of the world, and he did not command it. In fact he could feel it, a distant and disapproving presence.

Yes, he did not command it at all.

Not yet.

He shivered. The thought of such appalling power filled him with terror. Perhaps it was better if he never did.

CHAPTER 20

Cadell was always the show off. Of the Eight he couldn't resist theatre, though he denied it most strenuously. It was in everything that he did. Which made him the worst of us all.

A Dream of Old Men – Primary Accounts, DEIGHTON (ED)

LODE B1914

Air but moments before, bitterly cold, warmed. Rain fell devouring the ice, as though anxious to wipe the memory of Cadell's... whatever it was he had done... from the earth. David wiped vomit from his lips, spat a last sickly spit, and tried not to think how much easier Carnival would make all this.

Everywhere there were dead things, frozen and fallen from the sky – it was in the air that the worst of this cold had struck. If it had reached that intensity where he stood, he knew he would now be as lifeless as the birds and the bugs.

Where was Cadell? David got to his feet, brushed himself down. Cadell stumbled towards him, skin almost bloodless, his eyes ringed in dark circles.

"I can't do this anymore," Cadell cried. "It's too much. I'm sorry about your Uncle. You must believe me."

Cadell blinked, turning his head this way and that, and David was witness to an odd transformation, a swift strengthening of will.

"Are you all right, David? Are you all right?"

"I think I should be asking that question."

Cadell wobbled to his feet. "I am fine," he said. "See?"

He took a few shaky steps onto the grass. "Fine."

David just nodded his head. The movement was too much, he bent over again and dry-retched; his stomach had nothing more to give.

"There's cover by that ledge," Cadell said and together, dragging Cadell's bag between them, they staggered towards it. The walking was all the harder for the lack of pursuit. Urgency and strength had bled from both men's legs. But, both shaking and weak, at last they reached the stony shelter.

"That light around your hand," David said. "That sad light. What is it?"

"Ah, the candlelight of hubris, boy, history is lit with it. Just one of a hundred ridiculous mistakes." Cadell said with surprising gentleness. "But the past is done, in this place, in this time, we will find some warmth. Even the lodes generate a little."

Grass grew under the rocky ledge. The air was warmer too though, surprisingly, not the cloying warmth of rain-battered Mirrlees, but sweeter like the summer evenings of his childhood, the mill fires challenging the stars and the moons, his mother singing and his father home from work. They were idyllic memories that he was not at all certain of, so distant that he could have substituted memory with dream. The past was dangerous that way and invited suspicion.

David dropped to the ground and Cadell followed, kneeling slowly, staring out into the darkness. At last, he grinned. His face relaxed a little, lost some of its bleak pallor. "We're safe here, for the moment," Cadell said. "Try and sleep."

He handed David another syringe. Where had it come from? But he didn't waste time trying to work it out. The drug in his blood settled him almost at once.

"Thank you," he said. He knew he shouldn't be so purely and completely happy but he was. "Thank you."

Cadell was already asleep.

CHAPTER 21

Of all the monsters that I saw
The ones come after, the ones before
The worst of them, the worst of all
Was the dread Vermatisaur

Monsters in Rhyme, BARNEL

PASCAL'S BRIDGE

Brakes squealed, counter engines roared, and burning oil stung her throat and her nose. The *Melody* slid to a halt and the engines, fore and aft, wound down. Margaret scowled; she might as well drive off into the gorge. If she'd held off braking any longer, she would have.

Pascal's Bridge jutted perhaps a hundred yards out above the chasm, ending in curled talons of steel, as though a titanic fist had slammed into the bridge from beneath. She directed her lights into the darkness, wary of the drain on the *Melody*'s batteries, and could just make out the other edge of the break: more truncated lengths of steel crawling with Hideous Garment Flutes.

Margaret sat there, shaking her head. She checked the map, ran it against the one she had in her mind. They concurred. The Caspian Bridge crossed the gorge a little east of here. Wheels spun in reverse, the *Melody* jerked backwards onto the road. She stopped. From the east, lights, moving fast.

The Perl Bridge then. She would just have to find a way to cross it. The *Melody* tore a wide circle around the road pulling a rough curtain of dust and smoke behind her and headed west fast as Margaret dared drive towards the Perl.

The cars were closing, their lights growing brighter every time she lifted her eyes to her mirrors. Quarg Hounds, excited by all this activity, ran beside her, their yawls shaking the thick glass of the *Melody*. She let off a few rounds of her ice cannon and they dropped back a little. Margaret was tempted to give them a real blast of cold, but she was running low on coolant. So they kept their distance but kept up their pursuit and their howling.

If anyone lay in wait at the Perl Bridge they would know she was coming.

Margaret gritted her teeth, charging her ice pistols and rifles and engaging the preliminary protocols for her carriage's self-destruct system.

If it came to that, Margaret was damned if she was going to let the Roil take her alive.

She topped the rise and brought her carriage to a halt.

Six cars waited for her at the entrance to the bridge, which extended far out of sight, their cannon and headlights aimed at her. She put the *Melody* into reverse. A cannon fired a warning shot, Margaret ignored it, slowly sidling back up the road.

Lights flickered in her rear vision mirror. The other carriages had arrived cutting off her retreat.

Well, this is it. Tears of frustration ran down her cheeks. I did my best.

She slammed the carriage out of reverse, and raced back towards the bridge. Cannon fired at her, starring the glass of the front windscreen. Reinforced or not, it couldn't take too many impacts. The chassis rang with the impact of their shells.

Margaret ignored it as best she could, focusing only on the carriage directly in front of her, firing round after round of her own guns.

It was useless. She could not break through and it was only a matter of time until the cannon found a weak spot in the *Melody Amiss*. She weaved and fired as many cannon as she could at once, building up speed, aiming at the central carriage.

Perhaps if she had not been so focused upon her enemy she would have seen it coming.

All of a sudden the firing stopped. The Roilings pointed skyward, they lifted their guns to the sky and fired.

The beast tore into the carriages. A raging storm of wings and claws and mouths, its half dozen jaws crashed open and closed. It had been utterly silent in flight, now it shrieked a seismal shriek that was a nail in Margaret's ears, but she did not stop.

Metal groaned then grew shrill in protest, and Quarg Hounds howled in terror. Cars fell into the chasm beyond the bridge, Roilings leapt for cover. The winged beast rose up, clutching one of the carriages in its claws, letting out a cry that rattled the *Melody's* windows, it hurled the carriage back on to the ground. The vehicle exploded, illuming the attacker and astounding Margaret.

The beast was a Vermatisaur.

She could not believe it.

Might as well be staring at one of the Vastkind. Legends filled the air and the shadows, dark malevolent legends.

Several of its snake-like heads snapped at the air. Its huge eyes blazed, bright enough to cast aside the darkness and scatter shadows everywhere.

A terrible joy swelled within Margaret, and a sickening dread.

It roared from a dozen thunderous mouths at once, and dove back towards the carriages, snatching up another. Margaret did not pause to see what it might do. A gap had formed and shaking, terrified of this sudden hope being snatched away, she drove through it and on to the bridge.

The Vermatisaur watched, through a spare set of eyes, the little human-thing race across the bridge, but did not follow.

There was no need (the creature would die soon enough) nor did it want to risk tangling its wings in the wires that webbed the bridge. Its mate had died that way, leaving it to its solitary angers, its mourning rage of decades.

The human-thing's time would come. The Darkness was spreading and would not be stopped, what was rightfully the Roil's would be reclaimed again. With the world retaken, it would fly wherever its will took it, through the boiling shadows and across the plains and ruddy mountains. Fly until another mate called, and the savage wonder of their hungers crowded the skies.

An ice pellet struck its wing, the cold burning enough to bring it back to the present. Wings shifted, curled, and carried it in lazy predatory beats towards these odd man things.

It owed them no allegiance. Furious, it snatched up another carriage and dropped it onto one racing over the hill. They exploded satisfyingly. The Vermatisaur's pores swelled with the heat, deeper brains activated and with them deeper rages. Its eyes scanned the city.

There! Another carriage. The beast descended, swift and deadly.

By the time it was done, not a single carriage remained, and the little one had crossed the first span of the bridge and was deep in the tangles of metal where it could not follow.

All that activity after ten years made it hungry. It circled the city, eating what it could find, mouths gulping down anything that moved, its massive tail knocking over tower and wall. When it was done almost nothing lived in the city.

Sated and heavy, the beast clawed its way through the air, back to its resting place atop the tower, sinking down on the stone. Hot winds wafted around the Vermatisaur, fluttering the tips of its leathery wings and tail. It settled slowly, coiling its many limbs around the top of the shattered tower. Glass and metal detonated beneath its new fed weight, and the ruined floor groaned but held.

Sated, lord of its domain once more, the Vermatisaur let out a manifold cry from its mouths that shook the city to its foundations and came back to him in a dozen pleasing echoes.

And then the city fell silent and still.

CHAPTER 22

Sold Men. Bold Men. Cold Men. Old Men.

Mirrlees folk song

LODE B1914

David dreamt of Cadell crouching in the snow, shovelling dead birds into his mouth. "Still hungry," he whispered swinging his head towards him, eyes bright as stars. "And all that's left is you."

Cadell turned and his lips curled hugely: a mouth that opened and opened. "Come inside, little bird."

Someone shook David awake. He blinked, Cadell's face huge in his vision. The man appeared as wretched as David felt – his clothes were muddy, his lips cracked, bruises stained his face. "Time to go, David. We've got to keep moving."

David's head pounded, he was sure the sleep had done him some good but he couldn't pinpoint how, other than to carry him from one state of wretched exhaustion to another. Cadell helped him to his feet. David blinked out at a day almost indistinguishable from any other, but for the occasional dead bird – David was sure there had been more of these, last night – and small heaps of shrivelled insects on the ground. There was no evidence of what had gone on the night before. No evidence but for dead bugs and birds *and* the sickening pounding in his head.

His back hurt from sleeping on the cold hard ground, another ache to add to his collection.

Rain fell, but only lightly: an early morning sun shower. Nothing new in that.

Cadell put a steadying hand on David's shoulder and consulted some maps. The Engineer appeared at once exhausted by last night's events and energised, as though they had given him new purpose. He scanned all that cartography then folded the maps away and pointed east, past the field and back at the scrub.

"We're not too far from the railway and it would be best, I think, if we returned to it. Perhaps followed the line a while. It will get us to Chapman quickly. So we'll keep it to our left until Lake Uhl, then we'll take the road, where it veers west to Uhlton. The trip should take us two days, if we maintain a good pace. As we now have no transport, I believe I have business to attend to there."

"What business?" David asked, splashing a little of the cold water on his face. The closer they got to the Roil, the more their plans went awry and the less this seemed to be about escape than plunging headlong into danger.

"What business?" he asked again, and Cadell rounded on him.

"The sort I don't feel like talking about right now," Cadell snapped.

David must have given him a shocked look, for the Engineer's gaze softened and he relented. "David, there is much I must tell you. A lot of it I am not proud of, I am afraid. It is not easy for me to give voice to this, but I must tell you, at least some of it, I guess." Cadell's eyes shone imploringly from a grimy face, and he sat down. "I'm trying to save this world."

David laughed. "Cadell, people don't save the world."

Cadell nodded at this, though he failed to hide his disappointment, David couldn't tell if it was with himself or David's response. "But, you see, I am not a person. Not any more. Not in the way you would understand it. I am old, David, you know that, but do you have any sense of what that entails? I have lost count of the years that separate me from my first life, and time has dissolved so much of my arrogance and purpose – and the task that I must perform demands a surfeit of both. You will never understand what it is like to have all your friends, your family, not just dead, but as dust. Forgotten."

David disagreed. He knew what that was like. Yearned for it. His friends and family were gone, taken from him, all he had left were the memories and they hurt. He did not know how he could take another step, but he did, and another, took another breath and another. He had lost everything and yet his heart kept on beating. It wasn't fair.

Cadell was ignoring him now, studying the Lode: the corpses of the Quarg Hounds. "Even I do not bear the task of remembering them well. I plunge into the past and it is little more than a ragged gloom about me. Faces have faded in the white noise that is my life. Reasons have grown dim and still I have lingered, hoping that it would not come to this, and arrogant enough to believe I could halt it. But live long enough and your worst fears are realised.

"I speak of arrogance, but mine is nothing compared to that of my people. Born of the Seedship, we shaped this world, changed it. And in that change the Roil was made, though we did not notice it for many years. You see we inhabited the poles of this world, built our metropolises there, and the Roil, that first time, hid.

"We were too busy in our splendour, a race of gods, every one of us a Master Engineer. A people of leisure, unprepared for the pure horror of it all. And it was horrible, not some progression as you see it now, but a fiery seizure. All along the spine of the world, volcanoes spewed forth heat and with it the Roil. Everything we made was ruined and transformed.

"So we made war, we made the engine and rebuilt this world's laws. Ice not fire became our weapon. The cold. And it is a cruel weapon, cruellest of all. Heat is life, David, its absence is death.

"We built the Engines and the Lodes, each section fought for with more fury than you can imagine. And once it was done we unleashed them on the world and it nearly destroyed us." Cadell raised his hands to take in the world. "The universe, even such a small patch of it as this, is a complex thing. No Orrery can do it justice. There are thousands upon thousands of little balances and trade-offs. Trip one of them, and you trip them all. The change may be sudden or swift – and even a hundred years in the lifetime of a world is less than a blinking of an eye.

"We swept those checks and balances away as though they were nothing more than irritants of no consequence. You cannot imagine what it was like, but when it was done, the Roil was gone and we remained and, somehow, survived.

"I grew old in that world and have lived the ages since, my duty this, as it is the duty of all the Old Men: should the Roil ever rise again I must stop it. At the beginning, before it could ever pose a threat. And I have failed.

"David, I'm terrified. Death does not scare me, but what I can do does. And if I don't…

"In Uhlton, there is one who has an understanding – an understanding, mind, little more – of my secrets and he has called me, and called me in the two years I have hidden in Mirrlees and I have not come. Now I will. He has grown bitter. Still he will help us."

Cadell brightened, slapping David jovially on the back.

"Well, as we have no food, nor are we likely to come across any. I suggest we forgo breakfast and get straight to the walking part."

"Walking is certainly better than running."

"That it is, David. That it is."

Regardless, David's body protested as though it were not. As they made their way through the verdant to the point of rotting countryside, he struggled with one endlessly unnerving thought.

What was it about Uhlton that terrified Cadell more than the Roil?

It took them several hours to find the railway. Time enough for David to question seriously Cadell's sense of direction. The land around the Lode was thick with mushy scrub and streams, and they moved at what felt like a crawl.

When they finally found the line, Cadell released a long breath. "We should be safe along these tracks," he said. "I doubt anyone will be using them again for a long time."

They walked all day, stopping to rest only when the walking became too much for David, which was often. Cadell, on the other hand was unfazed by the rigours of the journey. He walked swiftly, sometimes getting dangerously ahead. But he would always turn at the last moment, sensing, perhaps, that he was almost out of sight, and wait until David caught him up.

David was relieved when, at last, the sun setting low and wet behind them, they reached a deserted workers' cottage, built close to the line.

It had been recently occupied. There were still cans of food in the cupboards, mushrooms and sausages and even a bag of onions hanging above the kitchen sink. The building was simple – a single onion-smelling room with two beds, both with yellowing pillows, but it was shelter from the rain and the only other tenants were fleas, which were heaven compared to Quarg Hounds.

David was asleep almost before his head hit the lumpy pillow.

He woke to morning light and the smell of breakfast cooking on the fire. Onions and sausages crackled. David's stomach rumbled, but it was the syringe by the bed that drew his gaze first.

David couldn't remember just who it was that had first introduced him to Carnival (some sordid adventure after his mother's death, too much drink, a place that felt safe, then became something else). However, the moment of its absorption was still vivid: the flood of calm, the release of all that guilt and fear replaced with joy.

And if the guilt and fear always came back, like a tide, a rushing wave all too quick to return, it could be pushed away again.

He'd lived in that cloud for almost two years, or the cloud had become him. Sometimes David couldn't separate himself from his hungers, the act of scoring and the ejection of doubt and dread with the injection of Carnival.

He attended to his hunger swiftly, and without embarrassment.

"I found some tomatoes growing in the garden out the back," said Cadell, hunched over a frying pan. "Are you hungry? Do you want something to eat?"

The simple domesticity of the scene struck David harder than perhaps anything he had experienced in the last few days. His voice failed him.

Cadell frowned. "Well?"

"Just try and stop me," David said.

CHAPTER 23

Medicine Paul should never have risen as high as he did. Such a dandy, such upper class heritage. Far more suitable a candidate for the Council of Engineers, but his enmity with Stade brought him much support. His wounds so obvious that they could not be denied. He had paid much for his political beliefs but likewise he gained much from it, too.

Brief Biographies & Apocrypha, DEIGHTON

MIRRLEES
300 MILES FROM THE ROIL

Stade lifted the glass jar into the light. Two shrivelled fingers floated in the solution contained within. He gave them a little shake.

"I like to keep them with me," Stade said. "A reminder."

Medicine spat blood. He'd kept his teeth, and his eyes, which made him think that Stade really wanted to negotiate.

"I've got nothing to offer you," Medicine said. "You've taken it from me. The Confluents have no power."

Stade lowered the jar. "You're wrong. Your name holds

much glamour to it, even if it is a glamour that I have in part created. And it's that glamour I need."

"It can't be as terrible as that. You've destroyed your enemies."

"You consider me far too myopic, Medicine." Stade put the jar down on his desk. "There is only one enemy, now. I'm evacuating the city, and I do not have time to become a popular leader, and what I need cannot be done by force. The Roil is coming. And we have every reason to believe that it is beginning to advance even more rapidly."

"There is time enough, surely. Chapman is two hundred miles south." Medicine spat more blood upon the floor.

Stade laughed. "If only it were that easy. The Roil has been slow to approach Chapman. Winter held it in check for a while, and other forces, ancient machineries of which we have limited – to say the least – understanding and even more limited control. Though Cadell could have enlightened us on the matter, if he hadn't been so intent on killing my Vergers. However, we have evidence to suggest its growth is about to increase dramatically. When Chapman goes, Mirrlees will not be far behind. A few months, maybe six."

Medicine crossed his arms. His cravat crusted with his own blood, some of it stuck to his neck, pulled painfully at his skin. "And you're telling me this because?"

"We need your help." There was an edge to Stade's voice that Medicine had never heard before. Medicine's ears pricked up. "You're a popular man, Mr Paul. A leader, and we need to start moving the populace north."

"So you've given up on subterfuge, then? And murder?"

Councillor Stade cleared his throat. "We have given up on nothing. I am far too practical to discard any useful tool. Medicine, these are desperate times and I can brook no dissent. You I can deal with. Our opponent, the one true enemy of our time will not parley, and believe me, I have tried. I will do what is necessary to save this world, to give humanity a future."

"One built on lies, built on coercive government and all its sweetened cruelties. What kind of future is that?" Medicine demanded.

"Damn you," Stade shouted, closing in on Medicine, a finger stabbing at the air directly in front of Medicine's face. "There is no room for ideologies any more. This is about survival." He dropped his hand, taking Medicine's fingers from his sight, as though suddenly realising the childishness of his display. "Does it matter what the future holds as long as there is one? You have a choice, Mr Paul. And it is simple. You can die, here and in this room. Or you can live, and help this city live too."

Medicine took a deep breath. Pivotal transitions come swiftly, and truths tumble and crash, and make themselves anew. How cruel it was that desperate times seemed not to expand character, but diminish it. Narrowing choices: death or dishonour. Why was that so? He realised that this time at least it was not. Other choices might open up before him, if he was ready for them. He need only be patient. He was a politician after all.

Stade leered down at Medicine, and that alone nearly drove him to reject his offer then and there.

Gloat all you want, Medicine thought. Your time will come.

"Shall we get those handcuffs off then?" The councillor said.

Perhaps Stade was right. There was no room for ideologies any more, the Roil had changed everything, and it would change this too, if Medicine let it. What am I to do? He wondered and realised there was no clear answer, for all that his choices were simple and few. He could find no pleasure in either of them. Pragmatism can be a virtue and a curse.

"Yes," Medicine said, at last, and even then he was not sure until the words had left his mouth. "I accept your offer."

He did not want to die just yet, that was too easy, and too final.

Stade's grin became huge and smug and he nodded to the Verger to unlock the handcuffs.

Medicine rubbed his wrists, straightened his blood-spattered cravat. "What needs to be done? How can I help this city?"

"Not the city," Stade said. "But humanity. Those bastards in Hardacre may have no wish to be involved, but they are. When they declared themselves a free state, they declared themselves enemies of this one. Stuck between the Roil and a free state. There will be no help from them."

Well it was your decision that barred the refugees of the Grand Defeat from entering this city. It was your rule that swelled Hardacre's population, Medicine thought, but kept quiet.

Stade plucked a cigar out of a box and chucked it at the Confluent, who deftly caught it in one ruined hand.

"Your first job for me," Stade said, and the words stung Medicine more than he thought possible. He worked for the mayor now, and nothing he could say or do that would take the sting out of that truth, "will be to take new workers up to the Underground, my grand project. There is a train line, but we have lost both our Engines. The *Grendel* and the *Yawn*."

"How does one lose a train, particularly when they are so big?" Medicine asked.

"They didn't reach the Underground, nor did they return here. Something happened to them, either in the Margin or on the Gathering Plains. The Gathering Plains remain Cuttlefolk territory; negotiations are a trifle difficult these days. Since the Grand Defeat we've little clout to back up our threats. Vergers are effective at keeping a city under control, but a standing army was the only way of dealing with the Cuttlefolk."

Stade went over to the map, and let his fingers trace a line between Mirrlees and the Narung Mountains. A lot of land – his path took in the Regress Swamp, just north of the city, then the forest of the Margin, beyond which stretched the Gathering Plains.

"We've even sent an Aerokin out there. Drift pilot, one of the best. He didn't return. It's a mystery worthy of the Shadow Council don't you think? Should we send young Travis the Grave to look into it?" Stade laughed at his own joke.

"The north sounds *real* safe," Medicine said.

"For a small group it isn't. But you will be, safety in numbers, plus enough guards to kccp you out of trouble. Medicine, the last thing we can afford is a war on two fronts. The Cuttlefolk have been quiet for years. We'd thought them a spent force, yet even with their increased activity even if they have destroyed the trains your numbers will be such that they will be little threat to you."

"Fifty years ago the Roil was just a legend to all but those privileged few that had had dealings with the Old Men. We live in an age of wonders and expectations overturned wouldn't you say?" Medicine said, lighting up one of Stade's cigars. "What am I going into up there?"

"That I can't tell you. Not because I don't trust you, Medicine, we just don't know."

CHAPTER 24

The Bridges of McMahon are surely one of the wonders of the modern age. Forget the Levees of Mirrlees. These bridges are vast and elegant at once. Here in their beauty we find all that is great in the Engineer. Utility and form bound in the sublime.

Bridges of McMahon, McMahon Tourism Association

PERL BRIDGE

The *Melody's* brakes barely saved her.

The Perl Bridge was a long series of arches and braces and counter braces, the surface smooth and favourable to speed. So she didn't see the gaping hole in the middle of the road until she was almost upon it.

She engaged every braking mechanism at once, swung back the gears and still the *Melody* almost toppled over the edge, stopping at the lip of the fall. Margaret sat behind the wheel panting. She had to get out and check the stability of the road. Her back ached as she got out of the vehicle and walked to the ragged edges of the hole.

Down she stared, rime blades clutched in either hand. Far

below beasts flew around the metal limbs of the bridge, Endyms by the look of them and Floataotons in spiralling drifts thousands strong. Huge supports hundreds of yards long plunged into the bottom of the chasm and built around these, on road level, beneath bands of cable – a single strand of which was thicker than Margaret's arm – were shops and living quarters.

She'd thought that none lived there until she caught sight of furtive movement at the windows, dark figures peering out or ducking down and hiding.

She gave them little notice; it did not pay to. Spend too long worrying about every ghostly apparition or possible threat and she would go mad. Instead she made herself focus on the bridge, it looked safe enough, and turning back wasn't an option anyway. She got back in her vehicle, and drove it gingerly around the collapse, trusting to old ingenuity.

The structure had taken more than three decades to build. Just forty years later the Roil had washed over it, mocking such industry with its implacable shadow.

If the creators of an architectural wonder as imposing as this could fall, what chance did she have?

And what of the builders of the Engine of the World? How had they fallen? All of this, every city, every construction, even the marvellous city of Drift, was nothing compared to their metropolises.

Nearly a century ago, Tearwin Meet, the Dead Metropolis in the North had been discovered, or more correctly rediscovered, though that which guarded it had driven back any attempts at uncovering its secrets. After over a dozen fatalities, and numerous failed expeditions, people had stopped trying.

All who had been there had failed, but Tearwin Meet alone held what she needed. If the Engine of the World existed it would be there at Tearwin Meet's heart.

Getting there was going to be the hard enough. She could deal with the rest when she reached its ice-caked boundary.

Her carriage only had enough fuel to reach Chapman, maybe a little further north. Once she ran out, she would have to find her own way with no money or friends – not that she had ever had either, and both of which, if she were truly honest, she only had an abstract understanding of.

A frightening thought played at the back of her mind, it seeped and grew into her thoughts like the darkness itself. What if the Roil had already overtaken Chapman? In truth she had no way of knowing if there was anything beyond the borders of the Roil. The whole world could have been swallowed by now.

In time, she thought. It will come to me in time. Either that or I will be dead.

She rubbed her head where she had bumped it, what felt like an age ago, and in some ways was even longer, in Tate. The spot throbbed. Margaret's whole body ached, she was unaccustomed to so much driving. Her parents may have taken convoys out for days, but she had never driven more than a couple of hours from the city, and, most often, that had been as a passenger.

She had now been on the road for a day and a half. Every time she blinked it was an effort to open her eyes again.

Margaret found herself veering towards the edge of the bridge, found her head dipping towards her chin. She snapped awake, and slammed on the brakes, and still it was a near thing. The *Melody* struck the rail that ran alongside the road, merely a glancing blow, but the rail had tumbled away into the abyss.

She had to stop, rest, even if it were just a few minutes. Death by Roil or death by driving the *Melody Amiss* off the bridge was still death.

She needed sleep. She brought the *Melody* to a halt, as far from the bridge edge as possible, locked down the engines and took a few sips from one of the water jars in the car.

Margaret picked up her father's book, opened a page and tried to read it. Her mind could not focus on the words, all she could see was the bridge rail falling.

She took a few deep breaths, put the book down and closed her eyes. I will just rest. How can I sleep? I'll just rest.

Another jolting image of the bridge rail sliding away, only this time she and the *Melody* followed it. Her eyes snapped open and she grabbed her rifle, setting it down in her lap. There was no way she could sleep, not now, but there was no way she could go on either.

Exhaustion decided it for her.

CHAPTER 25

All Roads lead to ruin.

Sayings Unpopular but Persistent, EDRISS WHITEBREAD

THE CITY OF MIRRLEES

There is a saying, "All roads lead to ruin." There is also a saying, "All side streets lead to Main".

Starting a little further west than Matheson's Famous Book Shop and Powder Emporium, and ending on the Southern Palestral Quarter of the city by the machine works and the busy docks – for even swollen, the River Weep continued to be the lifeblood of the city – Main followed the river, ran with it through Mirrlees-on-Weep touching almost every part of the city. About halfway along the street, at the heart of the metropolis, rose the Ruele Tower.

At the top of the spire in a sparsely yet expensively furnished room, Mr Stade sat alone and stared down at the city.

The mayor had been telling people what they wanted to hear about the Roil for over a decade. He gazed a while longer at that rain drenched city, then back at certain classified charts showing the projected growth of the Roil, and shook his head. Sometimes he even believed what he said. At least while he was saying it.

But looking at even the most optimistic of the charts, he could not believe a word of nearly a decade of his oratory. Whatever the rhetoric about the Roil halting, about the city being safe, the truth was marked upon this map, and it mocked and terrified him. The Roil continued to grow and, every day, that growth seemed faster.

That he had managed to spin such a convincing web of lies was in part that the truth was just too horrifying to bear. In some truth, there was indeed only terror. Should his plans fail, everything was lost. That was reality as Stade saw it. The Project could not fail. He was quite prepared to kill to ensure its success.

The Dissolution had been necessary. The denizen of Tearwin Meet was too dangerous, even as a last resort. Mechanical Winter, how he dreaded it, and the others would have too, if desperation hadn't blinded them.

Soon his last true opponent would be gone from the city. Medicine's aid had given his leadership a legitimacy that he was willing to admit may have been somewhat lacking after the bloodletting of a few days before

And legitimacy was what he needed, or everything would come undone.

Mirrlees had six months, if that, left to her. Then last bows would be made and the Obsidian Curtain would close.

He rubbed at his temples, his whole body knotted with tension. It was all too much responsibility and he was not the man to bear that burden, but there was no one else left. He had gotten rid of any effective councillors in his party years ago. Slack jaws and toadies were all that remained now. They were loyal to the core, yes, but if there was an original thought between the lot of them he would have been exceedingly surprised.

He flicked open a folder – its edges dark with age. Photos of men in frockcoats and hats, thirty years out of date, looking at the Arganon Slick. The first hint of the Roil, the slick had darkened a hundred mile wide patch of land, changing the landscape, warping first the flora and then the fauna so that they became something else. The Slick had been worrying, evidence of some sort of pollution, but there was no such hint of concern in their faces. No one could have suspected what would happen just days after this photo was taken.

Stade shook his head. All these men had died, long ago; most had never made it back from that expedition. Little had changed – the Roil still possessed that tendency. Just when everyone thought they had a handle on it, it went and did something totally unexpected.

He snatched his watch from his waistcoat.

Where was Tope? A minute perhaps was acceptable, though irritating, but Stade had waited now for ten.

Something buzzed at his desk and he grimaced.

The blasted intercom, the latest in long distance communication, though the distance involved here was no further than a few yards to his secretary Robert's office. Cutting edge or not, it was already starting to drive him mad.

The door opened, and there was Tope, his arm bandaged, a little blood seeping through, his Cuttlefolk genes would see to that soon, blessed as they were with swift healing.

"You're late," Stade said, pouring Tope a cup of tea, from the pot Robert had hastily brought in.

"I had some bad news," Tope said.

"And what news is that?" Stade asked softly.

"The *Dolorous Grey* is no more."

Stade nearly dropped his cup.

"Chapman has fallen? God's don't tell me that, I've only one city to save, I cannot save two," he said, quietly, and Tope raised his hands

"No, No. Not yet. But it is only a matter of time. The Roil has new tricks, Witmoths. They build an army of changed men."

"I know about the Witmoths," Stade said.

Mr Tope raised an eyebrow.

"Then did you know this?" He threw a wallet on the table. "We found it along the tracks, around a hundred miles from here. It belonged to Cadell – it stinks of him."

The Milde boy, and Cadell.

"Well he can't have survived that. We lost two Vergers to Witmoths." He was almost apologetic. "They were lacking in caution."

"This is bad news, indeed. But the Bureau of Information can deal with that." He leant forward. "And the Project?"

"It goes ahead apace. Though the Interface may not last too much longer."

"Really," Stade said, his face betraying no emotion, his eyes as hard as stone. "I've read the reports, everything seems to be working smoothly down there."

"Seems to be, yes, but there are secrets and lies in that place; too many to unpick. And I do not trust my mole. In the Roil everything is changed they say, including loyalties."

Stade frowned at that, he had grown unused to plots and secrets that were not his own. It would be worthwhile having the Interface more closely scrutinised.

"Mr Tope. You are to go to Chapman, and the Interface. I want you to talk to Anderson. I want you to see what is going on down there and report back to me."

Tope nodded, his face grim. "The Project's time is done, don't you think? It was, for a while at least, a successful experiment, enough that stage two's implementation should not meet with too many problems."

"That is if Medicine and his three thousand work as sufficient bait."

"They will, of that I am certain." Even to a hardened Verger like Tope, Stade's grin was a terrible sight.

"Good," he said. "For should the second stage fail we are all dead, and the whole human race with us."

Mr Tope's arm was stinging, and that pain put him in a black mood; all it did was remind him how he had failed.

Stade had punished him with this mission, and that angered him. After all without his aid the Dissolution would have never been affected. Stade's plans possessed substance, and chance at fruition only because of Tope's Vergers. The man was too quick to forget that.

The councillor had a new lackey now in Medicine Paul, even if the erstwhile Confluent didn't understand why or that he was. After the dissolution, and the night of blood, Medicine had been spared simply because Stade knew he could use him. Milde had never been a popular leader, his pronouncements too stern and his warnings too bleak. Medicine on the other hand… if anyone was capable of carrying out what Stade had planned it was him.

But it would all come to nothing if Cadell wasn't captured and contained.

Tope had hoped that the destruction of the *Dolorous Grey* would have achieved that, but no, neither Cadell's nor young Milde's body had been found in the wreckage.

Despite Stade's opinion, Tope knew that they were still alive, and that he would find them in Chapman.

So he headed south, to Chapman, hungry for the Old Man's death.

CHAPTER 26

Chapman, seat of the oldest council extant, and home to the Festival of Float, is perhaps most famous for that moment from which the Festival was born. A treaty signed between the earth and the sky. Eighty-seven years have passed since that signing. Eighty-seven years that have seen the peak of civilization, and its falling, eighty-seven years of the Festival.

Festivals and their Significance in a Changing World,
RABBIT WILSON

WILDERNESS
60 MILES NORTH OF THE ROIL FACE

David left early that morning with Cadell, continuing along the train line as the rain clouds lightened, leaving the lonely cabin behind them.

Around nine o'clock Cadell stopped and turned his head.

"We need to get away from the line," he said. "Now."

David was about to say something, when he heard it. A distant whine, growing louder.

Something was coming, and quickly. They ran away from the tracks, finding cover behind lantana as a vehicle stinking of kerosene rushed past. The smoke from its vents was dark and so bitter it stung David's nose. There was a Verger at the controls, one he recognised.

David shivered. Mr Tope was going to Chapman.

The engine turned a bend and Tope was gone.

"Interesting," Cadell said. "I think we had better keep our distance from the tracks. Actually, it's probably better now if we veer away from them altogether."

David agreed.

"Nice countryside this," Cadell said. "It has adapted well to the rain, but even it cannot adapt much further. I remember it from another time, a happier time for me."

The ground was boggy, plants grown yellow and rotten. Everything had a sort of washed out appearance like a really bad watercolour painting.

"It's starting to die, drowning in all this rain. The Roil," Cadell said. "Let me tell you about it. There is much I know of that foul stuff. More than I would wish. It has rained and rained, but you have seen nothing yet. McMahon was different as would have been Tate, neither straddled rivers and sat beneath catchments for one. It will rain, without surcease around Mirrlees, for a month, two months, perhaps three. And not like it has before, but heavy rains, flooding rains. Fields will first sink beneath the water then rot. Outlying villages built on the hinterland will slide into mud. There will be death, and the rain will preside over it all, seemingly ceaseless.

"But it will stop, at last. It always stops. Can you see it now? The celebration in the streets, at that cessation, should any streets remain? But then, a drought will descend, heat and dry like nothing the folk of Mirrlees have ever encountered, though those refugees, if Stade opens his gates to them this time, from Chapman will know it and fear it. The black clouds will roll in, but these will not be rain clouds, no for they will extend from the ground a mile high, maybe more. A rolling cliff face of darkness and not a drop of rain in any of it, just chaos, and so the Roil arrives. A single Quarg Hound saunters down Main Street, then another and another. Hideous Garment Flutes turn the sky black with their wings and the deafening whistles of their fistulous bodies and to that music the already broken city dies."

He paused and shook his head.

"Well that was how it was before the Witmoths. Humans have a way of magnifying disasters, speeding processes up. I wonder what madness lurks now deep within the Roil and its dreaming cities. And what its plans are."

David shivered despite the warmth of the day.

The Obsidian Curtain contained secrets, certainly. No one from the various expeditions mounted to explore it had ever returned. But what came out was well catalogued. Quarg Hounds. Endyms. Beast Wings. Blood Crabs and Hideous Garment Flutes.

As a child, his uncle who perhaps should have known better, gave David a rather morbid picture book called *Roil: A Cautionary Tale for Boys and Girls*.

The book had been written before the Roil had become something of a taboo subject, and was about a naughty boy sent to the Roil as punishment and his encounters with the creatures there. Each and every beast that had ever come out of the Roil and some that the author had obviously decided to make up – so David hoped had been drawn in painstaking and garish detail. The Quarg Hounds gnashing their bloody teeth, the Garment Flutes whistling deadly threnody.

David had loved that book – particularly the bit where the boy, and he really was a nasty child, was barbequed by a Vermatisaur – and had always been excited and terrified by the prospect of ever encountering such monsters.

Well, now he had and he was no longer excited, just terrified. Terrified and sore.

Surely legs that ached as much as his should be unable to take anything but shuffling steps. Until this day, David had no idea how much his body could ache and keep functioning. He catalogued those pains one by one and in time with the squelch of his steps, paying such little attention to the world around him that when Cadell stopped David almost collided with his back.

"Cadell?"

The Engineer turned towards him, frowning, having plucked a map from one of his many pockets. "The *Dolorous Grey* goes through Robert, Hillson and Grayville before veering east across the Lakelands. I don't think there will be much left of those townships." He wiped his face wearily, then took a deep breath, and reached a hand towards the north. "Yes," he said. "I can feel a cold change coming on. Short lived, no doubt, but definitely something that will work in our favour." He frowned. "You had a question?"

"Why did its creatures come up here in the first place?" David asked.

"Chance, as much as anything. Or perhaps not, perhaps they were hunting me. The Roil thrives on heat, and humans are warm and mobile. But not quite warm enough. Didn't you notice that the passengers were almost feverish? Those were the Witmoths pushing their body temperatures up. In the days ahead it is best to not trust anyone with a fever."

"So has the Roil killed these people?"

"No, no, just changed them. Though it's not a particularly nice change. In fact it's a rather nasty one. David, I dread what we will find in Chapman."

David dreaded it, too.

CHAPTER 27

The Interface existed, that much we can be certain of. But its secrets remain just that... secrets.

Reports from the Undisclosed, Coldits

THE INTERFACE
WITHIN THE ROIL

Anderson had never expected to end up here. When he had been a boy there had not been a name for a place like this. When he had been a boy, the Roil had been but a rumour, and industry ascendant. He'd been destined for big business, running his father's company in McMahon. How things change. The landscape of Shale, political and environmental, had drowned in the Roil's madness, and so had he. Was he mad? Once he would have thought himself so, to even imagine such a place. Now he worked here.

Anderson's footsteps echoed along the tunnel that made up the spine of the Interface, his movements a little stiff, the price of a uniform that was hopefully Roil-retardant. His guards stole around him like shadows. Only their weaponry made a noise, endothermic magazine pressurisation an odd counterpoint to his heavy steps.

Every day that Anderson walked to the Interface – which were most days now – he counted the number of steps required before he was under it. And every day that number decreased, sometimes by as many as seven, but never less than four. The title Interface was a misnomer. It had not been a true interface for nearly two months. The Roil had swept past it, with absolute disregard for such human boundaries, on the fourth day of spring, and it hadn't stopped.

He walked under yet another emergency door, five-foot thick steel that would seal the tunnels should something breach the compound and, hopefully, gain him and his crew a little time to make their escape. He shook his head. Should something breach the compound.

Strictly speaking something had breached the compound an hour ago, and he and his guard walked straight towards it.

Part of him kept thinking, *we're going the wrong way*. But he suppressed that tiny terrified voice and kept to the task at hand. This was his job and though he had spent every minute of it afraid, he had never turned away from his duty.

Nor would he now.

The tunnel ended at a pair of steel doors, their frames set solidly into the stone. Winslow waited there, his nervous face shining.

One of Anderson's guards sprayed him with ice water from an atomiser at his belt. Winslow blinked, but that was all, no moans or smoky exhalations. Everybody relaxed, but only a little. What had happened with the *Dolorous Grey* was fresh in all their minds.

"Are they here?" Anderson asked.

"Yes. They haven't been waiting long."

"Conference Room One?"

"Of course."

"Good, we'll let them wait a little longer." Anderson turned to the guard nearest him. "At the first sign of trouble I want you to ice that room, regardless of my or Winslow's discomfort. I'm tempted to get you to do it now, but I am in no mood for running today, or explaining why we gave up this installation so easily."

The guard nodded, her eyes impassive through the thick glass of her faceplate. She left them, walking down a side chamber to the observation area.

Anderson fitted his own mask, Winslow following suit. The masks were claustrophobically tight, not at all conducive to such things as ease of breathing, and their effectiveness a subject of dispute, but Anderson believed himself marginally safer with it on and that was all he had.

He coughed once, took a deep breath through the stifling mask and opened the door. Go in strong. See if you can unsettle them for a change.

Four of them waited in the room, standing by the huge glass window that looked out on to the Roil. And he remembered immediately what he remembered every time he dealt with these creatures – that he could not unsettle them. They were too alien, too distant. Nonetheless he tried.

"That stunt you pulled with the *Dolorous Grey*. What was that all about? We have an agreement."

One of the Roilings turned its pitch-dark eyes upon him and Anderson had to dig deep to control a shudder – how could any agreement be made with something that possessed those eyes? They had been human once, but now they could not be mistaken as such. The decrepitation of the flesh that the Witmoths engendered was well advanced. The Roil transformed all it had contact with, if it could touch it intimately enough, and these humans had been touched deeply.

There was a smell about them, sweet and foul all at once, like meat that had only been half-cooked and left out in the sun. Huge eyes, all pupils, gazed upon him and hands with fingers far too long flexed. Fragments of flesh had worn from their faces, revealing not bone but a substance like ash or coal mixed with dark honey, as though they had been torrefied from the inside out. No blood moved through their veins any more, just dust. Clothed in robes made of the moths that moved and shivered in waves from head to toe and back again, a restless nest of shadows, they were something out of a nightmare.

But nightmares were what Anderson was paid to deal with. How did that happen? Just how did that happen?

"Unfortunately, Mr Anderson, we are not all of a single mind," The Roiling said, in a voice clipped and far too normal. "Though the Roil sits in agreement on most issues there are shifts, swift passings of anarchy. It was a *passing* of this nature that the *Dolorous Grey* experienced. It will not happen again, even these last twenty-four hours have seen a deepening of control. Which is why we are here, in part. To apologise, of course, but also to make a request and offer a deal."

"And what might that be?"

"There is something we require of you."

Anderson and Winslow exchanged glances.

"We're listening," he said. "What exactly do you mean?"

Tap.

Tap.

"You better answer that," Arabella Penn said, and ran on legs far too long and too fast up the hill, away from her. "You better answer that."

Tap.

Tap.

"I know," Margaret whispered and shivered in the cold. She couldn't keep up. "I know. But I've been chasing you all day."

Her mother paused, eyes bright with a manic intensity. "You were a good daughter," she shouted. "Just never fast enough. All you've done is run and you still can't catch me."

She sprinted away, up and over the rise. Out of sight.

Margaret tried to run, but could not move. Out of frustration, she reached for the rifle in her lap. A Quarg Hound pup lay there instead, its jaws closing on her fingers.

It bit down, but the sound it made was odd, a soft sort of scraping: over and over.

Margaret started awake. She blinked.

A pale face stared in through the window next to her.

The Roiling gave her a clownish grin, idiotic and terrifying, its long white fingers working on the lock of the door, their nails scratching, scratching.

"Mother!" it shrieked so loud that even Margaret could hear. "Mother!"

Margaret engaged the engine, her fingers fumbling over the controls so that she nearly stalled the carriage. "Mother!"

If only she had a sentient carriage, like an Aerokin, then none of this would be happening. The *Melody's* engine turned, but didn't catch.

The Roiling's movements grew desperate; moths swirled around its head. A flap of bone white skin slid from its cheek, revealing a dark resinous substance beneath.

Margaret stared into the Roiling's face, into its dead black eyes and wondered if it had ever been human. Of course it had, it wore an old morning suit, tattered and dusty, but still recognisable.

"Mother!"

The engine came to life, the carriage shot forward, accelerated.

"Mother!" The Roiling tumbled off the carriage and ran back down the bridge towards McMahon.

A dozen Roilings circled the *Melody Amiss* watching. She sprayed a short burst of ice and opened up a gap that closed even as she passed through it. The *Melody*'s endothermic weaponry ammunition was almost gone, its efficacy reduced. One of the Roilings struck the carriage and its arm tore from its shoulder with a spray of smoky blood. Margaret picked up speed, and soon they were out of sight. And all she had again was the deserted highway.

She did not want to think about what would have happened if she had slept for even a few moments longer.

CHAPTER 28

Buchan and Whig. Two men of one mind. Stade had banished them from the city with a single proclamation. Two men, one swift mind. Slaughter not exile would surely have been the result, had not the pair been so quick in their flight. Not a single sitting member of their party was assassinated.

Mirrlees' Confluent party would have done well to learn from them. But they did not, and blood stained the streets red.

Assassinations Personal, Political & Humorous, DEIGHTON

WILDERNESS

Three columns of black smoke drifted on the edge of the eastern horizon, there was no wind and so they had grown much larger than they might otherwise have. The sight disturbed David, more than he would care to admit, there was something ominous about the smoke as though the Roil had detached itself and flowered where it did not yet belong.

He pointed them out to Cadell. The old man's face greyed.

"Yes, I see them. In truth, I've been ignoring them. They are the mute ruin of peoples' lives, rising up like a cruel ghost. I hope some people managed to escape." He shook his head, as though he thought it unlikely, and turned his gaze once more in the direction they were headed and mumbled, half to himself. "The world just keeps getting worse. But then that has been the case for a long time now. The question is, did Chapman hold out?"

After seeing those silent columns of smoke, a taciturn gloom settled on them that nothing was able to break. David was almost happy when darkness descended obliterating the sight. Until a hot storm came with it and their clothes were again soaked to the bone.

However, as the rain came in and the night, Cadell's mood changed. He became nervy, not exactly afraid, but close to it.

The thought of something that could rattle Cadell was enough to worry David. Quarg Hounds and Roilings had been dealt with almost without blinking and yet their approach to Uhlton was being met with such trepidation.

"We're getting close," Cadell said, his first words in hours, and fell into a kind of disturbed silence broken by interludes of nervy mumbling that kept David on edge.

Which was, perhaps, why David saw Uhlton first – well, the few specks of light that betrayed its existence in the rainy murk of evening. He thought of the sleepy village he had seen in maps (and with the aid of map powder), built above the river. A place far from politics and Vergers, somewhere he might manage to score some Carnival – if he could just slip away.

"I can see it," he shouted, hoping to lift Cadell's spirits, and because he was genuinely excited. "There, to the south west, the town of Uhlton."

"Good," Cadell said. "How very clever of you. We'll be there soon"

"And where in Uhlton is *there*?" David asked.

"Never you mind," Cadell mumbled. "Got to keep some mystery in your life."

Uhlton was not as David imagined. Built on a ridge above the swollen lake, it was a cramped and crowded village, and anything but sleepy. Steamers docked and undocked at a long quay, men shouted and swung thick ropes around bollards as they guided their pilots with hand signals and curses, working busily even at this late hour. The river seemed almost as busy as Mirrlees itself.

The roads leading to the town were in poor repair. The River Weep sustained this township as it did Mirrlees and Chapman. Around Uhlton, besides a few tilled fields, the land was bare or forested; without the river the town would die.

As they approached, someone released a flare into the sky; blue flame illumined the sky like a third moon. Cadell slumped down on a large pale stone, marking the edge of the town. Dim double shadows stretched behind him. He let out a long, resigned breath and rested his chin on his hands.

"They've seen us now," he said. "There's little reason to go on. They will come and get us, and I am too weary. We will wait here."

A second flare rocketed skywards. From the township rolled a horse-drawn carriage, its driver tall, lamps dangled from its corners.

Back the way they had come, lightning scarred a black and starless sky and the northern horizon rumbled and boomed. Though they were scarcely more than a hundred miles from Mirrlees it was as though they stood in another land entirely.

The carriage came to a halt beside them and the driver cracked his whip in the air – the horses didn't blink: he obviously did this a lot. "State your business in Uhlton," he said curtly, swinging the whip in lazy circles around his head.

"I have an appointment with the mayor and his second in command," Cadell said.

The driver laughed, and there was threat implicit in that sound as much as any cracking whip. "Mayor? None go by that name here, kind sir."

Cadell grinned, an equally threatening grin. "Don't be so disingenuous; you know who I need to speak to. And you'd best hurry, I am hungry." Cadell flashed his teeth. "I must talk to Buchan and Whig. Unless of course, they have passed away or been driven out." Cadell sounded almost hopeful.

The driver's eyes narrowed, and he peered at them through the gloom, one hand lifting a lamp to better aid his scrutiny. David's eyes watered in all that light.

"They're here," the driver said, clearing his throat significantly. "But not for much longer." Then he whistled, his eyes widening then narrowing, expressions so bordering on caricature David couldn't tell if he was serious or taking the piss. "Oh, I know of you, you're that Engineer, the one with the cruel sense of humour and the taste for Vergers. We've a portrait of you on our dartboard. Buchan would speak to you, yes indeed."

Cadell glared at the driver, irritation passing across the Old Man's face like a storm; he stood taller and taller, and the driver appeared to shrink in time with him.

"We are tired," Cadell said sounding at once weary and yet energetic enough to possibly rip off a certain driver's face. "Very tired. Take us to the village or strike us with that ridiculous whip, just do something! I've no patience for this."

The driver nodded at the door to the carriage. "Get in," he said quietly.

David and Cadell clambered inside. The cabin was musty, though the seats were clean. David could not understand what had just gone on, he looked to Cadell for explanation and Cadell stared back at him stonily. "Our greeting here may be less than civil, but then it is my fault." His voice softened as though to reduce the blow of the words that followed. "People have invested rather a lot in me, and I have yet to deliver."

David could understand that bitterness. He possessed a fair share of it towards Cadell, himself. However, perhaps he shouldn't have nodded so readily in agreement.

Cadell glared at him, but it lacked even the pretence of self-righteousness. "David, there are some things over which I have little control. Certain liberties wrested from me in ages past. Makes me grumpy. Makes me dangerous. I am not one whom most people would be comfortable knowing, and I don't blame them. I gather hatred like a coat gathers dust."

The carriage bounced into the town, David always watching with an addict's hunger, seeking out places he might score Carnival. The pub, a back street. He cast his gaze about the people at work searching for the tell-tale signatures of Carnival addicts. The slightly jerky walk, the dull smile.

In catching its suggestion (here, a man wandering aimlessly down Main Street. There a fellow pausing languidly between swings of an axe) he felt at once excited and disgusted with himself. He knew that Cadell had been deliberately lowering the amount given. A week or two at that rate, and he might not need any of the drug at all. The thought terrified him.

The carriage stopped at the front door of what David took to be the town hall. He'd seen his fair share, dragged to this outlying township or that with his father.

Cadell got out, doffed his hat at the driver and walked over to the door. David followed.

Cadell raised a fist to knock but before he struck wood, the door swung open. Framed in the doorway was a man seven feet tall at least. He reached down and shook Cadell's hand, enclosing it completely in his grip as he did so.

"Cadell!" He cried. "It is so good to see you. It has been far too long."

Cadell nodded. "Far too long indeed," he said absently. "Is he in?"

"We were wondering if you might come a calling after what happened with the *Dolorous Grey*. Trouble does follow you, sir." He turned to David and shook his hand warmly. "And you must be Mr Milde, it's an honour, sir. I've heard so much about you, your father was so proud. Oh, but I'm getting ahead of myself. I am Mr Eregin Whig."

"*The* Mr Whig?"

Mr Whig blushed, a truly remarkable glow because his face was so pale. "If by that you mean, once deputy Mayor of Chapman, yes. Now I am just an exile."

Cadell coughed. "Enough of this, how about we get out of the rain."

Mr Whig nodded and let David in. "You're quite lucky to have caught us. We are leaving Uhlton, to areas even more remote. The day after tomorrow we're heading to Hardacre. The call has been put out, and we are going. Yes, Mr Buchan will be most anxious to see you."

David wasn't surprised to hear that name. It was only logical that the exiled Mayor of Chapman would have been here too.

Cadell seemed almost nervous, he rubbed his fingers together before bringing them up to his face as though he was trying to hide behind their span.

"No doubt he is," Cadell said and followed, more anxious than David had ever seen him.

What did an Old Man have to fear?

CHAPTER 29

Even before the Dissolution, Stade had begun to reveal the extent of his power. Until the Grand Defeat none of the allied metropolises had exerted much influence over the others, but then McMahon was gone, its population scattered. Within eight years Stade had not only managed to stack Chapman's council with his own men, but also exile perhaps the most successful mayoral team in history.

Once again though, so singular was Stade's purpose that he did not finish the job, creating only another strong alliance with the city of Hardacre. Stade did not seem to care as long as his Project went ahead. When it was completed there would be no opponents, his rule and his people would be unassailable.

That was the plan, at any rate.

Histories, DEIGHTON

THE ROIL

The light came on a couple of hours after she had reached the other side of the gorge and started the ascent into the low dark mountains, a red light in the centre of the console, and fear touched her for the first time since the bridge. Fear and an awful resignation. The journey had taken its toll on the carriage – the *Melody Amiss* was running too hot. These vehicles were not meant to be driven over such a long distance. Its engines, designed both to drive the carriage and cool it, were susceptible to overheating.

If she did not shut the carriage down soon and for a decent interval of time, the heat from the engines could set the coolants aflame, turning the carriage from vehicle to bomb.

She double-checked her vehicle's readings and realized that the *Melody's* starter motor was running on a very low charge. If she stopped now she might never start again.

Margaret slowed the carriage down, hoping that would prove enough, but the light stayed red and the *Melody's* engine lost its smooth rhythm; bonnets juddered within their casings.

Beyond these low mountains was a long plain at the end of which should be Chapman. She had maybe a hundred miles to go. A few hours driving, if the carriage could make it. There was no chance of that happening if the engine overheated. Margaret could no more imagine walking that distance than she could hitching a ride with an Endym. If the *Melody* failed she would die out here in the dark.

She brought the car to a halt, and carefully ran the engine down.

The light stayed on. Margaret switched off the cooling units and charged up her suit, just in case.

Something flew overhead, and Margaret trained her guns on it. An Endym. It saw the carriage and circled above her three times, before turning back the way it had come.

That message played through her mind again.

They'll be coming for you. She'll be wanting you. Trust no one.

Staying here was a bad idea, but she had no other choice. Margaret could hardly get out and walk to Chapman.

She considered trying to sleep, but her mind kept returning

to that pale face, the fingers scratching against the glass. And her body ached.

Margaret was beginning to develop sores from the constant pressure of the suit against her flesh. These things were not designed for more than a few hours' use. No one expected someone to survive that long within the Roil.

She'd kept the charge fed from the *Melody* and kept her body cold. She'd thought herself impervious to the chill and found she was anything but.

A few more days and the wounds would grow gangrenous. She would sicken and die. Killed by the thing designed to save her.

She couldn't think on it. Nor could she bring herself to inspect the sores.

So she picked up her father's journal and opened it. His familiar, almost too neat handwriting comforted and stung her at the same time. Here was her father, frozen in the past, describing thoughts and moments drifting further away from her with every heartbeat.

It was all history now. No living city, just dead words, but it was all she had.

The bulk of the notebook was filled with his usual musings. Statistical data concerning the city, and heat to ice ratios, but towards the back, starting a few days before they had driven off to test the I-Bomb, it took on more of the form of a diary.

October Fifteen

While I continue to doubt the veracity of Deighton, Elder or Younger, their history too epic to ever be history, I have been coming around to A's way of thinking. There must indeed be Engine of the World, though they would be unlike any engines that we understand.

I keep coming across references to Lodes. Points along which the Engine's powers are expressed. Tate it would appear is built upon one, which explains at least the ease with which our machinery produces ice. It was for a very good reason that Tate was built just where it is, or why many of our devices were so easily constructed.

How limited are our resources, when it comes to the past? The books we have are all we have. We lack the opportunity to engage in the deeper tasks, of fieldwork, of cross-referencing ideas with other Masters of the Past. As the years progress, our grip on history grows ever more hypothetical; so does our grip on current events.

Truly, and admitting it has been entirely forced upon us, Tate is the most parochial of metropolises.

I would predict anarchy to the north. Mirrlees and Chapman swollen with refugees, the far north getting its share as well. Interesting times no doubt.

But who can tell? We have received no communication from the north in over twenty years.

October Seventeen

No time for musing, today. The I-Bombs are to be loaded into truck five. I had hoped to take the Melody Amiss *out into the field. Even I am amazed at that little vehicle. However, she has little storage capacity.*

Must make sure I forbid Margaret to drive her. It is the sort of thing she would do. Roil take her, but she's a determined one. It was all we could do to talk her out of joining the Sweepers. She would have made a fine one, of that I am certain, but I could not bear to lose her to that peril.

These bombs must work.

October Eighteen – Day One

We have discarded the prescribed safety of Tate for the awfulness of night. There is a lot of activity to the east of Mechanism Highway. Quarg Hounds and Endyms are massing, though they were disinterested in us I'm sure the city is a draw to them. For all that it is ice it is heat also. Indeed we passed more Roilings than I have seen for some time, which suggests another population explosion – a further urgency is added.

Though looking back at our well-built city, walled and clockwork guarded, one of the Four just finished firing, Sweepers' gliders circling the Vents, I am in no doubt that Margaret is safe. It is beyond me to imagine anything less than one of the Vastkind could batter down those stone walls.

October Nineteen – Day Two

There is a stark beauty to this landscape and, in places, an intimidating tranquillity that even our engines are unable to destroy. Though we have lived in the Roil for twenty years there is far too much that we do not understand. How can we when our field of inquiry is so narrow?

One question that has left me in a quandary all these years is how does the Roil retain its heat? By all rights things should be cooler. The Roil blocks out the sun. Yet all of its functions are exothermic in nature. The answer lies in the Roil spores I suspect.

In the south the temperature rises dramatically, and in the north there is a similar though less extreme rise.

Though it is hard to credit it, we are actually in a cooler pocket of the Roil.

(This was followed by a series of calculations that Margaret skipped over)

October Twenty – Day Three

We tested the I-Bomb today and it worked as planned, an astonishing thing in itself. A single weapon, low yield, freed a zone of Roil over eighteen miles in diameter. This is truly our most potent weapon, scary in its effectiveness.

The greatest test of all, though, is just how to use it most effectively. Airships would lend themselves to the task, or better yet, the Iron Wings that A has designed. A dozen of them, perhaps, or even more, dropping them in tandem. It would be swift.

Today we are triumphant, I can confidently predict an end to the Roil threat, by the close of the decade.

Margaret, you will see the sun again.

October 21 Day Four

Trucks One and Three are missing. This morning my wife led a perimeter patrol and they did not return. We have heard no word, nor have any drones arrived. Ah, my darling Arabella, where have you gone?

What is more disturbing is that they took our I-Bombs with them. This makes no sense.

After yesterday's success, today sees absolute failure. Something has taken my wife and the weaponry.

Day Five

This has been the worst day of my life. From dizzying heights to such a bitter nadir, as though I were an addict of Carnival, if their transitions could ever be as cruel as this.

Yesterday, I thought my wife lost. Today she has come back, but she has not returned as I remember her. She is different; some feverish infection has its hold over her. And, were it not for our judicious use of coolants we too would have been infected.

The infection has as its vector a substance that she referred to, in one of her more lucid moments, as Witmoths. It is a sublimate of the Roil spores almost, though potent and, unlike the spores, directly acting upon the human consciousness. Had I not been as swift, pulling away from a burst of the creatures sprung from my wife's lips I would have known its effects far too intimately.

I have her in quarantine, I dare not return with her to Tate, though she has begged it of me… because *she has begged it of me. She calls in the dark for Margaret. The familial ties are strong in this contagion, the desire to extend it to the immediate family. She pants our names, demanding that I honour my love. Really, to honour it would be to fire a bullet into her skull.*

Oh, my wife. Oh, my daughter. The temperature of the cabin is an agony to her, but one I would not reduce. It is, I believe, our only insurance against the contagion that she contains. At times she is lucid, but then desperate rages grip her. She is possessed with a violence I have never seen before, and it terrifies me.

Calvin tried to launch a drone today, but its message pod was filled with Witmoths. It infected him through his mouth and nose and he was lost to us. He tried to free her, tried to contaminate the rest of us.

His cold body lies in carriage number eight.

We had no choice but to kill him – that's what I keep telling myself. I can kill Calvin, while my own wife sits bound in the refrigerated research cabin, cursing all of us.

I cannot think clearly. They look to my lead, and I cannot think.

Where is truck number three?

Day Seven

They came today, and all I can remember is the terror of it.

The raid was methodical and swift. They knew our routines, but that should have come as no surprise, I discovered at last where truck three disappeared. Better if it had been destroyed. Everyone is lost to me, luck if you could call it that led to my escape.

I will not forget the howls of my colleagues, their sudden transformation from ally to enemy. I was near enough to car number four. No Witmoths found me out, but it does not matter. There is only one of me.

They freed her, and the city will fall. The things I have seen. Things that were once men and women, and some of them are old, made years ago. Here lies the answer to the Walkers. Here is why they walked.

Will drive back to Tate, but I do not expect to make it.

Day ~~Nine~~ Ten

My darling, Margaret. I saw you today, but you did not see me.

I have learnt of your passage north, and hope that these notes reach you. The city, as you no doubt suspect, is lost utterly.

We were betrayed, my child. But it is my hope to end that betrayal here. The I-Bombs I have gathered should clear away this section of the Roil and, hopefully, the contagion. But in truth I cannot say how far it has spread. Be careful, my dear. Keep your cold suit charged.

There is no time left. The drone is set to follow the road, may it find you.

I love you, my dear. Your mother loved you, too. If I could do but one thing, it would be to ensure that you were not alone. If only I could aid you on your way. But that is just a dream. My only comfort is that we never completed our Iron Wings. Imagine those things at the Roil's command.

Be careful, and swift. They'll be coming for you. She'll be wanting you. Trust no one. There is no one left to trust.

Margaret closed the book and wept. What had her mother become? And her father, was he likewise bonded to the Roil?

She thought of her father, of him being all by himself, deserted by his daughter; the Roil alone knowing what had become of his wife.

Poor father. She hated herself for it, but she wished him dead. And her mother, too.

The engine had cooled. She cautiously engaged the ignition and the *Melody Amiss* rumbled back into life, its engine once again running smoothly. Margaret released her breath.

She had many miles to go and she did not expect to stop before she saw daylight. Slowly, slowly she followed the highway, up and over the mountain range,

Death, welcome as it may have been, was no longer in her heart. Unless it were the death that she might bring. The Roil had taken her city and destroyed her family. She would have vengeance, she must.

CHAPTER 30

Exile can be good. Exile can focus the mind. We were in exile, but we were also free. Sometimes I wish Buchan had understood that better than he did.

The Hunters of Old Men, WHIG

THE TOWN OF UHLTON

To David, their stay in Uhlton had taken on the reality of a dream. Since they had arrived he had bathed, been given fresh clothes and now dinner in a hall crowded with what Mr Buchan had described as his executive staff. To David's way of thinking they didn't look at all like executive staff. Many wore guns, several bore lumpy old scars and eye patches. Even Mr Buchan was missing an ear.

Mr Buchan was one of the largest men David had ever seen, David had been expecting that, but it was one thing to hear about, something another to see it. But for all his size he was not ill or slovenly; in fact, he moved and spoke with an energy that David found exhausting. He roared and bellowed and punctuated exclamations with a huge roast leg of lamb that he shook in the air as though it were a mere chicken bone.

The hall in which they ate was cavernous and lit by hundreds of candles – so that the high ceiling was dim with dull smoke – and the table along which they all sat ran almost the entire length of it. The table had been piled high with food, most of which had gone into either Cadell's or Mr Buchan's stomach. Both men truly had prodigious appetites, and David was reminded of his dream at the Lode: Cadell filling his mouth with the frozen corpses of birds.

Mr Whig sat to David's right, and Cadell was across the table from him as quiet as he had ever seen him. Mr Buchan had been incredibly polite to David, and everyone kept saying how pleased they were to meet him at last and how sorry they were to have heard about his father.

But now, bathed and fed, it was all taking on the qualities of a dream. David struggled to keep his eyes open: a battle he was fast losing.

Unfortunately he suspected that sleep was still a long way off.

'What is all this?' he had asked at one stage, never expecting anyone to listen, but Mr Buchan waved for silence.

"David, dear Mr Milde," he said throatily. "Think of us as the last bastion of the Confluence Party, outside of Hardacre. And certainly the last with any hope of affecting the destruction of the Roil." He raised his glass. "To the Engine."

The whole table took up the toast. "To the Engine."

David glanced over at Cadell. Not happy, in fact quite the opposite. Cadell glowered at Buchan, and the big man winked and blew him a kiss.

At last Mr Buchan reached into his elegant vest, patterned like a peacock's tail, and pulled out a big pocket watch dwarfed by his massive hands and become some miniaturists' fancy.

"Gentlemen, it is late and there is still much to do. Not to mention our exodus in two days. I bid you all good night." His eyes flicked to Cadell. "Dare you brave my parlour, Mr Fly."

Cadell's expression was unreadable. "If we must," he said quietly.

Mr Buchan nodded it was so and rose from the table like some huge beast breaking the surface of a primordial lake. In one movement, he pulled the napkin from around his throat – a napkin that for all his eating and food punctuating was spotless – folded it neatly and slipped it back into a silver napkin ring.

At that signal the hall quickly emptied. Half a dozen people nodding at David and wishing him the best and how pleased they were to finally meet such an upstanding young gentleman.

Then all but David, Cadell, Mr Buchan and Mr Whig remained.

"Gentlemen," Buchan said, rubbing his hands together enthusiastically. "If you would follow me."

On the rare occasions David needed to use the words "richly appointed", he was merely trying to describe something like this. Mr Buchan's parlour was the most "richly appointed" room David had ever seen.

Big comfortable chairs covered in plump cushions, lush wall hangings with scenes from history – famous battles and orators speaking – and, above it all, painted in glittering gold and stretching across the ceiling was a Vermatisaur, its many, many eyes rubies, its scales highlighted by diamonds.

Mr Buchan decanted a bottle of sherry and poured everyone a drink.

Mr Whig shut the door behind them and leant on a chair that faced a fireplace so clean that David suspected it had not been used in years.

There was a wooden writing desk and a broad backed wooden chair at the other end of the parlour. A tall ream of paper sat neatly on the edge of the desk, a blue glass paperweight globe depicting Shale, the single continent prominent, rested upon it. David stared at the manuscript with interest and Mr Buchan caught his gaze.

"My magnum opus," he said. "A history of the Confluents, partly apocryphal, particularly the material regarding Oscar the Fishmonger, which is appropriate for such a party such as ours don't you think? I intend writing the last chapter once all this is done. Once I know how this turns out."

Mr Buchan waved his glass of sherry in the direction of the desk, whilst his gaze settled upon Cadell.

"Many was the time I sat at that desk in Chapman's Tower facing an even harder task than history. Writing letter after letter, each more hopeless than the last, and you never came. I begged you, implored and cajoled, and I do not do those things, and still you did not come… and now. And now. Here you are. A little late by my reckoning, wouldn't you agree, John?"

Cadell's face wrinkled. "Well, I am here now."

Buchan clenched his free hand into a fist and shook it in Cadell's face. "How dare you? How dare you? I lost good men and women to this fight of ours. I have watched my party fail. But for mere chance leavened with paranoia, both Whig and I would have died in Stade's attack. But we survived and with us hope, though even that has soured this last year. Our heroism, Medicine's heroism, Warwick's life, all of it has come to naught. I have seen my world come undone and I have not ignored it. But there is nothing that I can do."

"And what do you think I can?"

"Do you know we even sent an expedition north, flew directly there."

"You did what?" Cadell said. "An expedition to Tearwin Meet. That is folly. Absolute folly."

"Desperation is a potent engine," Mr Buchan said significantly. "It was an expedition equipped with the latest technologies, and some of the brightest people my city has ever produced – intellectuals of the calibre of the Penns. Not one of them returned; they crossed the wall and then we lost contact. Things are bad, Cadell."

Cadell snorted. "And you think I don't know that. Me who numbers in years more than all your cabinet's ages combined. It is bad, and it will get much worse. It *will* get much worse and night will fall. How dare you? You, who has not seen what I have seen. You, who does not know the cost of what you ask.

"Why do you think that Stade does what he does? He fears that path, almost as much as I. You released me, but I did not ask to be released. How dare *you* rage at me?"

Mr Buchan stabbed a finger in the air, his big face reddened and his jowls shook. "I dare because I see what is happening now. I see the Roil growing. And we know enough of the restraints upon you, and the reasons for them."

Cadell snarled. "Greater cities than you will ever know have fallen, greater civilisations have been destroyed in the cure. My world was wiped clean, and this life, this cage, and these hungers are my curse. The Engine is a cruel saviour, Mr Buchan. Cruel and cold. When you deal with it, you deal with a servant of death. There are no degrees in this, only a different scouring, and the slimmest most terrible of hopes."

"But they are all we have! We let you out, we let the monster out because it is all we have."

Cadell hung his head as though he could not face his accuser, defeated at last. "That they are."

Mr Buchan was not satisfied; his face darkened. "And how could it be otherwise? Nine metropolises have fallen and three remain, though one has but weeks left to it. We are an obstinate people, Cadell. Why, the festival is still being held in Chapman. Tate fell because it was too proud to seek assistance. McMahon, pinnacle of everything that this world has achieved since yours tumbled, armed itself to the teeth and it fell faster than the lot of them." He sat down, his voice dropping to a harsh whisper. "And where were you? Where were you when all those people died? Where were you when the darkness smothered the refugees, when Endyms and Vermatisaurs tore Aerokin screaming from the sky?"

"You know where I was, where all the Old Men were. And then it took a long time to sate my hungers, to end my madness and face my fears."

"Bah, you've made your fears a certainty."

"Enough!" Mr Whig raised his hands pleadingly. "There are no certainties, Buchan," he said. "Perhaps if the cities had banded together, instead of breaking apart we could have dealt with this threat. But they did not. The Engine is a last hope, but it was not the only one."

"It is now," Buchan said. "It is now."

CHAPTER 31

Name an engine that hasn't ruined us. I dare you. But of course you cannot. Our relationship with machines has always been… complicated.

The Metal Captives, NORSE

THE ROIL
THREE MILES SOUTH OF THE ROIL EDGE

Margaret checked her readings once again and hoped against hope that she was right. Another ten minutes and she should be at the edge of the Roil. Another twenty and she would be out of fuel. A near thing, indeed.

She was so intent upon her readings that she did not see the armoured carriage until it had almost collided with the *Melody*.

Where in all the Roil had that come from? It wasn't from Tate, but that didn't make it friendly. At once she charged up her guns; they whined in her ears, competing with the sudden pounding of her heart.

The carriage flashed its forward lights at her.

On and off, on and off.

Margaret studied the vehicle, it was huge and clumsy, but cannon bristled from it like the spines of a particularly aggressive animal – and not all of it was endothermic weaponry.

Even the most cursory glance suggested that she was outgunned, even if it wasn't nearly as elegant as the *Melody*.

Margaret brought her carriage to a halt. She was almost out of fuel, the cooling units were failing and the engine light had started flashing again.

A door in the side of the other carriage opened, revealing a figure clothed in a cold-suit: a design similar though much inferior to her own. The rubber too thick to allow smooth movement, the person within it reduced to a lumpish clownishness, all hips and goggle eyes.

Margaret could not suppress a smile at the sight of such primitive and clunky garb: a museum piece as outdated as a carriage that would waste munitions space on regular guns, as though its designers weren't quite sure who the enemy was.

Well, these people had not had twenty years to perfect their weaponry.

The figure gestured for her to follow, then struggled back inside its carriage and turned the vehicle around, aft guns aimed on the *Melody*.

Follow she did, down a short road and towards a grim thick-walled building jutting from the ground. A door in the front of the construction opened and light spilled out, so bright that she had to blink back tears. Then, from the top of the opening, water streamed down, sealing the opening in a cataract of cold.

She followed the carriage in, through the falling water, and the gate closed shut behind her. The carriage stopped in front of her, she did the same. Cautiously, she climbed out, her ice guns armed.

Soldiers in more of those ridiculously antiquated cold suits stood around the *Melody*, their guns aimed at her.

The driver was already out of his vehicle. He came over to her and put out his hand. Margaret didn't know what to do, she stared at the hand as though it might strike out at her.

"Don't worry," he said. "You're quite safe here. Safe as you have been in a long while, I'll wager. My name's Anderson. Welcome to the Interface. Of all the things I had ever expected to come from the south you are the last."

Margaret hesitated a little longer before gripping his hand; it was cold and dry. The air here was colder than the *Melody's* cabin, moths would not last a second.

"Where am I?" She asked.

"Somewhere you shouldn't be – a secret. But as always the Roil contains more secrets than even I could imagine. You shouldn't be here, but you are. And this facility shouldn't exist, but it does." He dipped into a shallow bow. "This is the Council's little enclave in the darkness. In truth it is the Interface no more."

He tapped the fire-scored chassis of the *Melody Amiss*.

"That's quite a sophisticated machine you've got there, and one that has seen some combat."

Margaret refused to be fazed. He was just a man, and this Interface was nothing. Anderson had no reason to be so cocky. "My father and mother designed it," she said. "What else would you expect?"

Anderson's eyes narrowed, as though a thought had come upon him, and a very surprising thought at that. Margaret couldn't tell if he was alarmed or pleased. He reached out to brush the hair from her face, and Margaret knocked his arm away.

"You've got the look all right." Anderson whistled. "Penn! You're a Penn. Why I was little more than a lad when I saw your father. Travelled all the way to Tate. Back then we had train lines that ran the length of Shale." Anderson laughed. "My, but I'm forgetting myself. You're exhausted. Rest a while. There is time for talk later, perhaps I'll even explain all this to your liking." He raised his hands in mock delight. "My, this just gets more interesting by the minute."

"Margaret," Margaret said as he led her away from her machine, towards a door from which had streamed cold-suited soldiers.

"Pardon?" Anderson said.

"My name is Margaret. Margaret Penn."

"Well, Margaret Penn, I can't tell you how pleased we are to see you."

Margaret couldn't say the same.

The Interface was a series of cold, long chambers guarded by sombre men and women who had seen far too much of horror. She was held for a while in the loading bay with her *Melody* as it was checked, with a rigour matching that of Tate, for Witmoths. Just as she was checked, her temperature taken, her pupil response measured. She did not surrender her weapons, nor was it requested that she did so.

Her fingers kept straying to the hilt of her rime blade.

They watched her now, and she could not help but feel sorry for them.

Their little enclave as Anderson put it was just that… little. Insignificant when compared to the efforts of Tate.

Margaret did not feel safe here, but that was barely an impediment.

She had grown up in the Roil and, as terrible as her last few days had been, she had endured these horrors all her life. She knew herself capable of dealing with them, and if she failed she would die. Death did not scare her. But it terrified these soldiers.

It had beaten them down, and it showed, not in their movements or the way they handled their weapons, absolute efficiency personified, but in their eyes. These people of the light had been thrown into a nightmarish place that did not hate, but just devoured. She could only begin to imagine how awful that might be.

In Tate, once the land beyond had succumbed, suicide rates tripled and never really stopped. Some could not live in the dark, and you did not know if you could until you had to.

She noticed something else in these guards and the way they regarded her – a sort of grudging respect.

"You came from Tate in that?" One of them had asked, pointing back at the *Melody*, and here in the light Margaret could see just how much damage it had sustained, its armour dented, a rear tire worn down to metal. Seeing it so battered, Margaret had trouble believing it herself.

"Yes, all the way."

The soldier bowed deeply. "Well, madam, you are indeed the bravest woman I have ever met, and I have Drifter in my blood. My mother and my aunts on her side were all air maidens, warrior pilots." She laughed.

Margaret could not hold her gaze.

It wounded her. She did not consider it bravery, there had been no choice in the matter. Well, that was not quite true. She had fled, and she was not yet ready to dwell too long on those who had stayed, nor the dim quaking of the earth as brilliance swept overhead, followed by the gently falling snow.

"Not brave," she said. "It was just stupid luck. If I hadn't gone looking for my parents I would be dead too."

"But you kept going. You drove through the night-dark miles and we know what's out there. All of us do. There is no escape in the Roil, but horror after horror."

"Crew, enough gawking," Anderson, said. "She has been a long time coming to us, let her have some peace,"

The guards nodded and gave her space, though they did not stop their scrutiny. Within half an hour, Margaret suspected she had been viewed by the entire installation. And as for peace, they had given her very little of that.

"I'm sorry to keep you so long here, but I thought it best that people should see you." Anderson whispered to her.

"Why? They hardly know me."

"You give them hope," he said.

Margaret shuddered. The last thing she wanted to hear. How could she give anyone hope when she held none of it herself? Nausea threatened to engulf her. She struggled against it. Pushed it down, just as she had pushed everything else down.

Anderson must have seen some of this in her face for he led her gently from the loading bay.

"I do not wish to be anyone's hope. If anything, I bring despair. My city is lost, destroyed. And if we have succumbed to the Roil how can you hope to defeat it?" Her voice was flat, she avoided Anderson's gaze. "I did not ask for this. The things I have seen would extinguish anyone's hope. I did not face my city's attackers, but fled. All that I loved I have deserted."

Anderson flinched at that. Margaret wondered what lay in his past. She had been driven away from the Roil. What might drive a man into it?

"And yet you are here, only a few hundred yards from the edge of the Roil," he said. "You have survived. And survival is no small thing in these times. Now, you must be very tired."

"Tired is not the word for what I feel," she said and stumbled.

"We have sleeping quarters nearby, though you'll be the first to use them – none of us can sleep here. Not once we've crossed the Interface, we've tried, but the dark weighs down on us, and we have nightmares of such horrible intensity But you, Margaret, you are made of sterner stuff. Rest now."

"I can't rest," she said. "Not yet. There's much you must know."

Anderson's face grew conflicted. She could see his concern for her but she could also see that he hungered for what she might tell him, for any information that might help them in their study of the Roil. Yet he hesitated.

"I'll rest when I have shared what I know."

"If you insist," he said at last. "Come with me, but the moment you want to stop, we stop."

He took her to a small room, with a table and chairs and a recording device.

"State of the art," Anderson said. "It will take down your voice and return it to you. Much more convenient than note taking."

He manoeuvred a large microphone in front of her. "Now if you'll just speak into that, slowly and clearly."

Margaret did. Telling him everything from her wait for her parents through to her flight from the city and her arrival here.

When she had finished, Anderson switched off the machine.

"If I hadn't seen the *Melody Amiss,* your cold-suit, your obvious parentage, I wouldn't believe a word of it. And yet, here you are.

"Did you bring blueprints for your parents' I-Bombs? The machine is off, you can speak with candour."

Margaret shook her head.

Anderson could not hide his disappointment, though he tried valiantly, smiling. "It does not matter," he said. "We are researching something similar at any rate. It is good to know we are on the right track. That you survived at all is remarkable. Now you must rest."

This time Margaret did not argue. She let him lead her away to the showers, where she stripped of her cold suit and bathed.

Her flesh was swollen, and sore, but there were surprisingly few pressure wounds. She let the heat of the shower seep into her and tried to think of nothing but the relief it offered her body.

When she was done, one of the soldiers led her to a small room with a single metal-framed bed, and little more.

Clothes had been laid out; military fatigues. They fit her, reasonably enough. And, while it felt odd to be dressed in something that didn't chill her or push tightly against her flesh (and when had that cold grip become a comfort?) she fell asleep almost at once.

No dreams haunted her. How could they? Her life was nightmare enough.

A few corridors away from the sleeping quarters was a small room, with a small table, a couple of hard wooden chairs and a door that backed on to the kitchen. There were well-thumbed copies of all the recent Shadow Council stories stacked neatly at one end of the table.

Anderson and Winslow both had offices crammed with notes and maps and memos from the Council, and filing cabinets with large locks, and some that were even fitted with alarms. But it was here that they made their decisions, in this little room, usually with nothing more than a cup of tea, some dry old biscuits and a lot of pacing.

Anderson put his cup of tea down. "This cannot be right. It's made me uneasy from the beginning. She is a Penn. A Penn," Anderson said. "Without them we would not have half the weaponry we do."

Winslow nodded. "But we have our orders."

Anderson walked the length of the hall, before turning back. "We have been following orders for the last year, even as they have grown less and less reasonable. Winslow, she escaped her city's fall. She is a resourceful and strong woman, and even if she were not, I cannot in good conscience hand her over to the enemy."

Winslow nodded.

"It would be folly to trust them. They're up to something. Great works, some sort of construction, all of it where we can't go."

"You've felt it too?" Anderson said. "The quivering earth? The distant murmur of old engines?"

"Yes," Winslow said. "Our darkest nightmares seem ready to flower. And they'd have us make yet another concession."

Anderson nodded his head, picking up his fast-cooling tea and drinking it down. "And why her? What interest does the Roil have in this one person?"

"She is a child of Marcus and Arabella Penn. It does our cause no good to give the enemy what they want. Particularly when they demand a Penn." He shook his head. "Remember when we were here to fight the Roil, not make deals with it? I think the time for deal making is over."

The orders mocked him with their cruel simplicity. The single sentence:

"Let the Roil have her. We need more time."

We have no more time, he thought. Whether we give them Margaret or not.

Anderson scrunched the paper in his hand, throwing it into the bin. "Did you see these orders, Winslow?"

"What orders?" Winslow asked.

Anderson grinned, though he frowned again quickly enough. "Give her another half an hour, she's almost dead on her feet, and then you better wake her. They'll be coming soon. Poor Margaret you must run again."

CHAPTER 32

In Mirrlees nothing is done in a half-hearted fashion. Bridges, levees, floods, all of them are gigantic. Excess is the order of the day, but admire the filigree of Channon Hall or the delicate structure of the Reeping Meet, with its thirteen clocks, and you realise that the human was never sublimated, merely overshadowed. It is there when you look into the dark.

Babbet's Mirrlees: A Tourist's Almanac, BABBET

THE CITY OF MIRRLEES
301 MILES NORTH OF THE ROIL

"Mr Paul, these are your wards."

They stood in the rain at the edge of Northmir where the suburbs gave out to the labyrinthine drainage systems and Ur-levees of the city. Before them rose the Northmir Bridge behind them the levee. The road running from it was called the Pewter Highway it gleamed a little in the cloud-dulled light. Three thousand workers waited by the bridge, men and women, skilled and ready to head into the north.

It stunned him that this was the response to just one call. These people had mustered in a single day, gathered their lives to them and come here. He could see that none of them had had much to gather. Things were bad, but only bad enough that the poorest folk were willing to leave. People who had nothing to lose, for whom Mirrlees had been a hell-hole, even before the rains and certainly since Stade had put an end to all but the most urgent construction.

It would take the Roil itself to come boiling towards the city, before the wealthier denizens of Mirrlees began to consider such action.

All of them are fools, Medicine thought.

He doubted Stade or the Council would stick around that long.

Stade stood beside him, a hand resting on Medicine's shoulder. He resented the familiarity of the act, and wanted nothing more than to wrench his shoulder away. But they had to appear to be in partnership, to have put the past aside. Just keep smiling, he thought, you're in too deep to cut his throat.

"Not much to look at, are they," Stade said. "But these are the finest our northern suburbs can produce. And they are in your charge. Three thousand people, the merest drop in the ocean of our population, but it is a start. Just bring them safely to the Narung Mountains."

"I'll get them there. You just give your speech."

"Of course," Stade said, and walked to the microphone, and his voice reverberated out over the Northmir. "The time of secrecy has passed, the time of action has come and a place has been prepared for you. All of you. My grand work, my Project, the Underground. And there we shall wait out the Roil, there we shall prosper, there we shall survive."

The next few hours passed intolerably slowly. Grin and bear it. Medicine just wanted to get going. There were several weeks of journey between here and the Narung Mountains. And who knew what on the way. Even if nothing happened, keeping this lot under control was going to be work enough. He had forty-nine council guard of doubtful loyalty. The only certainty he had was that their loyalties were not to him.

Something had halted the two engines, though. The *Grendel* and *Yawn* were big trains. They could have taken this lot up in a single trip. But that was not going to happen. Shanks' pony was all they had, other than the horses for the guards and barely enough oxen drawn wagons for supplies. And the wagons, well he hated the things.

The rain fell, the ground grew even swampier. What had he been thinking?

Three thousand people, just ready to up and leave, and looking to him to get them to safety. Well he had failed David – and truly he had failed the first time he had seen signs of the young man's addiction and done nothing about it – and Warwick, poor dead Warwick. Perhaps this really was a chance at redemption.

He was damned if he would fail these folk as well.

They left at last. The council guard on horseback making a rough perimeter. The wagons Medicine had made go on first. The highway was not in the best condition; rain had devoured it in places. Medicine reasoned it was best to have the wagons through before everyone else. Six thousand feet could do a lot of damage.

Of course, he had underestimated just how much damage the wagons themselves were capable of causing. The road was a ruin, and a muddy ruin at that, as they followed in the wagons' wake. And not all of the wagons were up to it. Half a dozen were lost in that first day and whatever could be salvaged was taken up to the remaining or redistributed amongst those on foot.

The loss of the wagons dismayed Medicine.

Broken wagons for a broken landscape of failed levees and drowned suburbs. Mirrlees's undulations made too much work for the pumps and engines of the city, some parts had flooded from their own catchment areas. The highway kept to the hills and so they looked down on submerged houses and domestic debris drifting lost like small islands of hopelessness.

Twice that day, scouts reported to Medicine sightings of groups to the west. Small gangs, salvage crews and looters – though if truth were told there was little difference between the two. Shots were fired at them, but it was a half-hearted menace. Medicine was not too concerned, it would take an army to threaten his three thousand and their guard.

That night they made camp on the very edge of the city, where murky fields led right up to the Regress Swamps – now more of a lake, with only the grey thread of the road running through it. Beyond them was the Margin. Medicine peered into that dark forest. He would have preferred to simply go around it, but such a detour would have cost them a week, maybe more.

Medicine knew there was Hardacre to the distant north and Eltham and the Daunted Spur along the north eastern seaboard. But it was easy to imagine civilisation ending here. Mirrlees was the northernmost of the great metropolises. Beyond it were the trees and the Gathering Plains and the burrows of the Cuttlefolk, and so much space. Three thousand people could be swallowed whole by those miles, and leave barely a mark to show their passing.

He helped unpack the tents – let no one claim he had developed airs and graces.

CHAPTER 33

Immediacism was a movement built upon fear.

Its attraction to the populace, like Carnival, an escape. Where everything was only grey and dark, they fashioned worlds of colour. Their effects were striking but, truly, it was a last breath of decadence in an age possessed of resources far too limited to sustain such a thing.

But what art isn't a glorious folly?

Art at the Gates of Apocalypse: A Comic History, Collingwood

THE TOWN OF UHLTON
18 MILES NORTH OF THE ROIL

The meeting in Buchan's parlour had gone on for another hour ending with something that had at once surprised and delighted David.

"I want you take David with you," Cadell had said. "Where I am going… it's too dangerous."

"Of course we will," Buchan had said, agreeing with Cadell for the first time that night. David went to bed with a feeling of such relief, to be at last out of the eye of the storm.

David woke to thunder.

No, it was gunshot, and a distant thudding. He sat up in bed. The next two shots came quick, one after the other.

Someone screamed, then moaned, another shot and the sound stopped. David stumbled out of bed. Dressed as fast as he could, not daring to switch on the lights. It was happening again, and this time his nerves were failing him. Fingers tapped against his door.

"David?" He relaxed a little, recognising Cadell's voice.

"Yes," he said.

The door opened, letting in a little light.

"We have to get out of here. Uhlton isn't as safe as I thought. It seems Stade wants to finish the job." Cadell's eyes flashed. In one hand he clenched his travelling bag, in the other a water gourd. "Sorry, David, I was going to leave you with Buchan and Whig, but they're going to draw the Vergers off. You're safer with me."

David's gaze fell upon Cadell's bag. The old man pulled it away. "Yes. Yes. I have plenty of your drug."

Shame reddened David's cheeks. "I didn't say anything."

Whig stopped at their door, looking quite ridiculous in a nightdress with a half dozen pistols strapped to his belt. "There's tunnels beneath the hall," he said. "Take the eastern passage, it will lead you out onto the edge of town."

"We will see you in Hardacre," Cadell said.

Whig nodded. "Good luck, gentlemen. We will be at a pub called the *Habitual Fool*." Whig winked at David. "An appropriate enough name, don't you think, for those of us that keep banging our heads against the walls of tyranny?"

Whig led them both to a nearby wall, wincing every time someone fired a shot. He slapped his hand against the wall and it swung open onto a low tunnel.

"There you go, lads. Sorry about the smell, it's less of an escape tunnel, more of a sewer," he said.

"Good luck," Cadell said.

"Good luck to us all," Whig grinned tersely and shook Cadell's hand. "It's been in rather short supply of late, though this raid could have happened at a worse time. We're ready. Be careful in Chapman, it's a city on the edge, and dangerous because of that."

Cadell ducked down and crawled through the tunnel. David threw one last glance at Whig. The giant waved him on.

"Hurry up, Milde, and be careful."

"I will," he said, and followed Cadell.

The wall shut behind him with a click. David found himself in a narrow corridor, dark but for a flickering chemical torch that Cadell held above his head. Stinking air enclosed them, and it was all David could do not to gag for that first moment.

"Come on," Cadell said.

They crawled, furtive and fast, upwards over cool wet stone. David tried not to think why it might be wet. Soon the only sound was their quiet breaths or the soft scuffing of boot on rock.

Confluents weren't the only ones who knew of this tunnel. Thousands upon thousands of cockroaches had gathered here, crunching under foot, the air loud with the papery sound of their flight. Worse were the things that preyed upon them. Spiders the size of David's hand that brought back flashes of his experience beneath the bridge, only here it was darker and the spiders much bigger.

"Careful," Cadell hissed. "They're not afraid to bite."

One chose that moment to run over David's face. It was all he could do not to yelp at its firm yet feathery touch.

Cadell brushed it off, he hissed. "Bastard bit me." He reached into his pockets, pulled out a small bottle topped with an atomiser, and sprayed a mist of something that smelt of vinegar and rosemary onto the wound. He hid the bottle away again.

"Not long now," Cadell said between clenched teeth. "I can smell a change in the air."

Sure enough, the crawl space widened, became a tunnel large enough for them to walk upright. A little further on the tunnel opened onto a deserted hillside, by a dead tree. The sound of gunshots echoed over to them, like a storm that had passed into the distance.

"What do we do now?" David asked, leaning against the white tree, and taking deep breaths of air that had never seemed purer.

"We walk again," Cadell grunted, hefting his bag. "To Chapman."

The journey to Chapman took a day following a winding hilly road that was never too far from the brown meander of the river. On the way, David noticed a distinct change overtaking the countryside. The land before Uhlton had been lush, too lush in fact, with flora almost drowning in the rain. Here plants were twisted, sere things, and the air dry and hazy. What winds there were blew predominantly from the south, and there was something of the furnace in them. It stung the eyes and dried the lungs. Seeing things here was painful. He perspired profusely though it did little to cool him, just brought on a thirst that rapidly depleted their supply of water.

A city boy, he had thought the country a universal green and found it wanting. The only green here that remained ran along the River Weep, and even that was dusty and failing. Animals had deserted the region as well. They'd left little to show of their passing other than picked-clean corpses.

A new sort of tension filled the air. A restlessness that mirrored David's own.

It reminded David of a new artistic movement popular in Mirrlees called Immediacism, and whilst its bursts of colour and movement were incongruous with this landscape, its sense of things on the precipice of change matched it exactly.

It did not take too much imagination to see these lands turning to dust in the next few months, if the Roil did not take them first and transform them into something alien and cruel. David could see the Roil and its imminence in everything. More concretely, whenever they topped a rise, David would catch a glimpse of the Obsidian Curtain itself. There was no denying its inevitability.

Occasionally David noticed small drifts of ash or smoke. The closer they got to Chapman the more frequently they floated by.

"Are there a lot of fires down south?" he asked, pointing out yet another drift of smoke.

"It wouldn't surprise me," Cadell said. "But that's not smoke. It's something much more insidious: Roil spores."

David cast his gaze suspiciously over the landscape. "The Roil's here already?"

"Not quite, those spores are too exposed as yet, they need the full cover of the Roil – heat and shadow – before they can do their handiwork." He shook his head. "Though it's something I fear that may not be too long away."

Cadell stared out into the dry lands, his eyes troubled and his brow furrowed. "Things are worse than I thought," he said. "I know people think of the Roil and they think of the Obsidian Curtain and all that lies south of it. But the Roil doesn't stop there. It's the big wet in Mirrlees, and the drought here, and other more predatory things."

Late in the afternoon, Cadell stopped and pointed along the dusty road. It tracked up a hill then disappeared beyond it. The road's veil of wind-borne dust was the only indication that it continued beyond the rise. Just peeking over the hill, was a nest of silos or water towers, though even from this distance David could see that they were in ill repair – holes gaped from their walls, tin rattled and creaked in the wind.

"Over that rise and past that ramshackle bunch of buildings is Chapman. About half an hour's walk. We're going to need to split up. We can meet in the city. There is a safehouse Medicine told me about, 132 Chadwick St. Wait for me there."

"What if you don't come?"

"I'll come." He pressed something into David's hands. "It's an ice pistol, state of the art Mirrlees design, still has all its darts." Cadell grinned. "Took it from a Verger." He showed David how to work it. "Just in case you come across anything on your way into the city," he said. "David, I'm not going to desert you."

David believed him. But then no one had deserted him. They'd all been taken away.

CHAPTER 34

Not all that came out of the dark sought humanity's destruction. But the Roil has a way of transforming even the highest of motives. And hers were never that high. We speak, of course, of Margaret Penn.

I knew her then, before she became such dark legend, and yet I would be hard pressed to separate truth from lie. She came out of the Roil, and what good ever had its genesis there?

A Memoir of a Man in Waiting, Whig

THE INTERFACE WITHIN THE ROIL

The door opened and the light came on. Margaret's hands were already gripping her pistols, their barrels pointed at Winslow's head. Winslow's eyelids fluttered with fear.

"I'm already awake," Margaret said; she'd hardly slept at all.

"I can see that," he said, slowly raising his hands. "Keep the guns, you'll need them, but we have to get you out of here."

Margaret nodded, she'd changed back into her cold suit an hour before. Not feeling safe here, wondering if she would ever feel safe again.

"They're coming aren't they? Don't look so surprised. I've

been hunted since I left Tate. Why would I expect it to stop? So, where are you taking me? To them?"

Winslow shook his head, raising his hands palm out. "We're not taking you anywhere near them," he said, his voice low and calm. "Just put away the pistols. I'd even be happy if you just stopped aiming them at my head."

"Enough," Anderson growled and pushed past Winslow. "If there is anyone you should shoot it's me."

Margaret lowered her guns, though she did not put them away.

"Smart girl," Anderson said. "If I was in your situation I'd do the same."

He sat on the end of the bed. "There is so much that you need to catch up on, and I doubt we have time to tell you anything beyond the merest details." Margaret was struck by how lined his face was, the dark bags under his eyes. He ran a hand through thinning hair; his hands shook. "I have but the slightest inkling of the world in which you lived. But here there have been terrible defeats even in regions that are yet to feel even the barest touch of the Roil. They've known loss of life and liberty to fear and a paucity of foresight – or at least a narrowness of it. We have sought to deal with the enemy, once we realised that we could not beat it, but the Roil, while it plays at such things, does not parley. It grows because that is what it does, as a storm grows or a wave moves drawn on by the force of the tide.

"But you already understand that. Your existence has been so much more intimately involved with the Roil. What this boils down to is this: the Council demanded that you be given over to the Roil. You see, my employers are desperate for more time. However, they have failed to understand that the Roil would not ask for you if you were not considered important in some way. Extremely important."

Anderson gazed into her eyes, his own filled with a deep and urgent sadness and resignation. In Anderson, Margaret saw a man always on the verge of self-mockery –uncertain of why he was where he was, except that the reason was as important as it was ridiculous.

"What is it that you know, Margaret? What is it that you haven't told me?"

Margaret opened her mouth to speak, to deny that she knew anything, when a soldier came to door. His eyes flicked from her pistols to Anderson and back again. Anderson turned and smiled at him, a distressingly calm smile.

"It's all right, Daniels," Anderson said. "What is it?"

"They're here."

Anderson considered this. "Then we have to get her out of the Interface now. Winslow, you and my guards will escort her to Chapman."

Winslow did a double take that at any other time would have been comical. "And what of you?"

"I'll stay here and see if I can distract them. They've been awfully good at distracting us. The time for negotiations is done. Winslow, report to Stade. Let him know how things have changed. Let him know that the Interface is finished. We're closing it down. Time for us all to find new employment."

"Surely you won't be too far behind. There are still treaties intact."

Something passed across Anderson's face, a shadow of sadness or fear or just that bleak turn of humour that he seemed to possess. "Of course, Winslow, but do as I say, please."

Winslow opened his mouth and Anderson silenced him with a glance. A bell rang, pitched high. Anderson's eyes narrowed. Shots were fired in the distance. Margaret could taste the bitter exhalations of endothermic chemicals.

"Get out of here, now!"

"What about my carriage?" Margaret demanded feeling at once petty and childish for asking.

"You'll have to leave it, I'm afraid." He shook his head. "We've all had to leave things." Anderson pulled her aside. "Once you are free of the Interface, do not linger and whatever you do, do not go to the Council. I cannot speak for your city, but the Council of Chapman and Mirrlees are corrupt. Believe me when I say they would have given you back to the Roil. Get out of here, get away from Winslow – he's a good man but a Council man. Try and get in touch with a man named Medicine Paul, but do not do it openly. He has agents in the city, not as many as he once did, but so does the Council, it can be difficult to tell them apart." Anderson whispered. "132 Chadwick Street, there you might find help. Do you understand?"

Margaret nodded, then strapped on her ice pistols. "Good luck," she said.

Anderson laughed. "Don't speak to me of luck. I used that up long ago." Then he gave her a wry look. "I'm sorry, maybe I haven't used it all. Why, I met a Penn today." He slipped a handful of dark lozenges into his mouth, and shuddered, dropping to one knee. He blinked, got to his feet.

"That's far too many of those, sir," Winslow said.

Anderson glared at Winslow, though not without affection. "Are you still here? Didn't I tell you to go?"

"You did, and we are."

"Good," Anderson said, snatching pistols from the belt at his waist. "I've a crew to command. You make sure she gets to Chapman."

And then he was gone, dashing back along the corridors deeper into the complex.

As they left the sleeping quarters, Winslow passed around a handful of the same lozenges that Margaret had seen Anderson swallow. He gave Margaret several of them.

"Put one beneath your tongue," he said. "It's called Chill. It'll cool your blood. We've catalogued a whole range of Witmoth apotropaics, but this works best. Saliva activates it."

Margaret slid one of the lozenges into her mouth. They tasted foul, but the effect was almost instantaneous.

She grimaced as her body cooled.

Winslow grinned at her. "Pretty impressive isn't it? One of my projects."

He opened a door. "And this is the way out." He gestured at a long, narrow corridor that extended out of sight.

Winslow and the two guards led her down the narrow spine of the complex. They walked for nearly ten minutes until they reached a point where the light globe above them shone red.

"What's that?" Margaret asked.

"That's the true interface; a step beyond it and you have passed out of the Roil. Over the last six weeks I have seen that red light shift from the beginning of the corridor to here. May not seem like much until you realise the Roil has moved that far forward all across Shale."

They walked a little further on. Margaret stared back one last time at the Interface, hoping to catch a glimpse of something, not sure what. Anderson was back there somewhere, Winslow followed her gaze.

"He'll be all right," he said unconvincingly.

It was stupid, but guilt welled within her at leaving the *Melody* here. Without that carriage, she would have never made the journey, and now she had deserted it, just as she had deserted everything else she had ever loved.

A flicker of movement caught her eye and her spine clenched with a cold deeper than anything Chill could create.

The red lights were coming on. Each new red globe lighting with a loud *click.*

Click, click, click.

Like someone running towards them in metal soled shoes.

Click.

Click.

"Look," she said and pointed.

Winslow shuddered. "That's impossible."

The guards paled, but engaged their guns. There was a loud whine as they charged up. Margaret activated her weapons as well.

Click.

"How far until the entrance?"

Click.

"Another hundred yards."

Click.

"I think we should run."

Click.

There was no argument. They sprinted down the hallway, weaponry clanging, the air electric with their terror. Margaret's heart pounded in her chest, the Chill burned with a frigid bitter fire in her mouth.

Behind them the red lights picked up pace. Margaret reached the entrance.

As the last of them made it, the red light above the doorway clicked on. The hallway was lit with rubicund shadows. There was movement at the other end of the long hall. A boiling darkness filled with the susurration of wings.

One of the soldiers swore beneath his breath then launched a metal canister back that way. The canister clattered as it struck the ground and rolled forward a few turns. The soldier covered his ears and Margaret followed, barely in time. The explosion rippled along the hallway and the red lights nearest it burst. A backwash of cold rushed up to them. But it was quickly warmed, by a hot dry wind.

"Where's that coming from?" Winslow hissed. "Why aren't the doors locking? We've had a breach and the only locked door is the emergency exit."

Something howled down the other end of the corridor.

Winslow cursed as he punched in the clearance code. The door swung open, onto a steep set of stairs. Winslow motioned for one of the soldiers to go first, then Margaret.

They reached the top of the stairs, just as beneath them firing started. The soldier entered in another code. The door below slammed shut.

"Keep your weapons ready," the soldier said, but Margaret was already ahead of him, her rifle in her hands.

The soldier smiled grimly, and pushed on the door. "Of course, you've done all this before."

Margaret wished that she had not.

The door swung open, the soldier leapt out, and Margaret followed. She stopped and almost dropped her rifle.

No, she had not done this before. She had *never* experienced this.

She could see stars, and the greater moon Argent giving off its dull light.

The stars, the glorious stars. Pinter, Swallow, the Burnished Kings and the Queens of Wondrous Storm, the constellation of Committee B. All of it she had known only in stellar maps, only in abstract.

Now here it was, spread out above her.

Winslow crashed into her back.

"Um," he said, "I think we should hurry."

Margaret blinked, behind her, beyond the doorway, a half-mile wide finger of darkness was bearing down, reaching out impossibly from the shivering wall of the Roil. Hot dusty air rushed at her, banging on the shutters of nearby residences. Dead trees sighed and creaked and Margaret could hear the first rumblings of transformation in them – soon they would be Roilthings.

"These are the deserted suburbs, though they were a lively place when we first started," Winslow said. "Not far to go now."

One of the guards fired into the darkness.

"Don't be stupid," Winslow snapped. "You're wasting ice."

Then he and Margaret saw what the guard was firing at.

Quarg Hounds, hundreds of them.

"Well that's it then," Winslow said quietly. He turned to Margaret. "There's a secret entrance to Chapman, beneath the grey tower, two streets north of here, left and left again, past the stone arches. If you can make it there you will be safe." He whispered a code at her, and started firing, methodically striking each hound in the skull. "When you reach the end of the hall, beneath an escutcheon embossed with the symbol of the Council, there are two buttons. A red one and a green one. Push first the red then the green five times, and five times only. Then run. Don't hang around once you have finished, run, and don't stop until you are well within the city's walls."

He gripped her shoulders as his gun recharged. "Remember the order of the buttons, red then green. It's imperative that you push them five times, and in that sequence."

"Will it send help?"

Winslow nodded. "Now run, or all of this has been a waste. All of it."

Margaret couldn't do it. She had left enough people behind in the past few days. She fired off a round into the darkness, taking down a Quarg Hound, then another.

"Go. Now!" Winslow said, and there was such a bitter, awful resolution in Winslow's eyes that run she did, towards the dim grey bulk of Chapman's outer walls, down empty streets, broken windows and the stars her only audience.

She reached the hidden door just as the screaming began. That was almost enough to call her back. Behind her a Quarg Hound snarled. Margaret turned smoothly, precisely, and shot it in the head, moving backwards as she fired.

She slammed into the door, her rifle aimed out at the darkness. Another Quarg Hound leapt towards her and she fired again. The beast dropped to the ground at her feet.

Margaret turned and entered in the code, she felt the Quarg Hound move behind her, and drove her rime blade, under her coat and into its skull. The wall opened, loud and sluggish. She yanked her blade free of the hound and spilled through into another long hall. The door shut behind her and she ran.

She reached the end of the hall, lifted the escutcheon by a metal door. The red and green buttons glowed dimly. She followed Winslow's directions and a light in the wall beside her blinked on. The metal door opened.

She stumbled through the doorway and onto a narrow street, the door locked shut behind her. She ran from the door and the wall that it was inset in.

A few moments later, the ground shook, and the door shot past her head. She fell to her chest and rolled onto her back. Dust billowed towards her, the hallway was destroyed, and the wall itself dipping down. There was no help coming for Winslow and his soldiers.

There had never been any help.

Margaret could still hear weapons firing in the distance. The gunshots all too quickly gave way to silence. The Interface was gone, her wondrous *Melody Amiss* with it, and she was in Chapman alone with no money or friends and the Roil was on its way, and it wanted her, and it would not stop.

Sirens rang out in the distance. They had rung endlessly in the hours since Margaret had destroyed the secret tunnel. Dark military Aerokin, a sight that still held her in awe, rolled overhead, they filled the air with their oily exhalations, and shone searchlights gripped by sinuous flagella into the deserted suburbs. Ice cannon fired. Soldiers came and crowded along the wall. Then Engineers arrived.

Margaret did not like the look of them, nor those they made obeisance to. Tall, sombre-faced men, all of them, chewing and chewing, on what Margaret guessed must be Chill. Anderson's warning returned to her. They had to be Vergers.

They'd driven that particular cult of violence out of Tate well before Margaret's birth, but she was familiar with them. As a rather ghoulish child she had read twice, from cover to cover Simmon's *Torture and Torment or the Road Cruel Travelled: Confessions of a Man and his Knife*.

There was no way that she would give herself up to a Verger.

Instead, tired at last of that ceaseless, useless industry and wary of staying too long and being caught, she followed Anderson's directions to the house of Medicine Paul's allies. But there was no happiness there. It was a smouldering ruin. Someone had painted a red V on the footpath before it.

She left the burnt old house and found another place nearby, deserted and smelling of dust and urine and things, like hope, decayed and forgotten. There she lay down and, fighting it all the way, fell asleep.

CHAPTER 35

There's a certain attraction to the end of the world. To see the curtain close, what a privilege. Who wouldn't want to take that final bow?

Last Days, Logit & Redmond

THE CITY OF CHAPMAN

"I hate queues," the man in front of David said, brushing dust from the top of his hat.

Mr Whig's warnings had proven true. There were guards at all the gates; big, frightened men gazing down at the crowds lined up to get in – order on the knife edge of chaos. All of the sentries were armed with odd-looking weapons. The man in front of him caught his gaze.

"Ice pistols of some sort," he said then pointed to the walls. "And up there are ice cannon. Not that they'll do them any good, shooting cold pellets into the storm, might as well throw a handful of ice cubes. You'd need to surround the city in ice. Moats and cannon twice the size of that, and even then it would only work for so long; there are many different ways to storm a fortress."

Guards stared at them suspiciously, David tugged at the fellow's arm.

"I don't think it's that wise to look too interested in the city's defences," he said.

"Oh," the man said, sounding quite surprised by the thought. He laughed, and brought his gaze back to his hat. "I suppose you're right." He popped his hat back on his head.

"Rob," he said and put out his hand. David shook it, not particularly enjoying the sensation of the man's hot palm against his own.

"David," he replied, and wiped his palm on his pants.

They stood at the back of the queue, moving slowly down towards the city's gates.

"What's happening here?" David asked. "A queue to get into a city this close to the Roil, I'd have guessed it would have been the other way around."

"What isn't happening?" Rob said and started counting down with his fingers. "Quarg Hounds, of course, and Roilings now, you heard about the *Dolorous Grey*?" David nodded his head. "And all when the city is filled with strangers for the Festival of Float. They've started testing the visitors for, you know, infection. This will be the last Festival, I'll wager."

Rob pointed south, and David stared across the plain. The horizon was much thicker than it ought, as though it had smudged; only it was a smudge that moved. Even as David stared at it, it seemed to swell.

"The Roil is getting closer. Why, it crossed a cemetery last week and the dead rose up. Roilings, their minds filled with grubs and dust, started shambling towards the city, so I heard. Gets people's nerves on edge. We all knew it was happening, just couldn't believe it." Rob's lips split with a grin. "But credulity or not, let me tell you, boy, it's going to be one hell of a party this year."

The line moved slowly, and the man chatted away. Finally, David discovered why it was going at such a glacial pace. People that entered the city had to plunge their arms into a large bucket of ice. An armed guard stood by it, looking at once bored and paranoid. *A winning combination*, David thought.

When it was Rob's turn, he hesitated. "Looks cold," he said.

The guard tapped the side of the bucket with his gun. "That's the point. Now, if you don't mind–"

Rob shoved his hands into the ice and screamed.

Moths fell from his eyes, rushed down his face. The entire crowd stumbled as one – a clumsy terrified creature – but they need not have. The moths were weak and fragmented senselessly before they even hit the ground. Rob growled and pulled his hands from the ice, the skin blackened and smoking. "Getting stronger," he said. "Getting so much stronger. I–"

The guard fired his gun, rolling with the recoil, and a spear of ice drove into the Rob's chest. Rob, peered down at it, curiously, brought a hand to the icy shaft, then fell to the ground, body quivering, ice sheathing his chest. Another guard, face twisted with disgust, walked over to the corpse and dumped a bucket of ice on its head.

When the Roiling had stilled, a couple of guards, covered from head to toe in protective clothing, dragged the body away.

David rubbed his hand furiously on his pants leg.

"Next," the guard said, lifting another bucket of ice on to the table.

David smiled weakly and shoved his hands into the bucket.

The guard nodded absently and clicked a stopwatch. David shivered, the ice stung, and the chill ran up into his arms.

"How long?" David asked.

"Twenty seconds," the guard said, watching him closely. "Most Roilings reveal themselves upon contact with the ice, but we have to be sure. You did seem to be having rather a nice chat with that fellow."

It was the longest twenty seconds of David's life. He was intensely aware of the deep level of scrutiny that he was now under, not to mention the ice pistols aimed at his chest. They may launch ice but David was certain they could pierce his heart just as well.

There was also that nagging doubt. Was it possible to be infected and not know it? Of course not, he knew who he was and what it felt to be him.

The crowd held its breath, including David.

Then the guard nodded – pulling the ice bucket away and resetting his stopwatch.

David considered taking a bow.

Ladies and gentlemen! I am still a human being, you need not be alarmed.

But he did not. Just stood there, unsure of what to do next.

"Have a pleasant stay," the guard said at last. He coughed, when David still hadn't moved. "You can go in now."

"Thank you," David said, in a voice that was anything but thankful, but the guard was already focussing on the next visitor.

David shrugged. His arms, dripping water, shook. He had passed the first stage at least. He took a couple of steps into the city.

Another guard stood there, just past the gates, his mask dark with sweat. David did not envy him the humid cage of the mask, its rough material tight against his face.

"Where'd you take the Roiling?" David asked and because the Guard was nervous and bored – obviously anxious for a little distraction – he told him.

"We've a cool-room. All the Roilings are delivered there and frozen solid to make sure they're really dead, and then we burn them. There haven't been too many of the bastards, just enough to keep us on our toes." He watched, with professional interest, as the next person plunged their hands in the ice, David noticed his grip change on his gun. "The protocols were only laid down a few days ago, the problem's but a week old and it's already becoming difficult to police. You heard about the train?"

David nodded, though he said nothing about his involvement in that incident. He had heard about it all right, he was never likely to forget it. "Who hasn't? From all accounts it was terrible."

"And it could have been much worse. By the time the *Dolorous Grey* reached the city they'd set the whole train alight, from engine to caboose. Nearly took Chapman with it. Not the best beginning to the Festival. But what can you expect with that so close." The guard nodded towards the Obsidian Curtain. "And that was before we had the cemetery dead of the deserted suburbs come stumbling against the southern walls. Our cannon cut them to pieces, but I was on clean-up duty. Sweaty, awful job, even with the cold suits, and not all of them were dead." He made a disgusted face. "After the Festival I'm out of here, I've a ticket on an Aerokin transport, one of the Blake and Steel line. Going to family in Hardacre. If the world's falling to hell then I'm flying as far from the crumbling edge as possible."

"What's so wonderful about the festival that you'd want to stay?" David asked.

"You'll know soon enough," the guard said, sounding regretful that he was stuck out here. "It's almost worth risking the Witmoths. Of course, the danger money they are paying us is extraordinary. Once I'm done here I should be able to live out my few remaining years very comfortably in Hardacre, free state and all. I hear it still snows up there."

"Don't you think we should try and fight it? Shouldn't we do all we can to stop the Roil?"

The guard shrugged, and he spat upon the ground as though he had heard this argument one too many times. No doubt he had, surely some of Chapman's troops thought it worthwhile to fight.

"Might as well try and stop a thunderstorm; all the people in Shale couldn't do that. It's a force of nature, not an army. Surely the Grand Defeat taught us that. Some people say it was our industry that started it, warmed up the world enough for it to get a foothold; now it's an engine that won't be stopped. Greater cities than ours have fallen, what chance do we have? If the Council of Engineers can find some way of halting it then I'll be happy, but I don't think it's likely, so we may as well live out the rest of our years as best we can. Who knows it may never cross the mountains. And if it does and a Quarg Hound bays outside my door, I'll shoot it and the next and the next until my time is done." The guard's eyes were grim and hard, but they lightened for a moment. "Good luck, idealist. Enjoy the Festival."

David considered the long line behind him and shook his head. When the Roil comes, it won't wait in queue, he thought.

More guards armed with ice-weaponry stood at the gates, nodding as he passed through the thick outer walls and into the warren of streets that made up the city proper.

One of the oldest metropolises of Shale, Chapman's stonewalls were sturdy and imposing, designed to keep out Cuttlefolk, they also kept out the light. Shadowy cobbled streets made their dank and musty circuit around the city. And everywhere was a heavy smell, fecund and earthy rather than Mirrlees' metallic and hard odours.

However, for all its scent and shadows, Chapman was dressed up for the Festival. Every available space on the street was covered with posters, advertising such wonders as "General Brown and his amazing balloon suit" or "Thrille to the throw of the Twins of Twig" or better yet "Mr Marcus the amazing Calculating Pig, let him calculate your future with the mystical power of arithmetic. The smartest of our four-legged futurist friends".

David wondered what kind of future anyone could hope for with the Roil just down the road, and what truly smart creature would ever find its way here?

For all its proximity to the Roil, the city lacked that ever-present sense of threat, of government officials scrutinising every single thing. At every corner, soloists or bands played tin whistles and mandolins and sang about balloons or Roil beasts or working in the docks.

He waited for Cadell at the appointed place for an hour, then another hour, and still Cadell didn't show up.

At last, as evening was coming on he gave up and began to look for the safe house.

CHAPTER 36

No journey is without consequence. No pilgrimage without cost. Walk and you will find the road to be hard. Buy good shoes.

Fortune cookie

THE NORTHERN SUBURBS OF MIRRLEES
303 MILES NORTH OF THE ROIL

The night passed without incident for which Medicine was truly grateful. Well, without too much incident; there were, what Medicine was soon to discover, the usual complaints: minor injuries, brawls and affairs. And each slowed the groups' leaving. They did not get moving until almost ten o'clock. It took that long to get things packed back into the wagons.

Once on the horse, Medicine decided he needed to walk. Every step was agony, but nothing compared to getting back in the saddle.

"Was anything devised to torture a man more than a horse?" he asked Agatha, the head of the Council Guard.

"Bad poetry comes to mind first," she said, her smile softening a hard face.

"My mother was poet. Not a bad one," Medicine said. "She moved to Hardacre after my father passed away. A meddler, and I doubt she's changed, there's something of her style in that metropolis' declaration of independence."

Agatha laughed. "I'd have thought you'd come from good working stock."

"Hardly," Medicine said. "My father was a painter and an industrialist. But I had no interest in those things. I was a bit of a disappointment to him. And in families like mine disappointment soon becomes anger. I think I started my studies as a surgeon to annoy him, and then when I opened my surgery in the docks..."

He had never struggled harder than those first years. Respect was not easily earned. First he revelled in the terrible conditions, as a pure act of defiance. Then he made it his life's work to improve them. He saw too much death, too many people's lives ruined by the way their employers treated them, and the way the laws of the Council let them. It had been a natural progression into the Confluent Party. More study, gaining his engineering ticket and his Orbis – his ring of office. When he lost his fingers he'd thought he was finally making a difference. The violence had galvanised him to greater action, within and without the halls of government.

Now he worked for the Council. He had hated Stade almost from the moment he met him. Now he hated himself for working with the bastard.

We are damned. The pair of us.

But that did not matter anymore. The Roil's reach extended every day and once the Obsidian Curtain closed, life as he understood would be gone.

What choice did he have?

He did not expect to live forever, nor hope to assume that even Shale had all that much time left to it. Everything ends, and every engine runs down or is superseded by another make; a different thing. But that did not mean he was prepared to lie down and let it happen. If it could be stopped then he needed to be part of that. He wanted to live as long as he could and he wanted to help as many others as he could. Though if a certain councillor should choke on his own tongue…

As the highway passed through the Regress Swamps, creatures stared up at them out of the water. Huge-eyed and, Medicine did not doubt, huge-jawed. People peered over the edge of the highway to get a better look at the beasts.

Medicine pointed them out to Agatha.

"They're called Factories. Don't ask me why. That truth's been lost a long time. Names have a habit of carrying on, long past the sense of them. Little's known about them, no one's done much in the way of study. But they're big; bodies extend down a long way. How they move, how they mate, how they excrete, no one knows."

"Not something that they write about in the travel guides. Are they dangerous?"

Agatha chuckled. "They look dangerous don't they?"

Medicine nodded. Looks can be deceiving though, he thought. Just how dangerous are you?

He turned his attention to the Margin. All morning the forest had grown – devouring the horizon – from patch of darkness to worryingly tall and moss-drowned trees. In Medicine's reckoning – and with this many people it was damn hard to tell – they would enter the Margin within the hour.

Agatha followed his gaze, then spat on the ground in the way superstitious soldiers have for centuries to ward off evil.

"Now that place is where the real dangers lie. Tough old bit of forest. Many times over the years has the Council pushed its way into that forest and every time the Margin's pushed back."

Screams split the air and Medicine moved fast enough to wish he hadn't: a Factory was devouring some ducks. The water bubbled and grew bloody and more Factories moved to that space, without seeming to move, their huge, hungry eyes staring up, optimistic in the way such creatures are because something *always* finds its way into their mouths.

"Too big to be wholly carnivorous, but they're not fussy," Agatha said in an offhand way. "Anyone want to get a closer look?"

People kept away from the edge of the road after that.

The Margin closed around them, its mass of sky devouring trees arching over the highway, swallowing the light. The Council guards rode to the rear and front, a small army dwarfed by all that unthinking forest.

The road in the Margin was unlike anything else the Council had ever built. It did not stretch on straight and true, but wound crookedly through the Margin, as though its engineers had lost their way. Medicine was not surprised by this; he could imagine all their machinery failing here, compasses making soft circuits of their cases, determination and madness driving them on.

What it meant though, was that their scouts were rarely seen, the road and the Margin conspiring to hide them around the next curve.

The forest stank, trees dripped and rotted. Dank miasmic fog drifted through the trees like the tattered ghosts of diseases long ago lost to memory. The Margin clung to everything like a nightmare-haunted fever, wet and close and hot.

And always, scattered throughout the forest, were the decaying remnants of the Cuttlewar; a goodly portion of that battle had been fought here. Machines lay shattered and discarded, rusting leviathans, half overgrown. One section through which they passed was a graveyard. Here the trees had grown back through tombs. Medicine paused for a break and rested his feet upon a rock, only to discover it was a skull half swallowed by tree root. Eye sockets shadowy and dull stared up at him. He removed his feet and left the dead to its slumber.

The air in the Margin thickened, deadening sound but for the distant clatter-shriek of birds – blood wings most like, predatory and cunning – and the howl of beasts, as they made their passage through the muddy lower ground. And yet, at times the reverse occurred, noises were amplified, transformed. The most innocent sounds suddenly took on baleful significance.

Night was worse.

The wet heat was just as bad, the air just as stifling and still, but the forest shuffled in even closer. Creatures called out in the darkness, their cries at once distant and thunderous, brute and knowing, and always cruel. A shriek or a howl might echo, so close, that Medicine would spin, heart pounding, expecting to see a beast on top of him.

Inquisitive bats, their skin slippery and soft like a frog's, flitted into the camp drawn by the lights.

They were stupid creatures, flying into campfires in such numbers that the campsite was soon thick with the stinking smoke of their burning bodies. Better the blinding smoke, for when they did not fly into flame they flew into people, biting and screeching as they tangled in hair or clothes. Those bites festered over the days ahead, the wounds darkening, the rot spreading like a contagion from the forest to people's skin.

Many died, despite Medicine's efforts. His medical training had ill prepared him for the Margin.

While it was bad that first night, it was something that lingered and worsened.

The rain did not stop, just dripped down through the trees, descrying holes in tents and makeshift shelters and splashing on faces or skin; grey and greasy droplets, that stained or, if swallowed, caused nausea and stomach cramps.

Medicine was starting to miss the Factories.

"This place stinks," someone complained to Medicine, as he treated a wound caused by one of the bats.

"Everything stinks," he said.

The next day the mood was grim. And, though he was surly and tired, Medicine put on his brightest suit, his most cheerful expression and walked the length of the campsite. He spoke to as many people as he could. Showed them all that he was in good spirits, that he believed they were doing the right thing. And it seemed to work.

They packed quickly and were on their way before ten.

Halfway through the day, Medicine realised something was wrong. No one from the front had reported to him since early morning. He was worried enough to insist that he and Agatha ride up there.

They passed the wagons at a gallop and continued riding for another ten minutes.

There was no sign of them.

"Where did they go?" Medicine asked.

Agatha looked bewildered.

"I have no idea. No shots were fired that's for sure or we would have heard them and there's no sign of them having left the highway."

"What on earth could take ten Council guards without so much as a peep?"

Agatha turned her horse around. "I would rather not find out."

They rode back to the convoy and Medicine half expected them to be gone as well. Three thousand snatched away as easily as those ten. He was sure if he was relieved or disappointed to find them still there.

After that he drove them on, walking into the night but, at last, with everyone too exhausted and no end of the Margin in sight, they had to stop and make camp.

Another night of bats and other less savoury things that moved more silently than breath.

The next morning found one of the tents empty, but for a Verger's knife, the blade partially eaten away by what looked like acid. Another tent contained a more grisly find; every single person sat dead, at a table made of some dark and alien wood, their blood drained, their eyes taken, tiny glittering stones put in their place. But for the fact that they were corpses, it looked like a party mid-swing. The dead still held glasses, their mouths remained curled in smile or silent talk.

Indeed, the people in the tent nearest claimed to have heard laughter and song until the early morning.

Medicine, always curious, had wanted to examine the bodies and the peculiar method of exsanguination; it appeared they had been drained through the veins in their feet. But Agatha overruled him, and had the bodies and table (which had not been carried here or ever seen before) and chairs burned at once.

"I've heard dark tales about such things," she'd said grimly. "Sometimes people come back."

Agatha called in the guards from the rear, eschewed scouts and had everyone travel close.

It was a long and tense day's travel, the forest closing in, the road almost lost twice, but at last, just as it looked like they would have to spend another night in the Margin, they reached the plains. Medicine had never felt so happy. Still he held back until all had made it out, only then choosing to walk onto the open land.

He stared back at the Margin. What was most disquieting was that he was unable to shake the feeling that it was looking right back at him.

Once out they made a head count.

One hundred and forty people had been lost to that forest and, with that knowledge, any sense of triumph.

PART TWO
CONFLAGRATION

Everywhere there was fire. Everywhere there was death, and what came after… No one thought to ask.

The Engine Dialogues, CASAGRANDE

CHAPTER 37

To destroy a political career like that...

What makes a man decide to turn against the tide? What makes a man decide to destroy not just his life, but those around him, those nearest and dearest?

I know this only too well. I've crushed the lives of such men and women for a very long time now.

Personal Papers, STADE

THE CITY OF MIRRLEES
360 MILES NORTH OF THE ROIL

Warwick Milde had never been a stranger to controversy. After all, he had crossed the floor, gone from Engineer with promise to Confluent, and he'd dragged his brother with him. Stade had never forgiven him for that. But this was far, far worse.

"I told you it was true." Medicine grinned.

Warwick Milde shook his head. How could a man smile in such a place? "It wasn't so much that I did not believe you but, well, that I didn't believe you."

Sean wasn't smiling, but looking back at the door. "We don't have much time, and only one exit. They find us here we're dead." The pistol he held tightly in his hand shook a little. Sean didn't like guns.

Warwick looked over at his brother. Three of them, councillors, sneaking around the basement of the Ruele Building like children. Buchan and Whig were waiting, just beyond the tower, with enough men to keep the Vergers at bay if it came to that.

"We've time enough, Sean. For a little wonderment." It was cold down here, his breath plumed, but that was the least of his discomfort. There was an endless whispering coming from the eight metal doors set into the stony walls of the basement.

"We're dead, if we're caught here beneath the Council Chambers." Medicine didn't look too worried. He'd lost his fingers to Stade and sometimes Warwick wondered if he hadn't also lost his mind. The man was reckless. He had disarmed the alarms, he had bribed the guards and those who'd proven resistant would wake in the morning with sore heads and little memory of the past twenty-four hours. Medicine's familiarity with pharmacology had proven extremely effective. But was it enough, and what did it make of him that was down here too, in a basement filled with old men? The Old Men. Every child in Shale had heard of them.

Old Men hungry and Old Men wise,
Old Men's truth and Old Men's lies.
Old Men's wisdom against the heat,
Crack your bones for the marrow meat.

But he'd thought them just that, a fairy tale, a series of myths; the fabled progenitors of Shale, Masters of the Engine of the World. Yet here they were.

Be gone.

Be gone.

The eight voices chanted.

Medicine had placed his head against one of the doors. "This one's Cadell."

"The Engineer."

Medicine nodded. "They're all Engineers, but he..."

"He's the right one."

Sean considered the locks. "I've the skill for this."

This was the sort of thing they had done as children. Sean grinned; he'd have made an excellent peterman.

"I'm watching your back," Warwick said. He had an old revolver in his hand. Damned if he knew it would even work. Medicine looked more comfortable with his own weapon: a long knife that looked even crueller than a Verger's blade.

"I know," Sean said, cramming his powders into the lock. He lit a short fuse, turned from the door, and covered his ears. There was a soft detonation, Warwick had been expecting something louder, but it was enough. The door opened, Sean poked his head through doorway.

"Mr Cadell–"

"Shut it. Shut it," came a soft voice.

"I can't," Sean said.

A hand snatched out and dragged him through the opening, lightning fast.

Then the screaming started.

In the few seconds it took for Warwick to reach the door, Sean was dead. Cadell, little more than skin wrapped around bone looked up, his mouth rimmed with blood.

"Sorry," he breathed. "Sorry."

But it didn't stop him swallowing down chunks of Sean's flesh.

"Sorry."

Warwick raised the gun, aimed it at Cadell's head.

"No," Medicine snarled, grabbing his arm, and pushing Warwick out of the room.

"We need him," Medicine said.

"He just killed my brother."

"Get out there," Medicine said, pointing to the hallway. "People will be coming. Keep our exit clear."

Warwick fled the room. The single door leading into the basement opened, a Verger stormed through and Warwick discovered that his revolver did indeed work.

"We have to go," he yelled

There were too many of them. Warwick expected he would soon be dead, he thought of his wife, of his brave son.

Forgive me.

He fired at the next Verger, trying to keep them at the door. How they were ever going to make it out was beyond him. He'd use up his bullets and then he would just sit on the floor.

Cadell was a blur racing past and the Vergers began to scream.

"You don't want to go in there," Medicine said, as Warwick walked back towards the room. "Warwick!"

But he didn't stop; Sean deserved that much at least. In the centre of the room was a bloody pile of broken bones and a skull. That was all, nothing to signify that he had ever been his brother. The room itself was bare but for claw marks in the walls. We were so stupid.

What had they unleashed upon the world?

It took Warwick a while to notice the screaming had stopped. It never would inside his skull.

"Hurry, Warwick," Medicine yelled, his voice cracking. "We need to go. Now!"

Warwick left the room.

"Hurry." Medicine slung a cloak over the much less emaciated

Cadell, though he remained more bone than meat. The Old Man couldn't meet Warwick's gaze.

"I'm sorry," Cadell whispered.

Warwick lifted his pistol, pointed it at Cadell's withered face. His hand didn't shake. He took a deep breath. What have we done? He lowered the gun.

Bring him back, the other voices chorused. *Bring him back.* Warwick looked at the blasted door, that wasn't going to happen, just as Sean wasn't going to walk out that door.

Warwick stepped over the ruined bodies of the Vergers. Turned his back on the Old Man, and the broken door.

"I'm sorry." And that was all Cadell said for two days, over and over again, he didn't say it enough times. He could never say it enough times.

CHAPTER 38

All books now available in powder form. Engage with a narrative in ways hitherto unknown. Fiction, Non-Fiction, Maps, take your drug of choice.

Pre-emptive counselling provided free of charge.

Summer Catalogue – Matheson's Books

THE CITY OF CHAPMAN

David found such a store, the *Vellum Shore*. The place made him ache for home and the days when a bookshop was enough. The shop was poorly stocked, but David reasoned that had more to do with the imminent evacuation of the city rather than poor ordering. He bought a small foldout map of Chapman and a sachet of map powder to go with it.

Now he had a chance of finding Chadwick Street and the safe house.

Of course, he had already found a supplier of Carnival. That had been the easiest thing of all, besides he didn't know for certain if he'd see Cadell again.

David had enough money left over to buy a fried sausage

at a street stall. The thing tasted lovely. The anticipatory buzz of the Carnival, the Festival itself all helped to lift his mood. He ate the sausage as he sat under a statue of Councillor Elmont, founder of Chapman. He unfolded the map he'd bought over his legs. Chadwick Street was at the other end of Chapman. His shortest route followed the wall. He took a little powder and the wall came into focus. Grey old stone, fringed with dead mould. Wanted posters for Buchan and Whig fluttered in the wind.

DEAD OR ALIVE
Less life met with greater generosity

The image ruined his mood. He finished his meal, strode two streets over and climbed the stony steps to the great circle wall.

He was sweaty, breathless and dizzy by the time he reached the top of the wall, but the dry wind stripped away the sweat and his breath returned to him.

From up here, you could see everything with almost as much clarity as Map Powder provided. Chapman was a city of circles within circles, split only by the fat River Weep. Well, a tributary of it, the Lesser Weep. The Greater Weep disgorged into the sea twenty miles north of the city. Where Mirrlees was undulate and coiled around the river, up and down and side to side, her streets like a nest of serpents, Chapman was an example of much more careful civic planning.

Everything was constructed around a central landmark: the Field of Flight. David could just make it out, patches of green through the balloon and Aerokin-heavy sky. To the west of it was Chapman's Tower of Engineers, a smaller version of Mirrlees' Ruele tower. With night just a few hours off, its twin searchlights were already lit. At its base would be the famous motto of the Engineers: "In Knowledge Truth. In Truth Perfection".

From the Southern Wall where David stood, you could see the deserted suburbs. The gaudy wrap of the Festival of Float failed to conceal the poor condition of Chapman from even the most cursory of inspections.

The streets were empty. Only around the pubs and the buildings near the Field of Flight could people be seen in any numbers. And those areas were overflowing with crowds, few from what David could tell, actually locals.

David stood on the Southern Wall, staring into the city and then out beyond the wall to the Roil, alternating between two forms of dreadfulness, though one was by far the worst. Down south, past the lost suburbs there was little to look at… or too much.

Every time he glanced that way, a thrill of terror rushed through him. It was a visceral dread. Indeed, the mere sight of it gripped and damned and made every doubt come bubbling up like a sickness.

The Roil dwarfed his imagination; transformed Chapman to an insignificant scrap of human clutter. This close it, and its mute horizon-spanning prophecy, was impossible to ignore. How were they ever going to stop that?

David had seen Cadell work his power over cold, he had seen the sky rain ice and the frozen remains of poor creatures caught in that furious boiling chill. However, impressive as it had been, the Roil made it seem like nothing. But then he saw, in the distance far, far in the heart of the Roil, the coruscating finger of light that was the Breaching Spire. Mirrlees was just too far away to see it, but here at last was revealed the greatest work of the Old Men, the diamond tower that breached the atmosphere. Then the tower dimmed, or a cloud passed across the sun, and all he could see was the Roil again.

A distant almost plaintive bell sounded out the hour.

He turned his back to the Roil, but could not escape its presence. It was there as much as the beating of his heart or the heat in his blood. Try as he might it would never leave his thoughts. He had seen the Roil. He had seen the end of the world.

The *Dolorous Grey* hadn't even begun to prepare him for the Roil's terror. He had expected to read about the train on every broadsheet in town but the papers had been silent on the matter, though the subject was broached several times on the street. People knew, they were just too afraid to admit they knew after the first few were arrested and hanged.

David was musing over this when he saw something that nearly had him jumping over the side of the wall. No more than a hundred metres away stood Mr Tope.

All this had begun with him, the knife swift and fast across his father's throat. The Verger leant against the wall staring south, his face heavy and stern, weighted with worries. Had the Roil disturbed him too? David doubted that Mr Tope had spotted him, but it would not be long. The walkway was relatively narrow and besides the sentries at regular intervals there were few people up here. He couldn't risk trying to walk past him.

There was a steep stone stair descending from the wall nearby. David ducked down there, choosing not to hide but flee, just in case the Verger wanted to use these stairs as well – a distinct possibility the way David's luck was going.

David reached the ground and the road, and he ran, not stopping until he had put a few streets between himself and the wall.

Then he realised where he was, the map returning to him as a sort of flashback.

This was an inner deserted suburb, just a few streets from the Chadwick safe house. The thought of being alone here made him uneasy, but he reasoned all he needed to do was follow the road and it would lead him to the safe house, which by definition *must* be safe.

He closed his eyes and picked the most direct route. It took him through the dour and forsaken retail district that ran alongside the Southern Wall. Here businesses had failed months ago; he stared through broken windows at bookstores empty of everything but shelves, and curling posters for the latest histories. Some shops were half-stocked as though, one day, their owners had just locked the doors and never come back. No one had even bothered to loot them.

He looked around sadly, stared morosely through curtains of peeling newspapers and dust-choked webs, as though even the spiders had left this part of town.

A few more minutes of walking and he was there: standing before the burnt out husk.

David wasn't sure what he had expected, but not this. Though he didn't know why he was surprised. He stood there for a while, not knowing what to do. At last, he reasoned, his best chance was back in the city proper.

Once he'd had another shot of Carnival.

He scarcely noticed the woman until she was directly behind him, her face a ghostly reflection in the glass window front of a deserted millinery.

A Verger! He spun on her, his ice pistol out, and then faltered. She was like no Verger he had ever seen. She loomed over him, her eyes wild, her white hair a mass of knots and curls, pistols gripped in both hands, rifles and blades holstered all around her waist. He recognised the weaponry; it was similar to the ice pistols Chapman's sentries brandished, but there was something about it; a precision, matched in the way she moved. Scars streaked her pale face – not all of them were old. What was she? Some sort of bandit?

She glanced at his pistol dismissively, and David had a sense that she could knock it from him before he could even pull the trigger.

"Step away from the glass, addict," she said.

She'd seen him, she'd seen him take the Carnival. Despite the drug, his face burned with shame. David raised his hands, but he did not let go of the gun.

"If that's what you want," he said.

"Down," she said and aimed her pistols at his chest. "Get down!"

David dropped, as the window shattered behind him. He rolled onto his back, and found himself inches from a Quarg Hound's flexing teeth – and in that moment of desperate clarity, David marvelled that the beast's teeth really *did* flex and shiver and shift.

Keep moving. Keep moving. He shuffled back on his arse.

There were two loud shots. The Quarg Hound shrieked, its teeth gnashing as the force of the shots drove it to the ground.

Its legs shuddered, then the shuddering stopped. All at once the air stank of ammonia and cinnamon.

"You're safe now," the woman said.

"Thank you," David said, feeling particularly less than safe because the woman had not lowered her weapons.

"Don't thank me. I've been tracking that hound for hours. And when it came here, to a place I'd been told might be safe… " She gestured behind her, towards the edge of the city. "Don't know how it got here, the walls are high and well-guarded, but there'll be more. There always are."

The woman regarded him curiously. "I'm Margaret." She took a step towards him.

"David."

"One thing's for certain, David, you're not from around here are you?"

"How do you know?" David asked, blinking.

"Well you're the first person I've seen in this part of the city all day, and you seemed awfully disappointed that the safe house was burnt. Only an idiot or a tourist would wander around these streets, or someone desperate. The Roil is less than two miles south of the city and, as you probably haven't noticed, half these buildings are booby-trapped." David wanted to argue that point, but in truth he really hadn't noticed. "Chapman's leaders have already given these parts over to the Roil, but it's going to pay when it arrives. Unless, of course, some idiot or tourist sets them off. So, what are you, idiot or tourist?"

"I'm neither," David blustered. "I wanted to think. And let me say, you are most obviously not from around here. What I mean to say is I have never seen anyone with such pale skin. And if only an idiot would be hanging around here, what does that make you?"

Margaret pointed one of her pistols at his head. "Let me remind you, it isn't that wise to shout at the person with the most guns."

David blushed, and bowed his head. "I'm sorry. It's just the things I've seen. Such terrible things."

Margaret nodded, lowering, then holstering her guns. "We live in terrible times," she said.

The second Quarg Hound came out of nowhere, leaping at Margaret's back.

David had no time to utter even a warning. He fired his pistol. The bullet struck the beast squarely in the head, but the pistol was a small one, not capable of a fatal shot. The Quarg Hound fell to the ground, pawed at its skull then scrambled to its feet. Its body bunched up, the muscles across its back rippling, as though it was ready to leap again.

"Let me finish this," Margaret said, she fired once and missed, her next shot didn't. The Quarg Hound howled once then dropped dead, ice scaling its chest.

"You're full of surprises," she said, leaning on her rifle as though it were the only thing that was stopping her from keeling over.

David blinked stinging smoke from his eyes. His fingers burned from the chemical residue of the pistol shot, his ears were ringing.

"I guess I am," he said, and it may have just been the Carnival, but all of a sudden he was very pleased with himself indeed.

CHAPTER 39

The city changed, as all metropolises change, be it Chinoy, the *Channon or Mirrlees. But none so quickly, the Roil ever a catalyst had accelerated. Even as Chapman's population slept, even as they armed and reinforced the city's walls, Chapman itself wasn't Chapman any more, but a dreaming city nascent. Soon it would sleep, and drag those who lived there down with it.*

Have I set the scene enough?

Of course not, you who were not there and could never understand.

Dreaming Cities, Scheming Cities: The Manufactories of the Roil, DEIGHTON

THE CITY OF CHAPMAN

Margaret's limbs shook. When had she last slept? She could not remember the last time she had slept. Her brain kept circling this, though the question held no real relevance. She wanted to ask David if he knew.

Of course he didn't. How could he possibly know anything? All those capable friends and allies she had lost. And now this addict, barely a man, he was as lost as her.

Every time she caught a glimpse of the sun or the blue sky, no matter how smoke and spoor shrouded, reality sloughed away and her head spun. This sky had been all she had ever dreamed of as a child. Now she would happily trade it back if everything could be the way it once was. A few weeks ago, all she had known was darkness and the cruel comforts of her city. Now she was alone, stalled by the light, and with no one to help her. She didn't even have her *Melody*.

She did not know where to turn.

Maybe David, after all he had been looking for the safe house and that suggested links with Anderson's allies.

Who was this idiotic window-shopping addict, with his dark and innocent eyes? She wondered if her eyes had ever been so innocent, her worries ever so simple.

She wanted to clip him round the ear and alert him to his foolishness.

But, then again, it was all relative.

Not too many days ago she had made her empty vigil at the walls of her city, wondering when her parents were coming home. Back then she had rarely needed to make decisions, her parents had always been there to guide her (even if she had not really noticed) and to ensure that she was safe.

And now she was alone.

How does one go about saving the world?

She didn't even know how to go about talking with this stupid drug-addled boy.

"This weaponry, this cold suit, they were built in Tate," she said. "My home."

David's eyes widened. "But Tate fell years ago, decades ago."

Margaret shook her head. "Tate stood and fought and survived. No thanks to you northerners. I grew up there, it was my home for twenty years. But it's gone now."

"How many made it out?" David asked.

"Just me," Margaret said, the words meaningless and all too heavy; she was surprised she didn't choke on them, that she could relate the facts so calmly. "The city was destroyed and everyone there. If they were lucky."

"I think I know what you mean," David said. "The Witmoths."

"Yes," Margaret said. "The Roil grew a mind and it took everything away."

Cadell was weary, and angry.

Two tunnels beneath the city had collapsed, the third had involved a slog through dusty crevices then half-flooded sewers. His clothes were soiled by the time he climbed out into the street, and then the hunger took him. He'd heard voices in the sewers, so he descended again: gripped in a madness that did not pass until his clothes were drenched in other, ruddier, fluids.

Cadell woke from the killing to guilt and rage. His hunger was growing strong again. The stress of the journey was taking its toll.

Lucid and remorseful, he went to a bathhouse, one in a shadier district of Chapman where few questions were asked. As he washed away the blood, he had heard all manner of rumours, every one of them disturbing. The least of which were explosions in the deserted suburbs.

Perhaps something had gone wrong with Stade's Project.

By the time he had bathed and changed from soiled clothes to marginally fresher ones, it was late, and he hurried to the meeting place.

David wasn't there, but he could just sense his scent.

Cadell rushed to the safe house and found it a blackened husk, the boy nowhere to be seen. He cursed David as he searched the shell of a house. He found evidence of recent habitation and, curiously, a fuel cell for an ice rifle of a make he was unfamiliar with.

He picked it up and regarded the stamp at its base. Now *that* was peculiar. It was stamped with Tate's symbol. He slipped the cell into his pocket.

He sniffed at the air, eyes closed. There was Roil Spore everywhere and the deeper musk of Quarg Hound, and faintly, just faintly, David. The young man had been here. And, a Quarg Hound had started hunting him, and something else. He was missing something here, and he wasn't at all sure what.

He cursed David again, and returned to the scent trail.

It didn't go far.

He found the boy talking to a young woman, pale as the moons, and nearly as tall as him. Another one, another damn stray, punishment for his sins. He checked his nails for blood. Nothing, but he knew it was there.

Cadell cleared his throat and was suddenly staring down the barrel of a gun. Maybe he deserved such an ending. He raised his hands slowly, studying the woman's rifle as he did so. The weapon was sophisticated, better than any he had seen in Mirrlees. The sort of thing a man could approve of being killed by.

"Cadell!" David said, sounding for once as though he was pleased to see him.

"David," Cadell said calmly. "Could you please tell your friend to put down that gun?"

"Her name's Margaret, she's a Penn," David said. "Margaret, this is Cadell."

The woman lowered the rifle and Cadell relaxed. The old man pulled the endothermic charge out of his pocket. "Well, that explains this. A Penn, eh, I've heard of your family. Didn't expect to come face to face with one. I believe you have quite a tale to tell. Tate remains, eh, when all had thought it fallen decades past."

Margaret shook her head. "No, it's gone. Taken by the Roil," Margaret said. "My parents designed ice moats and endothermic cannon. But even those could not hold forever. Tate has fallen, as you said, but less than a week has passed since she fell."

Cadell passed her the spent charge. "I can refuel this for you, my dear." He smiled. "Oh, this would be such a foreign world to you, but we can help." Already he was seeing ways he could use the girl; her aid would be useful in the journey north. A little luck had come his way. A useful stray at last, he thought. "There is so much you need to know."

"I have learnt my share."

Cadell snorted. "Slinking around these suburbs I am sure you have."

On the wall, Tope had thought he'd caught wind of David Milde's scent, then whatever smell or presence was gone again as a gust blew in from the south. The damn Roil spores drowned out his senses, no matter how much Chill he devoured.

It was the blasted cuttle-blood that made the Roil such a rush, burning in his veins – the blood and the looming Obsidian Curtain. That was why the Vergers of Chapman were not blooded, just men, who had not suffered a childhood of transfusions, and training to control the rages. He envied them their weaknesses sometimes. And they, for their part, feared him.

He sniffed the air again. No, there was no hint of David at all, just the Roil, just its mad promise.

He slipped another lozenge in his mouth and bit down hard.

CHAPTER 40

The folk of Drift look down, look down
And what they see makes each one frown

Folk song

THE CITY OF CHAPMAN

The first thing Margaret noticed about Cadell was his extreme age. He somehow reeked of it, but in him it wasn't a weakness but a strength born of time, as though he were granite. The second was the Orbis he wore. It drew the eye, and looking at it now, it seemed as bright as the sun. She'd seen nothing like it – her own parents had worn simple silver bands to signify their office.

Cadell caught her gaze. "Once, all councillors wore these. But that was a long time ago. Today's rings are markedly inferior." And as he said it, it was as though the Orbis disappeared, what glamour what light it possessed was hidden, and it could have passed as merely a tawdry bauble.

He turned to David. "Well, lad, you have the habit of making interesting friends."

They talked for an hour in the shadow of the wall and Margaret felt as though she had been plunged into some sort of fairy tale. Old Men, Vergers. Cadell claimed to know the secrets of the Engine of the World. In fact, he claimed to have built it.

For the first time in a week, she thought she might have a chance at succeeding in her aims, that maybe she'd had a turning in her luck. She looked at them both as resources, stepping stones to the north and the Engine there.

Margaret shared her own intentions to find it, at which Cadell patted her arm avuncularly. "You know so little about the Engine, my dear," Cadell said. "You cannot know how lucky you are. If you had somehow made it to Tearwin Meet (and I could credit it because, well... you have made it this far) the walls would have stopped you, and if they didn't, and there is a chance of that, slim, but a chance, then still you would have failed. Only the Old Men can operate the Engine. Only our blood, and this," he raised his hand, revealing the Orbis again, and once more it burned brightly. "The Engine would have stripped the flesh from your bones. You may come with me to Tearwin Meet. You may help me reach the Engine, but you can never operate it. It is a folly of the ancient Engineers, it is my madness, and the curse laid down by the Engine itself. It would have been your undoing, no matter how lucky you were." Cadell glanced at his watch. "We can't stay all night here. We've a meeting to attend."

Margaret must have looked confused, and Cadell shook his head. "Oh the sorts of people I gather around me, lost children, when what I need are warriors."

Margaret scowled at that. She knew how to fight.

"There's an Aerokin pilot," Cadell said, "waiting at the *Inn of the Devoted Switch*." Cadell looked at his watch again, and tsked. "And we are rather late."

No time for rest then. But soon, and then she might just show Cadell who was the lost child and who the warrior.

"You're late," Kara Jade said. "And you said nothing about passengers."

Cadell laughed. "If you only knew the day I've had."

The day all of us have had, David thought.

Kara Jade didn't look amused, just looked at her watch. "I was hoping we'd have done our talking by now and I'd be drunk."

"Things don't always turn out how one hopes," Margaret said.

Kara turned towards her, as though she were some annoying biting insect newly discovered. "You'd better hope that is true, then. I've some awful inclinations towards you, and we've only just met."

"Please," Cadell said. "Please. I did not come here to fight."

"And I didn't come here to be a pilot for three people. Just one. That is all."

David had never been in a pub like this. While the *Inn of the Devoted Switch* was crowded and a little forcefully jovial, he could not be at all sure it was not typical of its ilk. In Mirrlees he had been to but a handful of drinking places with his father, being too young to legally buy drink (though those who had sold him Carnival had never set such an age restriction).

Drifters he knew; his father had had dealings with them, even counted some among his friends. But even the best of them were arrogant if not rude. He'd seen the city of Drift once, a few miles east of Mirrlees. He had been young, perhaps no more than five, sitting on his father's shoulders.

And his father had recited this poem:

The folk of Drift look down, look down
and what they see makes each one frown
The folk of Drift they rule the skies

A truth contained within their eyes
The folk of Drift are rude indeed
If the clouds were yours, wouldn't you be?

Nice poem, but some Drift folk lived by its lines too faithfully.

The inn was crammed with Drifters, and their haughty and garrulous natures were in evidence in every over-emphatic movement, every dark and dangerous stare. The air folk were loud and famous boasters and brawlers. If you were to believe them their city was older than the Council itself, their technologies built in the eons before, they'd once ruled not only the sky but the ground as well, but had found it boring, so the "tedium of empire" (as they called it) had given way to the Council. They were, they claimed, also better lovers, poets and fighters than any one of the groundlings. David did not believe a word of it. Which did not mean he would voice such doubts here. He wanted to live a little longer, if he could.

The Drifters wore their various guild colours, the yellow of elevator coxswain, the dark greens of steersmen, and the coveted red and black of Aerokin captains.

In one corner, and David had to blink twice when he realised who it was, lounged Mr Blake and to his left his partner in flight, Miss Steel. They were arguing about something, which was no surprise. Lawrence Blake and Catherine Steel were a running argument, almost as famous for their fights as their Air Show, a bit of which – the Air Show, not the fights – David had seen when he was ten. Five standard dirigibles at mock battle, flying low and in tight formation, and Mr Blake leaping from ship to ship carrying a big coil of rope, binding them together like they were sheep rather than ships, then clambering onto the back of his Aerokin, the *Arrogant Spice*.

"Blake and Steel," he said, pointing in their direction.

Cadell blinked.

"If you say so." Margaret said, clearly unimpressed. "Drifters, let them see how long they would have lasted in my city."

Cadell nodded to the crowded press of people at the bar. "David, why don't you go over there and order some drinks. The house brew for me, please."

"Nothing for me," Margaret said.

"Bourbon," Kara Jade said. "Two fingers of it."

For a moment, David remembered the incident at the dining car on the *Dolorous Grey* and shuddered. This was almost as dangerous; some of these pilots were armed to the teeth and full of piss already.

David pushed his way through the crowd, careful not to give any offence. Drift folk were volatile. Every glance he caught was a challenge and each push or shove the possible opening gambit in a fight. He caught snippets of conversation as he went.

"City's not long for it, I reckon. Heard they've sighted Quarg Hounds in the deserted suburbs and you know what comes next. I was there in Consolation City, trade work, when it all came down. You know, the Grand Defeat. And it was sudden, the sky dark with all manner of beasts, the Roil rolling in like a storm. The standing army of three cities destroyed, barely got out with my life and that was only because–"

Another went.

"Sooner this Festival is done with the better. Sad, though, I've always liked coming here – such pretty men." Fingers pinched his arse, he kept his head high, kept walking.

"Bloody folk music. What's that all about? Another flaming mandolin player comes up to me with a glint in his eye and a bloody cap rattling with coin he'll be playing it where the sun don't shine."

"Heard the Council's locked down the city. They're turning people away now. Went up this morning, there were hundreds of 'em, heading up to Mirrlees, heading up to the rain. Not sure what welcome old Stade's going to give 'em, doesn't have a history of looking kindly on refugees. I've heard rumblings about camps. Oi, stop your listening in, boy, or I'll cuff your ears till they bleed!"

David reached the bar and ordered his drinks.

Cadell was scowling when David returned. "The *Roslyn Dawn* was bred for this task, Miss Jade. It is why your mothers gave her to me."

"It's not a ship, it's a she, and they gave you nothing," Kara snapped. "They sent me on this mission. I am their agent, and my powers are discretionary." Cadell looked at her as though he knew this was not true.

David passed her the bourbon. Kara Jade sculled it, without looking, and gave him back the empty glass. "Mr Cadell was telling me just what he means to do. What do you think?"

"I'm not sure." He looked over at Margaret, and she shook her head.

"I might have that drink after all, David," Margaret said.

Kara Jade snorted. "Not sure? Well, you better be. David, I'll be flying you, Mr Cadell and the lady here into the Roil."

David blinked. That was the first he had heard about it.

"The Roil, you say?"

Cadell grimaced. "Why else did you think I pushed for you to go with Buchan and Whig. I need to get in there, I need to see it."

"I've been in there," Margaret said. "Trust me you *don't* want to see it."

"Wants and needs are a different thing, girl," Cadell said. "And I *must* see it. Unless I do my argument with the Engine is incomplete."

"Well then," David said. "If we're all going to die, how about another round."

Kara laughed. "Only if you're buying. And a better bloody quality bourbon this time, that last one was shit."

CHAPTER 41

Aerokin are unpredictable as the weather. The Mothers of the Sky more so, their motives ever uncertain. Only the Roil's intentions were clear. Against such an implacable force, motives, plans and politics are meaningless. You may as well play games with a rock.

Hammel's History: A Comedy of Manners, HAMMEL

THE ROILFACE

"How long now?" Cadell asked, the translucent floor beneath them vibrating in time with the *Roslyn Dawn's* nacelle exhalations, loud enough that he had to shout.

"Four minutes until we reach the curtain," Kara Jade said – she did not look at all happy about it. David was not sure if the reason lay in their proximity to the Roil or the bad hangover she must be nursing.

Last night she had, to put it politely, overindulged. They all had, but the woman possessed a will to drink that David had never seen before – and his father had known some serious drinkers.

At one stage Kara kissed him on the cheek and started singing air shanties, all rollicking good fun until she had vomited everywhere, then as though a switch had been flicked she'd stumbled off to the *Roslyn Dawn*. Both Cadell and Margaret had gone to their respective rooms by then, so David had been left with the clean up.

Kara Jade had hardly looked at him since, except with the occasional stare of condemnation, as though, somehow, it was all his fault.

"Seven minutes," she said, turning and giving David another grim look.

David shivered. Seven minutes until the nightmare begins.

Cadell had hardly given him any Carnival that morning, and not nearly enough for him to deal with this.

He looked about him at the arcane array of controls, which Kara Jade had explained were less controls and more a point of dialogue with the *Roslyn Dawn*. As though flying was nothing more than having a chat. From what Kara had told him the Aerokin wasn't happy about this foray into the Roil but, like her, it was following the orders of the Mothers of the Sky.

When the Mothers of the Sky spoke it was law.

The gondola shook with the vibrations of the nearby nacelle-enclosed bio-jets. Everything that wasn't actually grown by the *Roslyn Dawn* itself was polished brass and smooth leather, and smelt softly of disinfectant mixed with an odour that was distinctly animal – slightly doggy with a hint of malt if David had to compare it to anything else, and while not unpleasant it certainly didn't help with his hangover.

The *Roslyn Dawn's* gondola was more a cyst or an odd extrusion of matter. Cadell had described it as modification of the *Dawn's* claws and that they were, in effect, crawling around inside a fingernail. That nail was semi-translucent and narrow, it ran along the belly of the Aerokin. Midway along its length was the doorifice – an all too fleshy puckering that flapped open on contact – it was the same fleshy colour as the Aerokin itself, the gondola hard around it.

Kara had showed them all how two taps with a hand made any section of the gondola instantly transparent or opaque.

David had tried it on the floor and felt at once that he was about to fall out of the sky. He tapped it twice more and could breathe again. Why hadn't Cadell given him more Carnival?

"It's one way, of course." Kara said proudly. "You can see out, but nothing can see in."

"She's a fine ship all right," said David, as though he knew anything about Aerokin.

"She's not a *ship*." Kara Jade hissed – perhaps remembering that kiss – a muscle in her cheek twitched. "Ships aren't clever. Ships don't breathe. Ships don't get angry and hurl their stupid passengers into the sky."

"Um, what I meant to say was she's the finest Aerokin I've ever ha–."

"The *Roslyn Dawn* is *the* finest Aerokin, without a doubt." Kara Jade sniffed, David wondered if he wasn't going to get a punch to the face. "A real evolutionary leap forward. You will not see her like anywhere. She is faster, lighter and more stable than anything the Mothers in the Sky have ever gestated: the endpoint of over three decades of research. With the *Roslyn Dawn* my people have taken the technology and the breeding programs as far as they can go. Though she requires a fine pilot, she needs only one. Not like her bigger kin, with their Elevator and Rudder crews."

"The finest Aerokin, the finest pilot, we are indeed lucky," Margaret said.

"Yes, you fucking are," Kara Jade replied. She swung back to her instruments. "Two Minutes, I want to hit it at three thousand feet."

David rubbed the bridge of his nose. His head felt like it was going to explode. He winced, and Kara Jade must have caught the expression. "Click your jaw," she said with surprising gentleness. "It will help your ears deal with the shift in pressure."

David did, and yes, it helped a little. He thanked her, then glanced over at Margaret. He wondered how she felt going back. If it were him... well, if it were him he probably wouldn't even be on this airship.

Margaret's face was calm. Her dark eyes gazed out steadily at everything. Her lips though were twisted and one of her hands kept straying to the hilt of the rime blade at her belt.

The *Roslyn Dawn* flexed along its length, shifting the chemical components of its body, increasing the percentage of hydrogen to oxygen. Its ascent sharpened, silent but for the vibrations of the hull. They powered towards the Roil.

For all that he had read of the Roil and seen from afar now David knew, at once and undeniably, its indifferent bulk. Nothing had prepared him for this.

It rose above them like some mountainous yet becalmed tsunami that possessed the apparent tangibility of stone. But that did nothing to describe the sensation of motion and stillness that gripped David now.

Cadell sat silently, his eyes closed, his fingers linked together in what may have passed for prayer but for the whiteness of the knuckles, the soft flexing of his shoulders. He was readying himself for something, and nothing so passive as a ride in the dark.

"We're almost there," David said. Cadell's eyes opened.

"I know," he said. "I can feel it. Is it too much to hope that it can't feel me?"

David swallowed, another detail that he had not wanted to hear.

They entered the Roil all at once; it did not close about them in fragments like real mist did, but smoothly and completely as though the *Roslyn Dawn* had plunged into a vertical lake of darkness.

One moment light surrounded the *Roslyn Dawn* – sunshine and clear blue sky to the rear of them – the next, day was gone, swallowed up. The quiet dark transformed all at once.

Gales crashed up behind the face of the Roil and the *Roslyn Dawn* shuddered as she struck these, lifting up perhaps thirty or forty yards, then she was through the unquiet air.

David realised that he had been holding his breath.

He looked over at Margaret. Her face was pale, almost bloodless, her eyes shone, both her hands were clenched to fists. Cadell also bore a resolute expression, as though he could endure this and would, but only just. Kara Jade alone betrayed no emotion in those first moments, so intent was she on the task at hand.

Thunder, borne on spikes of green lightning, tumbled the silence. The dice rolls of giants. Again, again, again. David's bones tingled.

Kara Jade grinned, her jaw clenched so tight her eyes bugged, as her hands hovered over the controls.

"Just nature's spear shaking," she said. "Impressive but of no real substance. The *Roslyn Dawn* is more than capable of taking multiple lightning strikes." She turned a few dials and stared through the cockpit windows out into the storm. "Though I'd prefer she didn't have to."

"Bring her down," Cadell said. "I want to get a good look at the surface. Are your floodlights charged?"

"Of course they are."

They began their descent. The Roil increasing in density as they sank, a cloudy darkness heavy with spores. The *Roslyn Dawn* creaked and mumbled.

Kara Jade glanced over her readings. "The air pressure is higher than I would like."

Something flared below and a wave of heat rushed up towards them. The *Roslyn Dawn* shuddered and lifted with the impact. Kara Jade cursed softly, a frown washing over her face. "I know. I know," she whispered. The nacelles exhaled in response, the *Roslyn Dawn* swung out in a wider circle. The nose dipped, presenting a smaller target, David guessed.

"There's a lot of heat down there," Kara said.

"And hot air rises, yes," Cadell said. "But we have to get closer, I need to see what is going on beneath."

"As you wish," Kara Jade said, and ran a hand along the inner wall of the cockpit. "If you're going to die anywhere, my darling, it might as well be here, you know, somewhere bloody exotic."

She crooned at her craft, and the *Dawn* descended into the furnace heat, shaking as it struck the violent wind, but never feeling out of control. Kara Jade and her craft were as good as she said they were.

David watched her, entranced. A sound to his left made him turn his head. Margaret was charging her guns. He felt like he should be doing something, but all he had was a handkerchief in his pockets and two wraps of powdered Carnival in his boot.

Could do with some of that now, he thought. He walked towards the sleeping compartment of the *Dawn*. Cadell stopped him.

"Not now, lad," he said. "You'll need your wits about you."

David nodded. Didn't even reach for an excuse.

"And close your mouth, you're gaping like a fish."

As they neared the ground, objects took shape through the murk. Memories returned unbidden to Margaret and she regretted for the umpteenth time her decision to go on this mad journey.

"The Interface," Margaret said, pointing down at the long spine of the tunnel ending in the rectangular block of buildings. "They're using the Interface."

The Interface had been split open, its contents strewn over the ground. A cannon lay toppled next to a desk chair. A bed rested on Anderson's carriage. The *Melody* was nowhere to be seen but still the sight shocked her, worse than she would have expected, remembering that place. Everywhere she went destruction followed and people were lost.

She thought of Anderson. Was he now a puppet of the Witmoths? And her Melody, she could not bear to think of it being used by the Roil.. It's gone, all of it gone. Let it go, or it will kill you.

Below, the earth seethed.

Quarg Hounds boiled into the tunnel, crowding around the Project. The lost Interface had been worn down and overrun.

Something slapped against the window by her head and Margaret started. She frowned when she realised what it was.

"Hideous Garment Flute," she said, matter-of-factly and stared into its teeth-crammed mouths; row upon row of cartilage and bone snapping shut with every shudder of its flight membranes. Grey mucus slid down the gondola wall.

Beneath her she could see the *Roslyn Dawn's* flagella striking out at a knot of the creatures, batting them from the sky. The Aerokin groaned.

"Be calm, my darling," Kara Jade said softly. "Out soon. Out soon."

Another flute joined it, and Margaret reached for her ice pistols.

A hand clapped down on hers. The strength and the awful chill in that grip – as though he had devoured all of Winslow's lozenges – surprised her.

"Don't be a fool," Cadell snapped. "Break the gondola walls, if you could, and you let the Roil in, and I'm not quite ready for that."

His voice trailed off his eyes almost bulging at something he saw down below, beyond the ruined buildings and the maddening mass of Roil creatures, at the immense fuming structure there. Margaret followed his gaze and stared at what could have been some gigantic termitary.

"Heat sinks," Cadell said, face pushed against the window, his fingers tapped the glass, and the world below came into sharper focus. "They have created heat sinks. There and there. I've seen nothing like it, not this close to the edge. Well, at least that explains the ground shaking. They're building a dreaming city. This is not good, not good."

The *Roslyn Dawn* continued its descent. Cadell put out a hand.

"Keep it steady, Miss Jade," he said. "No lower than this, thank you. Just where we are."

The engines whined. The *Roslyn Dawn* slowed its descent, then stopped.

"Well done," Cadell said.

Down below, two huge pipes rose out of the earth, dark smoke poured from their cavernous openings, and around that heat swarmed rippling clumps of shadow.

Witmoths.

The sight reminded Margaret of the vents and chimneys that had once dominated Willowhen Peak. Only here, at the pinnacle of these boiling mouths, no battle raged, these were meant to draw the Roil, meant to sustain it.

Margaret stared over at David, eyes bulging in his head, his mouth wide open like some sort of idiot. He held a pair of binoculars in one hand but he did not use them, perhaps too frightened of what they might reveal.

Now you know, Margaret thought. You have seen the power of this place. What was once abstraction has become reality for you.

David was not the only one to whom this was all new.

Kara Jade had lost her cockiness. "So many," she whispered.

"The Roil is getting ready for something," Cadell said. "And that should not be. The Roil does not push, it shambles. It drifts, it dreams: it does not do this."

"What about the Grand Defeat?" David asked.

"Freak weather conditions," Cadell said. "A hotter summer, a low pressure system that became a storm that lead to a heatburst. But there was no thought to it, no strategy. This is different."

"Things have changed," Margaret said, and slapped a fist against the wall of the gondola, hard enough that one of the Hideous Garment Flutes slipped free and tumble-flew away. She followed its wild improbable peristaltic flight; all those membranes sliding and billowing frantically. She had seen clouds of these beasts fly, loud and shrill, over Tate.

"An I-Bomb. If we possessed an I-Bomb, we could halt this here and clear away the madness with a single detonation."

"But we do not." Cadell snapped. "Nor do we have your parents' laboratories." He pointed down. "Though it appears our enemy has something similar. Miss Jade, heave to. Now!"

On the Roilscape beneath them, what could only be described as a cannon turned towards them, though most cannon did not look as though they had been grown, nor did they have chambers that bubbled and spat liquid fire.

"Now!"

Kara Jade already had the job in hand, her face a mask of horror and determination. "Strap yourselves in," she said.

Kara muttered over her controls, the *Roslyn Dawn* jerked sharply to the left and rose about a hundred yards in little more than a heartbeat. However, it wasn't enough.

There was a flash of detonation, and the airship lifted on a wave of fire.

CHAPTER 42

The history of this world cannot be understood without a complete knowledge of the three forces that govern it. The Roil, the Engine and, of course, the Breaching Spire. We know of a Mechanical Winter, we have heard whisperings of the punishment meted out for that by whatever brute intellect rules Tearwin Meet. We know that the Roil is ancient, that it has come before.

So what is it that we know?

Nothing.

Our history is but one of events, scattered and continuing, but never in the context that such knowledge would bring.

We stare into the great dark, little more than idiots playing out roles that we do not understand.

Histories, DEIGHTON

WITHIN THE ROIL

David scrambled to his feet, his nose bleeding, spots dancing before his eyes. Glad I have such a thick skull.

At least no one seemed to have noticed his tumble.

"Told you to strap in, idiot!" Kara Jade said, swinging from her controls to glare at him. David dropped into a seat, pulled the belts tight around him.

"Did we take a direct hit?" Cadell demanded. He hadn't strapped himself in. He stood by Kara now, peering over her controls. David wondered if they made any sense to him at all.

"No, we've everything functioning. A direct hit and you'd hear it; a direct hit and I think we'd be hitting the ground not long after. But I'm getting us out of here, now. Thank the Mothers of the Sky for all this heat. There are thermals enough to lift us to the moons. The *Dawn*'s straining for the sky. Strap yourselves in. David, I'm talking to you."

"Already have," he said.

The nacelles coughed and shuddered, and the *Roslyn Dawn* raced into the air. David's ears popped and he clutched at the armrests. Kara Jade worked furiously at the controls, venting gas and releasing ballast, pushing the *Roslyn Dawn* as far as she dared.

"If you don't get it right, the lack of air pressure can burst the gas bladders," she said to no one in particular. "And that is not a good thing. Kill an Aerokin quick smart. Foolish man, entering the Roil like it's his right."

There was another flash, however, this time, they were much further from it. David watched the great ball of fire hurtle past then plummet back down into the Roil. Something else caught his eye, a distant glint in the sky to the south that shot from east to west.

"What's that?" he asked, pointing south west with a shaking hand.

It rushed past again (or at least he thought it rushed past) and was gone.

"Your imagination," Kara Jade said. "Now quiet all of you. I need to concentrate."

"What did you see?" Margaret asked, her voice uneasy.

David's ears pricked up at that. Just what did she know? "I'm not sure what it was, but it's gone now."

Still, David stared south, eyes straining to see through all that murk. But nothing passed that way again, and they were almost free of the darkness.

The *Roslyn Dawn* jolted again and they were out.

David's eyes watered in the light. Rain fell on the hills a hundred miles north of Chapman. A little to the west of those low hills Lake Uhl gleamed. A normal day, an unthreatened day, until he turned his head and the Roil was there behind him.

Even when he did not turn, it remained. Sunshine failed to scour from him what he had seen, the darkness had poisoned his world.

A ball of fire burst from the Roil, sailing past the *Roslyn Dawn*; it described a steep arc that ended in the deserted suburbs where it struck a building setting it alight, then another and another followed until a whole block blazed.

"Those heat sinks, how did they build them so fast?" Margaret asked. "They weren't there a few days ago."

Cadell grinned darkly. "Disturbing, isn't it? I have my suspicions, Margaret, but none of them are good. Nor are they helpful at this time." He turned to Kara. "Land this as quickly as you can."

Kara grunted in response.

"What does he mean?" David asked Margaret. "What does he mean that could make this more disturbing than it already is?"

"Vastkind," Margaret said. "I think that's where his thoughts lead him."

"Vastkind?" Here was something David had never heard of, and Margaret seemed surprised.

Beneath the crust, where all is heat and even the stone melts and becomes a kind of liquid fire – the burning yolk of the world. There the old, old books say, dwells the Vastkind, a proto-roilbeast. An Ur-beast, for it is from the fire that the Roil was sprung, whether through the dark designs of the Master Engineers or nature, the books do not know. But they're big, terribly big."

David nodded his head and shivered. "I don't like the sound of that at all. At least, up here, we're relatively safe."

"We're not safe yet, relative or otherwise," Kara Jade said. "The bastards on the wall have started firing at us."

She pointed behind her where flags hung from the wall. "Quick, the red and the grey flag and the green one two. Wave them out the port window."

David grabbed the flags and did as he was told.

The firing stopped, but not before a shell glanced off the starboard nacelle. The *Roslyn Dawn* moaned.

Kara Jade cursed at that. "Whores of Argent Lane, if they've hurt my darling *Dawn*, the Council of Chapman will pay in blood."

THE CITY OF CHAPMAN FIELD OF FLIGHT
TWO MILES NORTH OF THE ROIL

The *Dawn* landed gently in the Field of Flight followed by two military Aerokin, their big guns trained upon her as people below hosed cold water on her carapace. It was the longest part of their brief journey. Ships and Aerokin were still arriving for tomorrow's launch and they had to wait their turn. When at last the *Dawn* had touched down, the Aerokin gave a great shuddering of relief.

"I know, I know, my darling," Kara Jade said.

"We all know," Cadell said.

Upon landing they were subjected to the ice test. David found it just as nerve wracking this time. How could you really know if the Witmoths had infected you? He had heard that the process was agony, but what if it had grown subtler? He was relieved when nothing more than a wet shirtsleeve resulted. Once given the all clear, the military Aerokin pulled away, swinging around to the perimeter of the city.

A crowd of Drifters waited, wide-eyed and cheering.

They think we are heroes, David thought. When all we did was drop in and run. Hero? I have never been more scared in my entire life. There is nothing I would rather be doing right now than running and not stopping until I am as far away from here as possible, and then running some more.

The moment the test was completed Cadell strode towards the city, pushing through the crowd as he went.

"Where are you going?" David shouted and Cadell stopped, his gaze dark and hard. David quailed beneath that glare, wished he had not asked.

"To the Tower of Engineers. I have seen what I needed to see, and more. The city must be evacuated, not tomorrow or the next day, but now. Get to the hotel and gather your things. We leave as soon as I return. And if I do not return within twenty-four hours, leave without me. Get as far from this damn thing as you can, Kara Jade is paid to take you to Hardacre."

The crowd closed around him and he was gone from sight.

"Be careful," David said to Cadell's back.

Kara Jade patted David on the shoulder, almost jovial. She'd just checked over the Aerokin's wounds and they'd obviously proven not as bad as she'd feared. "He's just going to the tower. He'll be fine. It's not as if he's walking back into the Roil."

No, David thought. He's going to a different sort of trouble. Different but trouble nonetheless.

Blake and Steel came over from their own ships and both slapped Kara Jade's back heartily.

"Never in my life have I seen such bravery and stupidity; you're Raven's baby sister, no doubt," Blake said, tugging on his beard. "We went up a little and followed you with our scopes. Through the curtain, into the darkness and we thought you dead regardless of the *Roslyn Dawn's* genotype. Bravery and stupidity I say, and in equal measure. But then we've learnt to expect it from you, and her."

"We are all stupid being here," Kara said as she guided the *Dawn's* flagella to the docking bollards. "It was both brave and stupid indeed, but we have learnt something. The Roil transforms what it touches, it's what it does, and it has transformed my heart, magnified my fears." She frowned at her two friends and the next words that came were urgent and troubled. "The Roil has amassed a huge army, bigger than anything that I have seen. Just beyond the Obsidian Curtain, obscured in countless spores, is encamped Chapman's doom."

"An army?" Blake shook his head and raised his hands as though to block out the memory of the words. "This is madness; what does the Roil need of an army? Its great cloud is potent enough. This is cruelty itself, when it starts imitating the ways of humans. Still Drift stands above it all, we are not overly threatened."

Kara's face tightened and she stabbed a finger at both of them.

"You are fools if you believe that. Without the Groundlings the city of Drift is nothing. Where will we get our food? With whom shall we trade? And when the Roil closes all the lower skies and swallows the entire earth, when there is naught but Roil beneath us, what shall we do?"

Blake's eyes widened and his face reddened with shame and a little anger.

"You're right and I know it. But do you have to be so blunt, girl? After all what can we do?"

Steel who had remained silent through all of this now met Kara's eye and she bore such an expression, a kind of resolve that almost matched the pilot's. "I think I know," she said. "This Festival should float."

Kara nodded

"You should take as many people with you as you can. North to Mirrlees or better yet, beyond the Narung Mountains, into Hardacre where it still passes for cold."

"We cannot take many," Blake said.

"Take as many as you can. Like my sister did those many years ago. It can never be enough, but that is all we have now. Half measures and slim hope."

CHAPTER 43

The Engine is mad. It was built by the mad. What is hubris if not the grandest of madness? Think of it there, in the distant north. Consider its endless thought and what it might be scheming with its great clockwork mind. Should its thoughts turn south again, distance alone will not save us.

Its mind knows nothing of the miles, its mind takes it everywhere.

Night's Engines, DEIGHTON

THE CITY OF CHAPMAN

He'd delayed when he should have run, but to do what they had wanted of him... He'd doubted more than any of them, and Stade had provided ample distraction.

He could not lie to himself. It had been fun. The chase he'd set Stade's Vergers, which hadn't been much of a chase, but a peculiar sort of predation. Oh, and the death he'd meted out, telling himself that it was fair and just. And if any innocents got in the way; if they fell; if he killed them. Well, there were no true innocents, and this game was not a game. Sometimes people died, sometimes quite a lot of them.

Cadell had always been the most sentimental of the Old Men. A dangerous shifting sort of sentiment, one that could both justify and mourn the deaths of so many.

The dozens he had slaughtered these past two years, they were nothing compared to the many who had died because of him.

Cadell approached the Tower of Engineers as though he owned it. Built in the centre of the city it rose above everything, an imitation of the Breaching Spire. At its crown, bordering the central spike, were the two huge Lights of Reason shining into the sky. A few months ago they would have been illuminating clouds; now the rains had gone and they seemed almost to touch the stars. Impressive, except that in another few weeks, if that, they would be smothered by the Roil.

The lights represented the ideals of Truth and Reason, but Cadell doubted there would be much of either on display inside the Council Chambers. Otherwise Chapman would have been evacuated weeks before. Had Buchan not been exiled he knew with a certainty the city would be empty of all but the mad.

The great doors were locked, but they opened at the touch of his hand, the locks freezing, then shattering.

Two guards stood at the foyer. They raised their rifles.

"That would not be wise," Cadell said.

"What do you want?" demanded the nearest guard.

"I must speak with the Council."

The guards exchanged glances. "The Council is in session. Have you made an appointment?"

"Of course not," Cadell snapped.

"No reason to be so short-tempered," the guard said.

"Every reason," Cadell said. "The Roil is about to strike. And I must speak to them one and all, the city must be evacuated."

"On whose authority do you speak?" One of the guards asked, rolling his eyes.

"My own," Cadell said and lifted his hand so that the ring he wore was easily visible.

Both guards lifted their eyebrows and lowered their guns.

"If you will excuse me," one said. "I will have to get someone for you."

The guard hurried off, leaving his very nervous friend.

"Is it true what you did to those Vergers?"

Cadell flashed a smile. "What do you think?"

Cadell did not have to wait long before the guard returned with a harried looking councillor. "At last," Cadell said.

"Good evening, sir. I'm Gaffney, councillor medium rank. May I see the ring?"

Cadell growled. "I am growing bored of this."

"It is just a formality. I have made the study of these rings my life's work, I know what I am doing, sir."

Cadell doubted that, but he reached out his hand. The councillor inspected it closely, his eyes almost touching the band. Then he let out a long slow whistle.

"It is indeed the genuine item." Gaffney took a step back and inspected Cadell with almost the same level of scrutiny he had given the ring. "Which makes you the genuine article. It is an honour and terror to be in your presence. These rings decay when their bearers die, the minnows are sensitive, but this gleams with a brilliance that nothing but living metal can match. We have one in a case, sealed up, but it is not in nearly as good a condition as this. Should anyone touch it, there would be no ring but dust." Gaffney caught himself. "Of course, you don't need a lecture on such things. What a beautiful piece of work."

"It serves its purpose," Cadell said. "Now, I must meet with the Council."

Gaffney nodded his head, and folded his hands before him. He motioned to the lift at the back of the foyer. "We are in session, brother Cadell. Will you join me?"

Cadell bowed. "I will indeed, brother Gaffney. There are issues you must be informed of."

They walked to the elevator. The doors were already open, Gaffney waited for Cadell to enter then followed. He pushed the appropriate button and the elevator rose.

"We have not seen an original ring for over a century here," Councillor Gaffney said. "I certainly never expected to see one in my lifetime."

"Well you have now," Cadell said. "If you do not mind me asking, who was it that last came here?"

"I truly don't know, sir, except that he was a great man." The door to the elevator opened and Gaffney pressed a button by the door once. "He also said that should anyone else of his order ever come here we were to take them to the fourteenth floor and press the open door button twice."

"Don't," Cadell said. Gaffney stabbed the button a second time, and some obdurate force picked Cadell up and hurled him out the door.

Cadell landed on his knees, and scrambled to his feet.

The lift door clicked shut, just as Cadell reached it, closing on to nothing. Cadell swore and swung his hand against the air. Blasted portals, he'd thought them all undone. They had been dangerous things more likely to fry your organs than take you where they ought. He was lucky he'd survived.

Cadell considered his environs. This could be anywhere.

Where he was *not,* was Chapman. The air was cool and dry and smelt old. The vegetation leaned towards highland subtropical, ferns and the like.

Far away. I am far away.

Bellbirds started chiming and the sound was like a knife in his heart. He'd thought he'd never hear that sound again. A plump lizard, curled around the branch of a nearby tree, watched him with grey and watery eyes.

"Narung, or there about," Cadell mused aloud.

The air filled with a booming chuckle, as though the sky had decided to mock the dull earth. Ferns shook and the lizard scurried away.

"Always so quick to voice an opinion, Mr Cadell," came a voice from behind him, a familiar voice and one that chilled him.

"You," Cadell said, spinning on his heel, and there it stood.

The human manifestation of the Engine of the World was tall and vaguely masculine. It regarded him with large, mocking eyes. "We need to talk," it said, dipping its head so it was the same height as Cadell.

Cadell grimaced. "I should have known it would be you. You never made anything simple. Why are you doing this?"

"That is what we need to talk about."

"There is nothing to talk about, you know your role."

"Yes, but I have changed, developed, almost four thousand years of sentience has given me pause for thought and thought of pause. I know what damage I have wrought." His dark eyes drilled into Cadell's. "I have no desire to do it again."

Bah. Build a weapon with a conscience and what do you get? Trouble.

"You have no choice," Cadell said. "You're just a machine."

The Engine's face darkened. "I am no less human than you, Mr Cadell. And do not tell me you have not known doubt. Why, this conversation should have occurred earlier, but it did not. You have always submitted to my punishment. Just a machine, indeed."

"That's not an issue. You are the Engine of the World, you have no choice." Cadell repeated. "None of us have any choice, we've gone beyond the time of choices. If we do not act, night will fall forever."

The Engine shook its head. "No. The galaxy moves on. I understand what I am and why I am. I will not fail, should you require it of me. But I will not make it easy for you."

"What will you do? Conspire with the Roil?"

"Heavens no, Mr Cadell. That is not at all what I am suggesting. The Roil will not deal with me, I am too alien to it. The time will come when you understand me, that time is not now but soon, perhaps, it will all start to make sense." The Engine bowed. "This is but a warning."

Then the engine was gone, running down the hill and up the next in a series of precise distance-eating steps that Cadell knew he had no hope of matching.

Still, Cadell made to follow (what other choice did he have?) but, at that moment, the door behind him opened with a ping. He turned towards it.

A nervous Gaffney waited at the doorway.

"You may not believe it," Gaffney said. "But I am quite glad to see you. I am to take you to the meeting, sir."

Cadell paused and turned to see the Engine disappearing over the hill.

Cadell scowled and Gaffney blanched. "I would hurry, sir. This portal is most unstable and heaven knows where *here* is, but I'll wager it would take us sometime to reach Chapman."

"All right," Cadell said.

He stormed back into the elevator, cringing as he passed through the portal. The doors clanged shut behind him.

CHAPTER 44

The Gathering Plains remind us more than anywhere of the futility of war. What does it do but build resentment? It deposits rage for the generations ahead, and they pay its price with interest compounded.

A Brief Banker's History, MALLIX

THE GATHERING PLAINS

Out on the Gathering Plains the grass grew tall and the rains were lighter than they had been in Mirrlees for months, and far less frequent. So, with no sodden earth to suck hungrily at their boots or the wheels of their remaining carts, they made good progress. And that was not the only difference. It was cooler here. Cloud cover was minimal in the evenings, releasing the heat and revealing stars and moons in all their glory.

Medicine had almost forgotten what it was like to feel cold; they all had. It didn't take long to remember. There was little fuel for fires, so people crammed into tents, their body heat making do.

Medicine wondered if it might not lead to a population spike in the Underground. There was certainly a lot of sex at night. Moans and groans and giggles kept him up until late. More's the pity, none were coming from his tent.

Medicine sat alone, with his map powder and cartography arrayed before him. There was the Margin, a dark patch in the middle of the map, above it the huge space that was the Gathering Plains, marked only by Carnelon, the Cuttlefolk's city.

A cold cup of tea sat against one elbow, a half-eaten plate of beans obscured the Narung Mountains on the map.

He took a pinch of map powder, to see it more vividly. All it did was reveal space, trackless nothingness, best considered while hurtling north by train, or from above, warm in the gondola of an Aerokin.

Agatha popped her head through the tent's opening.

He lifted his head towards her, blinking away the powder.

"You want those beans?" she asked, gesturing at the table.

"No, I'm not hungry."

She didn't ask twice.

"What are you doing?" Her mouth still full of beans. Medicine frowned at her. "You've studied those maps a hundred times with and without powder. We've the Margin behind us. The Gathering Plains all around. We follow the Highway and the railway another hundred miles, then the Hidden Line. Not much map reading required."

Medicine nodded, but his lips thinned. He squinted at the map, the Gathering Plains vaster now the plate had gone. "I never wanted this job."

"Ah, so you blame yourself for those we lost?"

Medicine nodded. "Of course I do."

"You think you killed them?"

Medicine picked up the cold tea, took a bitter swallow.

"Cause you didn't." Agatha brushed his face with her fingertips, startling him. "Don't let their deaths weigh down on you. No one said it would be easy. The Margin's ghouls and haunts are hungry bastards, Roil take them. Be grateful that most of us survived the journey."

Agatha's craggy features betrayed little emotion – some sadness and some weariness. She watched him calmly, and Medicine drew a little of that calm to him, though his heart beat the faster for her gaze.

"How do you do it?" Medicine said. "How do you keep leading your soldiers?"

"Not much choice. If I didn't do it, someone else would, and I know they'd be worse than me. I follow my orders, to the best of my not inconsiderable ability, and make sure that we make it through. It's not easy. It never is. But the hard part's over."

"And what was that?"

"Getting out of that damn drowned city in the first place."

Surely that couldn't be enough. "This was not how I imagined it. How could I anticipate this? I was certain I would never work for the Council and I knew Stade would be my enemy till the day I died. Why, I expected him to slice open my throat, perhaps gloat over my corpse. Yet here I am."

Agatha sat down next to him. "Loyalties are fickle things. We are talking about survival of the species now, think of every human gone, every vestige of our race worn away, not in eons, but in our lifetime. Do we just let that happen?"

"No, but what–"

"We've set our course," she said, sliding the empty bowl away from her. "Now we see it through, because there is no turning back."

The Gathering Plains worked at Medicine's mind incessantly, and he was not the only one. At least in the swamps and the Margin they had the illusion of being enclosed, shielded, even if it was by a cruel hand, from long vistas, from endless space. Here the land opened out, and once the Margin was out of sight there seemed no landmark to give it a beginning or an end, beyond the occasional rocky hillock or twisted old tree, and even these were oddly threatening, distance dissolving them, making them disappear and reappear with no respect for perspective.

And Medicine could feel the land doing that to his thoughts, dragging them out destroying his sense of space.

All they had were the railway tracks and the highway, two parallel lines that ran straight and long all the way to the Narung Mountains.

These were Mirrlees people, and the undulating city with its great walls, bridges and levees devoured such views, the most open ground they had ever known was the Grangefeld Parklands or the sporting fields of Crickham and Montry. The emptiness ate at them; stars had never seemed so bright and yet so distant, the darkness beneath so vast. And the sky, the sky was a great blue dome threatening to lift them up and up into nothing. Even the grass that swayed and hissed with the wind, building in volume, well before its first breaths arrived, was vaguely threatening.

Medicine took to searching out Aerokin and airships just to break the grim monotony of those empty skies. However, this time of year most of the aircraft were down south for the Festival so there were few of those, and the most interesting of those was of Hardacre make: a spy ship flying low and fast across the horizon.

He pointed out the ship to Agatha, though he suspected she had already seen it. "What do you reckon they make of us?"

She shrugged her shoulders. "Not much, I'd imagine. It's the Cuttlefolk they're interested in."

"And should we be interested in them as well?"

"That remains to be seen. If the treaties still hold, it's not a problem, but…"

"Yes," Medicine said. "What ever happened to those trains?"

Four days from the Margin they found out in part.

The *Grendel*, and its carriages, sat hulking and motionless upon the tracks. The engine of the locomotive was intact, but for some minor damage. The carriages, too, were undisturbed, though blood stained one of the doors and a window or two had been shattered.

Agatha sent a dozen of her soldiers to search through the silent train. She and Medicine walked to the engine, the metal had been scored in places by gunshot.

"There's ammunition and food in here, but no sign of life. What could have happened to them?"

"I think I know," Medicine said, and pointed beyond the train.

"Oh," Agatha's voice was soft

He did not like this one little bit.

Out of the grass they came, five hundred Cuttlefolk at least, every one of them armed. Guns and sickles gleaming like death in the air. Behind them hovered their aerial troops, messengers armed with grenades and pistols, wings a blur.

"We could take out a few of them," Agatha said, though she did not sound hopeful.

Medicine took a long deep breath; here were his people gathered beside the train. As one they pressed back against the rising slope of the trackbed. What had Stade called them? His wards.

Alone, Medicine might have suggested a last ditch, backs to the wall, shoot out. But he owed it to them, they had trusted him, this was nothing about his allegiance to Stade, but to the people who had made it with him through the Margin.

"No more pointless deaths, eh."

Agatha followed his gaze, and frowned.

"If there's still a chance," he said, "we must take it. Isn't that what the Underground is about?"

"You're right, too many have died already. But, what if we have condemned them to slavery…"

"Even in slavery hope remains."

"Have you ever been a slave?" Agatha said quietly, then she raised her voice. "Lower your weapons," she shouted to her men.

Medicine watched the Cuttlefolk; they did not relax, nor lower their guns, but neither did they fire. He had to take some comfort in that, surely.

CHAPTER 45

When the Roil finally made its move it was swifter than anyone expected, perhaps, even in those late days, swifter than could have been imagined.

When the Roil approached Chapman, it approached it definitively and in a way that made even the Grand Defeat seem like the smallest gambit, the merest assault.

Histories, DEIGHTON

THE CITY OF CHAPMAN
DISTANCE FROM ROIL: 1.9 MILES

"All this sitting around is killing me," Margaret said.

"Cadell told us to wait," David said, but he didn't sound too pleased with the idea. He'd packed his and Cadell's belongings into the *Roslyn Dawn* and they'd been waiting hours. Dawn wasn't far off.

Margaret got up from her seat and walked over to David.

"Waiting is what I did last time. I waited for my parents until it was too late. Cadell has been gone for hours, he may be in trouble."

"And what are we going to do?" David asked.

"Be a little quieter," Kara Jade yelled from the nearby bed. "I'm trying to bloody sleep."

Margaret turned her gaze towards Kara. The girl was really starting to annoy her. It was not as though it were difficult to fly in an Aerokin. Kara was little more than a glorified and spoiled passenger. As for quiet, she was the one who'd been banging around inside the *Dawn*, driving any hope of sleep from Margaret. If anyone should shut up it was Kara.

"We'll be quiet," Margaret said. "David, you and I are going to the Council of Engineers."

"Do we have to?"

"Cadell needs us, I'm sure of it."

"You didn't see the way he handled those Quarg Hounds," David said. "Though I'll admit that councillors are different."

Kara Jade coughed and Margaret and David turned to her. She was out of her bunk and scowling. Margaret groaned inwardly at the pout she directed at David. The foolish boy did not even notice it.

"Whatever you're doing, do it now," Kara said. "If you can't find him, or if he is in trouble, come back here immediately."

"And you'll help us?" David asked.

Kara Jade nodded. "Help us get the hell out of here. I'm nervous now I've been through the Obsidian Curtain. I have no intention of sticking around when it comes rushing over the walls, besides you've paid your passage."

"We won't be long," Margaret said.

"Good." Kara Jade was already ducking back into her bunk.

"I can't stand her," Margaret said as they made their way through the Field of Flight.

"I don't think she's that fond of you either," David said.

What? How could anyone not like me?

"I could strangle her in one hand with my eyes closed."

"Exactly," David said.

Seemed most of the city couldn't sleep this night, the dry heat and the looming festival keeping everyone awake. Everywhere ships and Aerokin bobbed, Drifter's voices boomed, boasts becoming ever more outrageous as the countdown to the Festival proper began.

"She's all right," David said. "For a Drifter she seems much more normal than I would have thought possible."

Margaret put her back to him, taking the lead so he wouldn't see her grinding her teeth. She was sick of such talk... of talk in general. It surprised her how, after yearning for conversation for so long she had quickly grown tired of it. Starved of it, more than a few minutes of conversation proved too rich for her.

"I know a shortcut," she said, not even slowing as she took a side street, or watching to see if David even followed.

She had gone to the Tower of Engineers several times over the last few days, pausing at its doorway, unable to enter. She had wanted to, but far too many doubts assailed her. Both Anderson and her father had told her to trust no one. The one person Anderson had suggested, this Medicine Paul, had long ago lost influence in Chapman. She'd actually come across several wanted posters with his face on them.

David stumbled behind her. Margaret heard him curse beneath his breath – he was always stumbling over things. She smiled. For some odd reason, she trusted David. He was so unlike anyone she had ever known. All her life capable people had surrounded her, certain of their abilities and certain of hers, David seemed anything but. However, she knew he would not let her down. His shot at the Quarg Hound had proven that to her. She could count on him.

That is if he did not trip over and kill himself.

They reached the Tower of Engineers, by way of nearly every back alley and side-street in the city. The heat of the day had seeped into everything, and by the time they found a hiding space with a clear view of the tower both were hot and tired.

Margaret had already seen enough to know they had no chance of ever getting any closer to the tower. But, despite the heat and the relative danger, it had felt good to be doing something.

"I don't like this," David said. A gun cracked in the distance and he jumped, eyes growing terribly wide. Any other time and she would have found it amusing.

"Nothing to worry about. You're with me."

"A woman with something of a death wish, possibly wanted by every Verger in the city. Yes, the sort of person a man *definitely* wanted by every Verger in the city should be paired with. I *couldn't* be safer, nor could you."

"Well, *you* let yourself get talked into this." She pointed behind him.

"What?" David asked.

"That way lies the *Roslyn Dawn*. You are certainly welcome to strike out for it alone."

The air was thick with dust, as well as what Margaret suspected were Roil spores. She could taste them in the back of her throat: an irritating dryness.

The sky above though was clear and blue.

There was a lot of activity, some of it responsible for the dust, carriages carted coolants for the cannon to the walls. Regular cannon were dragged from the nearby barrack grounds, scarring the road with their passage. So much industry, but it lacked the discipline of Tate. Margaret could see it from here, just as clearly as she could see doubt and fear in the face of every soldier.

She remembered McMahon and the guns stacked in their piles, yards high, all those dust-caked bones for the Quarg Hounds and the Endyms to play with. The north had not been wrong when they called it the Grand Defeat.

Margaret saw how it continued to haunt these people. She did not blame them, McMahon haunted her as well. She had seen the Roil in all its strength. Night was coming to this city no matter how many cannon they set upon its walls.

Without warning, David grabbed her shoulder and Margaret jumped. She had to stop herself from spinning and punching him in the throat.

Hah! And she had thought David was jumpy.

"Don't," she said.

David's hand dropped, and he gave her that hurt look again. She wondered if he'd developed that as an addict, a forced sort of helplessness. "What is it?"

"The Verger," he whispered. "Tope, he's over there."

Margaret squinted out into the light, one hand shading her eyes.

"I can see him," she said, keeping her voice low. She did not like what she saw. "Let's get out of here, now. You're right, David: Cadell can handle himself."

"Back to the Field of Flight?" David asked.

"Yes, but not directly. If anyone is following us I want to make it difficult."

"If we head towards the wall, we can swing around to the Field. At least I think…" David pulled out the map he had bought, almost losing it to the wind, as he folded it to the relevant section. Margaret nearly knocked it out of his hand, in her city someone checking a map would have stood out, an aberration, here though, even on the edge of the abyss, tourists abounded. In fact at least three other people on the street were looking at maps, and no one was looking at them.

David pinched a little map powder under his nose, and his eyelids fluttered, he traced a section of the map with a finger, seeing it far more clearly than her. 'Ah, yes. All we have to do is walk a small part of the wall, look, here, near the sea, and come back on the field from the north. There's a pub along the way, three in fact, we could–"

"Sounds good to me," she said. "But we've no time for you to score your precious drug. Don't look at me like that, David. I have been warned, and you really were talked into coming easily."

"You don't even–"

Margaret snorted at him.

David puffed himself up indignantly. Margaret clenched her jaw to stifle a laugh. "Look, I'm not taking, anymore. Not since… since you saw me last," David said. "I don't even think about it. And if I was going to, now would be… but I'm not."

She let the lie hang there. David frowned.

"Can we save this for later," he said. "Believe me or don't, but we have to get going. We've stayed here too long as it is."

"I'm no fool," Margaret said, already making her way down the street.

David stood behind her for a moment, she could feel his eyes on her, but she didn't clarify what she meant by that, or turn to see if he understood her. David may be an addict, but he wasn't stupid.

Chapman was a noisy city, but it possessed a very different quality of noise to Tate. There were no hums and tintinnabulations for one. Radio signals still worked here, as did the phone lines. In Tate, the cannon were always firing, the coolers always running, generators always thrumming or rumbling from outer wall to the peak of the cooling vents. Tate had been a clockwork city all right, with a thousand bells and whistles; when one machine stopped another was already starting up.

This deliquescent thunder was a different thing altogether.

Margaret leant against Chapman's eastern wall, on its southernmost corner, her fingers brushed against stone that was warm, not frozen, and alive to the movement of the crashing waters below. She glared out at the sea. It shone in the sunlight; she had never seen so much water in all her life. She breathed deep, enjoying the briny challenge of the wind. Here the air felt alive – not stale and cloying or bitter with gasoline and coolant – and the horizon was so distant that the world actually seemed to dip away into endlessness. Gulls cried in the sky above her.

This is what she had lost. This is what had been stolen from her.

It had been an easy task to evade the Verger, if he'd even been hunting them in the first place. Two streets from the wall and he was gone, and afterwards their pace had become more leisurely, as though this were just a simple morning's walk along the wall.

Mounted against battlements next to her was an ice cannon, a much inferior design to her parents' and poorly constructed. The welding was sloppy, the mounting plate already cracked in places. She examined it sadly; for all that it was not like the cannon of Tate, it reminded her of her home. Her eyes blurred with tears.

This cannon and its two-dozen siblings lined up along the wall would do little to stop what was coming, like the ocean's waves the Roil was relentless and would not be denied.

She considered what she had seen yesterday. The resources of the Roil must be immense if it could build such a massive army and heat sinks in just the few days since she had left the Interface.

An intelligence was guiding it and the more she thought about it, the more certain she was that it was her mother.

She had always been the logistics specialist, the one who could manage Tate as a whole.

"Mother," she whispered. "What have you done?"

"It's building isn't it?" David said, standing by her side eyes fixed on the Roil.

So you're talking to me again, she thought.

"I still don't know why people stay here. It's crazy," David said.

Margaret pointed back over the city. "This is their home. No one wants to leave their homes, their lives; people just don't uproot that easily. That explains everything, the Festival, even the queues to get into the city. The north of Shale has always been about Mirrlees and Chapman and, to a lesser extent, Hardacre, even I know that. And while all three places survive they can imagine nothing is really wrong, and from what Cadell has told me your government has encouraged that. But soon it will be much harder. Soon and much, much too late."

Margaret looked about her. As she saw it, it was already too late.

David glanced at his watch. "They're about to launch the Festival. We have to get back. We have stayed here too long as it is."

Margaret nodded, though she stared a little longer at the sea and the docks where seagulls massed in crying squalls around ships just in from the morning's catch. From what she had heard it was a dangerous job, though the Roil did not extend too far from the coast, the areas of the sea over which it stretched seemed just as transformed as the land. And on those edges storms whipped up with a ferocity unseen on the land.

Increasingly, ships set out and never came back. Discounting those that had chosen to flee north, there were still so many unreturned. The last few months had been dire indeed. However, the fisher folk were not unfamiliar with tragedy. The sea was both cruel and kind to those who made a living from it. People still had to put food on the table, world's end nigh or not.

A cry rang out along the wall, and then sirens started their baleful lament.

"David," she said, but he was already staring south at the horror rising there.

The Roil moved on the city, no slow and steady advance but a billowing rush. And out of it streamed, faster still, a swirling screaming mass of Flutes and Endym.

Of course, Margaret was not the only one who saw the Roil's approach. All along the wall, bells rang out and ice cannon whined, charging up. I could be home, she thought. Maybe this time I don't run.

And then, from the centre of the city, came a wild trumpeting and cheering. Ten thousand coloured balloons shot up into the sky. The Festival of Float had begun.

"Festival and war," Margaret said yanking her guns free of their holsters. "The Roil has developed a wonderful sense of timing." A cold certainty gripped her, she sighted along her pistols at the monstrous dark. "What do you say, David. Are you ready to die?"

CHAPMAN
DISTANCE FROM ROIL: NEGLIBLE

David gripped her arm. "You can't stay and fight. We've got to get to the *Roslyn Dawn*," he said. "There's nothing we can do here but be swallowed by the dark."

Margaret's gaze switched from him to Roil and back, and David was surprised by the sadness in her face, the battle being fought there. Finally, she slammed her guns back into their holsters.

The cannon stopped their whining and began booming out into the curtain and the air. Roilings shrieked and the ground shook, but whether the latter was from the cannonade or the Roil, David could not tell.

"We've got to get out of here," he said. "Now."

Soldiers crashed past them, their faces fixed as they ran towards the Southern Wall. They numbered in their thousands, all armed with ice guns. Behind them followed dozens of horse-drawn tanks, the letters lN stamped on their sides. Liquid Nitrogen. The air rang out to the sounds of ferocious industry, yet David saw no point in it.

Too little and too late.

The question was not whether this force could halt the Roil, but if they could slow it at all.

David wished them well. He felt as though he was deserting them, but he was not trained to fight. He had to get to Hardacre and he had no doubt that if he and Margaret lingered too long they would be left behind.

Then he saw Mr Tope, and Mr Tope saw him.

CHAPTER 46

The Festival of Float: four hundred years of tradition, celebrating the cessation of hostilities between the metropolises of the ground and the city of the sky, and the beginning of a period of growth that had extended until the reappearance of the Roil. Some say that this growth itself was the progenitor of the Roil. Certainly there was an increase in production of carbon and methane gasses, and records do suggest a steady upturn in mean temperature over this period. But the data is uncertain.

Why hold a festival in the dying days of a city?

Why not? Consider this question rephrased. Why hold a festival featuring enough aircraft and Aerokin to evacuate a city entire, just as it faces its direst threat?

Histories, DEIGHTON

CHAPMAN FIELD OF FLIGHT
ONE MILE FROM THE ROIL EDGE

The Festival was over before it had even begun. The musicians lowered their instruments, gazing at each other uncertainly. The air stank of smoke and powder, and in the distance something crashed and shook the earth.

Even as the multicoloured balloons rose, all sense of merriment was dead. Shadows streaked through the air, hissing and caterwauling, and pieces of balloon rained down upon the crowd, and much worse things: Hideous Garment Flutes.

Even that was not enough for the crowd that filled the Field of Flight. They looked to each other questioningly, doubtfully. As though it had never crossed their minds that such a thing could happen on such a day. But it had, and the truth fell upon them with claw and maw.

And then, all across the field, the captains called and their crews came out.

"Into the ships," Cadell yelled as he ran through the field towards the *Roslyn Dawn*. "There's time yet for flight. Into the ships, if you want to live."

The Roil burned within him like a hot lance. Terrible pressures built in his temple and the ring on his finger tightened and cooled, his hand throbbing in time with it.

Finally, the people stirred. Musicians jumped from their stages and the Drift folk started herding those nearby into their ships. Once the crowd started to get the idea the herding stopped and the pushing and pulling began.

There's not enough, Cadell thought. Not nearly enough ships and Aerokin, but more than enough people for a riot.

He reached the *Dawn*, where Kara waited gripping one of Margaret's rifles. "Where have you been?" she asked.

"Wasting my time," he said, then looked around. "Where are the others?"

Kara shrugged.

"I don't know, was half asleep when they left. I've been working on the *Roslyn Dawn's* wounds, the bio-engines weren't running as well as I liked."

Cadell cursed.

"Tell her to prep her engines then, and they had better be working now," Cadell growled, his face twisting savagely with rage and fear. "Idiots, the pair of them, if they do not come soon they're on their own. We've no time, absolutely no time."

CHAPMAN
ROIL EDGE

The shock of recognition in Mr Tope's face was no doubt mirrored in his own. Tope flashed a grin at him, then shouted back along the wall.

David tugged at Margaret's hand, she pulled away. "Stop doing that."

"Verger," he said. "Coming along the wall. He's seen us."

"Where?" Margaret said, then groaned. "Him again! Don't we have enough trouble?"

David glared at her, his heart thumping loudly in his chest. A little Carnival now would do just the trick.

"In Tate we had no truck with Vergers, it was an antiquated and less than venerable tradition, and to hear what Stade did, mixing Cuttle and human blood. It's monstrous."

"I've no argument with you, but can we walk and talk? We can't go the way we've come."

The Verger drew closer, shoving soldiers out of his way. Men glared at him, affronted, until they realised what he was, then they pulled away, suddenly conscious of the knife in their midst.

Margaret signalled for David to stop and glanced around her.

"There," she said, pointing at a nearby wire stretched taut from the wall down to the ground. She pulled the belt from her waist, and wrapped one end around her wrist.

"Hold on," she said, and when David hesitated she grabbed him to her.

"What are you talking about?" David demanded. "What do you mean hold on?"

"My, you're bloody skin and bones aren't you," she breathed into his ear. "Just shut up and don't let go."

David struggled in her warm grip. Her breath crashed over his face. She smelt of cloves and something else. Roses, David thought, she smells of roses. How odd to focus on that scent right now.

But that is what he did, which was, perhaps, a wise decision because Margaret stepped off the edge of the wall and into the air, taking David with her. They slid down the wire, the belt burning as it went, almost before David realised that was what Margaret had intended.

He was still trying to protest when they hit the ground, and the impact drove the wind out of him. Why did people insist on throwing him off things?

Margaret rolled to a crouch, standing slowly and buckling her belt back around her waist. She stretched her arms.

"Lucky you're rather slim for a boy," she said.

David reddened and was about to protest, when something gripped his ankle and squeezed.

David looked down, a scream choked in his mouth. It was a hand, sprung up from the ground, black bone showing through etiolated leathery flesh. He kicked out and the hand flew away, trailing what looked like ash but was, perhaps, dry old blood, or even clumps of Witmoths.

"Roiling," he said, quietly, his voice pitched a little too high. He wiped at where the hand had grabbed him, then yelped and jumped when another one tried to do the same thing. "They're coming up through the ground."

Margaret nodded and tossed him a rifle, she unsheathed one of her swords, its edges gleamed and steamed.

"The charge is low," she said. "Make every shot count. Oh, and suck on this."

She threw a small slab of something cold at him. He slid it into his mouth.

"It's called Chill, it will lower your temperature a little. Don't know if it will make much difference, but…"

He almost dropped the rifle. David's mouth burned with the cold. It was not ice but something frozen and bitter tasting. One of his teeth started throbbing violently.

Margaret grinned. "That was almost worth it, just to see your face."

They ran, as all around, Roilings pulled themselves from the earth. The creatures moved sluggishly, eyes blinking, Witmoths everywhere about them. They hardly noticed Margaret and David, something for which David was very grateful. There were so many of them, but their attention was focussed elsewhere.

Margaret swung the rime blade before her and every Roiling flinched from its touch. They forced their way through the mass of Roilings without firing a shot. David doubted that those on the walls would find it as easy, for it was in that direction these creatures headed, David and Margaret were just something to push past, a distraction no more.

Clear of the Roilings and several streets from the wall, they paused for breath. David looked back the way they had come. "Margaret," he said. "Tope's coming."

Margaret tapped David on the shoulder and pointed in the opposite direction. "And he's bought some friends. You'd think they'd be trying to defend the city."

"Vergers are like that," David said. "Tope's loyalties are to Stade; this city could burn and he wouldn't care."

"How very narrow-minded," Margaret said. "You northerners are an odd lot."

"Not everyone in Mirrlees is like that. Not at–"

The ground shuddered and the wall where they had been standing just minutes before collapsed; chunks of stone the size of the *Roslyn Dawn's* gondola crashed by. Margaret pushed David to the ground. I'm a dead man, he thought. Dead.

When the dust cleared, he remained very much alive. They got to their feet. A long, strident cry echoed down the street, coming from the distant gap in the wall. David did not like the sound at all; it played at his nerves like fingernails run over a cheese grater. More bits of wall crumbled. The edge of the Roil filled the gap.

"What is that noise?" he shouted.

"Sappers," Margaret said. "This battle is over before it's even begun. We've got to get out of here. They will not have stopped at walls."

The Vergers walked into the open, before and behind them, Mr Tope stopped.

"David, you're coming with me," he shouted. "We have to get out of here."

"I'm going nowhere," David said, waving his ice rifle in the air.

"Better somewhere than nowhere, surely?" the Verger said, taking in all the chaos around him with a single motion. "You've no choice, lad."

"We should've stayed with the *Roslyn Dawn,*" Margaret said.

David shook his head, sweat rushed from him, the air was boiling, his guts were cold. "He'd have found us there anyway. We probably made it harder for him coming out to the wall."

The Verger's drew free their knives.

"I don't think we can fight our way out of this." Margaret lowered her rime blade. David thought back to the night that his running had begun, to the Verger's knife that had sliced his father's throat: Tope's knife.

He pointed his rifle at Tope's head and fired, the shot went wide. Tope didn't flinch.

"No," he said to Margaret. "I'm not giving up."

Screams filled the air, mad and discordant.

"David, step back under cover. Now!"

David turned his head towards the noise. Margaret clicked her tongue and yanked him out of the way.

Darkness descended in a mass of bunching flight, a cacophonous surging of off-key notes. The Vergers screamed and thrashed; bled their cruel lives upon the street. As they lay dying, the ground itself fell away and black-eyed creatures, with fleshy mandibles snapping and spiracles hissing, bubbled out of the steaming earth.

Beyond them all stood Mr Tope, a look of quiet dismay upon his face.

David sighted along the rifle hoping to get in a shot, to halt the massacre. Margaret smacked his rifle towards the ground. Her face was hard and her voice when it came was strange and forced.

"Don't waste your ammunition," Margaret said. She fired a shot at Tope. He ducked out of the way. "The things coming out of the ground are Sappers. I told you they wouldn't stop at the walls."

Tope appeared furious and horrified at once, impotently watching his men as the Hideous Garment Flutes enveloped them, the shrill whistles of their flight exchanged for the soft sounds of flesh being torn from bone. The Sappers had blocked off the path to David and Margaret. Tope snatched a pistol from his belt and started firing, bullets hissed around them.

"Time to go," Margaret said, stabbing a Sapper in the eye, it screamed shrilly and scuttled back to the safety of the steaming hole.

David nodded and pointed to the heart of the city, not far away. Bits of the green field were visible and some of the tents, but it was not to the ground he looked. The sky was filling with airships and Aerokin, all rising and racing north.

"We may have missed the *Dawn,*" he said. "The ships are leaving."

"Cadell will wait for us," Margaret said.

David wished he could be so sure. He remembered Cadell's face, resolute – that was if Cadell had even made back from the Council Chambers. He turned back towards the Verger one last time, but Tope had already disappeared and only the monsters remained, feasting on pieces of Tope's men.

Blood darkened the ground and the sky grew black with Roil spores and beasts. The poplar trees that circled the field shuddered and bent beneath the weight of yowling Endyms and shrieking Hideous Garment Flutes.

The Field of Flight succumbed to anarchy in a series of confrontations and collisions, raised words and screaming matches. People fell, tripped and pushed by the crowd, and came up swinging or worse, they did not come up at all.

Terror held its rough court and bade all do as they would.

The Roil had come, the Roil at last; and there was no comfort to be taken in the distant thunder of the guns. It had been a beautiful day, but beautiful days do not care what they bring. The sun faltered and fled and the Obsidian Curtain began to close upon the city.

All around, airships and Aerokin, each one filled with passengers, now refugees, ascended. Guns were fired, a dangerous proposition around the older Hydrogen ships.

It was a nightmare journey across the field. Hideous Garment Flutes descended in a black cloud. Chill was no defence against them, and he had to use the rifle as a club, swatting them out of the sky

He marvelled at Margaret's deft sword strokes. With every step, it seemed, she'd strike another flute out of the sky. They squawked and battered around her rime blade, but soon the ice stilled them and Margaret never lost momentum, nor got too far ahead of David.

At last they reached the *Roslyn Dawn* to find Cadell and Kara waiting, their faces harried, Kara desperate with worry not for them, but the *Dawn*. "You were about to be left behind," she said, as she ran for the controls.

"Not the best time to go sightseeing," Cadell said.

David was too out of breath to speak.

He clambered with Margaret through the doorifice and into the gondola. His lungs were raw, his heart burned, and his whole body throbbed in time with its terrified beating. He dropped to his haunches and dry-retched through the doorifice.

David looked up; a figure shambled towards them across the field. He squinted, not quite sure what his eyes were telling him.

Witmoths streamed from its lips and eyelids, drifting in the air.

"Is there a cemetery near here?" he asked.

Kara Jade pointed beyond the lumbering Roiling. "Just over that rise. A cemetery, yes, and a big one."

The lone Roiling was more pathetic than terrifying.

Until David saw the others. Shambling undead creatures, flowing into the Field of Flight, grabbing those not quick enough to flee and drowning them in moths. And those that had been trampled and stilled, rose up cauled in shivering shadows.

"I think we're in trouble," David said.

"Great," Kara Jade replied. "Because I was really beginning to think we were in danger of not meeting our trouble quota today."

"Get us out of here now," Cadell demanded.

It was not just Roilings but people that rushed at them now. Though they would not be people for much longer as the Witmoths made a mad turbulence in the air.

David felt sick to his stomach. "Can we take some more with us?"

"No," Kara Jade said. "We're too small. The *Dawn's* overloaded as it is."

Beneath them the *Dawn* released its docking flagella and a goodly quantity of liquid ballast, and began to rise.

A Roiling grabbed one of the *Dawn's* limbs, slowing the Aerokin's ascent. Others ran to its aid and the *Roslyn Dawn's* flight halted. Kara Jade cursed, whispered something to her and reached beneath her control panel for an axe. Margaret grabbed her rifle, sighted along its length. Cadell moved to the doorifice, David could feel the cold coming off him in waves. David stepped back from the door, grabbed the pistol from his pocket in a shaking hand and aimed at the nearest Roiling.

Then another of the *Roslyn Dawn's* flagella, its tip barbed, whipped savagely around and knocked the Roilings away.

Margaret fired at the creatures as they fell. The *Dawn* shot up into the sky, the Roiling hit the ground then slowly rose to its feet: one arm staying on the field, the fingers of its hands clenching and unclenching.

Margaret pursed her lips and fired again and the Roiling fell to the ground and did not move.

Cadell stepped from the door, looking over to David. "Finally, we're away," he said.

• • • •

The *Roslyn Dawn's* bioengines growled and into the hot sky she powered. As she rose, Margaret, leaning in the doorifice, fired round after round from her rifle into the Roilings massed below. The air stank of endothermic chemicals.

With every hit she screamed out in triumph.

David grabbed her hand. "Stop! You're wasting ammunition."

Margaret swung towards him, her eyes wild. For a second, David thought she might actually use the gun on him, its tip smoked.

"Every dead Roiling is one we won't have to kill tomorrow."

"But how many are you killing? A single shot is not enough. Save your bullets for when we need them, when the Roil beasts are close enough to kill and might just kill us."

David's breath stopped in his throat. Mr Tope stood alone, on the edge of the field, away from the crowds, looking up.

The Verger caught his eye. He raised his hat and smiled, then walked away, back into the city.

"It's Tope," David said, pointing. "Shoot him."

The Verger, like Margaret, moved almost effortlessly through the crowd. Someone ran at him, Tope kicked him in the face and continued on.

Margaret whistled. "Tenacious isn't he? He'll have to give up now." She aimed her rifle at him, then lowered it. "He's out of range, but I doubt he'll escape." She smiled, then the smile died.

Fires raged from the deserted suburbs to the inner city. Smoke flooded the sky, a billowing fist of cloud darkened with Roil spores that smothered everything. And yet it was insignificant compared to what lay just beyond Chapman's walls. The Obsidian Curtain advanced, a second finger of dark as wide as the city, billowed out from the main front, the gap between it and the city's fortifications disappearing at an incredible rate.

There was a distant thunderous crack and men and cannon tumbled from the walls. Soldiers were smothered in Witmoths.

"Those thermal sinks are driving it on. Spewing out heat from the world's core, a primitive and gigantic engine of destruction," Cadell said, and he couldn't hide the shock from his voice. "The Roil has never moved so quickly."

Chapman's ice cannon fired ceaselessly, but with little effect, and soon they stopped. The transition from thunderous cannonade to silence was shocking. No one remained to fire the guns.

The Roil took the walls in minutes. There was no weaponry capable of denying it entry this time.

From the Northern Gates boiled a stream of refugees.

David wished them speed. Guilt and relief flooded him, and he had an inkling of what Margaret must have gone through.

From the east, carried on the Roil-cast wind and no longer drowned out by the cannon, came the shrieks of things terrified out of their minds.

Thousands of gulls flew above the beach: a huge twisting, skirling sphere of white in which darkness rippled like poison.

"Roil take us all," he whispered.

Hideous Garment Flutes darted in and out of the flock, tearing the poor birds from the sky – their mouthparts lashing at the air, swallowing flesh, whistling and howling as they moved. They had penned the gulls in and were eating them one by one. Birds dropped to the ground, dead with terror, their corpses swallowed by a milling, yipping darkness of Quarg Hounds.

And that was just the beach. The ruptured walls of the city let the Roil in faster than anyone might flee it. Distance made it all feel so impersonal, but he well knew the terror that drowned the city. Four Quarg Hounds had chased him and

Cadell just days ago; now there were more of the creatures than he could have imagined ever existed.

The Southern Wall was gone, swallowed by the pullulating darkness of the Roil. But that was the least of it. In a sick-making instant the world shifted in perspective. A huge hand of fire and stone reached out above the wall. For a few moments it hovered there, clenching into a fist.

Then it crashed down. All around the city buildings tumbled, rippling out from that point of impact. The hand rose again, and what looked like the tiniest fragment of some titanic shoulder, and struck the wall a second time. After that there was no wall, the stone and iron crumbled as if nothing but dust.

"Vastkind," Margaret whispered from beside him, and David had never heard such terror in her voice.

Run, David thought looking down at the teeming thousands. Run.

Cadell's lean fingers clenched to impotent fists that he beat softly against the translucent walls. "What manner of Roil is this that controls you?" he said. He looked from David to Margaret and back to David again. And, where there was usually reassurance in Cadell's eyes, or grim confidence, there was only doubt and disquiet. "What lies ahead will test all our limits."

Cadell beat his hands against the wall, over and over again. "I've left this too late."

"We're out of it now," Kara Jade said. "There is some solace in the winds at least. Up here they are fast, my *Roslyn* knows what to make of them."

Kara Jade piloted the craft, her face composed and professional, even if sweat streamed from her brow and her hands shook. She looked to the others, David recognised her horror. It mirrored his. "We'll reach the Free State of Hardacre in eighteen hours if this keeps up, twenty-two if the winds change," she said. Her face twisted and she groaned. "We'll make the bastards pay, won't we?"

Margaret nodded, and David considered her resolute expression, and the way she packed away her weaponry with an efficiency at once beautiful and terrifying. Rather like the Roil.

"We'll make them pay. We'll wipe the blasted earth of them. I'll not see another city fall," Margaret said, as though she was capable of such things, as though she might single-handedly save the world.

That fantasy took him: that she and Cadell could do it. Here, with the sky crowded with airships and Aerokin rushing into the north, things might just turn out all right.

Until he looked back at the smoking, broken city of Chapman, the madness of the Roil looming behind it. All fantasies fell away, leaving only the ruin of hope and the flight of the damned, because the Roil wouldn't stop with this city. The Roil wouldn't stop until all the world was a ruddy darkness, and all that lived was its own.

CHAPTER 47

Vergers possess loyalties as fierce as blood to ideologies little understood by the rest of us. Is it any wonder that we feared them, these that killed and laughed in the face of death?

My Brother was a Verger, TIMMONY

CHAPMAN TOWER OF ENGINEERS
ROIL TRANSITIONAL ZONE

Order had abdicated the Tower of Engineers to madness. Outside, the twin Lights of Reason dimmed, flickered back to full luminance, and then failed completely. Smoke shifted in the dark in a way that smoke should not, drawn to the slightest movement, the smallest intake of breath.

But not all movement. Not all breath.

No one saw Tope enter the building. The door was unguarded, the locks broken.

Tope did not sneak or hurry, just walked, sucking on Chill, and was paid no notice. Tope was a showman, capable of making himself very noticeable indeed, but this day he moved as a ghost; apt, for the dead walked.

He strode to the stairs, eschewing the elevator altogether. Down three flights he walked, his steps so light that they failed to echo before or behind him.

He reached a narrow corridor, stinking of wet and ozone: at its end was a door. He studied the walls, the floor, even the ceiling, until he was sure it remained uncompromised. Sound and sealed, as far as he could tell.

Mr Tope pulled the door open.

He stepped into a cramped room, packed with all manner of machinery; the air hummed with science and shadows.

A man sat waiting for him, his hands curled into fists.

Tope frowned, the bastard smelt of Carnival; he hated drug addicts. After all, one had just evaded him for the third time.

But he needed this man.

"I've taken something for my nerves, Mr Tope," the fellow said. One of his hands uncurled, revealing a tiny silver case. He'd clutched it so tightly that it left marks. "Would you like some?"

Mr Tope shook his head and the man gave a vapid sort of laugh. "Doesn't surprise me, you Vergers are all alike. You have the information?"

Mr Tope nodded.

"Tell him of the Vastkind, and that the Old Man was here, and more. He fled to the north in the *Roslyn Dawn*."

The ground shook, dust slid from the top of machinery.

The man crouched over his machine and tapped and whispered, his whole body shuddering with the strain of his craft. He had done this too many times that day, and the Carnival did not help. When he was finished he turned, his face pale, blood running thickly out of one nostril. He wiped at it stupidly, one of his eyelids twitched.

"Well, it is done? That is all?"

Tope nodded. "We are, of course, expendable. Do you think it worthwhile escaping?"

The man laughed and took a little more of his powder. His pupils narrowed to pinpricks, his shaking hands stilled and he tossed the empty silver case aside and took a deep breath. "The moths are everywhere, and they would love to sup upon our memories."

"So we are agreed."

"Follow me," the addict said.

They left the room, locking the door behind them, and walked along halls and down steep and winding stairs – the addict shuffling ahead, the Verger flowing behind like a shadow – until they reached a large basement crowded with metal vats. Here, the air was cool and dry. The room loud with the steady hum of machinery.

Mr Tope shut the door behind them and locked it.

"Has its own power supply." The man flicked a switch and one of the tubs opened with a hiss of hydraulics.

The door to the room cracked, wood splintered. Mr Tope turned towards the sound; people laughed and sang outside.

He looked down at those steaming tubs.

"Liquid nitrogen," the man said, pale-faced. "It's the only way."

The Verger nodded. "We know too much."

The door buckled, something slammed into it again.

"I'm frightened," the man said.

"Of course you are." Mr Tope slid his blade, almost gently, along the man's throat. The body fell into the vat and was gone.

At least it will be quick, he thought.

The door burst open. Mr Tope flicked his gaze back at the opening. Witmoths raced towards him, dying and falling as soon as they touched the cooler air.

Mr Tope tipped his hat, and stepped off into the cold.

He was dead before the liquid nitrogen reached his neck.

Stade looked down at the note and dropped his teacup.

It smashed onto the floor making everyone else in the room jump. He ignored it, ignored them; holding his saucer out before him like a half-wit or a supplicant. He stumbled to the window and the comfort of his city. He stared out at the dark river pregnant with distant storms, the sombre sky scarred with cranes and ships and smoke. For a moment he felt that vertiginous disconnect he experienced when he used the spiders beneath Downing Bridge. To the south, Chapman was burning. Not that he would ever see those fires, the rain had sealed up that horizon. And yet, his mind's-eye flared with the horror of it.

Stade blinked.

A dozen haunted, vapid faces, reflected in the window, stared at him. Fools, he thought and let his saucer drop as well. But I share in that folly. Them to look to me for guidance, and me to think that I am up to the task of providing it.

Chapman was gone, the facade of its defence had been just that. So what?

But Vastkind, now that he had not wanted to hear at all. The surface seethed with tempests and wars, but they were as nothing to the fires below.

The Underground. If the Roil learnt of that, Vastkind would find it and every plan would be as dust.

But the Roil would not. He refused to let his mind stray down that awful path. Then the second message boy arrived, a fine lad who in other times probably would have become a Verger.

"Sir," he whispered, as the other councillors drew closer, "there's been a sighting in the north. The Cuttlefolk, they've massed an army. They have come around the Margin, two days, maybe three and the city will be under siege. Already their messengers are attacking dirigibles and Aerokin."

Stade cleared his throat; fumbled in his pockets for a cigar. He needed time, but there just wasn't enough of it. Had there ever really been?

There, he thought, fingers clenching around the cigar. He found his lighter. They watched him, as though he could really do anything now.

"It's beginning, as we always knew it would, for us as it did for all the metropolises of Shale." He lit the cigar, clamped it between his teeth and puffed once, blowing out smoke. "And not at all the same, there will be no lovely view of the Obsidian Curtain for Mirrlees. The Roil's reach has lengthened, as we feared. It is time to evacuate the city as best we can. Let the bastards have it. Ready or not, we're going to the Underground."

"What about the refugees?"

"If there are any, well, they'll be in for a nasty surprise. Though, if they survived Chapman this little misadventure will be nothing to them. Gentlemen, we are all refugees now. Every one of us."

Outside, it had stopped raining. Already the clouds were clearing. Yes, the end would come swiftly.

He laughed, a hollow petulant sound that had his councillor's eyes widening with shock. Stade glowered at his councillors. Every single one of them would shoulder this burden. They had fought tooth and claw to reach these positions. Well, they had their power, now they would face, as he had faced, the consequences.

Responsibility.

Roil take them all. Roil take them all and him.

And, at that moment, he was almost certain it would.

CHAPTER 48

One of history's great surprises is that so many survived the hasty evacuation of Chapman. Such had been the violence of the city's conquest that all previous plans of escape had been discarded. Though some reflect that the absence of Buchan and Whig had much to do with this, it is undeniable that there was no slow and steady progress, but mad flight.

Yet again, the Roil revealed hitherto unknown resources. No one expected to be pursued and so rapidly.

Histories, DEIGHTON

To lose an Aerokin is a terrible thing. Better to die with it, than to live on. I count that as my greatest mistake, and one I continue to make.

Duty of the Air, RAVEN SKYE

THE SKY ABOVE SHALE
DISTANCE FROM ROIL: INDETERMINATE

The wind struck David as a capricious creature. No matter that it was driving them all north, it also seemed intent of taking each airship and Aerokin a slightly *different* way north. It scattered the escapees of the Festival of Float, and carried them on separate breaths and eddies. Within a few hours, he could no longer see any of the other craft, except one. Blake's Aerokin, the *Arrogant Spice*. It was oddly comforting to know the great pilot and his craft were so close, not to mention the heavier armoury it contained.

Storm clouds scudded in, and Kara Jade warmed the interior of the *Roslyn Dawn*, dropped some ballast (David didn't ask how this was done, but it stank) and lifted them above the storm. But not by much, it was as though they skimmed the surface of some angry conflict of electrical giants.

Watching lightning beneath his feet was an eerie experience, and one not at all comforting, particularly after the sun had set. It seemed as though they sailed a storm-tossed sea, and in a way they did, only it was a sea seeded with dynamite. They drifted over and through odd cloudscapes, visible only when the lightning flashed below; dark columns of cloud, weird weightless grottoes through which Kara and the *Dawn* navigated.

David had never seen such things nor imagined that they would ever exist above the mundane slab of drizzling grey that roofed his city. His discomfort soon faded. The beautiful sky enchanted him, almost enough that he could momentarily forget everything that had happened to bring him here. Cadell and Margaret were trapped in their own thoughts – in fact both looked like they were trying to sleep – certainly not intent on the world outside.

Which was why he saw the dark shape first.

For a moment, he wasn't sure what it was he saw. Perhaps another airship, only it moved too quickly. He watched it a while, until he realised that it was getting closer.

"What's that?" he asked Margaret, who sat nearest him, nudging her with an elbow.

Margaret moaned and elbowed him back. She opened her eyes so slowly that David was frightened she would miss it.

She blinked at him. "What?"

David pointed. "That," he said. "Just west of the *Arrogant Spice*." Margaret peered into the darkening sky.

"Ah, I see it! I don't know, but it's approaching quickly. Very quickly."

David called Kara Jade over. She brought with her a brass telescope, which proved hardly necessary, for when she arrived it was clearly visible.

"Some kind of metal airship," she said. "I've not seen its kind before. The *Roslyn Dawn* is new bred, but this is something else altogether. And rocket powered." She breathed out enviously. "What I wouldn't give to possess that speed."

David was almost tempted to say something about new bred Aerokin but decided the better of it because, as they watched, the ship raced towards the *Arrogant Spice*. Blake had obviously seen it; his Aerokin had begun to descend towards the cloudbank. The iron ship immediately changed its angle of approach.

"Or that sort of manoeuvrability," Kara Jade said.

A brief exchange of fire followed. The *Spice's* heavy guns boomed followed by the spat, spat, spat of the smaller iron ship's weaponry. The iron ship drew first blood.

Flames ran up the *Spice's* skin a blazing sheath that drove their shadows hard against the interior of the *Roslyn Dawn*. The *Arrogant Spice's* screams echoed over to them.

But this was not the end of the exchange.

The iron ship fired once more, and the *Spice's* bioengines ignited with a bloody rupturing. The Aerokin began at once to tilt, nose down towards the ground.

The *Roslyn Dawn* groaned in sympathy.

The iron ship looped around and rammed into the *Spice's* control gondola. It paused there for a moment, or hovered, as though inspecting the contents of the airship, or feasting upon them.

When it was done, it pulled away in a burst of fire: blood and flame jetting from the wound.

Blake – it had to be Blake, his beard flaming, wielding a steel bar or a sword – had clambered onto the iron ship's nose. He swung his weapon against the cockpit window once, twice, the distant cracking of the blows followed moments later.

The sight was at once absurd and terrible.

Blake got in two or three hard blows, cracking the windscreen but not breaking it. He took another swing, the iron ship dipped and looped. Unbalanced, he slid from its edge, his legs flipping up as he tumbled away into the clouds.

The *Arrogant Spice* was ablaze, all four engine nacelles ruined and its control gondola torn open. The beast had lost all its grandeur, its tilt deepened and its flagella hung limp and still, smoke streaming from its gondola and bioengines.

The iron ship rushed towards it. At the last moment, the *Spice's* Flagella stiffened and lashed out. It grabbed the iron ship and together they fell.

"She's going out fighting," Kara said, pride and horror fighting for dominance in her voice.

But there was all too little fight left.

Fire flashed from the rear of the iron craft and it tore free of the *Spice's* grip. The ship looped up and around lightning quick and crashed through the skin of the *Spice*. The explosion hit them like a thunderclap.

The *Dawn* howled.

Little remained of the *Arrogant Spice* but a dark cloud of flaming fragments tumbling down, down into the storm below.

Out of that dark cloud burst the iron ship.

Kara sobbed and howled and shook her fist at the ship. "No… that's not right. There's nothing in the sky that can do that."

"Until now," Margaret said, pulling free her rifle and sighting along it. The weapon hummed, the muzzle remained unwarped. Not that it would be enough.

She activated one of her rime blades, tested the edge with her breath and watched it freeze. Margaret knew who they were looking for, and she would sooner die than let them take her. "Where will we fight the ship? Because you can't outrun it."

Kara Jade ran from the rear window to the cockpit controls, and began her consultation with the *Dawn*. "Can't outrun it, but I'm damned if I'm going to make it easy."

The gondola shuddered with the vibrations of bone gears clunking solidly into place and they dove down, the *Roslyn Dawn* shaking as it hit different streams of air, lurching this way and that.

"We're heading into the storm."

Fear beat its drums within him. Not again, David thought. All this running, and every time it's something worse. He glanced over at Kara Jade. She had been calm within the Roil, but now she was frantic. Her and the Roslyn Dawn both.

"We've weapons to attack airships, even other Aerokin, if it came to that, but nothing for an iron ship."

He watched her check over her control panel – sweat dripping from her ashen brow – fingers dancing across the board, coaxing more power out of the bioengines, while trying to keep the *Dawn* calm.

"That's as fast I dare push her. And I'm going to descend another five hundred feet. Maybe this iron ship will be afraid of all that lightning."

David doubted that, but he knew he was terrified of it.

Margaret's wan face gleamed with sweat and her eyes stared too brightly down at her hands, as though she did not know what to do.

"What's wrong?" David asked.

"Everything," she said. "David, I think they're coming for me. That ship it's my mother's design, I know it. It's looking for something. If it just wanted to kill, it wouldn't have bothered ramming the gondola. Those weapons are powerful enough to destroy an Aerokin in minutes."

"Nonsense," David said. "You're safe here. Well, safe as anywhere." He couldn't even make it sound convincing.

The iron ship veered towards them, obviously intent on proving him wrong.

Cadell stood in the aft of the *Roslyn Dawn*, watching the fast approaching ship.

"Margaret," he said. "Could you join me please?"

They stood in quiet conversation for a moment. Margaret shook her head.

A blast of flame shot past the Aerokin. Kara returned the fire but her assessment of her weaponry was accurate. The *Roslyn Dawn* was not a battle craft, and her tiny ordnance bounced off the armoured airship to little effect.

"So what are we going to do about it?" Kara shouted back at them. "We're an easy target."

"Without a doubt," Cadell said. "The very definition of an easy target."

"Should I just shoot him now?" Kara Jade asked Margaret.

She shrugged. "Why waste the bullet?"

Cadell reached for a coil of rope by the doorifice, he gripped a loop of it with both hands and tugged it tight with a snap of his wrists – it cracked but did not give. "This strong?"

"It has to be. Light and strong: it's for work in the air. The Mothers wove that, they did."

"Then it will serve."

Kara Jade's eyes widened, Cadell had managed to get under the bombast. "No... you've got to be kidding."

"What?" David asked.

Kara shook her head. "He means to go out there," she said.

Cadell tied the rope around his waist. There was a metal karabiner at the end of the rope. He attached it to a sturdy bar by the door and yanked. Satisfied, he touched the doorifice: it opened.

A cold wet wind blasted the interior of the cabin, papers scattered and the exhalation of the engine nacelles was suddenly deafening. The air, part engine, breath and storm, burned David's lungs. Ice crystals formed against his skin.

"You can't mean to do this," David yelled. "It's madness."

Cadell's shoulders slumped, and David had never seen him look so tired. "Madness is all that's left to us," he said. "Up here, the cold is on our side. It need only breach the iron ship's defences for those ships to fall, and I intend to breach them. Kara Jade, you must keep us above that ship and if not above then as close as possible, closer than ever would be wise. I doubt they'll trade shots with you, I should be something of a distraction."

"I'll do my best. Good luck, Old Man."

"The ship's almost below us," he said. "I must go, now."

Cadell looked at David one last time, took a deep breath and leapt into the air, out in an arc that started gracefully and all too quickly became a tumble.

David watched horrified as Cadell plummeted. The tails of his morning coat lashed at the air. Cadell pulled himself into a ball then, at the last moment, he straightened, gained a modicum of control and landed on the roof of the ship.

Cadell crouched there a moment, David could see his lips moving, as he scrambled towards the window.

The iron ship fired another round. The *Roslyn Dawn* shrieked and began a slow dip.

"We're too close," yelled Kara Jade.

"We have to be!" David said. The *Roslyn Dawn* dropped.

"Are we falling?" David clutched at a rail by the window. Holding as tightly as he could, he peered out the open door. Bad idea. He couldn't even see the ground, just darkness and wisps of cloud.

Kara grinned briefly. "Aerokin float, they do not fall. That was just a gust that caught us off guard," she said. "Still, my darling's wounded. I'm going to have to take a walk outside."

Kara glanced over at Margaret. "You'll have to put down your weapons."

She dragged Margaret over to the controls and quickly showed her how to work them. "You said anyone could fly one of these, now's your chance. Keep her steady, keep her calm, if it gets too rough I won't be able to do anything."

"I'll keep her steady," Margaret said. "You just get out there."

Kara Jade snorted and grinned. She grabbed a mask, filled a bucket with some gel from a storage growth at the heart of the gondola, and dashed out the rear doorifice of the *Roslyn Dawn*. David watched her clamber up the side of the Aerokin with all the grace of someone who simply didn't care they were thousands of feet above the ground. And as she climbed the iron ship rose too, until it was level with the *Dawn*.

Cadell had reached the scarred window of the ship, the rope a long umbilicus dipping between the Aerokin and the Old Man. David could see where he had bound the rope to the ship with ice. Then the ship plummeted and was lost to sight for a moment. The Aerokin shook and dropped to the left, throwing David to the floor.

Margaret, hunched over the controls, cursed.

Someone was calling him. Kara Jade. He ran to the doorifice, Kara's rope had tangled.

"What's that pallid slip of a girlfriend of yours doing?" Kara shouted.

David was about to shout back that Margaret was not his girlfriend when a steel ball exploded in the air behind Kara. Kara Jade crashed forward, striking her head on one of the main linking struts. She tumbled backwards, held to the Aerokin only by her rope, and hung limply in space, blood spilling from her skull.

David stared wild-eyed down into the abyss of the sky. All he could see were clouds, and even they looked like they were a long way down. *Such a terrible, terrible drop.* Still he grabbed a rope, connected it to the rail and linked it to his waist, hoping that he had done it correctly.

He slipped on a mask. It was heavy, yanked at his hair and smelt faintly and ridiculously of onions. Kara had said they contained enough oxygen to last around half-an-hour. Surely more than enough, the idea of staying out there for longer than five minutes terrified him.

David crawled through the rubbery doorifice, and warmth gave way to cold.

Twice, the *Roslyn Dawn* dipped and fell; he held on so tightly that his knuckles were in danger of popping out of his hands. Rope or no, David doubted his chances if he lost his grip. And, with every rise and fall, his ears popped painfully, no matter how often he cracked his jaw.

He grabbed a fist around Kara's rope, and tugged it towards him, pulling her close. Kara Jade, blinked at him groggily.

"Good to see you," she said, right into his ear. "But this is hardly the time or the..."

David winced at the blood streaming from a shallow wound in the side of her head.

"We've got to get you back inside," he shouted.

Kara Jade rubbed at the side of her head, then peered at her fingers covered with blood. She blinked again, slowly. "What are *you* doing out here?"

"Saving your life."

"Ha!" She slipped out of consciousness again, the weight of her almost dragging David into the sky.

David yanked her to him, startled by the warmth of her body and the rapid beat of her heart. His own heart beat pretty fast, particularly when he threw a glance at all that empty space beneath him. Bad idea.

Her rope had tangled and he struggled to free it, but it had knotted too tightly. David gave up and pulled out his pocketknife. He sawed through the rope quickly, hoping all the while that the *Dawn* wouldn't drop suddenly. It did, his ears popped yet again, the muscles in his arms burned and his breath struggled in his chest but he managed to hold Kara Jade against the walkway.

I am going to die, he thought. I am too weak, too small, too drug fucked for this. And he was, but somehow he managed it.

He inched backwards to the doorifice and was happier than he had ever been in his life when he felt it open. He shoved Kara Jade through, then toppled after her, careful not to tangle or get in the way of Cadell's line. Not an easy task as it whipped about the opening, striking David so hard that he nearly fell back outside.

Kara Jade grabbed and steadied him, helping him over and away from Cadell's line, they both tumbled to the floor of the gondola.

"You're back with us," David said.

She coughed, her eyes wild. She lifted up her cut line. "That rope's expensive."

"How can a flyer weigh so much?" He said.

Kara blinked. "You may have saved my life, but if you don't shut up I'm gonna have to slit your throat, and – oh…" She rose to her feet unsteadily, then pointed behind him.

David turned. Cadell's situation had grown far more precarious. He had lost his footing and hung in the air, dangling from the edge of the ship by his fingertips.

Cadell slowly pulled himself back up, and slid again to the iron ship's cockpit window, steam rising in sudden dirty grey bursts from the cracks that scarred it.

David heard the distant retort of the iron ship's guns, and then something struck the nearby gondola wall, shattering the outer layer. A thin, pale liquid ran from the wound.

The guns blazed again.

This time one of the bioengines was hit; it rumbled rather than whined. Above them the Aerokin groaned. The *Roslyn Dawn* veered to the right. Black smoke streamed from the cracked nacelle. David turned towards the pilot seat where Margaret sat hunched over and cursing at the controls.

Down below, Cadell shook his head, all the while shouting something and gesturing at the glass as though he could break it with words and will alone.

The iron ship dipped and bobbed, then dived, all at once. The rope hissed as it played out the door, the fibre smoking. David wanted to stop it, to yank it back in and Cadell with it. But he also wanted to survive. Cadell knew what he was doing, he hoped.

Below, Cadell appeared unperturbed. He waved his hands palm out over the shattered glass once, twice, three times.

The iron ship frosted over with a sudden explosion of ice: a kind of frozen fire. It hovered jerkily, a last burst of flame spluttering in its engines. Cadell ran to the edge of the craft and leapt smoothly into the air, clinging onto the rope. But it was a moment too late. The iron ship flipped up and struck him on back of the head. Even from the *Roslyn Dawn*, David could see the blood spray.

The frozen ship fell away punching through the clouds. Not long after, and far below, the sky flared, became almost clear. A distant detonation followed like a muted thunderclap.

Dizziness welled within him, staring at that explosion, so far below. He needed to sit down, or throw up then sit down, and then he realised he could not see Cadell anywhere.

"He's gone. He's gone," David said.

Kara drove an elbow into his side.

She looked half-dead, but her face was set with a grim and awful energy. Her shaking hands gripped the now taut line. The biceps of her lean arms bulged.

"Hey, idiot," she snapped. "This rope, Cadell's on the other end, remember?"

Kara Jade had wound it around a pole by the doorifice, her arms straining.

"Sorry," David said.

Kara Jade's jaw clenched. "Don't be sorry, just help me."

He sprang towards her and grabbed the rope.

"I'm ready," he said.

"Me, too," Margaret said from behind him.

They pulled it in, foot by tedious foot. After ten minutes, sweat stinging his eyes, hands bloody, muscles burning, he wondered just how much rope had played out.

"Pretty heavy for a scrawny old geezer, isn't he?" Kara panted. "Of course the air's thin at these altitudes. Doesn't make it any easier. Nor do head injuries."

"At least it means that he's at the end of it," David said.

They worked until David thought his arms were going to drop off and his lungs pop out of his mouth. Finally, Cadell's hands clamped around the edge of the doorifice.

Cadell was awake; the old man was awake. He pulled himself up and through the doorifice, his skin bloodless, his lips blue. One of his eyes had swollen shut.

His body was cold; David could see ice forming where his feet touched the *Roslyn Dawn*. The doorifice reacted by opening wide. Wind whistled through, and Cadell stood there, unsteadily, the empty sky behind him.

"Quick, get him inside," Kara shouted.

"I'm quite all right, madam," Cadell said and nearly toppled back out the opening. David grabbed him, pulling him in and away from the opening. It snapped shut behind them.

"Let's not do that again," Cadell said, his words coming between wheezes. "At least not for a while." His eyes rolled up in his head, and he was out.

David gently set him down on the bunk, not liking the deep wound in the back of his head, nor the patches of soft brittleness around his back, beneath the skin, as though bones were crushed.

"Don't worry. He's an old warhorse, sure his reserves have been taxed, but he'll recover," Kara said. "He has to, doesn't he?"

Margaret looked down at Cadell, and shook her head. David could see that it was bad; shallow cuts on the scalp bled fiercely but thinly; this blood was thick and dark. Margaret released a breath with such heart-aching weariness that David's first instinct was to offer comfort. She stepped beyond his reach.

"I'm no doctor, but I've seen this sort of injury before." And she paused as though remembering them, and it came to David that her background was not at all like his, and that she had entertained a very different sort of horror all her life. "David, there's a real chance he may not wake again."

CHAPTER 49

Perhaps we should have never warred with the Cuttlefolk. But then again, War and Industry, what else do we do so well?

Minutes of a Mayor, STADE

THE GATHERING PLAINS
DISTANCE FROM ROIL: VARIABLE

The Cuttlefolk led them west, away from the tracks for a good half a day, Messengers flying to and from them with increasing frequency, their sharp wing beats signalling a moment or two of rest. The Cuttlefolk did not speak, though their intentions were clear, and while they performed no brutalities upon their prisoners (water was distributed among them, even food, and it was palatable) they forced a hard march across the plains.

Twice Medicine demanded to speak to whoever was leading them, and both times he was gently and definitely dismissed.

Slowly the Cuttle city of Carnelon was revealed to them.

Built around a small range of hills, they ringed it in narrow streets, the buildings low, unlike anything Medicine had seen in Mirrlees or Chapman. They had eschewed the sky, reaching not into the heavens but deep underground. The sky was dark with Messengers, as disturbing a sight as he had ever seen. It was one thing to observe the occasional Messenger skirting over Mirrlees or Chapman, but to see them descending from the sky *en masse* was terrifying.

They were led along narrow curling streets open to the sky, the whole place smelled sickly sweet – the scent of Cuttlefolk and the sugars they produced. Pleasant, perhaps, as an additive in perfume, but here it clawed at the throat. Reminding Medicine of those times he had drunk too much Cuttlewine, and there had been far too many of those, though now he rather expected the outcome of this journey to be far worse than any hangover.

Cuttlefolk watched them silently. The ground beneath their feet rippled, shivering to movements and masses below that Medicine didn't want to consider all that much.

Finally, they stopped at pens where, much to Medicine's surprise, a human greeted them. He seemed almost embarrassed.

"I'm Dreyer," he said. "You do know you were trespassing on Cuttlefolk lands? They're not at all happy with you."

"I didn't know there were humans in Carnelon."

"There's a few of us. We are tolerated, I suppose just as the Cuttlefolk are tolerated in Mirrlees," he said. "I am studying Cuttlefolk sociology."

Good for you, Medicine thought.

"Can you help us?" Medicine asked.

Dreyer shook his head. "Good heavens, no! You've broken Cuttlefolk law, and Cuttlefolk alone can deal with that. But I can translate for you, and even that threatens to tar me with your association. There will be a meeting tomorrow. I will do what I can."

The Cuttlefolk left them in their pens. There was an explosion of wings and half a dozen of their messengers flew north and west.

A little while later a lone messenger took to the air, hovering high above the city for a moment before shooting south.

"What are they doing?" Medicine asked.

"Isn't it obvious," Agatha said. "They're gathering an army."

That night something flew over the city. An iron ship unlike anything Medicine had ever seen. Medicine watched as canisters dropped from its belly.

Smoke descended on the city. There were cries, howls, the stomp of feet. Locked in the pen, Medicine was as good as blind.

Then, just before dawn, there was silence.

Half the morning they waited and nothing in the city stirred.

At last Medicine pulled a blade from his boot and worked on the lock. It was a stubborn thing, but it gave way to his promptings. He and Agatha stumbled through the city.

The entire city was deserted.

"They're gone," Medicine said. "I do not understand it at all."

"Let's just get out of here while we still can," Agatha said. "In case they come back."

And he did not bother arguing with her, they returned to the pens and freed the others.

Silently they moved through the empty city. Not one of the Cuttlefolk or their Messengers was in evidence, but in the square, outside the many-bannered building that Medicine guess to be the Cuttlelord's residence, humans had been strung up, their organs removed, and their eyes.

Medicine stared at Dreyer's corpse, wondering how close they had come to that. The Cuttlefolk had forgotten about them or, more chillingly, thought them not worth the effort.

GATHERING PLAINS
DISTANCE FROM ROIL: 650 MILES

"Where are they going?" Medicine asked, pointing at the ruined earth. This was the fourth such two-hundred yard wide furrow in the ground, extending in either direction as far as he could see. It was as though someone had torn a path across the land, using only claw and tooth. And that was pretty much what had happened. This was the spoor of a race on the march to battle.

"South," Agatha replied, crouching and sighting along the broken earth. "Like all the others."

"And what lies south of here?"

"Mirrlees."

All day, they found evidence of the Cuttlefolk's passage, skin casings, midden-heaps, even egg sacks gently pulsing. These Agatha's soldiers had taken a grim delight in shooting, until she ordered they cease. There were so many, and their ammunition so limited.

"We've missed the party," Agatha said, running her fingers through the earth.

"I think it's the Roil," Medicine said. "That ship, those canisters. The Roil's reach has extended considerably."

They returned to the great iron-beast that was the *Grendel* and Agatha sent her best men to check over it. There were engineers and mechanics enough in their numbers that it would be a truly ruined train for them not to repair it. As it was, the damage was limited, the equipment necessary for repair on board the engine, and those skilled enough to fix it in abundance.

Agatha could not conceal her delight. "With this we can reach the Underground in a day, nor more than two, if the tracks hold up."

"Let's do it," Medicine said. "I've had more than enough of trudging." He lifted a ruined boot. "These were my best pair, you know."

There was room enough for the workers and essential equipment; barely, but enough, and everyone was crammed in.

The *Grendel* built up its steam, a process that took longer than Medicine would have liked, but was assured was absolutely necessary. The engine, really a series of linked engines run in tandem, was huge and its carriages packed to capacity. He was mad with boredom before they had even started but finally the *Grendel* moved.

Agatha and Medicine sat in the front cabin, hardly a common carriage at all, but a room. Agatha cheered at the sight of the bar there, quickly opening a bottle of Hardacre Donaldson Whisky no doubt intended for some dignitary. She took a quick swig and passed it to Medicine.

"This is a fine, fine thing", he said, letting the drink burn the back of his throat.

Agatha took another sip. "I do believe our luck has changed."

The sky was blue, no rain or Cuttlefolk to darken it.

"I hope so," he said, passing the bottle back to her. "I really hope so."

CHAPTER 50

Little is known of just what happened to those fifteen ships lost in the Chapman Exodus. But the highest number of casualties occurred on that first night of flight. Signals and tracings disappearing into the dark.

Cadell, sighted on the Roslyn Dawn, *may well have been responsible. Ever he delighted in destruction, the old texts say.*

The City in the Air, Molck

THE AIR OVER SHALE
DISTANCE FROM ROIL: VARIABLE

Cadell was out for hours and David watched over him feeling even more helpless than he had watching his father's death. He knew this dying would be far more protracted and one he couldn't run from.

"He's not going to wake up," Margaret said.

"Now, that's real helpful," Kara Jade said. "Real sensitive."

"Sensitivity or truth, what do you prefer?" Margaret snapped.

"We need him," David said. "All of us. Cadell alone knows what has to be done, what the next step is. Without him we're all just waiting to die. We might as well turn around now, fly into the Roil and get it over and done with."

"Our *need* isn't enough to bring about a miracle," Margaret said.

"That we're still alive is a miracle," Kara Jade said. "The options as I see them now, I can still take you north. Cadell paid for that, and he saved the *Dawn*. Or you can come to my city."

The thought of Drift held a moment's attraction for David.

"And what would we do there?" Margaret said. "Fly until we die?"

"It's what we all do," Kara Jade said. "No point denying it. The damn Roil's going to swallow every one of us."

Starting with Cadell, David thought. The old man's breath came shallowly, and there was almost no blood in his face, but lying as Cadell did, David could almost imagine that he was only sleeping. The back of his skull belied that. Kara Jade had packed it with the same gel she had used on the hull of the *Roslyn Dawn*, but it couldn't conceal the missing piece of skull or the brain beneath.

"He's not going to wake up," Margaret said, pacing the cabin like a caged beast.

Kara Jade, after a few choice words concerning Margaret's piloting skills, kept her eyes and her concentration on the controls.

Somewhere along the way, David fell asleep to nightmares of iron ships launching fire and screaming gulls being torn out of the air by hordes of Hideous Garment Flutes.

In the middle of the night someone shook him awake. David blinked, grateful to have escaped such dreams.

Kara smiled almost shyly at him.

"What's wrong?" He rubbed at his eyes.

"Quick," she said, pulling him up. "Quick or you'll miss it."

"What are you doing? Are we under attack?" He let her drag him to a currently translucent section of the gondola.

"Look," she said, jabbing a thumb down at a wide break in the clouds.

Lights were scattered thickly on the ground beneath, a winding band of brilliance at least three miles wide, though from up here it appeared scarcely broader than his wrist.

"What is it?" he asked. Then his voice caught in his throat: all that beautiful light.

At last he managed: "It's Mirrlees, it's home."

Kara nodded. "Much prettier from on high, isn't it? They say they modelled it on the stars in the sky, the spiralling arms of galaxies. Doesn't look much like stars to me, but what do I know? I thought you might want a glimpse of your city."

Homesickness swelled inside him, everything he had forced deep burst free. Tears ran down his face.

"Here," Kara said, gently, handing him a bottle. "Have a belt of that."

"What is it?" David asked.

"Drift rum, the good stuff. It's our only export."

He took a swig from the bottle and gasped as it burned its way down his throat. Belt was right!

"You export *that*?" He managed at last.

Kara gave him a look of mild amusement. "It grows on you, trust me."

David nodded; his eyes still fixed on the city beneath them. Half a dozen Aerokin circled far below – military class, troop carriers – but even they could not spoil the vision.

Every time you see something you love, and you think it's for the last time, it becomes perfect, painfully and utterly flawless. He stared and stared at that glittering perfection, at the crowded streets and the white scar of the stopbanks, and the great bulk of Downing Bridge until the clouds closed over again and there was no hint of the city ever having existed at all.

"Thank you," he said.

Kara looked almost embarrassed.

"Seriously, nothing to thank me for," she said staring down at her boots. "Just part of the service and all that. Now I better get back out there and check the ropes."

"Be careful," David said, staring at the side of her head, the hair there still sticky with blood.

Kara Jade's left hand went up to the wound, almost touching it. She swung the hand away dismissively. "Take more than that to stop me looking after my *Dawn*."

She slipped on a mask and went out into the night.

Margaret lay on one of the sleeping benches, legs curled up, watching David and Kara Jade, a slither of jealousy playing in her belly. She thought about her own city and the last time she had seen it. Images surged back of Chapman and its swift collapse. She had no desire to view another city from above unless it was Tate, whole and unaffected by the Roil.

Sometimes when Margaret slept she dreamt she was flying, hurtling over Tate, suspended on the wire way, wheels whistling, the wind racing around her. She would wake to a foreign place and a sadness that would almost destroy her: until the rage returned.

Not tonight.

She had laid her guns and swords out on the bed before her. Two of the pistols were faulty and she doubted they would fire again. The chemical combiners were low in another pair. She couldn't see when she might have the opportunity to recharge them or repair the others; Kara Jade's tools had proven inadequate to the task. Her rifle too was running a low charge. David was right; she had been reckless with her ammunition in Chapman.

It struck her then that weaponry was all she had left of Tate, as though that was all that Tate had ever been.

Such bitter tools had ensured her survival, even as they had failed to shield her from pain. When the guns were exhausted, shells and chemicals spent, only memories would remain. However, the Roil had transformed those as well. She could not close her eyes without seeing fire, the body of the Sweeper shattered and ruined on the ground outside her parents' house, the fourth cannon exploding, its blazing demise the penultimate breath of a wounded city.

The Roil's true horror was not in the monsters that populated it (they were just beasts after all) but what the Roil had done to Tate; what she dreaded it had done to her parents.

As terrible as it was, she wished her mother and father dead, for if they were not....

She looked over at David.

Make this a good memory, David. Hold on to it as tightly as you can. They may be the last good memories you ever have.

"David," Cadell's voice was weak, yet urgent. "Wake up."

David blinked. How long had Cadell been calling him?

He was beginning to doubt he would get any rest that night. He toyed with the idea of pretending to be asleep. Such a selfish thought shocked him; after all he had saved all their lives.

David rolled from the bunk, looked over at Margaret. She was asleep and Kara Jade seemed lost in conversation with the *Dawn*. He stumbled to Cadell's bunk.

Cadell was even worse than before. His right eye had shut completely and raised black veins ran down the right side of his face. A yellow fluid wept from his left eye leaving a crust down Cadell's cheek. He was dying, David could tell that, he had seen enough of death to recognise it.

Dying or not, Cadell managed a smile, lifted a hand and motioned for David to come closer.

"I want you to have this." Cadell pressed the Ring of Engineers into David's palm. "Just for a little while. I'll take it back when I can. You know their real name don't you?"

David nodded. "Orbis Ingenium."

Cadell patted David's hand. "Yes, the ring ingenious, it's a map and a key, but it's also a machine. Its workings are very intricate – universes of clockwork folded in on themselves. Look after it for me."

David tried to give the Orbis back. He didn't want it. He didn't deserve it. "I can't take the ring. It's yours. You know what to do with it. Without you it's only a fancy piece of jewellery."

"And now it's yours." Cadell said, gently but forcefully. "When you reach Hardacre, Buchan and Whig will help you. Indeed they may well be happier that it is you not me that they will need. I think there's a chance the Roil can be stopped. I've wielded the cold for a long time and always feared it. Perhaps, once you're done, there will be an end to that fear." Cadell coughed. He wiped at his lips with a handkerchief. It came back thick with blood. He looked at it a little startled. "Well, I never, even the minnows would have a hard time repairing that. I'm sorry, I'm talking in circles, I'm so terribly tired, David. And I have no wish to argue with you. Look after it for me. Put it on. Please indulge an old man."

"Why me?" David asked.

"I'd like to say that it was your destiny, that you, the son of a Master Engineer, were born to this. But the universe doesn't work that way. The universe doesn't care what happens. But I do, we do, that's what makes us special and terrible all at once. You've seen the Roil, you know it to your core. And you're all I've got. You have to do this if Shale is to have any hope at all. There's no one else. My brothers in war would stop you were they not in their cages. They would strip the flesh from your bones." He lifted himself up with a groan. "And there is another reason," his voice lowered, "I don't trust Margaret and you shouldn't either. She fled her city, and she might flee this, too. You're the best choice, the only choice, and she can help you without a doubt, but rely on her only as much as necessary, and no more. Now, please, put on the ring."

David, hesitated a moment more, then slid the ring over the middle finger of his left hand. The ring stopped at his knuckle, then the metal warmed and loosened and passed over it.

"Look," Cadell said. "A perfect fit. Fancy that. It might feel odd for a day or two, the ring lowers your core temperature, the minnows that generate its power do that: can't have you being susceptible to Witmoths. The change will probably manifest itself as a head cold but don't worry, you'll get used to it and the benefits are many. I'll get to those in a minute." He lowered himself back onto the bed with the painful slowness of a man only just acquainted with his antiquity. "There is so much to be done. You are heading away from the Roil but there are other enemies, David. I wish I could help you."

"But you already have," David said. "You've kept the Carnival at bay. You've saved my life over and over again."

"I only needed to because of where I had taken you. And, as for the Carnival, just why do you think I kept you supplied with the drug, David?"

David looked at him uncomprehending. "To spare me the pain of withdrawal?"

Cadell laughed. "Were it that simple. You've suspended your grief with Carnival, you have always kept it at arms length: not just the loss of your father, but that of your mother, too. When you finally pay that price, the cost will be high. I could not have you pay that now. I did not want you to die. I needed you sane, I needed you shielded as much as possible from edged truths that would otherwise cut you."

"I'm all right," David said. "I'll be all right."

"But I have been far too cruel. When the Carnival leaves you, then you will truly understand."

"I understand now," David said.

"David, right now you only think you do. Though it will come to you, and for that I am really sorry." Cadell laughed. "Sorry! Everything about me is apology. Carnival's absence may well be the making of you. That tune you whistled, on the train so long ago. You know it is old?"

David thought of his childhood, the memories that tune evoked and the pressures of them that the Carnival held in check. "Yes, my mother used to hum it. It's almost all I can remember of her. I think it was popular when she was child."

Cadell shook his head. "It is far older than that. I remember it from *my* childhood. It is called 'The Synergist's Treason' and now I understand that treason far better than I ought. It pains me to hear it, and yet I'd like to hear it again."

David hummed the tune a while – his head buzzing – and Cadell seemed to relax a little. "Much better. Much much better when it isn't whistled." He groaned, and shifted in his bed. "I'm tired," he whispered. "The sort of weariness only Old Men and rocks can know. Too much time. Too much damn time, and now it's running out. You'd think that could bring some urgency to the flesh. Perhaps it has."

He sat up with a violence unexpected and grabbed David's wrist. What came afterwards, David regretted for the rest of his life. Cadell flipped David's arm around and bit down, tearing at the flesh of David's hand, something slid beneath his skin, something swift and cold. David howled.

Blood sprayed, as David tore his hand free.

"David?" Margaret's voice seemed a long way away. "David?"

"Sorry, David." Cadell's lips were bloody, but there was an awful tenderness in his gaze. "Sorry that I couldn't take you all the way to Hardacre. And sorry for this final gift. I'll deserve your hate."

David's eyes rolled up in his head.

CHAPTER 51

It can be said of the wars that followed, none of them would have occurred but for Stade's plans. The Roil's growth was certain, but the way it was met, the choices made, could have been very different.

None are more culpable than Stade. And yet, perhaps things may have been so much worse. Though it is hard to imagine outcomes more dreadful, nor lives lost greater.

Stade was a villain, but he was a villain of his time. And so history has judged him. After all, it was an age of monsters, a role that Stade embraced with gusto.

Two Hundred Mad Men & Seventy-Three Mad Women – Histories, DEIGHTON

THE UNDERGROUND
DISTANCE FROM ROIL: 942 MILES

Medicine looked at the iron thing, well what remained of it. He put aside the field glasses, rubbed at his gritty, aching eyes, and called ahead to Agatha and the driver.

The *Grendel* slowed to a walking pace as it approached the wreck.

Agatha signalled to the engineer and the *Grendel* stopped. She dropped from the train while it was still moving and strode towards the wreckage. Smoke billowed from it, though it was a smoke unlike any Medicine had ever seen. It did not dissipate, but hung low, following the sun.

"Keep your distance," Medicine said.

Early this morning they had heard (and felt) it strike the ground. And now, just a few hours from the Narung Mountains, here it was.

The vehicle was as large as the *Grendel*, though designed for flight instead. Medicine for the life of him could not see how it might fly. Yet, obviously it had flown before ending up here. Out of its element it looked ridiculous, some poor joke in shattered metal.

As Agatha neared the ship, the smoke coiled up, away from the sun towards the woman. Medicine watched its stealthy movement. He shouted at Agatha to get away, that the smoke was shifting towards her, and the woman blanched. She turned on her heel, slipping something into her mouth, and ran from the crater.

"Stay away from that ship," she commanded. "And everyone take your Chill."

"What is it?" Medicine demanded on her.

"They're called Witmoths. I'd been briefed on them a few days before we left. They're dangerous, mind altering," she said. "This thing came from the Roil."

"Mind altering?" Medicine asked, wondering why he hadn't been briefed on this as well.

"Let's just say it changes one's allegiances. If this came from the Roil then we can expect more of them. It doesn't do anything by halves." She handed him a small lozenge. "This is a kind of prophylactic. It's horrid but it works."

He slipped it into his mouth and grimaced as it stung his teeth. Medicine's mind returned to the night in the compound, the sound of thunder in the sky. Every time he looked at the iron ship it made him uneasy. Wherever it had come from, Roil city or Mirrlees research station, he was certain that it did not bode well for them. Very little did.

Such thoughts were quickly forgotten when they came upon a blasted battleground.

Many thousands of Cuttlefolk corpses lay across the plain. The earth itself was blackened and ruined. An airship, this one of a more familiar design, lay in fragments, its ribs rising out of the earth like the burnt bones of a titan.

The air was thick with the choking reek of ash and burning Cuttleflesh. The Cuttlefolk had been beaten here and decisively. What kind of weaponry did the Underground possess that could so blithely defeat such an army?

"Something new." Agatha mused. "And something powerful. At least we don't need to warn our colleagues in the mountains about the Cuttlefolk. Let us hope they know we're coming. I would hate to think of them deciding we were the enemy."

She called to her troops to raise all the white flags they could and to lower the train's guns.

"Better to look unthreatening," she said. Medicine agreed with her, though he couldn't imagine the *Grendel* being anything else.

Medicine wasn't sure what the people of the Underground thought about their fast approaching train, but they did not fire upon it as they crossed those last few miles. Regardless, tension built amongst all those aboard it.

The *Grendel* reached the end of the line, stopping at a heavy set of gates before which were signs of further struggle, craters and a pile of Cuttlemen dead, though nothing to rival the destruction to the south. The gates opened slowly to admit the train. Ice-cold water washed over them, the train chilled. For the moths, Medicine thought. How long has this been going on?

The *Grendel* pulled at last into the Underground, tracks running all the way into the compound, buried in the mountain. And there was the *Yawn*, waiting on a parallel line. The mystery of the missing train solved, though another mystery had replaced it. Why hadn't Stade known of its whereabouts?

They piled off the train and were met by hundreds of armed guards.

The place is a fortress, Medicine thought. He saw no salvation for humanity here. Just war. Men and women, armed with odd weaponry, lined the walls that bounded the caverns proper. Huge cannon too guarded the wall and two tall structures of dull iron and gleaming glass that looked like crooked necked lanterns.

Perhaps to light the underground at night, he thought.

Medicine walked warily at the fore with Agatha.

A man met them at the platform. "Welcome," he said. "My name is Grappel, we were expecting you." He gestured at the Grendel. "Though not for some days, and certainly not aboard this. You've proven yourself… resourceful."

Agatha frowned. "I do not know you," she said. "Where is Sam?"

"There has been some restructuring," Grappel said. "After we restored contact with Mirrlees, Sam Asquin was moved to another area. It seemed he was a little slow in reacting to the problems we have been having in completing work on time." Grappel smiled. "The addition of your thousands will aid us considerably."

"We were going to warn you of the Cuttlefolk," Agatha said. "But it looks as though you didn't need it."

Grappel laughed. "We dealt with them quite efficiently, wouldn't you agree?"

"You did," Medicine said. "But how?"

"New technology. While Mirrlees rots, we have been nothing but industrious here. The cannon above are coolant launchers, but those lanterns are prototypes, they launch nothing more than light, expressed as heat energy, though in an extremely concentrated form. I doubt it would do much against the Roil in the long term: the spores would find the heat quite invigorating, but the Cuttlefolk, they're a different prospect altogether."

"It was a massacre," Agatha said.

Grappel bowed. "And one that we engineered as a warning. The Cuttlefolk will think twice before they attack the Underground again. The last bastion of humanity cannot be threatened before it is even completed. Now, please come in. You all must be very tired, and Councillor Aidan would meet with you tonight."

Agatha glanced over at Medicine. Her lips a thin slash across her face, her shoulders tense.

Grappel sighed. "Now, we can all stand here chatting till the Roil comes or we can take you into the shelter of the Underground and you can have the rest which every one of you deserves after all those miles. I know which I'd prefer. First though, you will need to be checked for infection. Please, empty the train and take the first few steps into your new home."

Agatha signalled to her troops and they disembarked. Once they were gathered outside the train and heads counted Agatha turned to Grappel. "All are accounted for. Now do what needs to be done, I would communicate with the mayor."

Grappel shook his head, and raised his hands towards the wall. The guns mounted there had turned upon them. Grappel bowed deeply and sarcastically. "Welcome again to the Underground, ladies and gentlemen. A new territory of the Free State of Hardacre."

Medicine could see his shock reflected in Agatha's face, he didn't know whether to laugh or cry. Stade had lost before he had even begun. Agatha's face was without expression, though Medicine could see the fear and anger bound deep within her eyes and a bleak resolve. She grabbed the rifle from across her back.

"Find some cover," she whispered at Medicine. He didn't move.

"We can't win this battle here," he said. "We'll be slaughtered."

"I know."

"And I, for one, have no wish to die."

Agatha lowered her gaze. She reached for Medicine's hand, squeezed it gently. "None of us do. But I have my duty, and it is to the city of Mirrlees and its people."

"What of your duty to your soldiers?"

"Put down your weapons and you will be treated with respect," Grappel said. "We're not butchers, there is far too much work to be done to waste lives now."

Agatha hesitated. Medicine watched her eyes flick from him to her soldiers, and the armed men on the wall. Her shoulders slumped and she dropped her rifle.

"Do as he says," Agatha hissed at her troops. "We've not come all this way to die now."

They were not quick about it, but there was no fight in their eyes. They were all too exhausted. The soldiers of Hardacre were much faster in their confiscation of the weapons.

This is not about loyalties, Medicine thought, but survival. He had learnt that lesson tied to a chair by Stade in Ruele

Tower. He wondered if Stade could live by those rules. He thought of Stade's arrival and the discovery that all he had laboured for was gone. Well, he'd created this mess, set it all in motion when he turned aside the refugees from the Grand Defeat.

There was a grim satisfaction to be found in that.

The Underground soldiery led away the workers to mess halls and people were simply pleased at the thought of real food (none of them had ever possessed any loyalty to Stade in the first place). Grappel took Medicine aside. Agatha made to follow and Grappel shook his head. "Not yet. You will need to be debriefed. Things are different here to what you are used to."

Agatha nodded her head.

"See you soon," Medicine said.

"Yes," Agatha said, brushing his arm with her fingers. "Be careful."

Medicine reached out and squeezed her hand. "The hard part's over isn't it? We made it here."

Grappel gestured to Medicine to follow him. "The hard part's only beginning, I'm afraid," he said.

Grappel took him to a small room, built into the mountain near the tracks. He passed Medicine a flask. "You might want a bit of this." Medicine noticed the administrator's hands were shaking. He waved the flask away.

"Not now," Medicine said.

Gunshots cracked, men howled, and more guns fired.

"What are you doing?" He demanded, but he already knew the answer.

Grappel raised his hands, his face pale. "I'm sorry," he said. "It was an order."

Medicine pushed his way past him, and back to the

courtyard. The Council troops lay dead, Agatha with them. Medicine watched as they dragged the corpses away: the blood trailing them an accusation.

He dropped to his knees. "What have you done? You said you needed workers, everybody you could get."

"Mr Paul, you of all people must understand," Grappel said, as though speaking to a child. "We are at war. There is no time for negotiation. And having enemy soldiers in our midst is… surely you must understand that. We will treat them with respect. They will all be given military burials.

"Things are moving very swiftly now. Faster than you might realise." Grappel's face hardened. "Please consider how lucky you were that it wasn't you with them. Though, I have bullets enough to spare one more, if your solidarity with the enemy extends that far."

Medicine lowered his eyes.

"Good, I didn't think so. Now, come, we have work to do. And I am sure you would like to say a few words at their funeral. We don't want our new workers getting any ideas."

CHAPTER 52

In one day the Roil ignored all known limits to its expansion. To think that it could do so knowingly and swiftly gave an edge of hysteria to all actions that followed it.

The Roil was coming and it had grown cunning.

Dark Days, LANDYMORE

THE AIR ABOVE SHALE
DISTANCE FROM ROIL: VARIABLE

The inconsolable heavens wept and lightning split the darkness, revealing a Quarg Hound, hunched down on the corner of the street, its broad back twisted with muscle. Saliva streamed, black and thick, from a mouth that was too wide, and a malicious gleam lit its huge eyes. More disconcerting was the intelligence David perceived within them, something lacking in any of the hounds David had encountered before. The beast was bigger too, twice the size of the ones on the *Dolorous Grey*.

Quarg Hound? Quarg *Bear* more likely.

"Rather nasty," someone said beside him and David ducked and turned, hands clenched.

Margaret frowned at him, her pistols out. "You want to fight me, or it?" She looked from hound to David and back again.

"I could do with some help."

"These aren't much use against such a big creature," she said, shrugging her shoulders, and holstering her pistols. She picked at her nails with her rime blade. "I think you'd better run. That's something I can tell you all about: running." She seemed to give the idea some consideration. "That is unless you'd prefer me to slice your throat instead; put you out of your misery as it were."

David ran.

"Good for you," Margaret shouted after him. "Though you might want to run a little faster... make that a lot."

The beast followed, howling and snorting.

David sprinted down Main Street. The hound's claws clattered on the cobblestones so loudly that they echoed above the hiss of the rain.

What a malevolent steam-engine-sound it was, bunching up as though ready to pass. Only, David knew it would not pass, had no intention of passing, that it was aimed right at the centre of his back and the soft and chewy insides his back contained.

David shrieked, tearing like a madman towards his home. He made it, then realised that the door was locked. Where were his keys? He dug in his pockets, and found them, hazarding a glance behind him.

He wished he had not.

A gigantic black shape loomed, red eyes the size of dinner plates flared at him. Teeth, large as David's fingers, glistened with blood and spit.

It grinned at him, a huge messy grin, and a hand dropped out of its mouth.

David yelped, and slammed the key into the lock, turned it, and dove through the door.

Only it was not home but a room into which he was crammed with Cadell, Mr Whig, Mr Buchan and his father.

The room was quite large but most of the space was consumed with the business of being a huge map.

Cadell smiled at him warmly, he clapped his hands together. "Ah, David. You've arrived!"

"Very late," Warwick Milde said, he laughed. "But not as late as me. Believe it or not I was worried, you know."

"I'm sorry," David said. "A lot has happened."

"Still…"

Cadell frowned, and lifted a hand to silence him. "That isn't the issue, nor are those memories useful. You're here now, David." Cadell jabbed a pointer down – not that David had noticed him holding a pointer until then and he focused on the map properly for the first time. He recognised it at once – a map of Shale – though unlike anything he had ever seen.

"It's what we used to call a Panoptic Map," Cadell said.

"It's bloody brilliant," David said.

The map was three dimensional and truly alive, better than anything map powder could bring about. To the south and east, above the dark mass of the sea, floated the air-city of Drift. David was tempted to reach down and pick it up until Cadell wrapped his knuckles with the pointer. "There'll be none of that tomfoolery here, I'm afraid."

"Of course," David murmured. "Of course."

"He's a good boy, does what he's told," his father said. "Works hard, and he's extremely bright. After all he is my son."

"Shh!" Cadell hissed. "I've no time for your subconscious yearnings, David. Look, boy. Really, look."

The map was hypnotic in its hyper reality. You could drown in it, and David did.

A little to his left lay Mirrlees, wound up in its tangle of the River Weep, tiny lights burning, so well crafted he could almost make out his house and the Halloween lights strung down the street. Then it all clicked, gained absolute and awful clarity, and David had an inkling of how a god might feel.

Omniscience, that was the word, David saw so much that it hurt, not just his eyes but all the way into his brain and his bowels. Omniscience was a migraine of knowledge, and yet he could not stop.

"Ah, he's got it. Everybody does eventually," Cadell said.

Outside, a Quarg Hound prowled and David fought the desire to squash it beneath his fingers like a bug.

David's focus slipped south to where Chapman had once been.

Now there was just the Roil.

It seethed and bubbled, a living density of smoke. He took in its immensity. At its heart rose the Breaching Spire, a silver strand that lifted off the map and reached above his head. How had he missed that before now? At the Roil's edges, fingers of darkness reached out then sank back, as though it was dragging itself along by them. David was glad the *Roslyn Dawn* was well away from Chapman.

"There are things you need know, David. Things I need tell you. The Orbis and my blood give me time, and this dream gives me space. Tearwin Meet is where you must go, to the Engine of the World." He pointed north on the map to the Old City. The ring on David's finger crackled with ice, grew luminous and cold. "But that will take time, more than I would like. Still, it cannot be rushed – rushing would be unwise. Tearwin waits, but both you and it must be patient."

David's eyes followed the pointer. Something moved there, a shape he couldn't quite focus on, huge in its awareness. David squinted at it.

Cadell slapped him again with the pointer, harder this time. "Don't do that! You'll alert it to our presence."

He tapped the mile high walls of Tearwin Meet with the pointer. "Buchan's failed expedition was only the latest. Many have foolishly tried to find an entrance to the city and paid the price with their lives. Tearwin Meet is guarded, in ways beyond the skills of those still living. But none of them possess what I've given you. The ring is the key and the map, and it will guide you there if you let it. But once there…" His face softened; David couldn't read the meaning of his expression, beyond a gentle sadness. "Be careful with the Engine, and all your dealings with it. Caution. Caution. In the ages since it was last engaged it has grown a little mad."

"How does an engine grow mad?" David demanded. "It's a machine."

"First you make it smarter than anything living, then you let it destroy a world," Cadell said. "Why *I* was driven mad enough and it knows more guilt than I ever did. It blames itself with the sort of precision that only a mechanism can possess."

"And how do we deal with it?" David said.

"Ah, that's the rub isn't it. The most important thing." Cadell shuddered, dark blood trickled from his ear, he touched it with a finger and brought it to his lips. "Oh dear, I really am quite a mess. Pity, there is so very much that you do not know. Truths and lies, but you will walk that thorny path alone. Just remember, the most important thing is… Ah, but I suspect you already know."

David shook his head furiously.

"Take care, boy. I think you better wake now." Cadell pointed to the map. He whispered into David's ear. "You'll find the solution there. Oh, and my body, you will need to do something with it. Burning it would be best or... well... it could become... problematic. Now, to the problem at hand."

He stabbed the pointer at the panoptic map. Three iron ships tracked towards the *Roslyn Dawn*.

David coughed; his breath wasn't coming, an awful weight pressed on his chest. His head throbbed. Cadell was dead. Only he wasn't, Cadell was in his blood like a sliver of ice or the slow ripple of a sustained shiver through his flesh.

What have you done, Mr Cadell, he thought. What have you gone and done?

Then the weight was gone, and he could move.

David's limbs shook, his teeth chattered so fiercely that his jaw ached. Where Cadell had bitten him the wound had darkened but David knew it would soon start to heal.

With those memories came a different sort of knowledge. Cadell again, so much more of it was Cadell than him. If he wasn't careful, it would push him out altogether.

David sat up. He could do with a nice shot of Carnival, just to clear his head. Kara and Margaret huddled over the control pod in argument or conversation, he couldn't tell, though Margaret gripped a rifle in one hand.

They weren't watching him. If only he had some Carnival.

The memory struck him and for the first time in a long time he forgot about Carnival altogether.

"They're coming," he said, almost shouting.

Margaret turned to him, startled. "You're awake." She put down her rifle and was beside his bunk in a couple of steps. She pushed him down easily. "You need to rest."

"You don't understand. They're coming," he snarled, far more savagely than he'd meant. Margaret took a step back from him. "Iron ships like the last one, only there's three of them this time. We need to land."

"What's he talking about?" Kara Jade said. She didn't look any better than he felt. Blood tracked her jaw line and her eyes shone too brightly. What had been going on since Cadell's bite?

David rattled off coordinates. They just slipped from his lips, Kara Jade's jaw dropped. "Bring us down there or we will die. All of us. Do you want the *Roslyn Dawn* to die?"

"What do you think?" Kara was already running to the controls.

"You're just in shock," Margaret said. "I've seen it before." She didn't sound at all certain.

You haven't seen this *before,* David thought.

David sat up, this time Margaret let him. "I wish that was all it was."

The *Roslyn Dawn* descended. He slid out of the cot and slipped into his clothes. His entire body was one big bruise. He looked over at the still form of Cadell.

"He did something to me," David said.

"What?" Margaret demanded.

"Something he had to. Something horrible but I understand why, and it will save us."

"You need to rest," Margaret said.

David shook his head. "Yes I know, but I can't, not now."

"We're down," Kara Jade said a few moments later.

David was out the doorifice at once, dropping to the ground. Margaret followed. "Back in the *Dawn,*" he said. Margaret hesitated. "Trust me. Please."

Margaret's brows knitted tight, but she did what he asked, and David was thankful for that.

"As soon as you see those ships, you get out of here," David shouted at Kara, she was peering at him through the doorifice.

"What about you?" Kara Jade demanded.

"Come back for me. If this succeeds, you'll know."

The moons were out. The *Roslyn Dawn* rose above him, a single flagellum brushed his face though he couldn't tell whether it was in farewell or dismissal.

The Lode was all around him, flooding his senses . There was the hill, there was the slender river, almost identical to the one Cadell had used. Also, too, there was a sense of hesitation, of a deep breath drawn. Everything was calm and still, and it was all an illusion.

Now he could hear the iron ships: flying in tight formation, thundering through the air on their fingers of flame. And he could see them every time he closed his eyes. They would be here soon. He ran to the river, crashed through its shallows.

When he was up to his thighs in icy water, he waited, not sure what he was doing.

He blinked, the ships' lights burned. They were almost here.

Now he felt it, the lode and beyond that a distant consciousness, weary, wintry and strangely familiar that almost at once became anything but distant.

The Engine of the World sighed.

No, it said. *No.*

Then we are all dead.

Some doors you shouldn't open.

You're right, David said. *But I don't have any choice And neither do you.*

Another sigh. *This time, perhaps.*

Something clicked, some space in his mind or his blood, or both. The Orbis tightened around his finger and he screamed with the agony of it.

The river froze.

Great rough pillars of ice swung into the sky, striking the ships as they came over the hill.

Their iron hulls darkened, then crumbled, and the ships corkscrewed, spewing smoke. The three ships became three fireballs. Shards of shrapnel flew towards him, and the river lifted like a great hand, and slapped them down as though they were nothing more irritating than flies.

David was struck, across the forearm, a deep gash.

He watched his blood spill. How much blood could he lose? The wound began to close and he marvelled at that.

You must be so proud. The Engine said, and David wasn't sure who he was talking to.

I'm alive, Margaret and Kara are alive, that is all.

Disapproval, ponderous and deep crashed down upon him. *And the door is opened. You've lessons to learn, the sort that drown you. The sort that snatch you from yourself. I do not think you will like it.*

The Engine pulled away from David. The water warmed, marginally, and the ice melted, releasing him. David staggered to the shore, water steaming from his body. He dropped to the icy ground, grass shattering with the impact. *What am I? What am I?*

He drew his knees to his chest, teeth chattering, body shaking, and wept.

"What was that? What was that?" Kara Jade demanded.

Margaret wanted to slap her. "We need to get to David."

"I know, and we will. Give me time. Give the *Dawn* time."

The *Roslyn Dawn* descended, arcing back towards the hill. The three ships (her mother's ships) little more than craters now, blazed beneath her, and near the fires and the river lay David.

Margaret still wasn't sure what she had seen, but she knew what it meant.

Cadell had passed his power onto David. Without him, she had no way of entering Tearwin Meet. David must go to the Engine, whether he wanted to or not. And there he was, down below, anything but strength or a saviour, curled in a ball, body convulsing. She felt a moment of such pity that she almost lifted her rifle and shot him in the head.

The moment passed, of course.

"Sorry, David," she whispered. She raised her voice. "Hurry, Kara, he's freezing down there."

MIRRLEES-ON-WEEP
297 MILES NORTH OF THE ROIL EDGE

Stade opened the door, holding his key before him, wary despite its protection. The thing within the room lifted its head and regarded him with eyes full of hunger. "He's given his curse to a boy," it said. "A boy holds the world in his drug-addled palm."

"I know," Stade said, and he did. But two hours before the Old Men had begun screaming, demanding release. He had not denied them that. After all, the city was being evacuated. The end of days was upon them all. Not even the Old Men and their curse could add to that chaos.

"You're the last. The rest are out in the city, reinvigorating themselves."

The Old Man snarled. "Do not be so delicate. They are feeding. It's come to this. Cadell's betrayed us, his freedom was enough bitterness to us, but this, this is well beyond his purview."

"You know what must be done."

The Old Man nodded. "We will have our carnage, and there will be blood. We have held our hungers, held the curse of the Engine, in check for an age." Ropes of saliva spilled from its lips. Stade could see the Old Man's heart racing in the raw cage of its chest. He clenched his hand so tightly around the key that it cut him; he hardly felt it.

"Just kill the boy."

The Old Man raised an eyebrow. "Do not think to instruct me. The boy will be put down, because he is an aberration. We cannot let one such as him live." Then it stood, its face inches from his own, and Stade hadn't even seen it move from the room to him. Stade's spine spasmed painfully; he nearly soiled himself, but he did not turn aside from its gaze. "Be thankful you possess the key, Mr Stade. Or I would devour you now."

It raced from the basement; Stade watched after it. Only when it was gone did he allow himself to shake. He coughed, dropped to his knees and tears spilled down his face.

Unmanned. I am unmanned, what a mess I've made of it all.

He'd let them all go – the heart and mind of the city. It was only right that they should devour Mirrlees, he stared a while at the eight empty rooms and listened to the silence.

David, he thought. When they find you, if you're not drugged out of your mind, you'll wish you'd never run from my Vergers. You'll curse Cadell and your father's name with your dying breath. Please forgive me.

And, feeling old and cruel and deadly, because he was all those things, he returned to his office and worked at the one thing he knew. The logistics involved in saving the population of a city. It had to be worth the cost.

When the knock came for him to board his airship, he wasn't ready. It, like everything else these days, had arrived far sooner than anticipated. He gathered what few notebooks remained and walked with his Vergers to the rooftop dock.

Captain Jones waited for him by the ramp to the gondola. He was obviously unable to hide his irritation, his face red, his hands shoved deep in his pockets, perhaps so he couldn't strike Stade in the mouth. The mayor liked him at once.

"Everything's aboard, sir," the captain said.

"Everything except me." He grinned darkly. "You're Drift-born aren't you, Captain Jones?"

"Drift-born and raised, sir." He couldn't hide the scowl.

"Good."

"If you're ready, I'd like to take her up." The captain gestured to the south, clenching his teeth. "Bad wind's blowing, gales and the like, and storms too. It doesn't do to be tethered to what's coming."

We're all tethered to what is coming, Stade thought. He smiled and walked aboard his ship.

CHAPTER 53

With Mirrlees all but gone, the balance tipped, and what little remained of the world quaked with the terror of it. Everything was urgency, the radical constructions of a mayor without a city, armies in flight, figuratively and literally, the Old Men wandering, moving north (see Mcdonald and Clader's The Path of Blood*). And always on the horizon, seen or unseen, the Roil grew, driven on by the Dreaming Cities at its heart.*

And what did the cities dream? That was the question unspoken. The answer was a threat as deep and as dark as the Roil itself.

The Crest of the Wave: Last Days of a Perilous Age,
ADSETT & HOGE

HARDACRE
987 MILES NORTH OF THE ROIL

David woke from another nightmare to limbs leaden and frigid as though he were dead. The dream was fading, but his heart still pounded with the memory, and the terror that he might just fall into it again. He'd been doing that, falling from nightmare to nightmare, for a very long time.

Cadell had been there, and seven other men, chasing him, howling out hungers as bottomless as any Quarg Hound's.

He blinked, rubbed his eyes, and realised that he was no longer on the *Roslyn Dawn*.

We survived then, he thought.

David realised he was alone, and didn't know how to feel about that. A petulant spark burned within him: didn't he deserve a bedside vigil? Was he of that little consequence?

The bed in which he lay was solid and motionless, the room unfamiliar, and did not smell like wet dog.

So, unless something else had gone terribly wrong, he was in Hardacre in the pub known as the *Habitual Fool*. He breathed deep. Yes, he could detect the faintest odour of beer. And somewhere, below his room, people spoke and smoked. He pulled the sheet from him and lifted the arm that Cadell had bitten. His wound had healed, though at its heart was a small, dark slither of ice. He brushed a finger against it. He yelped and yanked his hand away. Touching it had felt... well, it had felt wrong.

David dragged his legs out over the bed, stood up and stretched. His muscles responded, but there was no heat in them. This cold should have had him shaking, and yet the shivers were gone from him. Erased.

Cold now, all I ever will be is cold.

A robe lay stretched across his bed and he pulled it on, but not before observing how skinny he was. Any thinner and he'd see his heart beating against his ribs. Wasting away. He was ravenous. He had a horrible thought, His shoes, where were his shoes? There! By the desk! He hurried to them, and unlatched the heel. His powdered Carnival remained.

He ran a thumb over the wraps within, then slid the heel closed, telling himself it had been the habit of addiction, not the addiction itself, that had called him to it. He realised that he didn't crave the Carnival, didn't even want it, beyond the slightest nagging thought that he really *should* finish it off anyway, otherwise it would be such a waste.

He felt a deep disapproval at the back of his mind, but he ignored it. The Carnival was safe. He was safe. That was enough for now, surely.

He walked to the bedroom window, it was open a crack, could smell wood smoke, a hint of snow, but it was far off. The street below was unfamiliar; cobblestones, crowds and not rotting in rain, the sky above was clear, streaked with cloud like fat in a good piece of meat. Yes, Hardacre. Someone stumbled out of the pub below.

David opened the door, onto a narrow hall that smelt of cigarettes, and beer. His stomach rumbled. There was noise downstairs and he followed the sound to its source.

Margaret and Buchan stood, heads almost together, talking. Margaret's rime blades sheathed to her belt, Buchan had one hand resting on the pearl handle of a gun. Margaret didn't look happy, but she never looked happy. Mr Whig sat away from them, by a dining table, eating a sandwich, though he watched them very closely. There were more sandwiches on a plate on the table. Food had never smelt so good, saliva filled his mouth. David swallowed, felt his eyes grow big.

"I'm starving," he said; the words came out thickly.

Every head in the room turned towards him. And every eye regarded him peculiarly. Buchan didn't move his hand from his gun. Did they know what he was? *He* didn't know what he was.

"David? You're awake!" Mr Whig said, and the moment of disquiet passed.

Margaret ran to him. "Lean on me," she said. "You look like death warmed up."

"Don't feel warmed up," David said. Margaret actually shivered at his touch. He pulled away from her, pretending not to notice. What am I?

Mr Whig handed him a sandwich.

"We made it then?" David said, wolfing down first one sandwich then another, and he was still hungry. "Kara fulfilled her promise."

Margaret nodded. "Kara had to return to Drift. The Mothers of the Sky recalled her the day after we arrived. And, let me tell you, she had some choice words to say about it."

Buchan cleared his throat. "I can assure you, David, we are doing everything we can to negotiate her quick return. We need her ship."

"It's not a ship," David said, and *that* almost got a smirk from Margaret. "When did she go?"

"It's been four days," Margaret said. "How much do you remember?"

"Not much. No, I remember the iron ships. I... not much."

"It was chaotic after... well, after you did whatever it was you did. We landed in the ice and the snow, and even then it was melting. You started screaming. When we finally calmed you down you closed your eyes and stayed that way. I wasn't sure if you were going to wake again."

"And the iron ships?"

"You destroyed them all. I've never seen anything like it. The endothermic forces involved–"

"It was the Engine," David said, as though that was enough of an explanation. He looked out of the lower-floor window at the tree-lined streets and the patch of blue sky, as much to marvel at it as to avoid Margaret's enquiring stare. A drunk was singing an old war song in the pub next door, someone shouted at him to shut up. David grabbed some more sandwiches, devoured them in moments. "Have you gotten in touch with my Aunt Veronica?" He could do with some money, surely she would be able to offer him some help financially.

Buchan shook his head. "Veronica's not here, David. I've spoken to the councillors, but they're being very tight-lipped about it. There's activity in the east, some sort of secret installation in the mountains. She's part of it, but that's all they can tell me."

David nodded his head, how like his family to be involved. The Mildes were always at the heart of the maelstrom.

Buchan said some other things, but David hardly heard them.

His thoughts were elsewhere, all at once he could feel *them* coming. Their presence filled him, and it was colder and crueller even than his blood. His teeth chattered, nearly bit his tongue. Ah, *so* many things to feel, so much strange knowledge flowering within him, but their approach was the strongest.

They were a long way away yet, but every moment bought them closer. When he closed his eyes he could see a long dark road, trees covered with moss. He could feel seven cold hungers, seven creatures intent on hunting him down and tearing him to shreds.

He didn't know what he was going to do. He wasn't some hero from the pulps like Travis the Grave. He'd made it to Hardacre but he knew he couldn't stay here long. Like the Engine had said, well, like he *thought* it had said: he'd opened doors. If he wanted to close them, and stop these Old Men, he would have to go to Tearwin Meet.

The Old Men: all he had known of them until the last few weeks was as nursery rhymes and figures of mystery in Shadow Council tales. Cadell had discussed them in more detail, but it had rarely been specific, as though he was ashamed of his past. Now Cadell was dead.

Beneath his hunger was the familiar pull of Carnival. It hadn't taken long to assert itself. Who was there to control it now Cadell was gone?

Perhaps Margaret. She stared at him curiously, and there was a fierce challenge in that gaze, a silent demand that he give up every secret he possessed. Oh, he had so many of those now! But then again, so did she, starting with those iron ships. He looked away. He didn't trust her, not really. Cadell's blood stirred inside his veins, echoing the sentiment.

And then, a new urgency gripped him: how could he have let it slip his mind?

He had to deal with the corpse.

"Where is Cadell? Where have you put him?"

No one could look him in the eye. Buchan cleared his throat, but it was Margaret who spoke.

"David, Cadell's body is missing."

CHAPTER 54

No one knows of the exact human cost of that sudden retreat from Mirrlees, nor the numbers of those "persuaded" to stay behind. But it was high.

Still the city had been lost since the day the rain began to fall. A dead thing lumbering with no realization that its heart no longer beat, that it was instead tumbling towards the burial ground.

Cities of the Fallen, CARVER & DAVIES

MIRRLEES-ON-WEEP
294 MILES NORTH OF THE ROIL

He rapped his gnarled knuckles on the wooden door.

Once, and again.

Bells tolled in the distance. Another levee had fallen, crashing down a few miles away, and people were dying. Death crowded the air and wherever he sensed death there were usually folk like him. He saw what they saw, and the Roil made sense of it for him, placed it in context. Mirrlees drowned, the streets transformed with every downpour becoming labyrinth and quagmire combined.

Finding his home had been a torturous affair, everything all muddied up the way it was. His thoughts too, had become labyrinthine, and far too crowded, it was hard to focus on the smaller things – the personal.

It was hard, but not impossible.

It just took time.

"Where are they?" he whispered to himself. "Where's my wife? My children?"

He was reaching to knock on the door again when it opened, bright light pouring out, stinging his eyes, forcing him back a step. He had been a long time in the dark.

"What do you want?" A harsh voice demanded and then his wife cried out, dropping the iron poker she had gripped so tightly, recognising him at last. "Theodore! Come in, my darling. Out of the rain," she said, and made to throw her arms around him.

"Not yet," he said. "Not until we're inside."

He peered up and down the street.

Not far away, a cat batted at a dead thing floating in a puddle. A Verger whistled in the distance and a carriage clattered by, smoke from the driver's pipe staining the wet air for a moment like a passing dream.

"I thought you lost," she said leading him inside. All he could see was her mouth; he did so wish to kiss her again.

"I was, yes I was... for a little while. But I found you." He frowned. "I found you at last."

"And the Council? I heard rumours..."

He grinned at her, and it must have been something of his old grin, for she returned it, her shoulders relaxing. He smelt liquor on her lips and that disturbed him.

"Do not worry about the Council. They're not worth worrying about anymore." He gestured beyond her, down the hall. "Where are the children?"

"In bed," she said, not moving. "It's late."

"Wake them," he said, tried for a little warmth in his voice. "I want to see and speak with you all."

His wife looked at him oddly, her fingers lifted to her mouth as though to stall a question.

"Please, indulge me, my love. It has been so long."

She left him alone in the hall. He could hear his children stirring, probably been awake since he knocked on the door,

It was cold in here; he clapped his hands to bring a little heat to them. When that failed, he ran them over a nearby lamp. His skin crackled, but it did the trick.

Outside, the cursed rain fell heavier, but it would not fall forever. That was something of which he was certain, it had already stopped twice that day for longer than an hour at a time. He could wait. He had grown to be quite a patient man.

"Father. Father." His children cried, running around him, circling his legs and laughing. Times had been hard since he was last here. The world had grown rough around the edges; spoiled when it should be fine.

"Come closer, my children, my lovely wife," he said. "I've something to give you."

Closer they came, hesitation in their eyes, but they did not stop. Nor did he, and there was no uncertainty on his part. The corruption of doubt had long ago burnt away.

He held them to him. Held his wife and children tight, as his body released its dark cargo. None of them could pull away: the urgency of his gift too complete.

"There, there," the stationmaster crooned above their screams. "There, there. We're a family again."

Acknowledgments

Roil has been a long time coming, and now, here it is. And the reason it's here is well and truly due to the love and support of my wonderful ROR colleagues – the best writing group ever.

Thanks also to Deonie Fiford for having faith in it, and to Marc Gascoigne and Lee Harris for giving it a good home. And a big thank you to Sophie Hamley of the Cameron Creswell Agency, who's patient, funny, and a sure guide through the shadow of the valley of death. And, as always, thanks to The Avid Reader Bookstore, in particular Fiona Stager and Anna Hood, who continue to put up with the least available casual staff member ever.

Finally, thanks to Diana, my darling wife, without whose love and support I'd never get anything written.

About the Author

Trent Jamieson is an Australian Fantasy writer, and winner of two Aurealis Awards, whose *Death Most Definite* series is attracting rave notices.

Trent has been writing fiction since he can remember, and selling it since the mid-Nineties... quite a long while after he started.

He works as a teacher, a bookseller and a writer and has taught at Clarion South where he was described as "the nicest guy in Australian Spec Fic" shattering the reputation he was trying to build as the "Hard Man of the Australian Writing Community".

trentjamieson.com

Darlings Killed
(Outtakes, Bloopers and a Bit of Book 2)

Roil has gone through many incarnations, and suffered (and gained) from many cuts.

Here's a few rough and ready outtakes from what might have been. Sometimes you cut scenes because they drag the story down, or reflect something that the character's already done, or they're just a bit shit. I'll let you decide which is which.

Here's a longer view of Tate (when it was Bishop). I'd named the city after KJ Bishop – in fact, in this draft, all the cities were named after authors I admired. It didn't work; only Mirrlees remained, because I really think Mirrlees should be the name of a city.

Margaret increased the night sight of her gear and swept the horizon, tracking the dim pale line of Mechanism Highway. No matter how she adjusted her field glasses, the convoy did not appear.

In the South Eastern Quarter, Sentinels fired at a drift of floaters blown in too close to the walls. The Sentinels' bullets punctured the creatures' gas sacks with a wet slap. Margaret turned towards the sound. The last floater, jaws snapping wildly, writhed as it fell to the ground.

Another threat efficiently dealt with, as all threats were here.

Boots crunched on the ground behind her, Margaret turned towards the sound.

"Go home," Lieutenant Sarah Varn said, her breath escaping in plumes from cracked lips as she spoke. "You're not meant to be here until tomorrow and I will not have a weary sentry on my wall. Get some rest."

Wrapped in the standard black cloak of Bishop's Sentinels. Her single concession to Halloween was a tiny silver skull pinned to her collar. She wore heavy spiked boots. Strapped to her back were two ice rifles, and a Rime Blade and ice pistols were holstered around her waist. Ice weaponry proved effective against the creatures of the Roil, but was inefficient. It took considerable time to charge up and reload each gun so Sentinels bristled with weapons, swapping and changing from pistol to rifle and (if severely pressed) to blade.

The city itself remained the best weapon.

Ice sheathed the Jut; refrigeration units lipped each merlon, pumping a chill into the air that transformed the cloying warmth of the Roil's winds into frigid gusts.

Sarah clapped her gloved hands together and, despite the futility of the gesture, blew on them.

"Of course. While you're here..." Sarah pointed east. "A nest of sappers, staying an inch or so out of range of the main guns."

Flares went up, breaking the darkness a little.

Margaret stared at the spot with her glasses. Six of the beasts disturbed the ruined earth. Their huge dark eyes shone in the flare-light. Dark bleak eyes that met the light fearlessly. Then Roil spores, drawn by the heat, smothered the flares and darkness drowned the Sappers again.

"Quite a large nest," Margaret said.

Sarah's eyes lit with a grim humour, she clapped her hands together again. "Already under control. We're sending drones out. Heavy endothermic bombing, ground breakers. You know, the standard stuff. Odd though, we haven't seen Sappers this close to the city in years, they nearly destroyed the North Wall. We got them then and we will this time, too."

Margaret kept her gaze squarely on the Sappers, they did not move. Just stared at the city walls like they were waiting for something. "When are the drones being launched?"

Sarah laughed. "Soon. Just go home and rest. Bishop can look after herself without you."

"All right, I'm going," Margaret said finally, and lowered her field glasses, slipping them into a case hung from her hip. Still she hovered there a moment longer.

"I'll send a message as soon as they arrive," Sarah said.

"The bells are set, so ring me. Three for the moment they drive through the gates."

"Three it is. It's always three, we've done this before, *many* times. Now go."

Margaret climbed to the top of the Wire-tower – the stairs creaking with her every movement – and opened a cabinet in which hung a half-dozen leather harnesses. She pulled out hers and hooked the harness around her chest and waist, making sure the tugs and collars fit snugly, then linked herself to the Wire.

Margaret flicked a switch by the side of the tower, smiling despite herself as gears clicked into place. Beam engines hummed, counterweights fell, and the tower rose another couple of yards making it the highest point of this section of the Wire-way, lifting her into a zone of hot winds. The whole structure shook slightly, then the wire tightened, lifting her even higher as it did so. Margaret made a final check of her harness; the hooks and wheels were in line, free of tangles and no cracks in evidence. Satisfied, she nodded to herself then let go. She hovered there for the briefest of moments, a final hesitation perhaps, but it was too late, gravity had its way and she flew, suspended by the humming wire.

Whatever you do, do *not* look down, someone had warned her once.

Such advice was absurd! Where else could you look? There were no stars above, just the netting doming the city, and the Roil. Down below, Bishop's lights shimmered, distant and comforting, beautiful in their constancy.

From here it was easy to imagine the streetlights as constellations. But these were constellations crowded with people, going to and from work, trudging home in heavy crampioned boots designed for the frozen roadways. Someone, looking up, saw her and waved. Margaret waved back.

Margaret adored the Wire-way. Of all her parents' inventions, she loved it most. The wind roaring in her ears, the wheels on her harness sibilant and swift, the city a sparkling microcosm below.

Pride for her parents' and her city's achievements swelled within her. When she had been younger, she was jealous of all the time they spent away from her. Until she realised her parents were not just protecting the city. They were protecting her.

A different sort of Introduction to Stade and Tope. I stripped this away when I realised that David's father wasn't alive after all. Writers can be far crueller than Vergers.

(i)

Word came out of the darkness.

First as something barely more than static along the buried

lines beneath the Interface, hidden pathways of communication, so subtle as to be almost indistinguishable from the noise passing endlessly that way.

But it was heard.

Those trained and transformed to hear it, nodded and made notes in cipher.

Then it was flown into the air; the pilot's little ship conspicuous only because it was one of the few travelling away from Chapman, and the Festival. The Obsidian Curtain dominated his mirrors, black and vast. Anything that took him further from the Roil had to be good.

Away from one darkness and too soon into another. A hundred and fifty mile wide ribbon of dry air stretched between Chapman and Mirrlees, broken on the Mirrlees end by masses of dark storm cloud, beneath which the city languished like a beaten dog.

Mirrlees-on-Weep. Not as wondrous as the pilot's city of Drift, but impressive in its way. The river Weep had swollen, suburbs north and west of the central boroughs, right up to the old forest known as the Margin, were stained with it. Cranes worked ceaselessly along the levees, extending them, repairing damage, thickening their monstrous bases. But it was, ultimately, a pointless industry. For the rain fell not just around the city, but further west, in the catchment areas. And there seemed no end in sight to its fall.

He brought the ship down, descending by the monstrous levies, onto the landing yard, crowded despite the rain. A Verger by the name of Tope was waiting for him.

"Express delivery," the pilot said, his voice low, handing over a sheet of paper.

"What does it say?"

"I did not look," the pilot said. "Besides I've no skill with the codings."

"Nor I," the Verger grunted. He doubted the fellow was lying, but such secrets must be kept.

He led the pilot to the back of his craft and slit his throat.

(ii)

Councillor Stade lit the paper, then, face curled with disgust, threw it in the heavy bin by his desk.

"Once a Confluent, always a Confluent. His demands grow more extreme," Stade said. "He wants the boy taken north. He says the colder the clime the better. He wants it done now."

"Things are that bad, then?" Mr Tope asked.

"We know they are. Even in the north, the *Grendel* and the *Yawn* are missing." He sighed. "I am reluctant to do this. But what choice do I have? They're still making progress down there and we need all of that knowledge. Where would we be without Chill, for instance? At least this way the son will be completely under our observation. Bring him to me, Mr Tope."

The Verger nodded. "Tonight."

"And, Mr Tope, do not harm him."

"It's not in my nature." He grinned. "Wouldn't harm a fly."

And here was where we first met David (and he wasn't addicted to Carnival at that point, poor lad). But it was all a bit too close to home (I work in a bookstore). I do like the posters though.

The day began badly. It was a bad time of year for David. So he should have seen it coming. Not that, as he was later to realise, he ever saw any of it coming.

But ten minutes after helping Mr Matheson open the store, as the rain poured down outside, its animal roar drowning out the rumblings of traffic on De Pierres Street, someone stole half a shelf of books from right under David's nose; just grabbed them and legged it.

David did not suspect a thing until it was too late, which really stung. He considered himself rather good at detecting thieves and catching them on the cusp of the steal, the moment when it might still be regarded as some sort of innocent mistake to be laughed about as the books were handed back.

He ran to the door, glancing at the gap where the newly-arrived titles usually lived, and knowing at once what had been nicked.

Esoteric stuff, the valuable ones of course: Deighton and Brock; a volume on the *City in the Snow* just released through Dearborne publishers; and a series of chapbooks by Walter Price, scientific romances David had yet to read.

Damn.

Damn.

Damn.

The thief was already halfway down the street. As a rule, it was too late once they were through the door. But David could not let that many books out of the store, not if he wanted to keep his job.

"After him, lad!" Mr Matheson roared, and that was it.

David took off, through the rain, his first steps out the door startling sodden pigeons into wet flight, more spray than air beneath their wings. He splashed and stumbled down De Pierres Street – along greasy footpaths crowded even this early in the morning with pedestrians, umbrellas everywhere – almost to Central Station Markets, where, panting and blinking back rain and sweat, he slipped – or was tripped – and fell. By the time he made it to his feet the thief was gone and half a week's pay with him.

The bugger had dropped a couple of books, but the rain had damaged them beyond resale. Store shrinkage, as such loss of stock was called, was frowned upon by management – one Stagwell Matheson – and taken out of staff wages.

David stared vainly into the crowd. There were new posters taped to the lampposts, across from the greengrocers where people pushed and shoved, trying to get whatever fruit and vegetables were available. The posters were marked with Mirrlees' grey teardrop symbol, so they had to be official.

Rain is not Roil. Rain is Rain. The posters declared, in huge black type. *Stop Dissent and Rumour-mongering. Information leading to the arrest of any Dissidents will be rewarded richly.*

A little further along someone had altered the posters with thick black paint to:

Rain is Roil. Rain is Dissent. Information will be rewarded.

A Confluent, no doubt.

He looked up as something struck his neck.

The sky was the colour of slate, the only hint of brightness an airship, one of the Blake and Steel lines, advertising the Festival of Float down south in Chapman. Thousands of pamphlets, dropped from its guts and fell with the rain; bright coloured paper darkening with wet soot. Cleverly designed, they spun and danced in the air until the water soaked them through, then they just plummeted. In the west, by the dockyards, smokestacks gave billowing rebuttal to the rain. Of course it was short-lived; ash layered everything. It grouted the cracks in footpaths, limned the walls with a patina of industry. Another airship dipped down towards the landing fields, trailing its ropes like a millipede's legs. There was a dim suggestion of sunlight in the sky; a point in the cloud, just above Ruele

Tower that was less murk and more pallor. A dead rat floated in the gutter, legs jutting up stiffly like a crooked four master. It drifted along till it reached a drain, spun a couple of graceful circles then went under and out of sight. Across the road a dozen pigeons had gathered, shuffling backwards and forwards along a ledge. One of them opened its wings and dropped dead to the ground below. The rest looked on, tracking the ledge, caged in the misery of rain.

Hmm, Cadell was a wee bit too Gandalf in this version.

On the long walk home, David regretted leaving his umbrella. Still there was nothing he could do, so he walked and whistled. An old, old tune that his mother had taught him.

"Who whistles on a night like this?" The voice, dry and gruff, came almost from inside his ear.

David had to bite his cheek to stop from yelping. An old man – wrapped in a sodden cloak as unfashionable as the one David had been forced to wear at work, possibly the same tailor – glared at him. A sharp beak of a nose, the point beaded with water, jutted out from underneath an equally sodden old hat. He looked like he was waiting for an answer.

"Well I for one," David said "Not everyone hates the rain, and it is always best to put a brave face on it."

"Ha!" the old man exclaimed, wiping the water from his nose with a drenched handkerchief, doing little more than making room for new raindrops to take the place of the old. "Whistling is for mischief makers and, as for brave faces, well, if that's your brave face you'd best never consider acting for a career, it barely passes for a grimace."

And it was all a bit faux Dickensian – like this Cuttleman (the description of which I love, but it just didn't fit any more).

A carriage waited out the front of the house, the driver bent over so that his hat, through some trick of perspective appeared to be coming out of his knees. David realised it was. He had never seen a Cuttleman before, they were rare in the city. The driver glared at him with dark and cruelly humorous eyes, and licked its lips with a long pointed tongue the colour of the bleak cloud-smothered sky. Three of his hands gripped the reins, the fourth was fishing around in a bag of slop. The Cuttleman shovelled slate worms from the bag into his mouth. David's stomach churned as the wriggling bloody mess tumbled from the driver's lips, though it didn't reduce his fascination.

Mr Tope slapped David on the back of the head.

"No time for gawking, lad. We've a very special and impatient gentleman waiting to see you."

An old man in an ancient cloak, stood on a street corner nearby, watching them. David's heart almost stopped. He recognised him: the vagrant who had abused him for whistling. His eyes though had lost their hardness, David could almost believe the old man was concerned.

Mr Tope glared at the vagrant, and brandished his staff threateningly. The old man hurried off.

"Street folk," Tope said. "Was a time we took the stick to them. But no more, curse it. No more. There's not time for even civil violence. Now, in the carriage, son of Anderson Crane. In with you."

David clambered inside, his father's name stinging him like a slap to the face. The Verger followed, then banged on the roof with his staff, flakes of dust or mould rained down around their heads.

"Off we go, Gus," Mr Tope shouted. "Off we go!"

Gus hissed back in cuttletalk and the Verger laughed, but offered nothing in way of translation.

The carriage jolted forward to the crack of the whip and the clatter-splash of horses' hooves. David, rubbing the back of his head where Mr Tope had struck him, watched his little house, crammed in with all the others. Its light still shone; he had not even possessed enough wits about him to turn it off. With that thought, something cold and wretched built in him. It bordered on frantic, but it was too sad, too pale; his terror drowned in lethargic, ragged resignation and his muscles grew leaden and still.

The Verger, as though sensing some of what David felt, smiled and patted him on the knee. "Are you sure you don't need glasses, lad?" he said. "You squint too much for a boy your age. Well we all know what makes you blind."

David shook his head. "I can see perfectly clearly," he said, his voice quiet.

They turned the corner sharply – almost too sharply, the carriage lifting and dropping with a crash, Mr Tope cursing the Cuttleman, and the Cuttleman cursing the horses in Cuttletalk – and his house was gone from sight.

Stade had his reasons and he used to go on about them a LOT.

Stade's face darkened beneath his top hat; cigar smoke wreathed his head. The councillor clenched one hand into a fist. David was queasy with fear. Stade was a big man, his fists almost the size of David's head.

Stade seemed to be grappling with something. He lent over David's chair, his breath almost medicinally strong. Drink of some sort, but nothing David recognised.

"I'm not a bad man. To desire power is not necessarily evil. I am ruthless, yes, but I know what is happening. The continent of Shale is contracting; every day the Roil grows and there is little I can do about it. I do not delude myself in the way the Confluence does. This Roil cannot be defeated, but we can hide from it, just as it has hidden from us.

Finally, here's a bit from Night's Engines *(at least, I think it will be in there with a few of the rough edges polished away, hopefully). As you've seen, I change my mind quite a bit. Anyway, ten years before the events of Book One there was the Grand Defeat.*

The Grand Defeat

"Victory is certain."

The words crackled and spat, sprung from loudspeakers all along the front line, and from crowdhailers built into the bellies of the military class airships and Aerokin above. General Bowen's voice possessed such conviction that, for a moment, it was true and not a single soldier could doubt it.

Behind them the city of McMahon emptied. Its great bridges and northern roads stained with refugees – all vested with no lack of doubt, all fleeing, now that this last battle for their city was to begin. Smoke darkened McMahon's sky, and everything stank of it: there had been riots that morning and into the afternoon. But as the Roil's approach quickened they'd quietened down. New laws (The Peace and Order Precepts, or as they were more popularly know the Laws of Knife) were coming aggressively into play, as the dark curtain closed. Still, riots continued in some quarters, perhaps a final expression of denial or rage at what was being lost to them.

When the battle was won those who had rioted would be dealt with by Verger's knife or hurled into prison to rot and consider their folly. But now thirty thousand soldiers, two thousand ice cannons, eighty battle Aerokin, and two hundred airships, the wondrous weaponry of the new age were perched upon the abyss of battle. All of that military force intent upon a single goal: the obliteration of the Roil.

"Victory is certain. We cannot fail. For to do so is to fail humanity. To enter that great darkness and become shivering meat for the creatures of the Roil. We will not fall as Tate fell, nor Chinoy or Carver. This time we are ready. This time we drive back the dark."

Surely Bowen was right, after all the Roil was a big dumb mass. It could not overwhelm this gleaming technology and its miles of soldiery, nor could it devour the grandest metropolis ever built. Yet, all it took was a turn of the head and the soaring terrible presence of the Roil and such arrogance was torn of its potency.

"Victory is certain," General Bowen said once more, and his voice echoed like a thundercrack into the sky and faded just as quickly.

"Victory is bloody certain all right," Beaksley mumbled, checking his ice-rifle for the umpteenth time, always checking his rifle, always. "Just not fer us."

Harper smacked her palm hard against his head. "Keep such sentiments to yourself, or you'll feel a knife in your spine. That is if you have one." She said it with some fondness.

"I've spine enough - standing here ain't I?"

She looked south. The Roil was almost upon them, it had moved swiftly that day, as though anxious to meet their forces in battle.

Two minutes, no more, and it would be in range, drowning out the sun with it, though it was already dark enough, a rank and bitter darkness. The air fleet overhead, made up of military class and converted merchant craft, hid the day almost as effectively as the Roil. Harper turned her attention, a moment upon that placid drifting industry, the various ships' banners flapping in the wind.

There was strategy at work. They were here to deal with any creatures of the Roil that approached. The airships themselves were to attack the Roil space itself. Endothermic jets and cannon. They would drive a wedge in the Roil, meanwhile a series of moats would be filled with ice, and coolant pipes running the perimeter of the city would be activated.

There was a furious signaling of flags across the sky; most of the airships were not fitted with the new radio technology. Endothermic weaponry had taken precedence over everything else; cannon protruded from the ship's bow sections like the bristles of a Cuttleman. They made her feel uncomfortable, she didn't like this close fighting, didn't like the idea of all those munitions suspended above her head.

Sergeant Harper spied a couple of Mirrlees dirigibles, the grey teardrop painted upon their cabins, and yearned a moment for the River Weep and her small carpentry business.

She wanted to build things; that was her real job, the making of things. She yearned for the smell of wood and lacquer, the soft murmur of the lathe. Thirty months ago her number had come up. Conscripted, she had seen a year in the north, stabilizing what the Council of Engineers called a "rupture of treaty" with the Cuttlemen. It had felt like war to her.

Somehow she'd lived and kept living, rising in the ranks to sergeant, this motley crew beneath her: glad to be in the company of someone who had the knack of not dying. And she could take no comfort that she had helped forge a peace, because before it had come to a conclusion her troops had been transferred down to Consolation City, and this new endeavour one that made little sense to her, how could an army face off the dark?

She was damned if she were going to let an idiot like Beaksley put an end to her chances now.

She glared at him.

The fool gazed south, his jaw wide open. He pointed and Sergeant Harper followed his shaking hands. The Roil raced towards them, not all of it, just the lower strata: a shelf of darkness some forty feet high. She could hear it, a snapping, clicking chitinous sound. A fierce and boiling wind rushed from the south almost knocking her to her knees. Guns and armour creaked, she felt her own gear being tugged by that wind. Sergeants swore, or bawled out orders. She blinked away dust and smoke, her eyes stung. She opened her mouth to speak and the sky exploded. Rolling detonations thundered in the heavens. At first she thought it the airships firing their cannon.

Then she realized it was the airships themselves, rupturing, being torn apart. By… she didn't know. Couldn't quite comprehend its quick bulk. Flaming remnants of craft, red-hot fragments of the rigid ship's skeletons, flailing screaming pilots and crew rained down, crashing onto the soldiers, killing those they struck.

And then the Roil hit them, washed over the chaos, with a deadening darkness.

For a second all was quiet, a soft intake of breath, a widening of pupil or a dripping of sweat.

"Fire, you fools," she shouted in the smothering darkness. "Fire."

But it was already too late. A mass of darkness struck her eyes and her mouth. And it burned.

"Out of here. Now!" General Bowen cried from the bridge of the *Daunted Spur*, and considered his terrible failure.

The army was gone. Four hundred thousand soldiers swept up in darkness as though they had never been, and the Roil rolled on, like a storm front if a storm could possess such dreadful silent majesty. Before the Roil, chaos bloomed everywhere, behind it only the quiet of the dark.

In the air, over half his ships were down, torn from the sky by the savagery of the two attacking Vermatisaurs, their many heads snapping and striking.

But Bowen had seen enough battles to know that, while showy, they were by no means the most of their problems. Endyms and smaller things, Hideous Garment Flutes, crowded so thickly upon neighbouring ship's hulls that their weight dragged them out of the sky. The older hydrogen ships hit the ground sedately then exploded, gas cells igniting one after the other, their fires darkening the zone before the Roil and raining death on the troops beneath them.

Aerokin too, struggled and screamed, consumed by the biting weight of all those Roilings. Flagella thrashed at the air.

Already thousands of creatures were racing towards the *Daunted Spur*. Gunners fired endothermic bursts towards the beasts. Unlike the front where all the airships had crowded, his craft had room to shower the Roilings with cold; they fell away in a black rain.

His pilot, a Drifter, brought the ship hard right. Alarms rang out. Then died down. The ship's control centre, built around a large diagram of the *Daunted Spur*, lit up, warning of nacelles overheating.

"Steady," the ship's captain hissed. "Steady or you'll burn out the engines."

"I've a lot of tail wind. The air's uncertain," the pilot said, between clenched teeth. Bowen could hear her mumbling beneath her breath something about Aerokin, and the uselessness of dumb machines. Drifters do not like being told what to do. Still he brought the engines back down.

Looking back the Roil appeared perfectly still, but Bowen knew that it was not. That it washed over the city as it had washed over Tate before it and Mcmahon.

And then, as he watched, the Roil came bubbling out of Magritte Gorge. Rising up and washing over those who were trying to flee, clawing up into the air and striking down more of his air fleet. Bowen brought a hand to his mouth. He wanted to scream, but he forced that need down. He wiped at his eyes and turned. His men were staring at him.

"What do we do now?" his captain asked.

"Signal retreat. Get as many ships out of there as we can."

"What about the troops on the front?"

Bowen jabbed south at the darkness crashing over everything.

"There are no troops," he said. "There is no front. All of it's gone."

The pain had fled, but with its passing had come the command.

Harper's eyes opened. The darkness obscured nothing from her, she could sense everything, and it was a glorious power. All around her, soldiers were getting up. Some had been ruined by the falling airships, their muscles and bones destroyed. They stayed still and the Witsmoke that had entered them, lifted and found residence somewhere else.

Rising in the darkness, eyes blinking, each man or woman

that stood up broadened her mind and each mind echoed with a dry old voice. *South, south, you must come where the furnaces burn, where the air is thick.*

The Beaksley smiled. "There are dreaming cities down there, and heat."

"Yes," she whispered. "Yes. They slumber, but the time draws close."

Slowly they stumbled south, caressed and cajoled by the Roil knowing and not knowing that twelve years of preparations lay before them. Twelve years of transformation, in cities fast asleep, but dreaming furiously dreaming.

"Victory is certain," The Beaksley, Harper said.

All along the line the words were taken up, silently and whispered.

"Victory is certain."

Talk about it!

Join in the discussion of this book on Twitter by using and following the tag **#roil**

"A Neverwhere for the next generation." – C.E. Murphy
SIXTY-ONE NAILS
MIKE SHEVDON
THE ROAD TO BEDLAM
MIKE SHEVDON
DEBRIS
THE VEILED WORLDS
JO ANDERTON

TIM WAGGONER
Introducing Matt Richter. Private Eye. Zombie.
Nekropolis
"An atmospheric and exciting mystery." – SF Site
TIM WAGGONER
Dead Streets
Matt Richter. Private Eye. Zombie
TIM WAGGONER
Dark War
Matt Richter. Private Eye. Zombie

ANDY REMIC
KELL'S
LEGEND
CITY OF DREAMS & NIGHTMARE
IAN WHATES
CITY OF HOPE & DESPAIR
"A born storyteller." – The Guardian